HANAMI

«The cry of Sakura»

HARU YOSHIDA

I dedicate this work:
To the love of my life, my eternal love.
"It will always live in me"

PROLOGUE

Now yes! I already feel ready to tell my story after a few years. I was born in *Shirakawa-go*, known as *"the fairytale village"* in the Japanese Alps. As a Japanese woman in the modern era, I was fortunate to be born into a family dedicated to the teachings. Being my mother a teacher in early childhood education, and my father a prestigious and recognized Sensei, or Master in the Arts of Budō, I was educated and trained in various Martial Arts originating in Japan, thus being an expert Master in various martial disciplines; also graduated in Economics by the faculty of Gifu Prefecture, and graduated in the Spanish language.

I had only known happiness, fortune, and bliss in its entire splendor, living a dream life and love.

"Yes, I met true love, the eternal love!"

The *Sakura* tree and the *Hanami* (falling petals), have always been part of my life and my growth as a person. The meaning and philosophy of *hanami* go beyond the simple contemplation of the beauty of its flowers. It teaches us the ephemerality of life, in the same way that its flowers wither falling like a shower of petals..., thus offering us a unique, beautiful, and nostalgic spectacle at the same time; becoming every spring an event that floods the entire country. While I relate my training and way of life, I also explain the meanings of our words, and how we live our customs, ceremonies and traditions; from typical gastronomy to our philosophy and martial teachings; our way of loving and feeling; as well as our ethical and moral codes. From the Japanese Alps I moved to Tokyo, where I was still wrapped and sheltered in the security of the country, the family and the love of my life.

I continued with my perfect and wonderful existence, until "that moment" arrived, that "fateful moment," in which all the values that had been taught to me were affected; awakening in me those most feared and never imagined feelings in my precious and happy life: feelings of hatred, revenge and justice... I knew and felt the true horror. I lived and suffered the excruciating pain in my own body and in my heart.

"I completely broke!"

My own *"Sakura"* had cried *"tears of blood"* over me; warning me and advising me of the suffering and pain that I would suffer... In the teachings that were transmitted to me: *"the life is sacred,"* it is the most important thing to preserve! The life of every human being must prevail above all else, unless your life or that of your loved ones is really threatened and in danger. The circumstances and the facts led me to make a tough decision:

"I had to do what I had to do!"

In Japan, we say that you have to be sure you are not asleep when the sun begins to rise. Now, I know that I am wide awake and that it has already dawned. I will relate, with the ink charged with my tears and the blood of the "Cry of Sakura," how I survived...; how the life can change according to the events and circumstances that happen; how and why you have to be prepared for everything, because I really:

"I was born and died in the same day!"

I hope that the transmissions, that were taught to me, and that I am trying to convey, as well as the feelings that I experienced because of the horror and the tragedy, can help the readers.

And please: "Wherever you are: look, even when there is apparently nothing to see, and listen when it seems that everything is in absolute silence."

HARU YOSHIDA

I came to the world on the Day of the Shōwa era (1926-1989), called *"Shōwa no hi,"* on April 29, 1985 in Japan, the Land of the Rising Sun. It is a very important date that is celebrated every year, and was created in honor of the birthday of Emperor Hirohito, but after his death in 1989, the name was changed to *"Midori no hi."* Later, in 2007, it was renamed: *"Shōwa no hi."*

The Shōwa no Hi has a very deep meaning: the purpose of the Shōwa Era. This was a disturbing time in which Japan had many war conflicts, and a great war that it lost against the United States, World War II, from which it miraculously overcame, and resurfaced in record time thanks to the will and strength of the Japanese people; which was recognized years later as the famous "Japanese miracle."

Thus, the Shōwa no Hi aims to remind citizens of the turbulence of what happened, the triumphs, the hardship, and the harshness of the reconstruction of the country in that Era, and thus, transmit these teachings to the new generations so that it is never repeated again.

That is why from that day, April 29, begins the famous *"Golden Week,"* a week of holidays for the Japanese that generally lasts until May 5.

My birth, on that special day of celebration, took place in the Japanese Alps in the shadow of Mount *Hakusan* (located in the center of the island of *Honshū,* north of the city of *Nagoya*), in a village located in the valley of the *Shogawa* River called *"Shirakawa-go"* (which in Japanese means *'the town of the white river'*), located in the mountains of *Gifu* and *Toyama* prefectures.

All these villages were declared a *World Heritage Site* by UNESCO in 1995.

Currently they are famous as a tourist destination for lovers of the rural world.

Ogimachi is the main and largest village in the *Shirakawa-go* area. Their constructions style *"Gassho-zukuri"* stands out, which literally means *'like hands in prayer' or 'construction with the palms of the hands together.'* They are constructions with very high ceilings, of straw, and very inclined to support the weight of snow during heavy snowfalls that occur every year in the area. These buildings, also known as "farms" are considered as architectural masterpieces of carpentry.

They do not have a single nail; each wooden beam fits perfectly into the next, hence its importance in Japanese architecture.

In these populations, the cultivation of mulberry trees and the rearing of silkworms were the main activity of the peasant inhabitants.

I grew up contemplating the best views of the valleys and mountains that come close to the perfect definition of "postcard." Views that offer with each season of the year a wonderful spectacle for the eyes and the spirit. Each season of the year has its charm and attractive.

« Thousands of images and memories are piling up in my mind right now...! »

In spring, the *"Sakura"* or *"cherry blossoms,"* one of our best-known cultural symbols, fills the landscape with their white and pink flowers, like a rain of colors with different philosophical meanings.

Observing how the beautiful petals of these flowers fall, known as *"hanami,"* especially in early April, reminds us of the Japanese: that like the transience of the beauty of nature, we must also value the transience of existence and the fragility of life. Sprout new leaves of trees, and the shrubs show us their new flowers filling the landscape of colorful (flowers of all colors), and smells envelopes from poppies and lavenders of its meadows. The rustic stone and wood benches strategically located, invite us to sit down to enjoy their contemplation, providing us with a spiritual and mental relaxation that fills us with harmony and peace.

In summer, in this region, the agricultural plantations are boiling of colorful green, tinting the fields, and flooding the entire landscape with life and shimmering green. This nucleus of villages, since ancient times, is known as *"the fairytale village,"* which can give a representative idea of the place. The landscape, at this time, has as spectators thousands of slender pines, maples and firs forming a perfect symmetry, crossed by blue rivers of crystal clear and pure waters that cross its valleys, inviting us to swim and play at the pace of its calm current; go hiking or simply stroll under the rays of the sun, letting ourselves be seduced by the light that reflects the nature around it.

In autumn, the special season preferred by the Japanese, it is time to contemplate the landscape in all its splendor of contrasting colors. Japan has a climate at this time that is neither very hot nor very cold, and the skies are clear, revealing the attractive and captivating deep blue. From north to south advances the *"momiji,"* this translates as *'the changing color of autumn leaves.'* Wonderful and spectacular is the color of browns, reds and ocher of the leaves of the trees, especially of the *'Japanese maples,'* in Japanese: *"Kaede."* It is very typical of the Japanese to go on excursions and outings to enjoy the colors of their leaves, in a practice known as *"momijigari,"* which literally means 'hunting for autumn leaves.' This practice is the autumnal version of the *"hanami"* or *'contemplation of the cherry trees in spring.'* Namely, the word *"momiji"* comes from the term in *"kanji"* or *'han character'* (they are the ideographic signs used in Japanese writing): *"momizu,"* which means *'to dye red,'* and applies to all deciduous trees whose leaves turn red or yellow before shedding.

Attending *momijigari*, for the Japanese, is something traditional and transcendental, highly expected and mandatory.

In winter, the abundant snow covers everything, and this winter image with its houses completely covered by a white blanket is bucolic and enveloping.

The village of *Shirakawa-go* offers a picture that seems to have come from the imagination and invokes the past. It is like seeing through an old postcard, where time stops to give way to the slowness of the passing of winter life in this remote place. Surrounded by hundreds of ski resorts, we grew up sliding through its valleys dyed in pure and crystalline white.

There is so much snow that the houses accumulate up to more than half a meter on their roofs. The fir trees can barely support the amount of snow accumulated on their branches.

It is an alpine picture where the valleys wrapped by their immense mountains, with their villages scattered in the middle, give us an authentic and real Christmas postcard image.

« In that place, each season has its charm and its changes, just like life, and each one of them symbolizes each moment lived as unique, different and unrepeatable.

Yes, I am very lucky! I was born on a special day, in a unique postcard place, in a fairytale village, and in the bosom of a unique and wonderful family... »

They named me: HARU YOSHIDA. *"Haru"* means *'spring,'* and it is related to the *'rebirth of the world'* (something normal in Japan, where names are important for their meaning and must always be related to something beautiful or philosophical). It was not difficult, since I was born in the middle of spring, in the *"Shōwa no hi,"* and according to my parents: I was very expected and desired, so much so that life was reborn for them at that moment, filling them with complete happiness. And being an only daughter, I had all the attention and dedication that could be desired, as well as infinite and perpetual love.

My father's name is *Kenji Yoshida*, well known and famous in the region as *"Yoshida Sensei."*
"Sensei" means: *'Master.'*
He is a Master of *Budō* (Japanese Martial Arts or "the Way of the Warrior"), and my mother: *Kimura Yoshida* (in Japan when getting married, the wife loses her maiden name and takes that of her husband), also called *"Kimura Sensei"* (she takes the name with the title of Teacher, and not the last name, to avoid confusion with her husband, although many called her "Yoshida Sensei" as well), but as a School Teacher in primary education (*"Shōgakkō"* in Japan).
I clarify, for non-Japanese, that the term *"Sensei"* is not exclusive to Martial Arts. It literally means *'the one who was born before'* or philosophically: *'the one who has walked the path,'* from the kanji characters *"sen"* (before) and *"sei"* (be born, life).
It is referred to as a title to treat a teacher or professional in any area with respect and admiration. Normally it is added to the family name, except in peculiar or exceptional occasions. Outside of Japan, *Sensei* is used mainly in the world of Traditional Martial Arts (such as: Aikidō, Karate, Ninjutsu, Judo, Iaidō, Kendō, Kyūdō, Jōdō, Kobudō, etc.), and also is

used in the *Otaku* culture (referring to people who are fond of anime, manga or dorama).

According to traditional Japanese, they are called this way, because the only difference between a student and a Master or *Sensei,* is that this is simply *'born before'* and that he has both knowledge and experience, and is for this reason, that he can teach to others.

Being my parents *Sensei*, in public I always addressed them as the others, with the respectful treatment of *Sensei,* but in private they were "mom and dad," and as you can guess, I had the Masters at home as soon as I was born; a privilege of a few, and for which I am very grateful to have been born in this specific and exclusive family bosom.

« *I was always so happy in my family home and so loved and respected by my parents!* I can assure you that if I were to be born again I would not change anything about my childhood, I would repeat it a thousand times faithfully the same. »

I took my first steps on the *tatami* of my father's *Dojo:* Yoshida's School Dojo (*Dojo:* is the training hall where the Way of the Martial Arts is practiced, also pronounced as *"place of awakening");* which was located on one of the main streets of *Ogimachi,* the main village. My father's martial arts school was very famous in the region; there were continually students coming and going. They came from cities in other prefectures to receive his teachings. I was almost always there, because my father preferred it that way instead of my mother taking me to her school, and leaving me, while she was giving her classes, in the school's nursery; although sometimes, I was going with my mother, because my father had other things to do or traveled to take courses to other places. Many times he gave master classes in various areas of *Tokyo, Kyoto,* or in the North and South of the island; sometimes he was also called from *Okinawa.*

The *Dojo* for me was the best place in the world. It was made of wood with *"tatami"* (straw woven mat to cover the floor) and had the imposing wall of the *"Tokonoma"* (the most important wall of the hall), where is the *"Kamidana,"* 'The Shinto altar' (sometimes called with the Anglicism of *"Shintō"* or *"Shintoist"*), and it is located right in front of the *Dojo*. It is the most important wall, because it is where the spirits of the ancestors or *"Kami" (Gods)* are welcomed, and it contains traditional symbols and images of the founding Masters of the *Budō Arts*. These are represented on this altar to profess loyalty and respect, for the ancient teachings transmitted for centuries and generations.

It also serves to establish the warrior's relationship with the philosophy of life, including not only the physical part of the practice, but also the mental preparation through the practice of *"Zazen"* meditation (sitting meditation).

All this always governed by a code of conduct or *"Dojo Kun"* (rules written in 'kanji' or 'Japanese calligraphy'); announcing the precepts of the *Bushidō*, that help the practitioner to find a line or guide of conduct, and ethical thought and morals.

It is normal: to see in all the *Dojo* of the different martial disciplines this wall of honor with its personal altar.

« How I adored and respected that wall of the *Tokonoma!*

It is always present in my mind, and I feel its energy and strength. Although, I currently have my own *Kamidana*, my personal altar, which always accompanies me wherever I am for my protection and blessing, I still keep in my mind the clear and perfect image of the *Tokonoma of Yoshida Sensei's Dojo.* »

My parents say: That I began to imitate what the students did or what I saw *Sensei* do, until at three years old, I was able to enter the smallest class.

I remember the training sessions and games we did in the woods, and although we had a lot of fun, they were very hard. Walking and running noiselessly stepping on the dry leaves; camouflaging ourselves in the environment, and not being seen or heard by *Sensei*; climbing trees and remaining motionless for a long time; jumping and climbing up steep rocks and mountains, and holding on only with our bodies; rolling down the slopes while maintaining the control; or getting into the icy waters of the river, and swimming without moving the water. All this and more, we did both day and night. For us, it was not training. We saw it as a game, we were not aware of its hardness. I particularly, loved the night and night practices. I merged so much with nature that darkness was my ally, and my eyes adapted so quickly that I could see with total clarity, with or without moon. I never felt fear. I always felt safe. It was all part of the physical and mental preparation.

Sensei always repeats, over and over again that we must gain control of emotions and redirect them towards positivity, because the goal to achieve is the *"unification of body and mind,"* because he who achieves this will have an *invincible spirit*. Each and every one of the oral transmissions and teachings of essential concepts for life, or the importance of: *"staying alive,"* I can assure that they remain stored in my brain and flow in every moment or situation of my life in a natural way, without thinking.

They are entirely etched in my mind to show themselves to me when I need help, advice, or making important decisions.

All of them are part of my guide to walk the path of life. They are the unwritten teachings. These are transmitted to the disciple by his Master, which is called *"Okuden"* (*"Oku"* in Japanese means: *'interior,' 'heart,'* and its meaning together with *"den"* would come to be translated as: *'the deep and hidden transmission').*

« The teachings and transmissions received have shaped and carved my body, brain and spiritual trunk. And, when in the future I needed them…, they came to me naturally…! »

We were also trained in the handling of traditional weapons, all those that are part of the *Kobudō* (*"ko"* for 'old' or 'ancestral,' *"bu"* for 'weapon' or 'warrior,' *"dō"* for 'path' or 'spiritual way') which means: *'The ancestral martial way of the warrior.'*

The weapons of *Kobudō* or *Kobujutsu*, were instruments and agricultural tools used by the villagers, who in the need to defend themselves against samurai oppression developed their own fighting style that, over time, some nobles and masters decided to systematize and group all the knowledge of weapons in a methodical and organized way on the island of *Okinawa*, creating the *Traditional Martial Art of Kobudō.*

Yoshida Sensei is also a Master of *Ninjutsu* (the Art of the *Shinobi*, or better known in the West as the *Art of the Ninja*) and Master of *Kenjutsu* (the Art of the sword), which is called: *"Budō no Sensei" or 'Master of Budō.'*

Complete knowledge will lead us to any object becoming a deadly weapon in our hands, if we know how to use it properly.

All those weapons or tools were necessary for the formation of a good Martial Artist.

We had infinite weapons to learn to use, as well as their forms, handling and techniques.

It was virtually impossible to get bored in the trainings.

« I loved the *Taijutsu* classes, "melee training", from the different schools. I have to confess that *Ninjutsu* is my true passion.

Its history is fascinating and teaches us about the past so that we can preserve the present and the future. »

I also used to train at home with *Sensei*, because we had another small private *Dojo* where my mother also trained. My mother loved to train with the *Yari* and *Naginata* (Japanese spears), and although these were his favorites, was not easy to combat with *Katana* (samurai sword) with her. She always set out to beat my father in combat, but never succeeded, although trying to do so amused her immensely. The truth is: when the three of us trained together, it was very funny and special, because Yoshida Sensei is not as serious as the fame that precedes him. Outside the *Dojo*, he is funny, always smiling, very affectionate and friendly, despite his appearance of strength and his height, somewhat tall for the average Japanese. And although the features of his face are very marked and deep, he always transmits peace and harmony; unique qualities in one who has achieved great wisdom and knowledge along the way; something that is only possible in *"the one who was born before:"* the *Sensei*.

We also practiced the Japanese Traditional Dance *"Nihon Buyou"* every week. My mother practiced since she was a child, and sometimes taught other women and men at home.
« One day a week was exclusively for the three of us: family dance. I loved it! We had so much fun…! »

There are, in very general terms, three types of Japanese dances differentiated by their movements; on the one hand, the *"Mai,"* which are dances with slow movements and very firm postures; on the other hand, there is the *"Odori,"* which are faster and more cheerful dances; finally, we have the

"Shosa" which are dances where expressions and emotions are given more importance, than the steps of the dancers.

The *"fan,"* called *"osensu,"* is what defines traditional Japanese dance. It basically embodies their spirit. This was widely used in the theatrical dance of *"Kabuki,"* '*a type of Japanese theater of traditional origin,*' where the lower part of the body becomes relevant, and the rhythm is marked with light steps and pauses called: *"ma"*.

Other elements used in the dance can be: some kind of instrument, umbrellas, cherry blossom branches, etc.

The *dance* was part of the samurai training, because their complicated and difficult movements gave them agility for fighting techniques, and at the same time, softened the robustness of their movements.

The *Shinobi* or *Ninja* also includes the Traditional Japanese Dance in his training, since it helps to obtain a good coordination in his movements at the time of performing and executing the techniques.

But, what I liked the most, was the philosophy of the Martial Arts, and especially that of the *Ninja* or *Shinobi*, a philosophy of life that my father took care of transmitting it to me in depth, because he always states, insistently: That's what will always keep me safe and protected, because it is not enough to know the arts of war or fighting if the mind is not equally trained and prepared.

« The arts and knowledge of camouflage, concealment and strategy; as well of seduction, evasion, etc., and so many other things that were taught to me and that later on: I had the opportunity to put all that, and more to the test in my life.... And that, thanks to the instruction, perseverance, dedication and efforts in this martial way: *Years later, I survived a vital situation!* »

Now you know that: Yes, I am a *"Kunoichi"* (which means *'Ninja Woman'* or also a *Ninjutsu* or *Ninpo* practitioner woman)!

Sometimes, the trainings and classes were quite hard and combined with the studies at the same time, made the days always short and I missed hours in the day. It is that, to the classes of Yoshida Sensei, with dad, we had to add those of Kimura Sensei, with mom. She, in addition, was my teacher at school until I was nine years old, when I changed levels and teachers. To me, "logical," she always demanded more of me than others, and always had double of duties (or so I thought ...). But she always had words and tokens of love that made everything easier and more enjoyable. She had that indescribable art that always made you feel happy with everything. Perhaps, her appearance as a fragile and thin woman, with soft gestures, with a kind and always complacent look, is what makes you feel that calm happiness and sense of well-being.

She also instilled in me the love of reading and at home we read a lot. My parents loved to tell stories and tales.
I remember the many days of winters reading, telling, talking, and philosophizing about everything with them.
My mother also taught me English and French. At school they only taught English. She completed several master's degrees in these languages, as a young woman, and mastered them perfectly. She taught them to me from a very young age, so I learned them almost without realizing it.
It became almost natural for me to speak in Japanese, English or French.

All the children in the village played together almost daily. We were like a big young band running everywhere in the village, and inventing different games of all kinds. The shopkeepers of the place always gave us candies in passing. In the villages, a calm and peaceful life was lived in harmony with the place, and each one dedicated himself to his own: their businesses or their lands.

There were many sown fields and the peasants were always working on their crops.

At twelve years of age he was already helping *Sensei* in the *Dojo* with the classes of the youngest children. It was not until I was fourteen years old, that my father gave me the privilege of having my own group of children under my teachings and responsibility. I became his guide and Master for them. It was a great responsibility.

« It was a great honor that Yoshida Sensei would deposit that trust in me, and I felt very proud and happy! »

When I turned fifteen years old, I was given a precious gift: my first *real "Katana,"* my first *'Japanese sword;'* made exclusively for me ("with all the traditional rituals of protection and purification").

It was given to me and presented at the *Dojo* before all the students in a kind of ceremony. It was a huge surprise for me; it meant a very happy and fortunate day, because such honor implies responsibilities and spiritual growth.

« *It's my jewel steel! Is my great treasure, my samurai sword, the jewel of more value than I possess.* According to samurai philosophy: when unsheathing the *katana* blade, the warrior is revealing, at the same time, his deepest intimacy and his heart *(kokoro);* therefore, a strong link is created between the figure of the warrior and that of his weapon. It is an act of complete sincerity, of a deep search for oneself. »

It was customary in the samurai that when they turned fifteen years old, they could have their first real *Katana*; therefore, it is typical in Japan that many parents offer this gift to their sons when they reach that age, so it symbolizes "*The Samurai Sword*" in Japanese culture.

Namely that, in the Japan of the Middle Ages, the ancient blacksmiths, before forging a new blade, performed purification rituals designed to summon the spirits, so that the new blade would be favorable to the new owner, and keep him protected and safe in their battles and encounters.

The complete elaboration of a *Katana*, according to traditional methods, can take several months of work.

So that was an important age in my life: feeling happy with my own real *Katana*; studying, training, teaching my own *Budō* students and living my adolescence (smug and flirtatious, something normal at that stage of life ...).

I really, enjoyed everything that this bucolic and privileged environment offered me, in which I was growing and training as a person.

That same year, I finished what would become my junior high school studies, in Japanese: "*chūgakkō,*" and began my "*kōkō*" education, which would be equivalent to the high school years (in Japan, 100% of schoolchildren continue their academic education), until the age of eighteen.

My qualifications were usually good or very good. It was not difficult for me to study. I was quite applied and methodical.

At that stage of my life, I remember that I really liked going shopping with my mother, visiting the typical artisan shops of the place. We stopped and walked into most of them.

There were shops with local products, especially rice crackers "*sembei*" and sweet typical "*age-manju.*"

The *Mishe no koshō* store, was dedicated to the sale of Japanese pepper *"shichimi togarashi"* (it is a very typical condiment of Japanese cuisine, that consists of a mixture of seven spices of chili).

In those days, it was typical for stores to offer hot water with *shichimi*, pepper powder, which was an energy drink that the Japanese in the mountainous regions liked very much.

« Entering this store was like traveling back in time! »

We also went to the *"chashitsu,"* tea houses, and ceramic craft shops in the area. My mother always bought tea and bowls for the kitchen.

I perfectly remember a beautiful old wooden shop; it was called *Taka Yasai No Ie*, very popular for selling all kinds of multi-colored Japanese sweets using soybeans, mixed with legumes and peanuts. We always bought a variety of them to take with tea.

One day a week the open-air market was set up on the main street, and all the villagers came from the early hours to do their shopping. The peasants filled the stalls with the various products of their freshly picked crops. The whole street was flooded with different shades of colors and hues, with different smells in the air, flooding with people walking and shopping. At the end of this street was a famous store and restaurant called *Michi no Hajimari*, which means *'the beginning of the road'*. For more than 100 years, it has been an almost obligatory stop for all visitors who are heading to the beautiful temple *"Myozen-ji"* to take *"Miso aisukurīmu,"* and *"Umegae-mochi,"* a pastry with rice pasta and red bean filling that is eaten roasted on grills.

The name of this restaurant was the reference that marks the entrance of the way to follow to get to the Temple.

The *Myozen-ji* Temple was founded in 1748. It is located on the north side of the *Shirakawa-go* village, in *Ogimachi*, and both: the temple and the gate of the *Bell Tower* have thatched roof and are in the *Gassho* style.

At the top, is the local *Myozenji Museum,* in which all the materials and tools used by the local population are displayed for to preserve the past.

The center is lights up every day; you can enjoy the smell of old-fashioned fire and its manicured gardens, full of bonsai typical of the Japanese Alps.

The set of buildings is recognized as: *"Property of the people of the Shirakawa-go set."*

Another of my favorite corners of the village was the *"Shiroyama Viewpoint,"* located at the northern end of the village. Going up to the viewpoint, where the *Ogimachi Castle* was located, to enjoy the best views of the village and its traditional houses was, without a doubt, one of my preferences of the place. There, I spent hours meditating and reflecting. In that magical corner, I reconsidered and reasoned about the philosophical teachings of life that my father, Yoshida Sensei, taught and transmitted to me, as well as other training and teaching thoughts from my mother, Kimura Sensei.

« I always had a lot of things in my head to meditate and process; to redistribute and place in my brain; to adjust and calibrate in my way of believing, feeling and thinking... »

Both of them instructed and trained me, so that tomorrow I would become a "complete human being," and thus, be able to understand human nature, in its essence as a rational animal, and know ethics, to which we attribute the qualities and values that are exclusive to the individual himself. Such as: compassion, affection, understanding, generosity, and many other skills and virtues that are positive in the absence of empathy and compassion for the suffering of others, social poverty, injustice...

Disciplines such as music, philosophy, art and literature contribute to the sensitivity of the human being. And I wanted to train myself in everything, and gain a deeper knowledge of life and of existence itself. The humane treatment of all people is what we should aspire to in society, and act with humanity towards others. Only then, can we live in a common atmosphere.

« I wanted to understand and assimilate all that to become someday: *'that complete human being,'* what in martial philosophy is called: *Tatsujin.* »

I was about to turn sixteen years old, when Yoshida Sensei and Nakamura Sensei (another Grand Master of the prefecture) gave me, at the *Dojo: "The degree certificate with Teaching of the Art of Kobudō,"* which accredited me as a Teacher or Master.

Now they would address me as *"Sensei"* in this martial discipline.

« I remember that I felt: *'concern and responsibility'* »

That same year, a few months later, I was also awarded the *"Ken-Jutsu Teaching Certificate" (Ken-Jutsu no Sensei).*

But it was not until I was seventeen years old that I obtained the same *"Authorization Title of Teaching Ninpo-Jutsu or Shinobi-jutsu,"* also known as *Ninjutsu (Ninpo no Sensei).*

Obviously, to reach these degrees, one must have black belt graduations (with the respective levels of *"Dan:"* denomination of the levels of the degree system in Japanese Martial Arts; *"dan"* means: *'step'* or *'level,'* and refers to the professional category of *"Sensei"* or "Master").

When naming me, people preferred to call me by my full name: HARU YOSHIDA SENSEI, so as not to create confusion with YOSHIDA SENSEI, since this one refers to my father since always.

Things were always happening in my life, events were happening one after another, and the years passed too fast. Now I was about to enter another phase of my life.

It was very close to turning eighteen, and normally at the end of the *"Kokō"* (high school), the Japanese people face one of the most important and fearful moments of their lives: the university entrance exams or *"daigaku."*
Traditionally, Japan knew how to have an educational system of high level and performance, in accordance with its social standards, which promoted a high exigency to the students, but also demanded that they get ahead with great success, which exerted a lot of pressure not only on the universities or academies, but also on the faculty and students.

It was time for my college entrance exam...
...And I overcame my entrance exam!

With my good grades I was able to enter the "Faculty of Economics and Information Science" in Gifu Prefecture.
« Why did I choose this career in economics? You will think ... I have always thought that the economic aspect is a fundamental piece to analyze human existence, as well as the main factor for the study of the history and culture of countries. It is one of the main fields of study in modern society, due to the importance of the control of production on a financial and social level. There is also the branch of the philosophy of economics that deals with moral and ethical aspects to be applied in economic activity. »

I still remember the joy I felt on my first day of college. I longed for that moment in my later years in high school.

As *Shirakawa-go* is a place in the middle of the mountains, there are no trains, so the only way to get to *Kanazawa* station is by bus. These, left punctually every half hour and it took approximately one hour and 20 minutes (making transfers); then, at the station across the street, I took another bus and had another 20 minutes to the university.

I spent almost 2 hours every day in a journey to which it was necessary to add another 2 hours for the return. This it was like this every day during the four years of formation at the Faculty.

It is true that the Japanese spend half their lives on trains.

A high volume of people move daily on high-speed trains between major cities, and on hundreds of urban train (subway) lines in metropolitan areas. The distances in the country are very long. Japan has the densest railway network with the highest traffic in the world and the longest travel distance, as there is not a single town or city that is not connected to commercial or work centers.

Japan has a peculiar view of the world, everything that happens in this country may seem somewhat "strange" for the West, but it is that people live at a completely different pace from the rest of the world, and the culture of travel in public transport is very widespread.

The Japanese thought is that, as long as there is only one person in any part of the country that demands transport, an entire station is kept open only for that person.

Hence, it is normal to invert and add to the workday: one, two, three, and up to four more hours each day.

On my first day of college, I got up at five o'clock in the morning to go to class. It was April, and in Japan, on this date, the school calendar starts until March of the following year when it ends.

The school year is divided into three stages: the first from April to August, the second from September to December, and the third from January to March.

Students also have summer holidays (from the end of July to the end of August), winter holidays (from the end of December to the beginning of January), and spring holidays (from the end of March to the beginning of April).

Normal then, that on that date, shone a beautiful and bright day. I remember looking at the sky when leaving home, and I thought it was pleasant to be accompanied by such a bright day. Besides, very soon, it would be my eighteenth birthday so I felt very energetic and plethoric.

It was a medium-sized campus; there were several buildings between parks and manicured gardens. The place provided a lot of serenity within the educational stress.

My classes took place in the buildings located in the east and south wings of the complex, so I crossed the park garden between them several times a day.

I was able to combine the schedules and I signed up, within the same faculty, to *"Spanish"* classes.

« I was very excited to learn this wonderful and rich language! »

With the university, I no longer had so much free time, so my martial training went to only weekends.

Before I got to college, I had already flirted with some guys, but never gotten serious with any of them. In that sense, I was not doing badly; I attracted quite a few young people. It's not that I was a super beauty or anything like that…, but I did know how to provoke certain "reactions" in others, and to take advantage of my conditions and weapons as a woman.

Being trained in the *Art of seduction* had its advantages. The important thing is to know how to control: how, for what, and when to use it.

Regarding me, at that time, I had, and still have: very long dark black hair, very straight and shiny (like most Japanese women), very cared for by my mother since my childhood. She loved to take care of my hair; she took care of it so that it was always perfect. Physically, I was slim but well-fibered and strong, due to always training. That is to say: "with a good figure." As for my face: it was small and somewhat rounded, childlike in appearance and soft-skinned, with slanted eyes, of course, but somewhat larger and more open, than most Japanese.

« I think it was a 'normal' young woman, typical Japanese. »

One day in college, I noticed a boy sitting on a bench in the shade of a Japanese willow tree, on the north lawn of the campus. He had a book in his hands, and suddenly, he raised his head and stares up at the sky as if searching for an answer. He stayed a long time like this, without taking his eyes off the bright blue sky of that day. That specific gesture is the one that drew my attention to him.

I felt that he seemed like someone special, someone I would like to meet. I watched him carefully. He had a very careful appearance; I thought among myself that he was a *"Binan,"* which means that *'he is a handsome man'* and *"Kakko ii,"* which is equivalent to *'handsome,'* and is used to refer to his appearance.

The truth is that he attracted me a lot because he had a symmetrical body and face; he was slim, but I could glimpse between his clothes, that he was somewhat muscular and athletic, which gave him a very attractive virile aspect.

I thought that the safest thing was that he practiced some sport.

Also caught my attention his shiny black hair (like most Japanese men), well-groomed with a good modern cut which suited his rather small, triangular, youthful-looking face.

Weeks passed until I saw him again, and I was running down the hall because I was late for one of my classes. I braked right in front of him, on the verge of having collided with the rush; I stayed a foot from his face, and lowered my head without saying anything, running towards the class. I could see, in a tiny instant, her brown eyes with the edge of the iris very black. That caught my attention. I spent the whole day lamenting how bad I reacted, because I could have said something, like apologizing or simply a sorry.

That day I preferred not to meet him again out of shame.

It was not until the next day, at the end of classes that we met again from afar in the campus park.

We both felt we had to get closer. We played at a distance to look at each other without looking at each other, so that it wouldn't be too noticeable that we were looking at each other. We would take a few steps and stop, like I'm going but I'm not going....

« It is the famous Japanese oriental shyness that acts in this way and I played my role: I let myself be carried away in the game like any "normal" girl because that is what I wanted to show him. »

Most Japanese people start dating someone in college, with the arrival of adulthood.

The cultural differences between Asians, specifically Japanese, and Westerners are quite considerable.

In Japan, there is an *"ethical protocol of courtesy"* when meeting or introducing someone. This, also called *"etiquette code,"* defines the social behavior in the country, and is considered very important. As in many social cultures, the *etiquette* may vary slightly, depending on one's status in relation to the other person with whom one must deal.

For example: The eye contact, known as *"shisen"* literally means *'the line of sight,'* as if it were an imaginary line between our eyes and the point on which we are focusing, or *"shisen ga"* which means *'crossing of gazes;'* this is not common in Japan! Because the ethical protocol says that staring a person in the eye can be very rude, uncomfortable, and disrespectful.

It is preferable to be subtle, and not to be too direct in a Japanese flirtation if you want it to consolidate into a serious intimate relationship. It is necessary to abuse hints and signs; to look without looking; playing to lower and raise the head…; it is about "awakening the senses."

As a general rule, the Japanese are usually shy by nature. They tend to get nervous when it comes to performing more intimate and personal acts. Sometimes it is difficult, because both, the man and the woman are reluctant to take the initiative to take the step in the relationship.

Japanese men like "real" and "transparent" women, when it is to establish a serious relationship as a couple.

The cultural level and the way of being are also measured to see if they are compatible, as well as knowing how to behave and the education, since making profanes comments, or having rude, or inconsiderate attitudes are not acceptable. For any of these actions, one is rejected immediately and there will be no other opportunity.

To conquer the heart of a Japanese woman, it is very important that the boy shows that he is friendly, funny, that he likes to take care of himself, and practice sports.

Another trait that Japanese women adore in men is: the kindness. They like her that: he gifts her with details, be attentive, give her flowers and chocolates, and organize romantic dinners...; in short: she should feel that you are devoted to her and that there is no one else.

When going on a date, he should always present himself well groomed and well dressed, so that the girl can see how careful and scrupulous he is, because men who are absent-minded, and do not take care of their appearance and personal hygiene, have few options with Japanese women.
He should also make use of the smile in all its amplitude. The girls or women expect to be conquered, since it is the guy who has to take the initiative, although this aspect is changing nowadays.
For all that, it is becoming increasingly complicated romantic relationships flowing among Japanese.

The Japanese commonly use the last name as a social way of addressing others. The first name should only be used with people from the closest and most intimate circle, or among the family. Thus, when it is necessary to introduce oneself: the last name is said first, to establish a distance that allows treating and speaking with respect.
After, we can repeat (among the young people) saying the first name plus the last name. Then, you have to lower your head slightly and lean your trunk. It is one of the many courtesy etiquettes *("Aisatsu,"* the well-known *'Japanese greeting'*) that must always be respected.
Unlike other cultures, you never start a conversation without going through a process of protocol introductions.
To start the conversation with the person we have just met (never shaking hands or kissing), always start with the expression: *"Hajimemashite,"* which can be translated as *'delighted'* or *'nice to meet you.'*
When this word is pronounced, *"beginning"* is given.

Those who study Martial Arts will have noticed that the term begins in the same way as *"hajime"* (which comes from the verb *hajimeru*), and marks the *"beginning"* of a combat or fight in any of the disciplines that are practiced.

Another correct expression that can be used is: *"Dozo Yoroshiku,"* which also means *'delighted, it is a pleasure.'*

Then, you have to continue with the conversation, and for this, you use a way of thanking to the interlocutor for this new relationship, and for the future conversations that are going to take place by saying: *"Dozo yoroshiku onegai shimasu"* or also: *"Kochira koso yoroshiku onegaishimasu,"* this is how the reciprocity of feelings is expressed when meeting someone, and the unspoken desire that more encounters are desired.

Returning to campus with the flirting and approaching, we continued walking towards each other slowly until we cut the distance to two meters. We then performed the Japanese greeting, and proceeded to introduce ourselves, following the protocol described above.

His name was TAKASHI (name that literally means: *'praiseworthy, noble'*) YAGAMI (surname whose meaning is equivalent to *'eight'* or *'God'*). I loved his name, it defined him very well.

When I told him my name: HARU YOSHIDA, smiling commented that *"it was logical that I could not call me otherwise."*

« I didn't understand why he said that…! »

We finished the presentation meeting, remaining in something that comes to be translated as: "that we will continue to see each other here and we will continue talking on more occasions."

This is a success in Japanese relations for a first contact, because it means that we are both interested in seeing each other again and getting to know each other more. When there is no interest, at the end of the protocol they end up saying: *goodbye*, *bye-bye*, and that's it, there is no more to wait!

From that moment, I felt inside me that I would be someone worthy and honorable. I felt many things, it was what is known as *crush or love at first sight* or *at first contact...* Whatever it was, I returned home very excited, and with my heart beating faster than the train I was traveling on.

As soon as I arrived, I told my parents. I had met the boy I liked, whose name was Takashi Yagami. I told them how Takashi-San (*"San"* is an honorific suffix; it refers to courtesy treatment in Japanese towards other people and is equivalent to *Lord* or *Lady* regardless of age, and applies to all people except oneself; is used with both first and last name; except for being in an intimate and familiar circle) was physically, and that I had loved meeting him, and that we had agreed to continue seeing and talking...
My parents made a few jokes regarding my emotions, but seeing my joy, they decided to respect me and let me fly and dream. They wished me luck, and gave me permission and encouragement to invite him home whenever I wanted, and that they would remain eager to meet him soon. Of course, there were advice on the sexual issue, and they did not refrain from giving me all the advice possible or almost all, although they knew perfectly well that, in Japan, sex does not come so quickly, that it takes time to become intimate.

It had been a few weeks since I had started University, and my eighteenth birthday arrived, in the *"Shōwa no hi,"* on

April 29, and as I already told, it is a very special holiday and celebration in the country.

In the past, giving and receiving gifts on birthday or Christmas occasions, was not part of the most orthodox Japanese tradition, but western customs were gradually introduced. In our house, in our family we used to give each other gifts on certain and important dates for us. It should also be remembered that, in the past, the birthday of all Japanese people was commonly celebrated on the New Year. Currently, the western tradition has been imposed on Japanese practice, and it is increasingly common to share celebrations imported from other countries.

And, although eighteen years, are not significant in Japan because the age of majority is *twenty years* (which is very important in Japanese society), I had two very special gifts on that day: one from my parents; and another by *budokas* training partners of the *Dojo School Yoshida Sensei*. My parents gave me a *"Sakura,"* a *'cherry blossom tree,'* a little more than three and a half meters high, beautiful and already sprouting its flowers. I was impressed to see that great tree in front of our house.

There were many neighbors on the street watching the spectacle and applauding the *Sakura*.

They brought it in a huge truck with a crane, and I had to choose where in the garden I wanted it, but I had a hard time deciding because of its large size. The nice coincidence (which was no accident), is that the tree was eighteen years old, just like me. My parents said that, in that way, we would have a birthday together. Every year, I would give to the tree attentions and love for, and the tree would give me the rain of his petals on that day. It sounded heavenly music in my ears when I heard those beautiful words, and with that symbolism exclusively for me, a *Sakura* of my own that would last my entire existence...

At that point in my short life, there was a "new beginning" that would bring me changes: love, evolution, maturity, feeling that I was part of nature with my tree, and offering the maximum respect towards it; as well as valuing the day to day and the delicacy and fragility of everything around us.

There are two varieties of *Sakura*: one in white and the other in a pale pink hue. This one was of flowers in pink tones. Although there is a Japanese legend that says that, previously in its beginning, the cherry blossoms were only white.

« I had my own private *"hanami"*! I would see every year the delicate cherry blossom fall in its fullness with the wind before withering. This is also related to part of the *"samurai code"* in Japan. The truth is that the emblem of the samurai warriors was the cherry blossom. The highest aspiration of a samurai was to die in his prime, in battle, and not to grow old or "wither," just as the cherry blossom does not wither on the tree. »

There are beautiful legends of the *Sakura* that come from times of ancient Japan, when numerous battles were fought in which many warriors died, leaving the whole country mired in sadness. These legends leave beautiful messages about love, and how to overcome our own limits and survive.

One of these legends of the *Sakura* flower, tells how many women appeared dead, as many as men who died in battle. None of these women were killed; they themselves did so under the name of their "samurai husband" killed in battle. This act was always done in front of a cherry blossom tree that, with the blood it absorbed, its flower turned pink. After this, whenever a samurai came out of his house, he planted a cherry tree in his honor... And so, the legend goes it is how Japan was populated with so many *Sakura* trees.

In the end, I made the decision to plant my prized tree in the front part of the garden, in front of the house to the left of the plot entrance. To all those present there, from my parents to all the attending public and the gardeners who had to do the work, liked it and applauded the chosen place.
« There it was, majestically, my *Sakura* flooding our house with color and joy! »

At sunset, as it was the custom, the entire family we walked together to the temple to give thanks to have reached that day, and ask to live many more years. Halfway there my father said he wanted to stop by the *Dojo* to pick up something he needed. So, we changed course.
Upon arrival, my father opened the door and ushered me in front. There were all the high-grade disciples, all the black belts in the school! Everyone had remained absolutely silent until the door opened and we entered. It was a surprise they had prepared, in agreement with my parents, because they wanted to give me a present on behalf of all of them.
They delivered me a *stone slab* with a gold metal plate embedded in the stone itself, and an inscription with letters engraved in black.
The recording written in *kanji* (it is a philosophy of difficult translation) would come to be translated as: 'On this day-, this year-, this *Sakura* and the person Haru Yoshida Sensei turn eighteen years old; may they remain united and continue to fulfill, and celebrate together all the years to come and every spring that will have to flourish.'
I thanked, with great emotion and surprise, all the fellow *Budoka*, with whom I had lived so many years, so many experiences and so much love from all...

« It was an unforgettable day! There was no better gift! They are wonderful memories that I keep with my *Sakura* to this day, and that give me the joy of living. »

At the next day we placed the stone next to the *Sakura*. I liked very much seeing it there next to the tree, and reading the beautiful words of my group *"Buyu,"* 'martial friend or companion,' every time I contemplated it.

During the following weeks at the university, Takashi-San and I would meet every day, and we had conversations at the different moments that we coincided. We were already getting to know each other more. We talked a lot whenever we could.

He was nineteen years old, a year older than me; he was in the second year of Information Sciences (technological), it is a branch of science that studies the practice of information processing. Which arose in response to the social need to develop effective methods to collect, preserve, search and disclose information, as well as study algorithms and systems that store information and documents.

He was a good communicator and a good listener, just like me, and that made our conversations easier.

Takashi-San told me about where he was born and lived: in *Nagano (Nagano-ken),* which is located on the island of *Honshū.* About his family: his father is a businessman dedicated to electronics production, and his mother is a housewife at present, although she had studied pharmaceutical sciences. He told me that he played baseball for seven years, and belonged to the *Japanese Junior Baseball League* (Japanese passion), and also practiced from six years of age to seventeen the *"Kendō"* (the most widespread Martial Art in Japan), where the Japanese begin their practice as children in schools.

Armor and a sword bamboo or wood is used. *"Kendo"* comes from *ken* (sword) and *dō* (way).

So we had the *Budō*, the Martial Arts and the Philosophy in common. This brought us endless conversations about the training we both practiced, and how we saw the world due to this knowledge and preparation that the practice of Martial Arts provides. As he was as passionate as I was, it was easy for him to become fascinated by my life and all that around me. He felt admiration for my dedication and a lot of respect; so much so that he often called me *Sensei* (it is normal in Japan to show respect and recognition of a Martial Master). He was eager for I to teach him and demonstrate my skills, especially *"Ninjutsu,"* since he had always been attracted to the *Art of the Shinobi* or *Ninja*. He also wanted to meet the famous Yoshida Sensei. Also showed his desire to want to practice, but I evaded the subject, dodging and making his wish stronger, like a good *"Kunoichi"* (female ninja).

Finally, he also explained to me why, when he introduced us, he told me that "I couldn't call me any other way", and he said such nice things since my name mean: "spring," "sunlight" and "beauty;" and to him it was logical because I reflected that exactly when he looked into my eyes; that he saw before him a great person who radiated: strength, transmitting beauty, charm, coquetry, pride..., but which inspired a deep respect and calmness at the same time; that he was sure that I had to be someone of high status and knowledge; that he felt that I would be someone unattainable for him ... And more superlative things that left me blushing and ashamed, because no one had ever said such beautiful things to me ...

We ate every day on campus. We had many moments and opportunities from Monday to Friday, between classes, to be together, talking or studying.

Soon we began to see each other outside the faculty. We used to go for a drink or something to eat; sometimes we also met up with university friends.

It had been a couple of months, and we had almost told each other everything; we had opened up and been sincere with each other. He talked to me a lot about how he was attracted to me, and also kept telling me that he liked everything about me; also said that he was fascinated by my world, my life, my knowledge, my way of thinking and being; that he had never felt anything like this before.
I, too, dropped him, subtly, what I liked about him and what attracted me.

Both of us, deep inside, were thinking of *"Kokuhaku,"* which means *'confession,'* and is performed when a man or woman declares himself or herself to the person he or she loves and hopes that, with that declaration, both of them can change their relationship to a formal one of courtship.
If there is a most difficult activity for the Japanese, that is the *Kokuhaku,* because declaring the feelings to another person can be very hard on the ego, as you never know what the other person thinks of you, and you wonder whether to go ahead or not, if it will be worth a try... Because experiencing rejection is something that no Japanese or anyone else likes to expose oneself to.
Normally the *Kokuhaku* statement comes with phrases translated from Japanese, in style something like:
"I like you, please come out with me" (standard phrase used for both sexes).
This *"phrase"* marks the beginning of a serious and formal relationship. Perhaps the two people have already gone out alone on more than one occasion. However, it is not until the moment in which this phrase (or similar) is pronounced, that

both are considered *"boyfriends."* And in fact, it is not until the moment in which both accept their feelings that they can show physical affection (a kiss, a hug or holding hands); all this is reserved only and exclusively for formalized couples. This *confession*, although it may seem somewhat "ridiculous" to Westerners, it is not so much for the Japanese, since they do not go through the courtship with another person if there is no certainty that both want a formal and lasting relationship.

It is not even surprising that between adults, the confession includes phrases like: "I love you so much that I can't live without you, and I want to start a relationship to take it to the end (implying marriage)."

Therefore, it is not a simple "let's go out and see what happens next," no! In Japan after *Kokuhaku*, thinking of another person is excluded, totally out of the game.

Thus, the *declaration of the Kokuhaku* is not just anything.

It takes courage and being sure of the other person!

We meet one day to go for a walk together in the park of *"The way in Kanazawa."* It is a walk full of *Sakura* trees on both sides and, although the *hanami* had finished and all the flowers had come off, the trees were full of new leafy green shoots.

And yes, there, next to a Japanese cherry tree, the *Kokuhaku* occurred, he pronounced *"the phrase"* and I answered:

"Yes, that I liked him too! And yes, I also wanted us to go out together formally!"

« This is where our *'courtship'* formally began! »

Then, he took my hand and we started running. I didn't know where he wanted to go until we got to a flower shop. He told me to wait outside for a moment, and came out with a beautiful bouquet of *"Sakurasou"* flowers (these flowers grow since the *Edo* period, also known as the *Tokugawa* period: from 1603 to 1868, and are very popular in Japan, because the shape of this flower is similar to that of the Japanese cherry tree, the *Sakura*). In floral language its meaning is of *"desire"* and *"lasting love."*

« It was a very wise choice for the moment, which showed me and let me see that his mind and heart knew how to act together; that he did not react madly and without thinking (choosing 'anyone' or 'this same'); that he meditated his actions and feelings. I really liked his way of acting and the message through the chosen flowers. »

As I did every day when I arrived home, this time with my bouquet of flowers in my hands, I went to my mother (my father was always teaching at that time and arrived later in the evening), to tell her everything that had happened to me during the day; although that time, holding my bouquet, she had already imagined it because she exclaimed:

"Oh... Haru! It's a bouquet of *Sakurasou!* Did Takashi-San give it to you? And has he declared you the *Kokuhaku?* Tell me please...!"

I told her everything, and she was very happy. She insisted that I invite him over for the weekend. We talked for a while about all that and how I was feeling.

« It was comfortable to dialogue with Kimura Sensei every day. »

Then, I continued my daily routine: went to study, and then, went to the *Dojo* at home to meditate and train, because I needed it and I missed it.

That's how it was every day, sometimes alone and other times my mother joined in (when she didn't have to prepare courses or correct exams), until my father arrived and we had dinner together.

At that stage of my life, every weekend consisted of giving a class on Saturday mornings to my students at the *Dojo*, and when they finished leaving, I stayed training alone. After, I would meet with my parents (if I didn't have plans with friends). Sometimes we went to visit a family member. Other times, we would go to *Kyoto, Nara...* or to the center of *Tokyo* for a walk, to eat in a restaurant, to the cinema or to the theater.

We really liked *"Kabuki:"* traditional Japanese theater that is characterized by its stylistic drama, where the elaborate and striking makeup of the actors, and a very colorful and bright costumes, combine singing and dancing in very careful choreographies that are an essential part of this scenic art.

The *Kanji* that form the word are the conjunction of three skills: *"Ka"* for singing, *"bu"* for dancing, and *"ki"* for expression or ability.

The *Kabuki Theater* is currently considered "Intangible Cultural Heritage of Humanity," and first emerged in the 17th century, at the beginning of the *Edo* period. Although, originally, it was a show performed only by women, later it is prohibited, because they begin to make farces and pantomimes in the comedy that were considered 'very daring' by the authorities, who prohibit it in the name of "the moral defense of women" so that it would not be confused with prostitution (something that was beginning to happen), and from then on, it was limited to male actors, giving rise to the so-called *"onnagata:"* 'men playing the role of a woman,' and only it can be represented by mature men, who perform all the papers, including the woman's.

The *Kabuki* is one of the four genres of classical Japanese theater, along with the *kyogen*: an older style of spoken theater; the *noh*: musical drama; and the *bunraku*: known as puppets theater.

Other times we went on excursions and tourist visits (something that the Japanese do a lot within their own country) to different regions, or to ski in the *Northern Japanese Alps* where most of the ski resorts are concentrated (of the more than six hundred ski resorts that there are in all Japan, more than two hundred are in the Alps), and from home, we accessed it comfortably by Rail.

When I went skiing with friends, we usually went by car (the roads are often dangerous at night with snowfall in all the alpine mountains), so we used to stay overnight in one of the various hotels that are next to the ski slopes, and we would return the next day in the morning.

Normally on Saturdays, we always ate out of the house. On *Dojo* Sundays (alternatively), in the morning I trained with the high grade partners (black belts with *Dan* levels); sometimes indoors and sometimes outdoors, in the mountains, where else I liked, because nature is the essence and authenticity of the *Art of Shinobi* or *Ninja*. We trained strong among us, and sometimes appeared Yoshida Sensei and then ... it was worse!

Sensei pushed us to the limit and we were shattered. At that point, what we wanted to do was *really relax*. So, we all went to the *"Shirakawa-go Natural Onsen,"* the public hot springs, and enjoy bathing outdoors with the sound of the crystal clear waters of the *Shogawa River*, and contemplating the views of the *Hakusan Mountains*.

The massages in that *Onsen* were fabulous! You felt that the world stopped, and the pleasure and relaxation were a unique experience for the body and senses; you relaxed so much..., that you felt float in the air. We usually spent a couple of hours until we were as good as new and all aches and pains were cured.

The rest of Sunday, I tried to dedicate only to myself: to be at home reading comfortably and recovering energy to face the next week.

The other Sundays, when I did not have *Budō* classes, I used to dedicate it for a walk and go to the *"Jin,"* 'Temple,' to pay my respects and give thanks to the *"Kami,"* or *Gods:* For the fortune, for existence, for everything good that happened to me, also for my health and always for what is to come.

After thanking, I made my requests to the *Gods*, which generally consisted in: world peace (although it sounds like a beauty queen, and it is that in Japan is always present in the citizenship, due to so many years of wars in the past), protection and health for me and my loved ones, and that my spirit remain noble and kindly.

« I had always asked the *Kami* for the same thing throughout my entire existence (until that future day came when I had to ask for something "unimaginable" for me), perhaps because I had never needed anything more. I had the life I wanted and everything I wished for! I couldn't ask for more...! »

As I have already told before, I used to go to the beautiful "Viewpoint" of the town to contemplate the view of the villages and the mountains. I sat there, in "my favorite place," reflecting and meditating on everything that had happened, and what I had pending by to do. I was sitting there for hours with myself...!

I also walked by the villages of the place, talking and greeting to the neighbors, and friends that I met on the way.

I always bought some things in the stores (all the shops were open every day), or I ate a typical cake from the village; sometimes I used to do this with my parents or with local friends. Later, I was coming home to eat with the family, or were we going to eat out. In the afternoon, I dedicated time studying and preparing things for the faculty, listening to stories and tales from my parents, or conversing with them and reading.

Since I had met Takashi-san, I missed him on the weekends; ever I was thinking about him, and what we would do and say to each other in the days of the following week. He told me that the same thing happened to him, that *"I was his true love."* And we missed each other more and more, finding it hard to be apart, even for a single day.
« This is what happens when two people are so much in love, as we were! »

Since the declaration and request, as well as my acceptance, of "being boyfriend and girlfriend" officially, this was already known by all the students at the university, including the professors (friends had spread the word…).
In theory, it will take a few years to move on to the "next step", according to Japanese tradition. That step consists in that, when the relationship is already strongly consolidated, the couple announces their love to friends and family. In our case, we were quicker to take that step. As for the friends, it was not necessary, they were already expecting it, but the first date with the families was missing, and it is a tradition to do it when the relationship is serious, after of our declaration and acceptance. It is custom and tradition: to carry details or small gifts to like and win over the loved ones of the couple. My parents were somewhat more modern. They wanted to meet him from the beginning even though we weren't "official boyfriends," but Takashi-San's parents were somewhat more traditional.

At the end of July, we had vacations at the university until the end of August, and "my boyfriend" was already very anxious to come to *Shirakawa-go* and meet my family, especially my father, the *Sensei*.

He also really wanted to see me training *Ninjutsu* (which he was passionate about!), or to see me giving classes, and besides, he didn't want us to go a month without seeing each other (neither did I!); so I decided to invite him in early August to spend a few days at home.

Of course, I had already spoken to my parents, and I had permission to invite him.

« I remember how happy he was and how excited he was...!

It is considered an honor to be invited to the home of Japanese. »

At home, we prepare everything for their arrival (it is normal that, in these situations, the whole family gets involved and actively participates). We had a small room with an armchair, a table and closets (a lot of space was needed to store the *futons* (it is the traditional Japanese bed consisting of a mattress and a cover that is placed on the floor, on the *tatami* or mat, and folds and picks up every day), also for clothes and ski equipment, etc.

So, we made room for Takashi-San to open the futon at night and put his things.

I went to pick him up at the station, early in the morning. I saw him so nervous that, before taking him home, I took him to take something to talk to him, and calm him down. He was amazed with the place, the views, the village, being there with me... He was going to really know me: my family, my roots, whole my life..., and he would live with all of us for two days! All of this had him very nervous and thrilled.

After talking to him for a while, I managed to calm his nervous state a little...

We headed home. We went inside and took off our shoes (as is customary in Japan).

Whenever you enter a house, you shout: *"Tadaima!"* to the people that are inside. This expression can be translated as *'I'm here' or 'I'm back.'* My mother was in the kitchen, and while she came towards us, she answered: *"Okaeri nasai!"* (The closest translation of which would be *'Welcome home'*).

I made the introductions and they greeted each other, as the protocol indicates. My mother told us to go to the *Dojo* room, which is at the end of the house that my father was there.

She was glancing at me with mischief, as if giving me the go-ahead, affirming that she liked "my boyfriend."

We were at the entrance step, waiting... *Sensei* was meditating in front of the *Kamiza* (the altar) in the *Seiza* posture (the traditional way of sitting on the knees); when he finished, he stood up and turned to us bowing and inviting us to come in. Takashi-San's whole body was trembling and he couldn't control his nervousness.

We proceeded to the presentation. Then, my boyfriend apologized for his momentary absence, and went to get some gifts that he had brought for them (as marks the Japanese etiquette).

He handed a tray of *"Doyaki:"* which are some cakes with chocolate and sponge cake, of high confectionery, to *Kimura Sensei,* and a *"Keshōmen:"* a decorative surface of a piece of wood (flat source of carved artisan carpentry), engraved with a branch of the *Sakura*, or Japanese cherry tree.

My parents thanked him and welcomed him to our home. My mother tried hard to make him feel comfortable, but my father, on purpose, just stared at him seriously, and without saying a word.

Takashi-San looked at the *Dojo* and everything on the walls: pictures with photos, titles, weapons and old objects. I was explaining every detail to him, and trying to make him relax. He commented, impressed, on old photos of my father with his *Sensei* and tried to imply his knowledge of Martial Arts, and what he was passionate about, so that the *Sensei* would hear him.

He continued to hold the tension until Kimura Sensei told us: "Let's go to lunch!" (Lunchtime in Japan is between 12:00 and 1:00 p.m.).

It was 12:00 noon, and we all went to the dining room, helping to set the table, and carry all the dishes that my mother had prepared with great care.

She had prepared dishes of *Shichū* (Cream Stew), *Soba* (wheat noodles with *tsuyu* sauce), *Tepanyaki* (grilled chicken with vegetables and soy sauce), and *Sashimi* (finely cut raw fish and seafood).

For the drink, *Sensei* put on the table a bottle of *"Sake"* (also called *Nihon Shu* that can be served hot, cold, or at room temperature), but offered the version called *"Otoso,"* which means *'destroy evil and revitalize the spirit.'* Then, he began the ceremony by pouring the *sake* into the so-called *"Tokkuri,"* (it is the traditional bottle, of special handmade ceramic, which is used to serve wine), and filled the cups called *"Ochoko"* (these are like small glasses or cups without handles), serving the "guest" first.

We made the toast of *"Kanpai"* which means *'dry glass,'* before drinking, and it is considered a festive way to toast.

Thereupon, Yoshida Sensei spoke for the first time saying:

"Takashi-San, 'a father's kindness is higher than a mountain, and a mother's love is deeper than the ocean;' this is our feeling for our daughter, and what is yours?"

"My feeling is to reap the *goodness* in Haru-San to collect her *love*," Takashi-San replied. "Because I believe that *love and goodness* cannot be achieved without each other, and there is no reward without the help of those you care about. I hope to achieve this with the company and courtesy of both *Yoshida Sensei,* as it would be my greatest wish, and the greatest honor that can be granted to me."

"You have my support and blessing," said Yoshida Sensei (mother).

"If my daughter is happy you have my gratitude too," added Yoshida Sensei (father). "Let's toast to the newcomer to our home, *'Kanpai'*!"

« My father used an ancient Japanese proverb about love to examine and test Takashi-san, and he reacted by responding with a play on words, very intelligently, with other proverbs of wise men. »

This display of intelligence was notorious to my parents. In fact, it was praised by Kimura Sensei at the end of the meal; which made my boyfriend feel pleased and reassured.

The gathering consisted of wanting to know about him: his career, his hobbies, his family, etc., but not as an interrogation, but rather using the *"secret arts"* of making him speak, and open up in confidence. The truth is that he spoke almost alone (despite his shyness).

« Mastering this art of directing (manipulating), without the person realizing it: a conversation, an attitude, or even their own behavior, is very important.

The truth is that we all felt comfortable talking and laughing, although my father kept his composure… »

After lunch and the gathering, we walked from the house to show him the village, and introduced him to the neighbors and friends that we were meeting on the way. I showed him the stores, explained the celebration of the festivals and customs of the local villages. I also pointed out to him the mountain ranges that loomed majestically before us, and I told him about my childhood running through those hills and plains.

We arrived at the Temple and lit incense; we bowed and thanked the *Kami* (gods) for the happy events we were experiencing. The acceptance of my parents was something very important to both of us, and for that we were euphoric and happy.

We looked at the stalls selling amulets in the shrine, and he bought an *"Omamori,"* a popular *'Japanese amulet,'* which is a kind of cloth pendant whose primary purpose is: *'To protect and bring fortune to those who wear it.'* He gifted it to me saying: "I want that you carry it with you all the life."

The term *"Omamori"* comes from the verb *"mamoru,"* which means: to protect, to take care, and to defend; it also has the power: to avoid accidents, to take care of health, to attract luck, to help in love, to pass exams, etc.

Most Japanese believe in them and always carry one with them. The *Omamori* are usually carried in many places: in the pocket, on the mobile phone, in the bag or in the car.

The bag, *"omamori-bukuro,"* is a small silk sack in brightly colored, and has the name of the shrine where it is purchased embroidered on rear side. Inside and always closed to external view, it contains a rectangular inscription, which can be made of paper or cardboard; it also bears the name of the God or protector *Kami* for the occasion with a prayer written and blessed by a monk from the Temple of the place.

« That amulet has been with me ever since! I have always carried it with me! Takashi-San's protection and love always accompany me. »

That first night, it became extraordinary and unusual, not only for me but for my parents as well, accepting that new situation. It was the first time that a man, the boyfriend of their only daughter, their little girl, slept at home. I didn't know what they thought or felt, although they had been the ones who insisted that I invite him, and that reassured me.

« *'Their little girl had become a woman,'* for sure this was what was on their minds, especially in that of *Sensei*; I could see it in his face and in his nostalgic look... I knew him well, as he knew me. My mother always told us that *'we were like two soul mates!'* »

The next day we went to Yoshida Sensei's school. We had class. Takashi-San was happy and very excited because: He was finally going to see the training!

Takashi-San was marveling at the *Dojo,* made of ancient wood, and appreciated everything he saw: the wall of the *"Tokonoma"* (altar), the *"Kakemonos"* (fold-out scrolls with Kanji or ideograms writings), weapons and... More weapons on all the walls, more pictures, more titles... Everything caught his attention!

That class, on that day, was given by Yoshida Sensei to the high grades group and it was of *Ninjutsu*. When he saw me appear on the *tatami* dressed in my *"Shinobi gi"* or *"Shinobi Shozoku"* (the traditional black clothing of this Martial Art) he was dumbfounded, speechless...

Sensei said that on that day we would work on: "The balance with nature," consisting of executing the movements of the technique, in such a way that the three axes between man, sky and earth, are one.

This was worked without weapons and then with the different weapons of the *Shinobi* or *Ninja*. Yoshida Sensei was introducing parts of the philosophy of thought with nature, such as:

"The value does not focus on man but on Nature, and thus one can speak of 'Humanism' since the Heaven, the Earth and the Man form a single set."

The principles of Heaven (Ten), Earth (Chi) and Man (Jin) are a series of concepts, techniques and body forms to develop a natural martial ability.

Using *"Taijutsu"* or *'The Art of using the body,'* one learns about one's own body, and the hard training helps the student build the mental and spiritual character necessary to face a life and death fight.

Yoshida Sensei also explained and clarified certain concepts to the students in the class, such as:

"Martial techniques aimed at the destruction of the enemy, except in self-defense, are no longer used. They now continue to be part of the harmony of the natural world. The ancient techniques of war *(Bujutsu)* were converted into 'Arts of Peace.' Today the sword and the chrysanthemum coexist peacefully. Its moral and spiritual content are the instruments for the physical and ethical formation, thus provoking in Man the integration with Nature."

The class ended, and all the disciples performed the Japanese ritual of the usual greeting and respect sitting in *seiza,* in front of the *Tokonoma.*

« "The arts of war are the arts of peace. Train hard in conjunction with the principles of Nature for harmony and universal concord;" this was the message that *Sensei* transmitted at the end of the class that day. We had always remembered that class, and talked about it on multiple occasions, because for Takashi-San it marked a beginning in his new life, which he never forgot. »

Takashi-San was beside himself with what he had seen and heard. He spent the whole day saying that he wanted to enter the *Dojo* and participate in the classes; he wanted to practice the *Art of Ninjutsu.* He spent the day saying that Yoshida Sensei was a great master; which was the best thing

he had seen in *Budō* classes... I don't know how many
"Onegai shimasu," 'please,' he got to pronounce that day...!
I talked to Sensei, and we agreed that he should put on a
"Gi," or training *Kimono* (my father would leave the clothes
for him), and try him out to see how he would do in the class,
or if on the contrary he would give up....

The next day, I would give the class to my group of
students, and Takashi-San, with his *Kimono Shinobi Shozoku,*
joined to the group on the *tatami.*
I did that day a class of *"Shinobigatana,"* also known as
"Ninjatō" or *"Ninjaken,"* which refers to the sword used by
the *Ninja*, with the straight edge blade, instead of the curved
edge of the *Katana* or samurai sword.
The truth is: he worked and reacted quite well to all the
movements of the class. His years of *Kendō* practice had
served him well when it came to moving his body, and
performing the techniques, as his footwork and concentration
were very good. He had aptitude to develop any martial
discipline or sport that he proposed because his physical
preparation was quite remarkable.

Logically, when finished the training, he did not stop
magnifying and praising me with my aptitudes and abilities
as a practitioner and Master.... Without realizing it, all day he
addressed me as *Sensei,* and I had to continually tell him that
"we were outside the *Dojo*, and privately, so please: Call me
by my name 'Haru'!"

Takashi-San in those days that he spent in the family,
he was hooked with training and with our way of life. He was
constantly asking me to teach him other basic movements for
beginners because he wanted to train. When there were no
classes at the *School Dojo*, he spent most of his time at the

home *Dojo* practicing non-stop. I was continuously teaching him new movements and he was working on his own.

He even did Dance with Kimura Sensei, and he also participated in the family class that we had once a week, all together, in family.

When I got him to stop practicing, we went on excursion and enjoy the mountains and nature. He said he would like to live there, that the fame was true, and that it was like living in a fairytale place.

The week passed almost without realizing it, the days went by very quickly.

It was a wonderful week and we had a great time!

My parents were very happy with his arrival as well. They had a very positive impression of him as a person, which was very important, as parents and relatives are always very dear to your Japanese partner.

If you progress to the point of to meet and be part of your partner's family, this is considered: *"a turning point in your relationship."*

Therefore, getting "the blessing" of the family is very convenient to have a good future together, and from my parents' side, we already had their full approval and blessing. And as a well-known Japanese proverb says: "The longest journey begins with a first step."

« Takashi- San and I, never forget in our minds that first week together when he met my family, the world I belonged to, the place where I was born and grew up: *'The famous fairy tale village!'* »

From that moment on, Takashi-San asked Yoshida Sensei for permission to become a disciple of the *Ninjutsu* Martial Art, and to be able to come on alternate Sundays to train at the School *Dojo* and receive his teachings and mine.

The permission was given to him by both of us, and during all his time at the university he always attended as agreed, never missing a single Sunday. This way he could combine with his family, as well besides taking advantage for to study. It was good for both of us. So, we both had availability to go out with friends too, and miss each other when we didn't see each other.

« On vacation he always took advantage for staying in our house for a week or two, becoming part of the family clan as one more member. »

But we still had something pending: my introduction to his family, to his parents. We decided that, in the last week of vacation, the last Sunday: we would visit his parents and repeat the protocol in reverse.

He was born in the city, also the capital, of *"Nagano,"* which belongs to the island of *Honshu,* in central Japan. It is well known because it hosted the XVIII Winter Olympic Games in 1998. The prefecture has spectacular mountain areas and peaks that are part of the Japanese Alps. Hence, winter sports such as skiing and ice skating are especially abundant.

Also well known is the *"Jigokudani Monkey Park,"* where you can enjoy bathing with the famous snow monkeys. The main attraction of the city is the impressive *"Zenkoji Temple,"* which is attended by large crowds of Japanese and tourists.

Nagano is a small city that can be easily explored on foot or by bicycle.

I had been there many times. When I went skiing to that side of the *Nagano Mountains*, I always walked around the city and the surrounding villages. It is a nice and pleasant place with a lot of ancient samurai tradition, and it is eaten very well in the area, especially *"oyaki,"* a round pie or bun stuffed with vegetables or beans paste. It is a dish originally from the prefecture (many Japanese people travel expressly to taste it).

His family lives in downtown, on a street parallel to *Chuo-dori*, which is *Nagano's* main road, and runs through the city from north to south.
Takashi-San and I had arranged to meet at the station exit first thing in the morning on a Sunday. I carried my presents for his parents, and I hoped they would like it because I tried to find something nice but not sophisticated (according to tradition it should not be something of excessive value).
The day would consist of the presentation, and if I was accepted, I would be invited to lunch. We would spend the afternoon, and I would return at the end of the day by train.
I arrived at the station, and we walked; the house was about three minutes away. It was a typical Japanese house, old but renovated, and there was a small garden around it.
The house occupied almost the entire plot. There were many plants; you could hardly go through the stone paths that marked where to tread. It had a lot of charm and intimacy.
We were at the front door when her father appeared. He came from a small garage located to the right of the residence. He approached, very cheerful and smiling. He performed the Japanese greeting bow, to which I responded by bowing and showing my respects, and invited me inside.
« I had the feeling that he was a respectable and jocular man at first glance. »

Takashi-San opened the door saying: *"Tadaima!"* (an expression that I already explained is used when entering a house). A very pleasant woman's voice was heard that replied: *"Okaeri nasai!"* (Welcome home!)

We were taking off our shoes, and his mother was already bowing, telling us to "please come in."

« She reminded me of the beautiful high-society women described in the novels of ancient feudal Japan. »

The protocol of introductions began, and they praised me saying that I was a very beautiful young woman, and that their son was right when he told them about me.

« What were they going to say in front of their son if not...? »

Takashi-San's father's name is: *Jiro* (a name that refers to the *second son*), and his last name is: *Yagami* (*eight* or *God*). The mother's name is *Natsuki* (summer moon) *Yagami* (surname she takes from his husband).

As I was feeling a bit blushing by the compliments, I quickly moved on to the delivery of the gifts: I offered her a Japanese art sculpture that represents a *'Japanese lady'* in traditional dress (what a coincidence! as she is like the type of woman I described who reminded me of Natsuki-San!)

« ... and I told her about it...! »

It was a piece of porcelain produced in *Seto,* a Japanese city in *Aichi Prefecture*. The creation of these pieces dates back to the end of the 19th century, during the *Meiji* era (1868-1912).

I also gave her a tray with *"Mitarashi dango,"* small skewers of rice balls coated with sweet soy, typical of *Shirakawa-go,* my village (to contribute to the meal, if I was approved and invited to stay...).

I offered Yagami-San a beautiful Japanese *"bento box,"* lacquered in black and red, and decorated with flowers in gold lacquer that contained four trays (*bento* is a Japanese tradition with many years old); it consists of a box with several compartments of different sizes to contain different kinds of food, and take it to work, to the park, etc. I knew, from his son, who used it daily to take food to the company, and who used one he had had for many years already. I expected that he would use this new *bento* in his daily habit. They showed great joy and appreciation for the gifts. I liked that they were so expressive because it was calming and exciting at the same time.

Takashi-San confirmed to me with his eyes that they were very satisfied, that they liked it and that everything was going well.

He had told them all about our formal relationship: his vacation with my family and the treatment he received from my parents, which is always greatly appreciated by the other party.

« They went out of their way to make me feel good and I really appreciated it. I thought they were beautiful people! »

It was time for lunch and, yes, they invited me to eat! And as is traditional we went to the dining room table, and we all helped to prepare it (it is customary in the country to always offer to collaborate and help, unless they tell you that it is not necessary).

Natsuki-San commented that she had gotten up very early in the morning to get everything ready. She prepared several typical dishes such as: *"Sukiyaki,"* a sweet and salty dish seasoned with *"shoyu"* (a type of soy sauce), sugar, and *"mirin"* (sweet rice wine), along with beef strips with vegetables. She also delighted us with another tasty dish, the *"Tsukemen Ramen,"* it is served in two different bowls: in one the slightly cold noodles, and in the other the broth.

The last dish was *"gyōzas,"* Japanese dumplings stuffed with onion, cabbage, minced pork, soy sauce and garlic. And at the end, she placed my tray of *"Mitarashi dango"* (the rice ball skewers) on the table.

It was a great meal; everything was very well presented and very well cooked. The care and dedication was noticeable, and I thanked them with total and absolute sincerity.

The meal was followed by a good gathering in which they talked about them: when they became boyfriends in their time, when Yagami-San, father, practiced *Karate* as a young man... They related details and anecdotes of their son's childhood: of his sports such as baseball and his practice of *Kendō*...; we also talked about us and his vacation at my house; and of course of the *Art of Shinobi*, with which he had returned from the village so enthusiastically.

We also commented on the stories and legends that they had read or were told about the *Ninja* in the fights against the samurai, etc.

We drank tea; we continued talking, and time passed without us noticing, until it got late. So, I said goodbye thanking them for their attention and kind welcome.

They said that I had my house there for whenever I wanted, and that "I was welcome to the family!"

« This meant that they approved and accepted me, which made us both very happy. »

When we went back to the station to take the train back, Takashi-San told me why I was not nervous at any time (as he was with my parents), and why I was so serene... I tried to explain to him that, of course, I had worry and nervousness inside me, but that it was part of my martial training to know how to control and dominate not only the body, but also the emotions. I promised him that we would work on that, since he did have problems with emotions and control of his feelings towards others.

Taking advantage of the subject, I questioned him how he would know if I was cheating on him or hiding my real feelings, or if I was playing emotionally with him...

He had a clear answer to all that. He replied the following: "That he always looked into my eyes, because my eyes told him and showed him everything; that my look was very special, but that he had learned to read and interpret it, and most importantly: that he fully trusted me and my sincerity towards him, because he was also sure that when it was not so, I would let him know it myself without any hesitation."
« I liked his response, his words, the trust he placed in me, and knowing that he was making an effort to study me and get to know me, accepting my *"special,"* or not so common, *way of being and living.* »

When I got home, my parents were anxious to know how everything had gone, and what my boyfriend's parents were like. So, I told them everything and they were very happy for us. Although Kimura Sensei and Yoshida Sensei added that they were sure of my success and that they'd like me, because *"I knew how to please others and how to attract them."*
Yes, this was true! But I can assure you that I did not use any strategy, any sentimental weapon, or any trick or mask, because I did not need it.
I was totally natural and sincere, I was just me: real and authentic. I wanted it that way. It was my way of showing love and respect to Takashi-San and his family.

A few weeks later he confirmed to me that his father took the *bento*, I had given him, to work every day. Also, that his mother had the figure next to the television, and that to everyone who came to the house, she showed it and explained that it had been a gift from her son's girlfriend, recounting the comment I made about the resemblance of the figure with her.

We already had the family matter, on both sides, resolved in our relationship and that was important, because as a Japanese proverb says: *"If you have done everything you must and everything that is in your hands, the rest will be done by destiny."*

« It is incredible how the significant situations and moments lived throughout a life remain in your memory, recorded with all kinds of details, as if they had happened yesterday. Each thing, each place, each word that I relate here has been exact, to the millimeter, without adding, rectifying or changing anything, just as they are stored in my mind, just as I have lived them and felt them... »

The first vacation of the first year in college was over. Everything followed its natural path: studying, training, teaching...; Takashi-San coming to train as agreed, enjoying the little free time we had left, going to visit his parents when I could...

Everything flowed naturally!

Our lives continued, as our relationship grew stronger and stronger.

We grew internally and also externally, and just as we matured as people, we advanced in our education and training, in a joint vision of life that we were obtaining with the philosophy that we acquired and applied.

It was a non-stop in learning about our existence.

We felt happy and at ease with everything we had and did.

In my "second" year of university, "third" for Takashi-San, one day we went to visit my "in-laws," and after to walk around *Nagano,* through the *Matsushiro* area, one of the oldest areas of the city. We entered to visit the ruins of the old castle and the old samurai houses. I remember that, we sat on a stone; we had been talking about that samurai era and nowadays...

And if there is a place where legends and traditional myths mix with the reality, that place is Japan, and here it was not going to be less in the themes of love and the deepest feelings.

Japanese mythology is full of stories, legends and myths, but there is one legend that endures and prevails over all: that of the *"red thread:"*

"According to legend, human relationships would be predestined by a *red thread* that the gods tie to the little finger of those whose purpose is to meet in their lives. The legend is firm and solemn: if fate has arranged for you to meet a certain person, it will be so. What's more: it affirms that those who are united by the red thread are destined to become soul mates, and that they will live a great and remarkable story, regardless of the time that passes or the situations that occur in life. The *red thread* can tangle, stretch, tighten or wear out..., but never break...! It does not matter how long it takes for these two people to meet, but that moment will occur, without any doubt in our lives, and when that meeting occurs, they will never be able to separate."

It was because of this legend, that Takashi-San took out of his jacket pocket a *"string of red thread"* and rolled it, delicately and smoothly, around my little finger of the right hand, pronouncing:

"My heart will always belong to you!"

I took the other end of the string and the little finger of his left hand, and wrapped it with a few turns, with the same softness and touch.

"And mine will join to yours to beat together, at the same rhythm being one!" I replied him, while I noticed a loving tear sliding down my face, just as it did on his.

According to the myth, from that moment on, the bond is stronger, and that thread is already taut, and if we were to move away from each other we would feel excruciating pain.

« The legend has its charm, and the fact that sooner or later we will meet that someone determined by our destiny makes it even more magical. But I, who always analyzes everything, wondered about the legend: Why on the little finger? And it turned out that it has to do with blood: the ulnar artery (which runs from the inner edge of the arm to the inner side of the palm region of the hand) connects our heart with the little finger through the duct or vein *(red thread)*, and according to legend, that vein would spread throughout the world until it joined the artery and reached the heart of another person. »

I remember well that, after that magical and intimate moment, we headed to the city center to the famous *Chuo Dori* road, to enjoy the night walk along the famous street illuminated by wooden lanterns, which are characteristic of the city of *Nagano;* I remember, too, that we laughed a lot, because we walked with our red string tied on our fingers. We didn't untie our fingers until the moment we said goodbye at the station.

The years of university were passing, and I came of legal age for me when I turned 20.

On Coming of Age Day, *"Seijin No Hi"* is a national holiday in Japan, celebrated in all towns and cities in the country.

On that day, the transition to "adulthood" is celebrated for all young people who between April 2 of the previous year and April 1 of the current year have reached or will reach 20 years of age, and are considered "adults" of full right.

It is celebrated on the second Monday in January, and consists of a public event generally organized by each City Council.

There, gathered together, the local government officials welcome everyone to "adulthood" and inform them of the responsibilities and duties that they will have to face throughout their lives as adults in the Japanese society.

For the occasion, the girls wear beautiful and traditional *"Furisode,"* *'Kimonos with sleeves with long falls,'* and they wear make-up and hair for the occasion, a very careful style that costs families a lot of money.

The boys also wear dark *Kimonos* with *Hakama, 'pleated trouser skirt;* this would be the most traditional attire, but they can also opt for the western attire of suit and tie.

After the ceremony, many young people and their families go to the temples and shrines closest to their city to ask the favor of the gods, and take photos.

We went to the *Myozen-ji* temple, in my village in *Shirakawa-go.* It was the perfect place to see dozens of young people, boys and girls, in their formal attire celebrating *Seijin no Hi.*

In the afternoon and evening, young people usually meet with their friends to go out to dinner and party. It is curious to see, in such modern neighborhoods of *Tokyo*, like *Shinjuku* or *Ikebukuro*, a multitude of groups of young people in *Kimono*, or suit and tie, going out to celebrate and have fun.

In *Shirakawa* we were a couple of dozen young people who officially became "adults" in that year. We celebrate it by singing and dancing until late at night.

Takashi-san had celebrated it the year before in *Nagano* and dressed traditionally with *Hakama*.

I gave him a *"Japanese Crane ring"* (in gold) that contains two beautiful Japanese symbols: *the crane* and *the blossoming cherry tree.*

The crane symbolizes: peace, beauty, loyalty and longevity, representing Eternal Life.

The blossoming cherry tree *(Sakura)*, symbolizes the temporality of life. It is also a symbol of love, good luck and rebirth.

The crane ring was made, by a renowned jeweler, to bring: peace, beauty, good luck and revival to the wearer's life.

« From that moment on, he never took it off. He always carried it on his right ring finger… »

My parents gave me, apart from the *Kimono,* and beauty and hairdressing expenses, a beautiful pendant: *"Mokume Tsuba"* (the *"Tsuba"* is *the 'hand shield of samurai swords'*).

This pendant, made in exclusive jewelry and handmade, with the same metal technique of the swords; it was half with Takashi-San because he really liked the idea of Yoshida Sensei, and insisted that he wanted to participate (he invested almost all his savings).

The meaning of the word *"Mokume"* means: *'metal that looks like eyes in wood.'* The technique consists of forging a metal that actually looks like wood.

The creation process also contains the esoteric and hidden concept of "intentions" which means: the concentration of one's own consciousness, bringing *'unity and value to your life,'* reflecting courage, fidelity, as well as intelligence and clarity of thought.

In *Zen* philosophy, the *Tsubas* (from *Katanas* or swords) represent the symbol of *"The Diamond Sword,"* the same sword that, metaphorically, cuts the world of illusion, superfluous thoughts and feelings that deceive the human being, in order to bring him back to reality as it is.

Thus, the day of my twentieth birthday, became another day of fortune and gratitude, which I reciprocated and thanked with all my heart to the *Kami,* Gods, in the Temple of the village that saw me born.

« For all that this pendant symbolizes and means, I too have always carried it on my neck. »

The following year Takashi-San finished college (he was one year ahead of me). He got his "Bachelor's Degree," something we went to celebrate by organizing a big party with college mates and friends. I remember that it was a big party, how could it be otherwise that special moment in life in which one stage closes and another opens.
The student stage was over for him, and a new one was beginning: the stage of looking for a job, writing resumes and study plans to present in companies...
To know that, the bachelor's degree in Communication Sciences contemplates advertising and public relations to position any company well in the global market.
This university degree allows generating communication plans for companies, both national and international, and managing aspects from their social networks and commercial expectations. It also allows you to collaborate in the construction of communication strategies in the field of politics.

For my part, I was beginning the "fourth" and last year of my career in the university, while Takashi-San tried to build his future. He did not stop contacting all the companies in the country, going to many places and interviews.
Now, we no longer saw each other at the university but rather we met outside of it, when we both had free time.
We missed each other a lot. The cell phone became the most necessary thing between us, although I didn't like that dependence of always having my cell phone with me, but we had to be able to communicate, since it was very hard for us not to see each other every day.

After six months, he was called for an interview in response to the interest in his resume. Although he had done and attended other interviews before, he was "especially" concerned about this one, because it was a very important company and of great relevance in the country at a national and international level.

I had a feeling about it. I felt it was his time and I wanted to help him. We decided that we needed to work a little bit on the *"aptitude"* and *"attitude"* issue (since I knew how nervous he got sometimes, although with the practice of the Martial Art he was already controlling himself much more at that time). I wanted him to understand that these two concepts are very important in the labor market. Having them well defined, and knowing how to demonstrate them in a job interview is of utmost importance.

Attitude is the personality, the temperament that one possesses in certain situations, and the capacity to solve a work situation, or to know how to be in a meeting. It is the way of doing things.

Aptitude is the talent, ability or dexterity that we have. It is what we know, our acquired knowledge, everything that we have learned throughout our academic life.

Both are important, since you must not only contribute your knowledge, but also your motivation and ability to transmit that positive energy to your co-workers, since most of the time it work in a team.

When you have a job interview, you must be taken into account your strengths and weaknesses. The important thing is to know how to expose, not only the knowledge you have (your aptitude), but also the commitment you want to acquire when you start working (your attitude).

To know our aptitudes and attitudes we need to make an introspection to be honest with ourselves, and to know what our limits and our strongest points are.

« We had three days to work on this, Takashi-San had a hard time because of his great shyness added to the lack of control of his nerves and emotions, but he tried really hard! »

What was so difficult for him was natural for me, because all these concepts, and many others, of life or ways of acting in society, were taught to me by Yoshida Sensei and Kimura Sensei from a very young age to prepare me for my purposes in today's society.

They made mention of the "aptitude" and "attitude" reflecting that these must be taken at the beginning of any activity, whether it is a Martial Art or any other type of sport, art, work, etc., since when you study the basics, the aptitude facilitates learning.

For example: in a *Dojo* there are disciples with great capacity and faculties to practice the Martial Art, but there are also other disciples with less technique or skills, and not for that reason they are worse or better, they just have less aptitudes than the others. Those with less ability have to increase their motivation or attitude to improve their technique. For this reason, in a *Dojo* your physical fitness does not matter, because this will come, but do not forget to come with a lot of attitude and a desire to learn. And this balance, between both concepts, is applicable to any area of life, whether, I repeat, in social relationships, sports, work, etc.

Everyone knows that a Paralympic athlete has limited capabilities but this does not prevent or limit him/her from improving and striving to achieve their dreams. Their struggle to improve in their discipline gives them the strength and motivation to reach and achieve their dreams.

At the end of those three days of preparation, I saw Takashi-San more self-assured and much more confident in his strategic plan for the interviewer.

« This is the importance that these concepts have in the lives of all people to improve and continue walking the path of learning. »

The day of the interview arrived. Everyone was very tense for him, for how he would go... But I was very calm and very sure that he was going to do well, just as I knew that the position was for him, I felt that it was his destiny.
When the interview was over, he called me saying that he was very happy, that all the effort had been worth it, that his legs did not shake, that he performed and exposed everything we had rehearsed and that, at the end, he told him that he had liked it a lot his "aptitude" and his "personality"; that they would contact him in the coming weeks.
« Liked his aptitude and personality (attitude); it worked! »

He continued to send resumes, and attend other vacancies that he read, or told him about (while receiving refusals from some, and was waiting for others...).
He also kept coming to *Shirakawa-go* to train, to be together and to visit my parents..., while I continued with my daily routines.
The last year of college was taking up more of my study time, and with the *Master's Degree in Spanish* I was doing more overtime as well.
In August of that year (school vacation date), my parents and Takashi-San agreed that I needed to relax and rest, and they agreed that we should go on a trip for a few days somewhere.

We decided to go on vacation to *"Okinawa-hontō,"* *'Okinawa Island,'* an archipelago, the largest island in Japan, located southwest in the East China Sea. It is the furthest prefecture from Japan, and encompasses more than 160 small islands. The capital of the prefecture is the city of *Naha*.

It is a favorite summer destination for the Japanese due to its tropical climate, vast paradisiacal beaches and coral reefs, as well as its World War II sites.

We booked into an oceanfront resort hotel. The room was huge with wonderful views of the great white sand beach with crystal clear and beautiful turquoise waters.

On the ground floor there was huge Japanese *"Onsen,"* *'thermal baths.'* So, the first thing we did, was to enjoy the relaxing showers, the different pools of hot and cold water, the different types of saunas and, of course, the wonderful and relaxing massages.

After we were like new, we went for a walk along the most atmospheric street in the whole city, the *Kokusai Road*.

It was full of restaurants, cafes, bakeries and many stores focused on tourism. Along the same street you could reach the famous public market *"Makishi,"* where you could find all kinds of fish and seafood.

We decided to enter an *"Izakaya"* or 'bar' / 'restaurant,' and ordered the star dish of *Okinawa:* the *"Okinawa Soba,"* which consists of a noodle-based soup (it was almost mandatory to try it because of its widespread fame).

After lunch we strolled a little more through the surrounding streets and then went to rest.

The next day we planned the routes and visits that we would do in the seven days that we would be on the island.

Every day we did the tours, excursions and visits that we had in the planned plan.

We visited the *"Shuri Castle,"* which is a must-see for the Japanese because of its World War II history. The original castle was totally destroyed and what is visited today is a reconstruction.

Okinawa was formerly an independent kingdom until the Japanese government took military control of the archipelago, and since then it has been part of Japan.

During the war, in 1944, the island was militarily invaded by more than 500,000 US Marines. The battle was one of the bloodiest in history, killing thousands of soldiers and hundreds of thousands of civilians. It is estimated that a quarter of the *Okinawan* population died.

The island was totally devastated!

We went through more than 400 meters of tunnels, where more than four thousand soldiers organized the Japanese defense.

Here the commander of the Japanese navy committed *"hara-kiri"* (or *"seppuku:"* *'Japanese suicide'*), just before sending a telegram to *Tokyo* asking that the *Okinawan* population be remembered. *Okinawa* was invaded, and the Americans decided to drop the atomic bomb on *Hiroshima* and *Nagasaki*.

« The feeling of so much horror perpetrated there invaded us. To imagine what happened in that war leaves anyone dismayed... »

We went to the islands of *Kerama* where we practiced diving and snorkeling. We took ferries in *Naha* to visit the islands of *Zamami, Tokashiki* and others. One day we flew to visit other islands such as *Miyako* and *Daito*.

Near the hotel we had the Okinawa Aquarium, and we were surprised to see two huge whale sharks in there.

Another day we went to the north of the island, and we went through fantastic forests in the middle of nature to reach the *Hiji* waterfall, a splendid and unheard of place.

Of course, we went to the *Onsen* every day to relax, and the hot springs were a must!

We were enjoying everything and ourselves, letting ourselves be carried away each day on a new adventure.

It was the third day of our vacation, and I broached the subject of having our "first serious intimate relationship" to my boyfriend.

I was twenty-one years old and we were in our fourth year of relationship. I felt it was time, that I was ready!

Although Takashi-San had already given, on different occasions, signs of desire, with insinuations and attempts to go further, until the end..., I was holding him back waiting for that "perfect moment."

I wanted it to be something "special": magical and unforgettable (this was what my mother also told me in this regard, and that I had to choose: when, how and with whom).

In Japanese culture, unlike in the West, roles are reversed. Women are expected to make the first move and express what they want to do next in the relationship.

We were clear that a sexual relationship involves much more than the act of penetration (intercourse); it also involves enjoying, and feeling fully with all the possibilities that our body offers us, and that penetration is only one part of sexual contact. Kissing, hugging, caressing... are different ways of having that intimate contact (which is what we did until now). We both agreed to maintain that kind of contact, until I felt ready for the next step.

For my part, I wanted time to learn to feel and desire, to know my body and develop my sexual capacity.

I think that when you decide to have a first sexual relationship, being able to talk freely with your partner about what you expect, what you like, the contraceptive method, safe sex, etc., is essential.

In Japan, sexual art is considered a natural act and therefore is not associated with any concept of moral guilt; is very open and there are no limits, as long as it's consented to by both parties.

Consequently, the sexual act is a sacred duty for both men and women, and abstinence is considered a non-positive attitude in the relationship of a couple or marriage.

« Sex performs a necessary function in the human being to maintain the balance between body and mind. »

In the Japanese language we have the term *"ai:"* 'love' or *"aisuru:"* 'to love,' and the term *"koi:"* 'love' (but with the symbol of *"kokoro"* or 'heart;' *"Koi"* refers to a love for the opposite sex or a feeling of longing for another person. It can be described as "romantic love" or "passionate love." While *"ai"* has the same meaning as *"koi,"* it also has as its definition a general feeling of love. *"Koi"* may be selfish, but *"ai"* is true love. To be better understood: *"Koi"* is always to love. *"Ai"* is always giving.

With these words and meanings of the Japanese language, we played to continuously express our feelings of love. With this play on words we transmitted authentic poetry to each other, words with very beautiful and deep meanings.

Takashi-San was different from most Japanese men. He left his shyness behind and became expressive, romantic and open with all subjects and situations (here *Budō's* training worked the miracle, and without he hardly noticing it).

We had something very beautiful, and were living in a kind of permanent honeymoon; he had agreed to respect my decision to wait to go further in the intimate sexual relationship, until I was ready, so together we consented to take the next step that day.

« I was ready, it was the "special moment" that I had been waiting for, I wanted to give myself to him and let myself be enveloped by sensuality and passion…! »

Japanese women like romanticism in these situations. So, he got up, called room service, and ordered flowers, candles, and a bottle of *"Imperial sake"* or *"nihonshu"* (fermented rice alcohol drink).

He played with the lighting to create atmosphere, and filled the bathtub, which was in the bedroom by the window (I just watched as he did...).

The waiter arrived and left everything on the table; he put the candles, and placed the flowers in different places around the bed and the bathtub; then he took a flower, went to the closet, and came back with a small gift-wrapped package, and held it in one hand while he kept the flower in the other. He approached me and get down on one knee, while I remained seated on the edge of the bed. He stroked my hair and face with the flower. He told me that he had been carrying this detail with him for quite some time, for when that day and that "special moment" will comes. He said he loved me deeply, and gave me the gift: they were beautiful and radiant "earrings," from which hung an elongated "teardrop" of crystal or transparent glass that, depending on the reflective light, changed colors. I tried placing it in different places with the different lights, and they were very pretty.

I really liked it at one point in the room that changed to pink (like the *Sakura* flower), and as I moved it slightly, it went up in tone to almost red (color of blood); "I was very surprised by the effect, it was very striking!" At another point they turned emerald, at another more turquoise and then golden yellow... They were really very curious, almost magical... I put them on!

«I just loved them, they shocked me a lot. I had never seen such a beautiful object or jewel! I promised that they would always remind me of that moment: *"my special moment to give myself to my beloved totally;"* and that I would wear them with joy, pride and respect. »

We got into the bathtub; we had filled it with rose petals. We drank *sake* (a little for the occasion) and toasted to us and to our love.

With my feet I caressed his body gently, seducing and exciting him. We laughed and played sensually until... the desire overcame us, we could not wait any longer and...

… Without further delay we indulge in pleasure!

We gave ourselves to each other! Our bodies fused together with the fire of passion!

The next day when we woke up, we hugged each other tightly as if telling each other: That's it! We're already one; our love is consummated, sealed and ready to continue the path...! It was like a "magical awakening."

That was the day we changed the plan outlined while we had breakfast, because we wanted to do a *"Shinrinyoku,"* literally means: *'forest bath,'* and consists of walking through the forest, immersing yourself in it and absorbing it through the senses, forming part of the environment. To walk slowly and gently through it, observing, listening, smelling, tasting, touching and feeling…

Simply being present in nature and connecting with it (the *"Shinrinyoku"* for the Japanese, is something common and usual because they have that sensitivity with nature).

For the philosophy of life that we had of feeling part of nature, as *Budoka* (*Budō* practitioners), with the feelings that enveloped us that day, it was like a bath of pure love that made us feel the strength of our union.

Takashi-san had an assignment from his father, Yagami-san. The latter had a good friend of his who lived in *Okinawa*. He told him that they had grown up together until adolescence; that they practiced *Karate* together from childhood, until his partner moved with his family to live in the archipelago; that he was *Karate Sensei* there on the island (and that, for that reason, we would surely like to meet him too).

They had always kept in touch, but Yagami-San was eager that we would visit and meet him, and he also wanted us to give him a present from him, through the person of his son. His father's friend is named "Isamu Kobayashi," known as *Kobayashi Sensei* (*"Isamu"* is: *'courage'* and *"Kobayashi"* is: *'small forest'*).

He managed to reach him by phone, and they agreed to meet at the *"Naminoue-gu Shrine,"* a majestic *Shinto shrine* perched on a cliff, overlooking *Naminoue Beach* and the ocean, quite close to where we were, in downtown *Naha*.

It is known to be a place with a lot of spiritual energy.

« When we arrived at the temple, I knew inside me that Kobayashi Sensei did not choose that place at random. »

Upon arrival we identified him immediately; his appearance was that of a Master, he was unmistakable! He seemed to be in his 50s, of medium height, with a broad back and muscular arms. His face was oval, with a tanned complexion, small eyes with very bushy eyebrows, and thin lips; also matched his short dark hair with well-drawn gray. He had what is said: *a good aspect.*

We approached and introduced ourselves as protocol dictates. He, immediately, asked about his father and invited us to walk around the sanctuary, telling us about the place and its history. He spoke slowly in a firm but soothing and enveloping voice.

He led us to the cliff, and we sat contemplating at the wonderful view of that great beach. At that moment, Takashi-San handed him the package from his father with an envelope. *Sensei* opened the envelope and read a note it contained, smiled and put it back in the envelope.

He just said:

"Your father is a great person whom I respect and hold in great esteem, he loves you very much, and for that you have all my affection and friendship forever; of course, you too Haru-San."

« And he didn't open the package; he kept it in the little bag he was carrying along with the note and the envelope. »

He then asked us questions about us, our lives…, and commented that he thought it was a beautiful life with a lot of future ahead of us.

He told us about him that he was closing his *Karate* school, because he would go to live the following month in Paris (France). His wife is French and her name is Sophie Moreau. They met here in *Okinawa*, she came here on vacation fifteen years ago; they fell in love, and she came back to marry him and live here together.

They were very happy there, but his wife's parents had recently passed away, and they left him an inheritance house in Paris along with other rental properties. She has many acquaintances and contacts in France, so they have decided to relocate. His wife is taking care of setting up a *Karate Dojo* for him to continue his teachings there, while she will be in charge of managing the rents of their inherited properties, so he commented that they will be very well off financially.

« Kobayashi Sensei said something beautiful: that if she left everything for him fifteen years ago, now it was his turn to give her something back, and what better: than the place where she was born; and that he belongs to the universe, so he doesn't care where to live if you are with someone who loves your heart. »

We saw him excited about his new life in Europe, and somewhat saddened, as he looked at the sights of that beautiful island, where he had remained for so many years and now left behind to many of his disciples who had followed his teachings long time.

Sensei invited us to eat at his house where his wife was waiting for us. We walked to the *"Tsuboya"* district, known as the ceramic district. We took a detour that started from the main street, and a few minutes later, we arrived at a very nice and simple house, full of plants around it, with an old wooden door that opened just when we were in front of it. Then, a European woman appears smiling and waving in perfect Japanese.

Kobayashi Sensei made the introductions and we went inside. The house was decorated with a mixture of east and west together giving it an elegant and cozy feel.

She was short for a French woman (her height seemed more like that of a typical Japanese), her petite face with very light skin highlighted her green eyes, in contrast with her half-blonde and gray intertwined hair. You could see her elegance in her gestures; and her voice was nice and sweet. She spoke very fluently and as if she had known you forever.

We immediately appreciated that she was a lovely and very kind woman!

There was a large table in the center of the main room, presented and served for four people with a beautiful table linen and crystal cups. We were invited to sit down, and ordered not to move.

Kobayashi-San and Sophie-San (as she wanted us to call her) began to bring various dishes. Among several typical *Okinawan*, she served a French dish that prepared especially for us: *"Ratatouille,"* it was a recipe of stewed vegetables, with spices and various Provencal style herbs, which gave it a delicious flavor.

We were very comfortable with them and talked for a long time about their lives and, of course, about the world of

Budō, the Martial Arts, and it turned out that Kobayashi Sensei had heard of my father, Yoshida Sensei.
He said that it was his understanding that he was a Master who was highly regarded and respected in Japan.
« It was an honor to hear those words about my father from someone like him, so reputable and famous in *Okinawa.* »

When we said goodbye, he told me that I was very fortunate to be the daughter of a *"Dai Sensei,"* 'Great Master,' and to be so well trained and educated.
« That was true! His words were right, and there is not one day that I do not give thanks for having been so fortunate... »

Takashi-San and I were elated and happy about his father's commissioned, and to have had the honor of meeting *Sensei* and *"okusan,"* his 'wife,' Sophie-San.
They also invited us to go to Paris, that they would be delighted to offer us their home.
« Meeting them was "prodigious." The *Kami* made it possible. At that time, I could never have imagined what an important and fundamental role "Isamu Kobayashi Sensei" would play in our lives in the not too distant future. He would be part, without knowing it, of destiny! »

The holidays came to an end and we went back to the obligations and daily chores.
When I told Yoshida Sensei about the pleasure I had in meeting Kobayashi Sensei, he commented that he had also heard of him, and knew that he taught *"Shotokan"* style *Karate* on the island of *Okinawa*, and that he had many disciples.
Then we talked about the history of *"Okinawan Karate-Do,"* and how it spread to the rest of Japan. We talked about the predecessors and founders until we reached what we know

today. Disseminating Masters such as: the Motobu family, Seikichi Uehara, Kanga Sakugawa, Shoshin Nagamine, Sokon Matsumura, Anko Itosu (disciple of Matsumura), and so on up to Gichin Funakoshi, known as the *"Father of modern Karate or Karate-Do (Shotokan style)."*

We did a good review of history, teachings and learning knowledge.

I liked to educate myself about everything, I always wanted to learn and acquire knowledge...

As Carl Friedrich Gauss said:

- "It is not the knowledge, but the act of learning; and not the possession, but the act of coming to it that grants the greatest enjoyment."

« Of course, upon returning from the vacation trip, I told my parents about the step we took in our intimate love relationship Takashi-San and me. As I have already explained: in Japan the sexual act in a couple's relationship is seen as something natural. There are no taboos! There is talk of sex, although that doesn't mean including intimate details of a personal nature... »

It was a week after we returned from our trip, when my boyfriend received a call from one of the companies that interviewed him (the one for which we work on *aptitude* and *attitude*…), quoting him again.

This time he was called to appear at the *Building Center Tokyo,* the company's headquarters, located in the financial district of *Nishi-Shinjuku,* in the center of *Tokyo* (great building!).

He had an appointment with the *"Kachou"* (head of the section of the information department). To get to the position of *Kachou,* it usually takes fifteen years or more of dedication to the company.

We were at home with my parents that weekend celebrating the possibility that the following Monday, the day of the appointment, Takashi-San would be going to work for a company of that caliber, so soon and just finished college! My father and I knew, with total certainty, that he would be "chosen." Plus, he had already had that feeling when he attended the first interview, which was 'by' and 'for' that we had worked with the concepts of *"aptitude"* and *"attitude,"* so that he could overcome it successfully.

Yoshida Sensei said to Takashi-San, just as he was saying goodbye that Sunday:

"If you sit on the road do it facing what you have yet to walk and with your back to what you have already walked" (it is an old Japanese proverb).

Monday arrived, and what we all expected happened: He did it! He joined the prestigious company "OTARU NHK GROUP," a Japanese multinational with presence in several countries. This group is immersed in a wide range of business networks, from telecommunications to electronic commerce, technology, finance and media. It has a large number of departments with positions at different levels that allow the development of all professional potential.

The company, due to its large size, generates more than thirty thousand jobs, through more than 500 offices, providing various financial services with a need for international expansion and global dimension, and this is where Takashi-San's degree is useful (this it will be his job).

The way to follow in a Japanese company is to enter as *"Kaishain,"* the lowest level, at the end of university. When a company hires you as soon as you finish university, their goal is that you will spend your entire life with them, meaning that your job is practically guaranteed for the rest of your life.

Based on work and dedication, over time the employees go from the *Kaishain* level to *Kakarichou*; these are the supervisors who are in charge of assigning specific tasks to the lowest level employees; then to *Buchou*, that are the heads of each department (Human Resources, Sales, Research and Development etc.). Also belonging to this group are: the *"Shocho"* (Directors of one of the company's factories), the *"Shitencho"* (Directors of one of the company's headquarters), finally, with luck, at the age of 50, one reaches *"Kachou,"* and above all, there is the *"Shachou,"* the president of the company.
This is the standard structure of companies in Japan.

Takashi-San started working in a week, in the month of September, and although the work day regulated by law is 40 hours a week, Japanese people work a lot of overtime each week and there is a reason for this: and is that each extra hour is equivalent to the salary of a normal hour and a half, and companies pay them all. No employee is obliged to do them but most does it because it is good extra money, and it all adds up to climb future positions.
So, Takashi-San did not have an end time because instead of leaving every day at 5:00 p.m., when he wanted to, he worked two or three hours more. The good thing was that he had every weekend off, and that was important so that everything continued in the same way, and we continued to enjoy being together.

Happy for my boyfriend's future, it was the end of summer vacation and it was time to go back to college. Not only had I enjoyed and rested, but I had regained my energy, so much so that I was studying more than ever and training much more than I did before. I didn't stop! I pushed myself to the limit every day. My parents warned me to slow down, but

I was very focused on making the "big effort" until the end of my career, and I wanted to cover everything; I didn't want to give up anything.

That September a terrible event happened in the faculty that caused a huge uproar, and opened gatherings among the students.

It was about a student who was not doing well in his studies.

As I already mentioned: the universities in Japan are tough and demanding, but they also want to help you to be successful, because the recognition of them and of the teachers is at stake.

This young man was alerted on several occasions by the rectory of his backwardness and poor progression, and he did not respond well to the help that was offered to him, and apparently, the management urged him to a meeting to meet with his parents to discuss the matter.

He came from a high society family, of samurai lineage (like most of the noble and wealthy classes Japanese). He was the son of an important businessman in the country, so his future was already written: to succeed his father.

The pressure of not fulfilling what was expected of him and the offense it would mean to his parents, being called out for his lack of commitment or conflict with his studies... led him to commit *"Jisastsu,"* the Japanese word for to refer to suicide of a person (which is quite common among young Japanese nowadays).

But the surprising thing about this young man is that he performed the complete ritual of *"Seppuku"* or *"Harakiri"* (literally: *'belly cut'*), which is the Japanese suicide ritual by disembowelment.

"Seppuku" (the most commonly used term) was part of the *Bushidō*, the ethical code of the samurai, and was performed, usually voluntarily, to die with honor before falling into the hands of the enemy and being tortured, or as a death penalty

for those who had dishonored themselves, or caused offense to "their lord."

"Harakiri" has survived as a practice to the present day, despite its prohibition as a judicial penalty in 1873. Numerous Japanese military men did it during the 19th and 20th centuries, as a form of protest to show disagreement with some imperial decree, or to escape defeat, as in the case of World War II.

The code of the samurai written by *Yamamoto Tsumemoto* in the 17th century stated: *"The way of the samurai is death,"* and by this, he was referring not only to the warrior's death in combat, but also to his duty to commit suicide before to accept the surrender.

Seppuku was traditionally performed after thoroughly cleaning one's body, drinking *sake* (rice liquor), and composing a farewell poem or final statement *("zeppitsu"* or *"yuigon")* on the back of a war fan *("tessen")*.

The entire ritual consisted of sticking the *"tantō,"* 'knife' (white weapon) through the left side with the edge to the right, cutting from left to right firmly and returning to the center of the abdomen, ending with a vertical cut almost to the sternum.

The samurai, on the other hand, gutted himself by executing a horizontal and a vertical cut: it was the *"Jumonji"* style, *'number ten'* (from the ideogram drawn by the strokes of the cuts). The objective was to cut the nerve centers of the spine, causing long agony; for this reason, although it was considered honorable to do it alone, it was customary to use the *"Kaishakunin,"* that is: 'a second person in charge of decapitating the suicide during his agony, just after the cut.' It used to be always some great Master in the Art of the Sword.

All this had to do with the belief that warmth and the human soul resided in the lower abdomen and that, by opening it, its spirit was thus released, taking into account that the term *"hara"* (from *hara-kiri*), means at the same time and everything together: "belly" and "spirit," "courage" and "determination."

Noble women also performed *"Jigai"* suicide (so called because it was not technically considered *harakiri* or *seppuku*) for a multitude of reasons: to avoid falling into the hands of the enemy, to follow her husband or lord in death, to receive a direct order to commit suicide, etc.

The choice to assume such a responsibility was considered an honor, or a token of affection or recognition.

I cannot fail to mention the world-famous public case of the writer *Yukio Mishima*, who committed suicide according to this ritual on November 25, 1970, the morning in which he finished his last book, to rebel against a society that he considered had fallen in the deepest moral and spiritual void, and he saw a humiliating defeat in the adoption of the Western model in the economy of his glorious country.

The artist pronounced, among others, the words: "I am on the verge of the moment in my life when all the legs of the table have disappeared" or "I am exhausted...," are some of them.

The author then performed the *seppuku* or *hara-kiri* publicly: He opened his belly calmly, feeling how the steel was cutting the flesh and intestines, thus having the opportunity, the only one, to die slowly, as he had described in some of his books. It was opened in canal in the first phase of a ritual, that culminates when a comrade decapitates the head of the sacrificed with a single sword stroke ("kaishakunin," acting as second), but he had no luck; after several attempts by his assistant, it had to be his friend *Hiroyasu Koga*, who decapitated him, and finished the ritual that was to be a shocking gesture for Japan and Japanese literature.

In this way, the Country of the Rising Sun dismissed the one who was the most relevant writer of the 20th century.

Another famous case is reflected in the Japanese epic entitled *"The Forty Seven Ronin"* by *Ako,* written in the 17th century. Suicide after losing a battle or failing a objective was common in Japan, and today, it is still a country with a high number of suicides (being the country with the highest rate in the world), although they occur for very different reasons: social pressure, job loss, divorce, family pressure, social isolation, etc. Many people in Japan, especially young people, go to forest areas and use various methods to commit suicide, alone and even in groups.

« That boy from college was just twenty years old! »

Due to that event, I took the opportunity to speak to my students at the *Dojo* that weekend about the Bushidō and the samurai code of ethics. I wanted to know what they thought and how they faced with the concepts: "life" and "death," the two sides of the same coin. I wanted to convey to them the importance of "being and feeling alive." We know when we are born, but not when we will die; that is the only tangible truth.

Fearing death is fine, it is something natural, but the problem comes when fear is dominant. It is then when the day-to-day life is affected and arises: panic attacks, anxiety, the feeling of failure..., and is at this point: the time to seek help, or to fight to courageously face the feelings that invade us.

It turned out, that the class served for a disciple to confess to everyone that he, until starting the *Ninjutsu* classes, had had many moments in which he thought about "death" and "suicide." And, that he no longer thought as before, that now he was happier and loved life. We are all rejoice, I especially, that the Martial Arts help the weakest mentally, and help them to obtain the courage and bravery necessary to strengthen the spirit.

However, I was always attentive to that student, assuring myself that he was growing internally, and that he would never have those thoughts again.

Takashi-san was doing very well in the company, they were very happy with him, and that was reflected in his mood. He looked very happy and smiling.
« He always wore that shy smile that was contagious as soon as you saw him! »

Sometimes we would go to a *"love hotel,"* and rented a room. Love hotels are a cultural and normalized aspect in Japan.
In ancient times, in the Edo period, already existed the so-called *"otebiki-chaya"* or *"deai-chaya"* and literally means: *'meeting tea house,'* to offer a meeting place for lovers.
A love hotel is a hotel in which the rooms are paid for fractions of time, instead of for full nights as is customary in other countries. These hotels are highly extended throughout Japan.
They have a luxurious appearance and are fully automated. Their most typical clients are usually young couples who still live with their respective families, and therefore, do not have their own home to be able to have privacy and have sex.
Another type of clients are already married couples who want to give an exotic touch to their privacy and break the monotony.
And, of course, these hotels are also used for extramarital affairs.
In our case, it was because we were the typical young couple who lived with their parents, and we did not have our own house where we could give free rein to the passion of two lovers in private.

That same year, in February, Takashi-San told me that his company was offering vacancies in different departments, and among them, there were several positions in "economy;" that he had spoken with his superior that his girlfriend was about to graduate in Economics at the end of March, and replied him that there was no problem, that I should present the curriculum because the vacancies would not be filled until the month of June.

I remember that, at that moment, we dreamed awake with things like:
- Look if they give me the job and we work together...!
- Can you imagine?
- And both just when finished the college career…!
It made us very happy just to imagine it.
But that possibility was an opportunity that had to be seized, what it gave me even more energy to continue with my efforts. And, of course, I prepared the resume, and sent it through the official channels dictated by the company.

It was a beautiful winter day. I watched from the window of the *Dojo* at home, sitting in *"Seiza"* (kneeling posture), as the snow covered everything.
The village of *Shirakawa-go* and all the mountains that my sight reached, offered me that optical effect of the brilliant color of the white of the snow caused by the air, formed by ice crystals of beautiful hexagonal shapes and turning into beautiful flakes.
That bucolic postcard picture made me feel at peace, and also made me reflect on life, that of others and my own.
I thought about: What could I do to give something to others? How to transmit to other people and give them reasons to live and be happy…? Since, I had so many…!

In Japanese culture, we have the philosophy of *"Ikigai,"* which translates as *'the reason for being,'* and means: "a life that is worth living" and has "a purpose" for it. According to our belief, everyone has an *Ikigai*. It is that internal reason what makes us get up every morning. It is the source of our motivation, which helps us stay on track to achieve our goals.

Many have already found it, and are aware of it; others, without knowing it, carry it inside. And it is that, finding this purpose is essential to create a life plan.

The world situation in which we all live immersed is a good opportunity to stop and reflect, and discover which one is ours *"purpose,"* our *Ikigai*, for to live with integrity.

It may seem difficult to live such a life, but philosophies like this are also meant to encourage us and help us build the world we want.

It takes passion and effort; talents that give meaning to the days that pass, and make us give more the best of each one. In Japan, we use the technique we call *"Kaizen,"* which means: *'taking small, constant steps to achieve your goal.'*

You have to achieve these goals to be in possession of the happiness of the *Ikigai* philosophy, and if not, this must be your next mission.

« This feeling of wanting to share my happiness and knowledge to help others has always haunted me. My purposes in life have been: to teach others to be physically and mentally prepared to face life, learning to value what its nature offers us; make them feel strong in spirit and strive to achieve their goals; that they accept that life is short and the time is a gift that is offered to us to be able to live it fully, and that we can choose how we want to use that time; share my knowledge to also learn from others, since everyone has something to teach, and I want to gather that wisdom; I want to continue growing inside myself as a human being, as a person… »

Yoshida Sensei and Kimura Sensei made an effort to teach me the *"Do"* or *'way,'* but they also taught me that I would have to choose and that, at times, it would be difficult because there are many paths and with many intersections, and a bad decision could mean pay a high cost.

I had good "guides," and up to that stage of my life, I had not had to make too relevant decisions that could harm me or cost me a high price.

I had lived in a natural way everything that was happening to me. My life flowed by itself, I just adapted and accommodated to the small changes and situations that were occurring around me.

From that window, where I was still motionless and sitting in the position of *Seiza*, concentrating on the snowy landscape, and seeing my precious *Sakura* (how much it had grown in the almost four years that it had been transplanted!), I viewed and felt that I would leave the house where I was born, the one that had been my home and refuge, where I had had and felt so much love and protection, where I had been formed and lived since ever...

I was at that moment sensing the future changes that lurked and was approaching me rapidly... Then, burning tears began to flow from my eyes, sliding down my face; I barely caught a glimpse of my tree, and could hardly make out its snow-covered branches. A melancholic sadness began to invade me inside, I felt "a goodbye" to a part of me, to the part that gave me life, to the part that formed me and shaped me until I became who I was in that instant.

Suddenly, without any meteorological change, the *Sakura* began to expel snow, throwing it as if it were rain...

« It was crying just like me! It was the tears of the *Sakura*! Then, I knew with certainty that that *"sayonara,"* that "goodbye" was coming and was going to happen at some point... »

The final exams were coming and I was totally dedicated. My first confrontation was with the "Spanish" exam, which went quite well and... Finally, after four years... I got my longed-for *"University Master's Degree in Spanish!"*
I was very happy, because the language has one of the most difficult and complicated grammars in the world. That's why I chose it, and I really think it is the richest and most beautiful language on the planet.
Little by little the rest of the exams were coming, one after the other, one subject after the other..., my credits were very good and that helped, although I slept less and less....
I worked very conscientiously on my *End of Degree Project,* individually, and tutored by a full professor to whom I am immensely grateful for his help, dedication and supervision.
The end came and I put the books aside. It was time to wait for a few days for the results of the scores…

Although the snow was melting, as it was the end of March, the mountain peaks were still loaded, so I wanted to take my skis and go to say goodbye to the studies and of the winter skiing through my beloved Japanese Alps. I felt the air, still cold, on my face as I slid down its slopes. I was feeling free! And my shoulders and back were light; I was letting go of the weight that I had been bearing, and more and more the feeling of lightness and speed was increasing in the face of to the previous slowness and heaviness.
I spent hours enjoying that mental and physical agility that occurs when "you have finally finished something" or "you

have done what you had to do;" that were what I perceived and it caused me pleasure and satisfaction.

Finally the day came to know the results! I would know if I had passed all the exams and would collect my grades.

My mother asked for the day off from school to accompany me, either to celebrate together or to tuck me in and encourage me in case of failure; and no one better than her for the latter, since she has that special "something" or "skill" tranquilizer and solver for moments like that.
It was my turn and they gave me an average / high grade and my "Bachelor of Science in Economics."
My mother and I hugged each other jumping for joy, like most of those present there that day. We congratulated each other, acquaintances and strangers.
There was a lot of excitement all over campus!
It was a holiday for all the students!
Then I called Takashi-San (I never disturbed him during working hours but that day he was waiting and nervous) and with my shout and laughter it was clear to him the result. He said only: "Congratulations! I knew it!" over and over again.
Quickly, my mother and I went to Yoshida Sensei's School to give him the news, because he was also worried and suffered for me. We entered the *Dojo* screaming like crazy, and *Sensei* immediately stopped the class by running towards me.
He hugged me so tight that I could hardly breathe, while whispering to me:
"Congratulations and how much I love you!"
After, he hugged my mother, as if thanking each other and celebrating winning a match. A lot of emotions surfaced, and all there, in the middle of the *tatami* with all the students clapping and congratulating me.

The *Sensei* finished the class, and before the students present there he uttered a few words praising my efforts, my tenacity and persistence when giving myself in everything I did and started; thus instilling in all the values of the "effort" and the "rewards" that are collected.

He ended up saying to everyone: "That you have to sweat a lot when training because that will help you bleed less when you fight out there;" and that "all the efforts we make will always be worth it."

We went to celebrate at an *"Izakaya"* or *'restaurant'* in *Ogimachi* village, and all the villagers who heard about it came up to congratulate me saying: *"Omedetou gozaimasu!"*

During lunch, I received a call from Mr. Jiro Yagami and Mrs. Natsuki Yagami (my boyfriend's parents) congratulating me; they also spoke with my parents.

Everyone was very happy for me!

« In a couple of days, everyone in the *Shirakawa* group of villages had heard about it, and when they saw me, they all congratulated me enthusiastically. That place was like that! »

In the evening Takashi-san and I, went to celebrate it in Nagano. We walked the streets of the city and ate a famous *"oyaki,"* 'patty or dough buns made with wheat flour and cooked on the grill, which are filled with vegetables such as eggplants, mushrooms or squash.'

After, we stopped by his house so that his parents could see me and congratulate me in person.

Later in the evening, we went to a *"kaitenzushi,"* a *'sushi* restaurant,' where the dishes are placed on a conveyor belt that runs through the restaurant passing by all the diners; the dishes pass in front of you, and you choose the one you want, from among hundreds of varieties that circulate without stopping.

There we had arranged to meet up with my university classmates to celebrate together. We were about forty people approximately...

We were there for hours, and I still don't know how they could count so many dishes and drinks that were consumed; because in these types of places the bill is the result of counting the glasses of drinks plus each dish or portion that has been eaten, and there were hundreds...

We ended the night in a *Karaoke* (it most logical and typical in Japan) until the early hours of the morning.

Waking up the next day, with no alarm clock, no schedule to follow and no rush... clearly announced to me that the *"new stage"* of my life had arrived.

I decided that I would take a while. I would dedicate more to myself and my loved ones. I thought about training as much as I wanted without controlling the time I spent. I would help my mother more at home, my father in the *Dojo* classes, and I would also spend more time in the villages with the neighbors and villagers. In short, I wanted to contribute all the time that my college years had taken away from sharing; I wanted to feel part of all that again, because sometimes I had the feeling of having been absent for a long time from everything and everyone.

I wanted to recover that emptiness!

Of course, I was preparing my resume and selecting companies that might interest me, and I sent them, but I took it very calmly and without stress or rush.

« I felt that I would be called by the company where Takashi-San worked, but I didn't say anything to anyone. It was something that, simply: "I felt it in me." »

The announcement of spring was everywhere. At that time I just wanted to enjoy the *"Sakura;"* contemplate their flowers and observe their beauty. They always bloom before other trees.

There are multiple ways to enjoy cherry blossoms: contemplating the blossoms in silence, walking in the mountains or meadows letting spring itself is founded with oneself, or simply sitting under its shade and having a picnic (this is very common in Japan).

The *"hanami,"* 'the fall of the cherry blossoms,' continues at night and is called: *"Yozakura,"* 'cherry trees at night'.

In the evenings (most of them during the spring) I would sit in my garden under my *Sakura;* spread a tablecloth on the ground and put dinner on it. A dim light, coming from the lantern at the entrance, was enough to see slightly, since when it was possible to see, I preferred the light of the full moon, that beautiful moon phase when we are, precisely, between the Sun and the Moon.

After dinner, I'd lie down contemplating the new t shoots begins of its bulbs, and after a couple of weeks its flowers appeared, splashed with that warm yellow first and later lunar white. When at night, the petals fell through the air with that soft aroma over me it filled me with optimism and energy.

Sometimes the three of us lay down (together with my parents), and in silence: we surrendered to the pleasure of the feelings of nature.

By day, the petals fell like confetti floating in the breeze.

I hugged my tree (that we had turned four years more together, as the plaque at his feet showed), and I offered 'respect' so that he would bring joy to our lives and we could celebrate *hanami* for many more years.

« That feeling of "goodbye" that I kept feeling inside me did not leave me and it afflicted me. »

On the other side, I remember how well I was enjoying everything, and of the time available I had when my birthday came on the day of *"Shōwa no hi."*

At that time, I turned twenty-two years old, and that year I attended all the events that were held in *Shirakawa-go*, and participated in the events and parties, as well as the famous *'Golden Week'* (considered the holiday period by excellence for the Japanese).

Takashi-San spent all those days with us; he also needed a few days of rest and to disconnect from everything. Having a good time and enjoying ourselves was what we wanted.

There are many events and celebrations throughout the country, from April 29 to May 5; although it usually extended a couple of days more (it is the only time in the year that many Japanese people take so many consecutive days of partying).

The third of May is celebrated as *"Kenpo Kinenbi,"* Japan's 1947 *'Constitution Day.'*

May fifth of May is *"Tango no Sekku,"* *'children's day'* and young boys are honored.

Entire villages and families hang kites and streamers on the doors of the houses, representing the present of the young people and their future, wishing them strength and success in their lives.

During Golden Week, many festivals are celebrated around almost every city in Japan. In them, tours are common to see everything full of beautiful flowers, such as azaleas and wisteria, which surround the stalls with their handicraft and gastronomy products, while the different historical parades of a cultural nature pass.

There are always so many people every year, you can hardly walk! On the first day, my birthday, we wanted to celebrate with a meal of *"sukiyaki,"* (which consists of a 'pot with vegetables, beef from the region and everything is cooked with eggs'), in a restaurant near the temple, run by a very friendly lady who is a friend of the family.

We could hardly get there; we were making our way through the crowd.... We managed to get in and there was no room, but Mrs. Hiroko-San (a dear admirer of my parents, the *Sensei*) made room for us on the top floor. It was his private home, and there in her "private dining room," she sat us down and served us her *"famous pot of meat and vegetables,"* which everyone came looking for, because it was very famous and popular in the region ("Takashi-San commented that he had never eaten a *sukiyaki* as good as that one").

« There were reasons for it, because their meat was delicious and of great quality. The fame of the veal of the area is known for its breeding and the cuts, made with skill of its bovine pieces, for which they have many international recognitions. »

The celebrations ended, and spring was expanding everywhere with all its splendor of greens and flowers that lent its color to the landscape. The smell of flowers and the songs of nightingales, abstracted you away from the mundane entering into a state of wellbeing, something very much desired after such a cold and freezing winter.

One day in May, I received a call. It was from the company where Takashi-san works, telling me that they had attended my resume for the vacant positions in the various economics departments. They gave me a face-to-face appointment in three days. He named and listed the different economic departments to be covered, and that I should think about which of them I wanted to apply for. Upon arriving at the company, I had to request the assistant of the chosen department, and would be interviewed by the Head of that department and by the Executive Director.

« This is where I exclaimed a classic to myself: I knew it, I felt it inside me! I communicated it to everyone immediately. And the joy spread... »

In three days I would have the interview with the *"Kachou"* (the head of the department of my choice). The department I would choose was clear, the "economic development" department, because it is what I had based my thesis on and I had worked on it recently: the ideas and methods to be applied in the future to know and understand poverty; and to know how to intervene in the development of the most disadvantaged communities.

The department and the subject I had it insured. As for the concepts of "attitude" and "aptitude" I was not going to have problems there, precisely (if I trained Takashi-san in this, it cost him... but he did well...!). That part was controlled; in addition I had a couple more alternatives, just in case... like good *Kunoichi*. I also took into account that the *Kachou,* to reach that position, would have an age that would be around fifty years minimum, something important to be able to draw a profile, and if we added what a large company like that expect from its employees..., we already had the conditioning factors to which to give answer.

So I did not prepare anything at all. I had full and total confidence in myself.

Yoshida Sensei, on the night before the day of the interview, told me:

"Are you motivated? Don't forget that motivation is what drives us to act and to live, as well as to achieve our goals."

"Yes," I replied. "I have plans for a near future to realize with Takashi-San, and my ideals as a professional in the sustainable human development, and collaborating in the extinction of poverty in the world are enough motivations for me."

"Yes, they are, Haru!" said Yoshida Sensei. "I am pleased to see that you look to the future with hope, with the conviction of wanting *to do what you believe you have to do.* Our voluntary acts, not imposed, but carried out with conviction and free decision, will cause us satisfaction and bring us happiness. But that vital sense, related to the work environment, your occupation and how you interact, is linked not only to your reason for being, but also to what is happens in the world in which we move. This is not only intrinsic but also extrinsic, my dear Haru, and always remember that the soul is intrinsic to the human being...."

"I am conscious of everything and of my nature. Please don't suffer for me *Sensei,* you have trained me well! Thanks Dad!" I answered while hugging him.

« *Sensei* feared that my pretensions and purposes in working life were very high and that, if I did not achieve them, I could feel that I had lost the battle and give up or sink in purpose. But none of it! I have always known that it is a utopia, but for me "it is enough to know that I have tried." To contribute my seeds or my own grain of sand in the great mountain, as far as it is possible for me or I am allowed to arrive…, was and is my purpose. I am very aware that one cannot fight the world alone, a whole society is needed. »

The day of the interview arrived, it was a day of splendid sunshine and I headed to *Tokyo*, to the *Shinjuku* district, where the company's prominent 30-story-high building is located, occupying an entire city block. And there, on the 22nd floor, was Takashi-San working in his office.

For the occasion, I chose a suit jacket with gray skirt (summer would soon be here) and white silk blouse with matching handbag and heeled shoes (classic Japanese women's clothing to go to work, whether it is an office, in a company or in warehouses, stores, supermarkets, etc.).

I collected my long hair with a very elegant retro and Italian style bun that gave it its own, modern and serious style.

The first thing in Japan is punctuality; you can never be late for an appointment, much less work. So, like clockwork, I showed up punctually where I had been indicated.

I had to go up to the eighth floor (my favorite number because the 8 placed horizontally equals "infinity," it is a significant and important number in Martial Arts as well), so I had already started well.

I had to say what my selected department was:

"Economic Development and International Cooperation."

Then, they made me pass to a great office, and they told me that the interviewer would come right away. I waited standing. In a matter of seconds a good-looking man in his early fifties entered, with a very serious look on his face.

The courtesy greetings and formal presentation took place, as the Japanese tradition dictates. Immediately afterwards, I was invited to sit down, pointing to an armchair, and he began to talk about the company, its international extensions..., until he arrived at his specific department, which was the one that interested us: development capacity, available tools, plans, etc. After a correct presentation and description of the company came the questions. He spoke very correctly and slowly.

I observed that he was examining my *attitude* and composure; also that he was drawn to my eyes, my special look. But I felt comfortable, because after a series of questions, I took the initiative, having into account the concepts that I had captured in his previous speech; and I exposed the possibilities of sustainable human development of my degree project, and how the company could intervene benefiting from political, social and financial level.

Without forgetting my *attitude* and *aptitude* at any moment, as well as my composure, gestures, the right look transmitting confidence and security at the level of his eyes, which I observed to elucidate what my words and tones were provoking in his emotions.

When I finished exposing, he opened a folder, took out my thesis, and said that he had read it in its entirety twice because he had been very interested in it; that he needed to see the person who had developed it, if that person would have the capacity, the courage and the value necessary to empower oneself in these processes in cooperation at the international level, and if my sensitivity towards the most disadvantaged would not interfere in the processes…

So, I did a mental reading of demographic data, and focused on the large-scale and international level prestige which the own company could be endowed and benefit from, if it provided the necessary innovation and development components together with the human factor and the advanced technologies.

He began to feel a lot of enthusiasm and happened to converse, showing interest in my words.

I had his undivided attention! His countenance had relaxed, and he exuded at the same time that exempted some occasional smile.

Suddenly, he got up and apologizing himself, leaving very quickly and returning with another person whom he introduced as Executive Director (the corresponding introduction and greetings were made); then they went out together again... After a few minutes he came back alone and commented that we had finished, that it had been a pleasure talking to me; that he hoped to do it again very soon; and he was convinced that I was a valid and well-prepared person despite my youth.

He escorted me to the office door, we bow greeting and... It's over! A young lady accompanied me to the exit, very courteously said that they would contact with me very soon, and thanked me for coming.

« It is normal in Japan that, at the end of a job interview, they always have some detail out of courtesy and respect: to highlight something good or positive about the interviewee so that he/she doesn't feel bad, or to encourage him/her for the next time. I observed that, in my case, it was not just one detail, there were several and very positive, so I had no doubt that they would hire me. Normally, when I felt something, it always happened. I left happy and very satisfied, like someone who had achieved something or *done what he had to do*. »

I took advantage of the fact that I was in *Shinjuku*, one of the 23 districts of *Tokyo*, and took a tour of that frenetic urban paradise of immense area and tall skyscrapers, with its wide shopping streets and countless buildings complete with *karaoke*, cinemas, hotels, cafes, bars and restaurants, electronic stores and of all kinds, concentrating around them the most famous department stores in Japan, giving access to the most exclusive purchases in centers such as: *Isetan, Keio, Odakyu, Takashimaya...*, full of endless floors of designer clothes, cosmetics and perfumeries, decoration, jewelry..., and their basements overflowing with all kinds of restaurants and food services.

Here is also the *Metropolitan Government Building* or *Tokyo City Hall,* with 243 meters high being one of the tallest buildings in the city. The 360° views are magnificent with its two observatories at 202 meters high, and it has a spectacular panoramic restaurant (viewpoint) in the north tower.

There, contemplating the views of the entire city, I sat down to eat something and contemplated the *Shinjuku Park*, which is located at the back of the City Hall, and is like a lung in the middle of the city to oxygenate and stroll through its beautiful gardens full of *Sakura*. It is a place very frequented by workers in the area at lunchtime, and by many Japanese who come to enjoy the *"hanami"* watching the fall of the petals of its flowers.

On the way to *Shinjuku Station,* I could not restrain myself and did some shopping before taking the train back. I still had to spend the money I had been given for my birthday. I must confess that I spent it all on shopping!
That's the thing about *Shinjuku*, it's that frenetic and irresistible and one can't control oneself buying and consuming.
Its railway station is the busiest in the world. Really, the huge station building is the union of different railway stations. It is huge, it looks like an airport and you can see many tourists lost in its immensity and the large number of train and subway lines; as well as stores and restaurants.

When I got home, when they asked me how the interview had gone, I answered that it would start in June…
My parents knew what I meant. They know me well!
The next day, on Saturday, Takashi-San came to see me and spend the weekend, as usual. I told him in detail how the whole interview went. And we talked and talked, until we realized: that we were having a dialogue as if I had already signed the contract with the company…!
« It is amazing how the mind works, especially when the subconscious becomes conscious. That is: the subconscious emits messages at the conscious level and certain patterns are activated in rational behavior. And this kind of 'sensation' or

'sensitivity,' 'heart' or 'feeling,' is what drives us to perceive answers or see the 'hidden' or 'secret.' The subconscious processes what the mind does consciously. Evidently, all this has to do with the mental work that is done in the *"Budō"* or *'way of the warrior'* in Japanese Martial Arts. Its practice and training lead to open and expand the senses and develop the mind to a higher level. Some call it *"mental powers"* or also *"Ninja powers,"* but nothing further away from reality...! The years of a lifetime dedicated to martial training, and especially to the *"Art of the Shinobi"* or *"Ninja,"* are the result of developing the mind and the senses. »

Only four days had passed since the interview and they called me. I had to present myself for that week to sign the contract that would start on June 1.
The day of going to sign arrived and I showed up on time. It was very fast. They took me into a meeting room, and there were two company lawyers present, the Chief Executive Officer (CEO), and the Head of the department.
I read the contract..., and I signed! After receiving some opportune indications, they accompanied me and showed me what would be my small office, located on the 10th floor (with a large window and good views) so that I could see it, and when I start work the first day, bring the things that I want or need (I could even decorate it to my liking, but for me it was already perfect). They also gave me some huge company information tomes about the company to read before starting.
« In the middle of May I had my contract in the hand signed. It was done! Just as I had foreshadowed! »

Takashi-san and I would work at the same company, to only 12 floors away...!

We were very happy and decided to celebrate it with our families: Takashi-san's parents and mine (although they had spoken on the phone on different occasions, we had not yet made a direct personal introduction).

It was the perfect and special occasion to make the "official" presentation in the form of celebration and be all together.

We chose a very good and beautiful restaurant in the *Ginza* area, a *Tokyo* district, and a very commercial area of the city. The area is full of prestigious luxury boutiques, elegant cocktail bars and *sushi* restaurants. We chose one of among many others, whose specialty is *"Yakiniku,"* 'grilled meat' or 'Japanese barbecue.' These restaurants have charcoal braziers (*sumibiyaki*), which are part of the table itself, and each one cooks the pieces of beef and vegetables to taste. The important thing about these restaurants is the quality of the meat, this is cute very thin and it is boneless to facilitate the use of chopsticks. Once cooked, it is seasoned with a typical sauce.

« It was a bit expensive, but the occasion was worth it. We wanted the first meeting of our families to be perfect. »

Our parents connected very well, and the feelings in the environment were very affective and positive. They talked about many things and various topics, apart from also talking about us. I remember our trip to *Okinawa* came up in the conversation, and Yagami-San talked about *Karate* and Isami Kobayashi Sensei, of whom we all spoke wonders of him and, of course, from his wife Sophie-San.

It was a perfect night with a pleasant temperature and we decided to go for a walk. *Ginza* has a mobile and beautiful architecture. In fact, it is considered the best or newest in architecture, and because of that, it is one of the most luxurious neighborhoods in *Tokyo*. It is full of luxury stores with the most prestigious brands and firms of fashion and technology. It is an area where you have to be attentive to the new buildings that are continually being built, because in Japan they are very given to demolish buildings that have become old to make way for new ones. That same ride, the following year, is different with new buildings and spaces.

When leaving the restaurant, we opted for just that: strolling. We arrive at the *"Hama Rikyu Gardens,"* 'a traditional style Japanese garden,' famous for its pond of salty seawater, which enters directly from *Tokyo Bay,* and which has a natural effect on the level of the pond, which it changes with the tides. It also has a huge and beautiful tea house, on an islet above the pond, from which you can enjoy wonderful views that invite you to relax while having an exquisite tea. We were fine, but had to hurry back to the station to catch the trains (they run until midnight), so we took cabs (Japanese cabs are among the most expensive in the world) to the second railroad transfer station so we could catch the last train of the night to Nagano.

« It was a great meeting and a great celebration of all together. I have not forgotten a single detail of that beautiful night! It made us very happy that the families liked each other and that there was such a good harmony. We knew from both sides that our parents were delighted. It was the perfect beginning of the new stage that was opening in our lives from that moment on. »

My first big day of work at OTARU NHK GROUP has arrived!

Let me clarify some points to know about Japanese companies: Japanese company works like a big family. This has both pros and cons. On the one hand, it offers you a lot of stability, since it is very difficult to be fired in Japan. And, even if you have bad results, as a good family they give you opportunities, one after the other, as many as are necessary, helping you together to overcome that step.

The company provides you with all the bureaucratic procedures that represent the payment of fees or taxes, medical insurance, tax declaration, etc.

On the other hand, some companies will require you to "act of presence," this is to be present at any time, so Japanese people work a lot of overtime. The normal thing is to do 30 to 60 overtime hours a month, which are generally always paid; although the majority of Japanese choose not to request such remuneration so as not to harm the company.

Another point against are the endless meetings; there are meetings for everything. The working day in Japan starts, as a rule, with the first meeting called *chōrei,* which lasts about thirty minutes, and in which the different and varied objectives of the day of each department are presented; being the heads, *Kachou,* of each section who communicate the news, the casualties or incidents of any worker, and then, the company statutes are read. The day also ends with another meeting called *shūrei,* in which the results obtained are presented; the failures or mistakes made are analyzed and possible solutions are presented.

In our case, we did not have many of these obligations. Our schedules were established by law, overtime was voluntary and paid, and we could even request to release some Fridays a month (which we did on only one occasion for health reasons).

We had the same work schedule, which greatly simplified everything when it came to organizing ourselves.

On my first day of work, I went straight to the *Department of Economic Development and International Cooperation,* where I was greeted by the interviewer (who gave me a big smile welcoming me) and introduced me to my immediate superior: Shiro Takayama (*Shiro:* 'fourth son,' Takayama: 'high mountain'). They both accompanied me to what was already my office.

They were very interested to know if I liked it, if I would be okay or needed anything; they showed me company notebooks, the computer, passwords, programs, etc. The interviewer asked for permission to leave and instructed Takayama-San to 'take good care of me' (which was very nice of him and quite a detail!). My boss told me to accompany him that the first-hour meeting was taking place, *chōrei.* With my presentation to the other department colleagues and plans for the day, it lasted 40 minutes.

After finished, I went to *'my office;'* quickly sorted my things and took time to catch up.

At 12:30 p.m., a 45-minute lunch breaks. Takashi-San and I had arranged to meet at that time for lunch at the *"Shinjuku Gyoen Park National Garden,"* the famous botanical garden of about 60 hectares. It also has a former secondary residence belonging to the imperial family, an art gallery, two Japanese tea houses (where tea ceremonies take place), several rest pavilions, restaurants...

It is divided into three landscaped areas such as: the English garden, the French garden and the Japanese garden. On one side, there is also a huge greenhouse with thousands of tropical flowers and plants.

We meet next to one of the park's tea houses. Takashi-San was in charge of buying two *bentō* of food (a *bentō* is a portion of food prepared to take away, usually it takes rice, meat or fish and a garnish based on vegetables). It comes in a tray with single-use containers. It is something very usual, in the daily and traditional Japanese gastronomy, for many workers. We ate lunch together on the shore of one of the park's lakes and then had tea. It was another one of those beautiful and clear late spring days.

We talked a bit about how the morning's work had gone, and we said goodbye until 5:00 p.m. (the end of our working day), meeting us at the main exit of the company.

The workday passed very quickly, without even realizing it. When I went out, my boyfriend was already at the door and introduced me to his immediate boss: *Hiroshi Saitō* (*Hiroshi:* 'generous,' *Saitō*: 'blessed') in his early forties, very slim but modern and friendly. He also introduced me to several colleagues in his department. All of them were very nice. I could see that there was trust and complicity among all of them.

My boss, Takayama-San, was about fifty years old; he was shorter, somewhat stockier and stronger. More serious, or is that still, there was not that level of confidence.

That same day I was able to speak, although very little, with some colleagues from my department; they all treated me very well and offered to help me with whatever I needed, which made me very happy on my first day at work.

We quickly went to the station to catch trains. The train ride to *Nagano*, we did together; he got off at that station to go home, and I made one more transfer and continued until changing of the station, and take the bus to get to my home.

« This was the hardest part of every day, the amount of time we spent on public transportation on a daily basis. It was also the price to pay for living in the famous and beautiful Alpine mountains. »

In that first year of working at the company, my life consisted of coming home, having dinner, and going to sleep to wake up at four in the morning.

I dedicated only the weekends to my personal training. On Saturday mornings, I would share class with the senior grades (which Takashi-San attended as well), and on alternate

Sundays: one Sunday we would train and enjoy the rest of the day, and the other we would spend with our families or friends.

It was in that same year that *Sensei* and I granted to Takashi-San the degree of *black belt 1st Dan* (after previous examination before all the disciples and companions), which meant a great joy for him, but this implicitly entailed a great responsibility too.

Obtaining this rank means climbing to the top as a professional and an expert. It is the result of the path traveled, where efforts have paid off, but it is not the end or the goal (as many believe), but the starting, the beginning of another way: that of darkness and that of shadows, or in other words: that of evil and difficulties, because, it is from that point on, where the fight against oneself and one's spirit begins, to later be reborn in a new day. It is where the light shines after that darkness, and then, that gleaming black belt turns whitish (worn out by use) until, little by little, it returns to its original white, thus completing the circle of the own existence.

« This is the true way of the warrior. In times of peace, war is the daily struggle for life and for survival against all the invisible attacks and social spankings that must be lived with. This concept goes beyond the principles that lead a man or a woman to face a fight and not lose ethical and moral values. He or she must maintain the spirit noble and blameless. »

Takashi-San was already beginning to understand that in his training he had to go further. He had to open his mind and spirit to see clearly through the darkness. I always guided him, but I had to let him walk alone in this inner search, because he had to learn to "fight with himself:" the toughest and most feared battle a human beings face.

The changes became visible as time passed, as happens with all *Budoka* or 'Japanese Martial Arts practitioner' in any of their disciplines.

Takashi-San had managed to conquer, not only my heart, but my parents hearts as well, and especially Yoshida Sensei's. He had become a member of the family. He got with effort to achieve a union with the *Sensei*, a connection of *master and disciple,* like *father to son.* And that had become very important to Takashi-San, for how significant this is in Japanese culture.

For me that bond was very important. Conquering *Sensei* was not and is not an easy thing. He is a warrior forged as such, of samurai origin and lineage, who lived the transformations of other traditional times and adapted to new times. He always tells that the real change was made when he saw me born (older villagers tell it too). That at that moment, he understood that his heart was beating differently and that he liked to feel those beats that made him compassionate and soft (so he tells it himself), and that he swore that he would always love me and protect me.

My mother confirms the story, but adds that all that was wrapped in a cloth of tears, that she had never seen him cry before. She tells how, when I was born, he held me in his arms for a long time and that his tears were gushing down; that he did not want to release me until the nurse had to force him.

I liked to hear the stories they told. Now I was hearing them again with my boyfriend, who also loved to hear them. Our relationship was still beautiful and full of love, our infatuation did not decline, quite the opposite!

Every time it was getting stronger, and it was difficult for us to be apart, either during work or when we said goodbye every day and every night.

For these reasons and others such as: the distances, time and money we had to invest in transportation to go to the company daily, it was that: the following year, we decided to move in together and rent an apartment in *Tokyo,* close to work.

We discussed it with our respective parents, and it was fine by both parties. They didn't put any objection or rejoinder for that we not marrying. We wanted to do that later when our salaries were higher.

We were very lucky for the constant support we always had from them in everything we did.

We needed a few summer days off, a vacation, to look for our new home. But Japan works very differently from the West in that respect: In Japan, there are many holidays, but the concept of having a month of vacation in summer does not exist.

Japanese employees have three periods which are: *New Year* (at the end and beginning of the year), *Obon* (in summer, in the middle of July or August) and the *Golden Week* (up to one week, between the end of April and the beginning of May). The worker has about ten days off from paid vacations per year, which in many cases are not used, and when they do, it is usually for reasons such as getting sick. What's more, if you can't go to the office one day, you use a paid vacation day, although you can do more than ten days without charging them, and this is not done by anyone.

Therefore, something as simple as getting sick in Japan is really very hard, because on the one hand, paid vacation days are lost, and on the other, it is possible that that month will be charged less if you have already used all the days available that you had paid.

It is very difficult to do the ten days together, also because of the *"Japanese Giri"* or *'sense of duty:'* not causing problems or annoyance to colleagues or the company due to absence, and in case of taking one or more days off, the first thing to do when you return is to apologize for everything that may have caused you absence, and thank them for allowing you to do so (Japanese ethics).

The *"Obon"* festival was approaching, in the middle of summer, and many companies offer several days off in August to take the *"Obon holidays."*
Our company offered it, so we had a few days, about four days exactly. But we spoke with our co-workers explaining that we were looking for an apartment and we wanted moving; all of them were all delighted to support us. So, we took another four more days, and we would have a total of eight days to do it all...

Obon is a tradition that consists of a ceremony in which offerings are made to the ancestors who return home, lighting a fire to attract their spirits *(Mukaebi),* and thus honor their memory.
During the days of the festival, the tombs of deceased relatives and ancestors *(Haka-mairi)* are also visited. Then the *bon-odori* takes place, a traditional and popular dance that each region has its own way of celebrating it. And our prefecture is one of the most popular, which is why many Japanese come from everywhere all over the country.
This dance is to welcome the spirits, comfort and soothe them to return them back to the afterlife. It takes place in the central square around a small temple, accompanied by Japanese drums that mark the beat *(wa-odori)* and go through each of the streets of the village.
It is like a great summer festival full of joy and color!

While all this party and bustle wrapped everything up, Takashi-San and I were immersed in locating effective real estate agencies that could give us a quick solution.

We only had to say what we were looking for, how we wanted it, the conditions of the apartment, and above all, that it was close to the company and in a quiet area. And since we were in love with nature, we asked to be near the *"Shinjuku Gyoen Park National Garden,"* where we ate every day because it was very close to the company. Also, because being in a city as saturated and stressful as *Shinjuku,* it was important for us to have a view of the park, because it meant a lung of oxygen and an oasis of peace for us, coming from the mountainous Alps.

« In Japan's large metropolitan areas, it is not uncommon for young couples to cohabit in an apartment before marriage. »

The real estate agencies in the country are very efficient and usually take care of everything. Within a couple of days they called us to confirm that they had had two entries that matched our conditions, and that both were right in front of *Shinjuku Gyoen Park.* We had to see them as soon as possible because they would be rented quickly, as the demand in *Tokyo* is huge and continuous. So the next day we went to the address given to us. It was right in front of the gardens, a large block of buildings, which we call a *"manshon,"* what in Europe is a tall building with flats or apartments.

It was a modern building with a few years of construction, with a luxurious entrance on the facade. We went up with the real estate agent in the elevator to the fifth floor (which is really the fourth floor, because in Japan there is no fourth floor, no door four, or anything with that number, because of the belief that it attracts bad luck, since in Japanese 'four' is: *Shi* and 'death' is: *Shi*, although their writing in kanji is different, they are pronounced the same).

As we exited the elevator there were two doors, one on the right and one on the left. We headed for the latter, and upon opening we found a nice *"genkan"* or *'entrance,'* which encompasses a small area, at the same level as the exterior, where upon arrival you have to take off your shoes. There is a *"geta-bako"* or *'shelf,'* where shoes are placed and slippers are taken to wear around the house. Then you go up to another higher level, which is the level that the rest of the residence has.

As soon as we entered we loved it; it was very spacious and bright. It was very elegant and modern furnished, western style with some Japanese details. A nice living room with two large gray armchairs with gold cushions, several shelves on the wall, a large plasma television, and a dining area with a large glass table with four black chairs of the latest style. The floor was synthetic flooring in soft pearl gray tiles and white ceilings. The walls were partially combined in shades of white, gray and gold. On one side there was access to the kitchen, spacious in white and gray, fully equipped and furnished with all electrical appliances, and a pantry room with cupboards. On the other side of the living room there was a distribution to two rooms. One of them, very spacious, was for children, guests, relatives or assistant. It was western style with two small beds side by side, a wall of closets and a private mini office area. The other room was large and in 'traditional Japanese style' called *"washitsu,"* with a *tatami* floor and *"Tokonoma,"* the traditional place of honor for the family altar. There were *"shōji,"* which are vertical sliding partitions to cover the windows; an *"oshiire,"* a large closet with two levels to store the futons, and a very nice noble wood ceiling. In the middle of the rooms, there was a full bathroom with a modern style deep bathtub.

The living room had large sliding windows overlooking the great park and its lakes, and in the background: the great buildings and skyscrapers characteristic of *Shinjuku*.

It was a spectacular view for to be in the center of *Tokyo*! The apartment had 91m² totals. There was: telephone, wifi and a domestic internet connection. It was very spacious, designer, and everything was new. We didn't have to put or buy any furniture. Just bring our personal belongings (that's what we wanted). The agent said that she had another one very close by that we could look at as well. And we both said: no!

We saw ourselves there from the moment the agent opened that door. We felt that we would be very well off and that this would be our home.

The price was within our budget, since that year they had increased our salary for both of us.

In *Tokyo*, a typical rental agreement is for one year, and the agreement is renegotiated each year. The tenant pays the agency commission, the *"chukai tesuryo,"* as payment of fees and the *"shikikin"* deposit, which in our case, was five more months as a deposit for the "all furnished and equipped", recoverable if the apartment does not suffer any damage.

We rushed with the agent to her office, and made a reservation or *"tetsukekin,"* which is equivalent to one month's rent, recoverable when the rent is effective. In order to prepare the contract quickly, as the next day was a holiday, we agreed for the final signature, remaining payment and delivery of keys, for the next business day.

The return home was filled with joy. We did not believe that we were going to form a home and a life together, and it was imminent...! In two days we would open the door of our own home...

The feelings were on the surface of my skin with so much emotion and happiness. He went straight to his house to tell his parents about it, and I was in a hurry to share it with mine. On both sides of the families, they were happy for us and wanted to visit our new home. We agreed that they would accompany us on the day of the handing over of the keys: *"reikin,"* and so they would visit it.
We would all go together that day!

The next day, we enjoyed the *Obon* festival in *Shirakawa-go*. The two families passed it together, and we participated in all the events: the lighting of the fire for the spirits, the visits to the tombs, the drumming and the dance. The crowd of attendees was overwhelming. You could barely walk but we were all together laughing and dancing.

The day of the signing came in which we all went to *Shinjuku*. The first thing was to go to the agency to make the countless payments, and after signing and putting our stamps *"hanko"* (which literally means *'small stamp'*) on many, many documents..., we finished the transaction.
« In Japan, *hanko* is used in place of the Western signature for: contracts, picking up a postal package at post offices or opening bank accounts. The *hanko* is a seal used for personal or company identification. These stamps are used with a special reddish stamp pad, and the mark left by stamping the *hanko* on the surface is called *'Inkan.'* »

With the keys in our hands we walked to the apartment. When our parents saw the park just in front, they already made the gestures of astonishment and positive surprise.
We went up to the fifth floor and opened the door together, with one hand each on the key, and turned it slowly while looking into each other's eyes.

It was a very special moment for us. My mother said that the groom should take me in his arms, and walk through the doorway together to let love in. We all laughed, but Takashi-san put his arms around me and lifted me up, and just like a newly married couple, we passed the door.

He took off his shoes shaking his feet, while my mother took mine out, and he led me through all the rooms of the apartment until he left me standing in the living room. He got down on his knees, as our parents applauded, and said to me:

"We are in our home. Here we will form our home. We will fill it with love and joys!" he said this by adding the expression: *"Tokimeku"* which means *'to enter a crucial moment'* or that *'a crucial moment has come,'* and symbolizes *'the emotion by which we stand still as if time has stopped.'*

« It was a very beautiful and emotional moment that was engraved in my heart forever! »

The families really liked the apartment, especially the traditional-style master bedroom: *"washitsu,"* with its *"fusuma"* doors, that slide open from side to side. The decoration of these interior doors separating rooms is a true art. For centuries, this artistic and handicraft work is made of cloth or Japanese *"washi"* paper, and the motifs they represent are those of nature with mountains, animals, forests and rivers. The engraved motifs of our *fusuma* were the mountains above forests, crossed by a river and in front of the whole landscape: the branches in first dimension of the 'cherry blossom' or *Sakura.*

« There has always been a *Sakura* in my life that is imprinted on my own name at birth, symbolizing 'spring' and the manifestation of its flowering..., always there: enveloping, accompanying and reminding me how fragile and fleeting nature and existence are; enunciating to me to live the beautiful moments, because they are not eternal and just like the cherry blossom, they wither. »

That part of the house, the *"washitsu,"* is what they liked the most as they are quite traditional, but they recognized that the western design of the rest of the house was spectacular, and was done with great taste and distinction.

Our mothers got down to work, writing down everything that was needed, announcing that they would take care of some things like the *"futons"* for the bedroom, which consists of three elements: the *"shikibuton"* or mattress, the *"kakebuton"* or bedspread and the *"makura"* or pillow; also the *"Yukata:"* which literally means 'bathing clothes,' for men and women, although its use is not limited only to after bathing. Men's *yukata* have much shorter sleeves and are more muted and not as brightly colored as women's *yukata*. The *yukata* is composed of: a *"juban,"* a garment worn under as an inner kimono, *"obi"* or belt and *"geta"* or sandal. These are often seen in Japan on the streets or at festivals during the warmer months. Our moms also wrote down such things as: towels, tablecloths, kitchen and cleaning cloths, etc. The apartment was stocked with tableware, ceramics and bowls, kitchen utensils, chopsticks, etc.

The dads organized the transportation of our things because it was a complicated move, since it took about five hours by car (much longer than by train). And the moms took care of the shopping and their notes.

We only took care of packing, each one at home all the personal belongings that we would move.

We had three days of vacation left to get everything ready... And we did it!

The day before returning to the offices we were already in our residence fully installed (with some boxes still to open and place), and with the pantry and refrigerator full.

The families made it possible by overturning themselves into everything, and giving themselves completely to us and our well-being.

« How many times do I have to say how lucky we were...? »

Our new life was there, with our jobs a few minutes from our home and discovering our life together for 24 continuous hours.

Takashi-san and I shared everything together: shopping, eating, cleaning, clothes, etc. He was very active in everything; did it with pleasure, and always with his characteristic smile.

He said that everything made him happy because being together was what he loved the most, and that nothing in the world mattered more to him. My feelings were the same and we said them to each other very often, even if it was not necessary; because we both knew perfectly well what we had, *and no one could destroy or annihilate that so unique and ours that is called: "eternal love!"*

Gradually our lives were accommodated to the frenetic pace of Tokyo, although we had our philosophy of life, and we never stopped keeping our bodies and minds in the *Budō*, in the martial disciplines. In our *tatami* room at home, we trained almost daily after work hours.

As we were going to *Nagano*, at least two weekends to see his parents and to *Shirakawa-go* to see mine, I was bringing me my weapons and various *Gi* (training clothes or uniforms) and also my *Ninja Tabi* (footwear long cane with flexible rubber sole, used by *Shinobi* or *Ninja*).

I also had with me my highly valued *Katana* (gift from my father).

I still remember the day I took it from *Yoshida Sensei's Dojo*…!

I had it in my hands and I was looking at it, when *Sensei* asked my permission and grabbed it, held it for a few seconds tightly with his hands and unsheathed it while saying:

"We are going to do the cleansing ritual and increase it internal energy."

We took out the cleaning kit: a wooden box carved with *kanji* writings alluding to the arts of war, with the different elements inside: the metal hammer, called *mekugi,* a ball of non-abrasive powder, known as *uchiko*, lubricating oil or *koji* and rice paper, called *harai gami.*

All of these components are to be used in the cleaning ritual of a *Katana*, and are applied with the utmost respect, courtesy and reverence.

A *Katana* must always be kept clean and lubricated to prevent the steel from altering or deteriorating. Sweat, dust or blood itself affects the blade, and therefore, periodic maintenance must be carried out.

We cleaned it together and when we finished the cleaning ritual, he re-sheathed it on his sheath *(saya),* and performing the reverence put it in my hands reciting a Japanese proverb:

"You may only need your sword once in your life, but it is necessary that you always carry it."

« The *Katana* continues and will continue to be a symbol for all Japanese, reminiscent of feudal Japan, and continues to be *"The sword of the samurai"* in the contemporary era, along with *"Bushido"* or *'the way of the warrior,'* which contains the strict ethical code of loyalty and honor until death. All this is still valid in today's context and floats in the social air of the country. »

When we spent the weekend with my parents we always trained in the *Dojo* with *Sensei*, sometimes in the mountains, which in my opinion, there is where you enjoy, where you really learn and put all your knowledge and senses to work. To be able to be in that paradise now that we were in the middle of the city was to be invaded by pure air and nature.

Both his parents and mine also came to visit us in Tokyo and spent weekends with us. Having a guest room made it easier to enjoy them and spend more time together. We used to walk, went to the movies, the theater, shopping... There are always things to see in the capital as it is the political, economic and cultural center of Japan.

Tokyo is a large extension that has 23 districts, which in turn contain 26 cities, and each one with its multiple nearby neighborhoods modeling a puzzle that forms the Japanese capital.

Shinjuku city is the most important commercial and administrative center; only in its enormous station more than three million people travel daily, which makes it the busiest in the world; being the station itself as a complete city. It has a population density of more than 17 thousand people per square kilometer. This area is divided into two parts: the western part where the large modern buildings and skyscrapers are located, and the eastern part which is the commercial area.

When we walked through *Shinjuku*, alone or accompanied by family or friends, we visited the different temples such as: the "*Zenkokuji* temple," the "*Hanazono* Shrine," the "*Hōjōji* Temple," the "*Anahachimangu* Shrine," the "*Shinjuku Suwa* Shrine" or the "*Inari Kiō Jinja*" among others...

Other times we would go up to the *Tokyo Metropolitan Government* building, the city hall, to see the views by day or by night, both of which are impressive.

We also walked through the famous "red light district," which is called *Kabukicho*, full of brothels, cabarets, pubs, hotels, many pachinko (game rooms) and many neon lights, very entertaining and striking with its entrance through the *Kabukicho Ichibangai* arch. Or we crossed the alley of *Omoide Yokocho*, which is like traveling to the past of Japan, with its small restaurants that offer the best traditional foods; or *Golden Gai* Street, with a lot of nightlife to drink *sake* or beer, and just opposite, is the sculpture of *"Love,"* by the American artist "Robert Indiana" that is in many countries throughout the world; or we would go to shops and to the huge shopping malls, always with many people, and everything wrapped in many lights and colors, screens and giant posters. All this is by and for the insatiable consumption of the Japanese.

We were getting better every time in the company, we were climbing positions and we were taking on more responsibilities; which meant more salary as well.

Everyone knew about our relationship as a couple and living together. We formed a good group of friends who, at the same time, were co-workers; we used to meet to go out, go to lunch or dinner, to attend events or celebrations of traditional festivals... Many times they would come to our house or we would go to the house of another and celebrated anniversaries, special days or just because we felt like having lunch or dinner all together.

What's more, to four of them, passionate about Martial Arts, we taught at home or in the *Shinjuku Park* some *Ninjutsu* classes, the art of the *Ninja*, and *Ken-jutsu*, the art of the Japanese sword, and this served to keep us both in practice and in teaching.

Even Saitō-San (Takashi-San's boss) and Takayama-San (my boss), alone or with more colleagues, we went out together for dinner or drinks, and they had also been as guests at our house on different occasions.

When they found out that I was *Sensei* in Martial Arts, everything changed in the company. Both the coworkers and the superiors began to call me *Haru-Sensei* or *Yoshida Sensei*, instead of *Haru-San* (something normal for the Japanese to use the teaching title in the name as a sign of respect).

In Japan we have the *"Nomikai,"* which means 'to drink alcohol after work with the bosses,' to improve the relationship of trust inside and outside of work, and to strengthen ties that improve the climate. This is a common tradition, where the company bears the expenses of the meeting. And, as it was well known that we were not used to drinking so much alcohol, there was always food and other beverages.
Our bosses were great people. We couldn't really ask for more: we were slowly climbing the corporate ladder, we related well with everyone, and everything around us was positive.

Time passed at high speed, without us even noticing it. From time to time we did some extra hours in the afternoons at the company, and we made our good savings for whims.
During the years that passed, we made many and diverse trips through the country (as good Japanese), and some of its islands, apart from *Okinawa*, such as: *Miyajima* Island, *Miyakejima* Island, *Dejima* Island, *Aogashima* Island, *Hokkaido* Island, *Shikoku* Island and the *Amami* Islands.
We also went outside of Japan: Hawaii, New York, Los Angeles, Canada, Holland, Austria, Rome, Venice and Florence, these three in the same trip, as well as Barcelona and Seville at the same time, in Spain. We loved to travel, and we often said that we should know at least most of the Earth and its continents before we die. To see all the beauty

of the planet where we were born and lived. Value it and understand it. Assimilate the knowledge and experiences that the different countries and their cultures offer us, as well as to obtain a different perspective and vision to recognize our own place in the world.

« Everything learned and known makes our life always worth living. For all this we kept thanking the *Kami* or Gods for the fortune bestowed upon us in our lives. »

All these thoughts are part of Japanese popular culture; it is understood within the philosophy of *"Ikigai,"* making reference again to that element that becomes our reason for being in the world, the motivation we need and that drives us to act and live. It is about seeking happiness in some way, identifying our purposes, and doing what is necessary to achieve them, even if our purposes change. We just have to recognize them again and make a commitment to pursue them.

« With our philosophy of life, our way of being, thinking and feeling, we were building our *"place in the world,"* where we always started from two elements, which for us were irreplaceable: "love" and "respect."

And when you can say that you have found that place you call "home," that place in the world that belongs to you and where happiness is possible, then you are in the place where your heart belongs. »

One day, I was asked by the executive director (CEO) of the company to carry out a "social project" as a "pilot test" in the fight against poverty, and inequality in the most disadvantaged areas of Japan. This is to make municipal economic aid for social inclusion more effective, promoting social activities in the most affected areas.

I carried out a project, almost illusory and to my particular way of seeing, where it would be invested directly in people, in their districts and neighborhoods, improving their entire local environment immediately by making job placement policies in social aid, employment, housing aid, and the municipal collaboration of the affected areas.

I remember that I prepared it by dedicating time and special attention to it, and after two weeks I gave the dossier to my boss.

A few months had passed, when one day in the company they announced and congratulated me, because my project had been approved by the territorial council to launch as a "pilot test" in different cities of the metropolitan prefecture.

In the company we all celebrated it together in style, and I received congratulations from the management and the presidency. I was given a *"membership,"* which means: it allows the employee to have the right to demand a new job in the company in his job, for any reason or circumstance, disappears or dissipates. In other words, it has in its favor to earn *"keep your job with the company for life"* options. I was also given an envelope with a "fairly good financial reward" for the work done.

Most Japanese workers aspire to that peace of mind and security in their jobs.

«It meant a lot to us, especially to me; if my project benefited the most disadvantaged people, it would have fulfilled my purpose of the *"Ikigai"* philosophy and the reason why I had chosen this career. It was like making my most unrealizable dreams come true...

I can't describe my feelings in words! But I'm sure you can imagine... »

Our relationship was growing stronger and stronger, as was the stability in our jobs. This prompted us to talk about "wedding" and "having children." We had been living together as a couple for more than five years, and we felt it was time to *"seal our love forever officially before the world."*

Although we were very comfortable in our apartment, we started to think about a house with a garden for our children. It was the "financially" perfect moment!

So we were looking at areas that were ideal for us around *Shinjuku*, no more than a couple of train or subway stations from work, so as not to waste too much time daily on distances.

We spent hours talking and planning our wedding. Before the law, we only had to present a declaration in the city hall with the official seal and the confirmation of two witnesses, registering later in the *"Koseki"* (the Japanese civil status registry); from then on, women take their husband's name because the law does not allow couples to have different names while married. We wanted to celebrate both types of wedding: the traditional Japanese or *"Shinto"* wedding and the Western or *"Christian"* wedding.

This decision of the type of wedding, almost never has to do with the preferences or religious beliefs of the couple. In Japan, weddings are not religious ceremonies; these only consist of celebrating together with family and friends the union of the bride and groom, whatever the type of celebration chosen. Generally it is just a matter of taste, preferences and budget.

Many Japanese couples choose the Western wedding, because the traditional wedding involves a huge financial outlay. And it is also very common for the bride and groom who can afford it to have both ceremonies.

Traditional Japanese *Shinto* weddings are mostly celebrated in spring and autumn, with November being the most chosen month, since the number 11 is: a very important lucky number in Japanese culture.

Pending to set the favorable date, according to the astrological calendar of *"Koyomi"* (in which there are favorable days and forbidden days for a ceremony like this), we already had everything planned and in agreement with the families. The decision to hold the ceremony in *Shirakawa-go* came from both of us, but Takashi-san was the first to express it, and I absolutely agreed!

For families, the choice was also excellent; since we all wanted the ceremony of our official union was in *"the village of the fairy tale,"* in the *"Myozen-ji Temple"* from the year 1748, a temple that evokes the most ancient Japan.

The *"Shinto"* which means: *'way of the gods'* is the native faith of Japan and is as old as the country itself. It has no kind of sacred text, no founder, and no absolute God. It is based on the teaching of ethical principles, but has no commandments. More than 80% of Japanese people practice *Shinto*. Shrines, in the culture of the country, are places of rest filled with a sense of the sacred and a source of spiritual vitality. They are considered by the Japanese as their spiritual home.

The shrine that we choose is located on the north side of the *Shirakawa-go* village, and its main hall, made of Japanese wood: *"zelkova"* (the *zelkova* tree is widely used for the construction of houses, boats and luxury furniture due to its precious ornamental characteristics and great hardness), with its thatched roof, diverse and attractive entrances and views of the manicured garden…, represented the perfect image of our dream ceremony.

We would hold the *Shinto* ceremony in the main hall of the shrine. My parents knew the entire administrative committee of the temple and the priest or *"Kannushi"* very well, so they would coordinate the dates with the availability of the shrine.

Shinto weddings are known for their beauty and distinction in their clothing, their exoticism and originality in decoration, as well as everything that surrounds them, but also for their extreme rectitude, sobriety and seriousness in protocol.

The wedding ceremony begins with the entrance of the exclusive guests to the venue (this type of wedding is only attended by the couple's closest friends), and later the bride and groom enter. The girlfriend always enters accompanied by her mother and the boyfriend by his father. Then the *Shinto* priest arrives, who is the last to join.

The priest performs the ritual of purification and blessing of the couple before announcing their marriage to the *kami* (deities), and recites a prayer in classic Japanese, giving way to the exchange of the *"juzu,"* 'an ancestral rosary' and the rings, which consists of drinking sake three times, a ceremony called *"San San Kudu"* which means: 'Three-Three-Nine,' and symbolizes the union between heaven, earth and the human being, which will bring happiness to the couple. Once the *sake* has been drunk, the couple must deposit the cups at exactly the same time, since tradition dictates that whoever places the cup later will die sooner. After drinking the bride and groom, these offer *sake* to the parents, as a symbol of family unification.

The ceremony lasts approximately 20 or 30 minutes, during which there can be no signs of affection on the part of the bride and groom, they can barely touch and they cannot kiss either.

The bride is dressed in a white silk *kimono*. In Japan, white is the color of death, and means that the bride's singleness dies, returning to be reborn later as a married woman, which is at the later moment when she changes her *kimono*. Sometimes they wear one with red motifs on top, as these two colors symbolize the joy of life and rebirth, and wear on their heads a big cap called *"wataboshi,"* which is a white silk headdress in the form of a hood, which serves to hide her face until the end of the ceremony, not revealing the elaborate and beautiful hairstyle with golden details, called *kanzashi*, and her face is painted white as a symbol of purity.

To the *kimono* we must add the *Nikai zori*, the Japanese sandals, with velvet straps and mounted on a double platform of rice straw, being the groom who gives it to the bride for the wedding day, and this is because the double platform symbolizes the union of the boyfriends. Also important is the white *tabi* (white socks) for the *zori* and a small handbag.

The bride's wedding *kimonos* are called *"shiramuko."*

The groom wears a *"haori"* jacket, which is a traditional Japanese jacket that reaches the height of the hip or thigh, similar to a *kimono*, and unlike the *yukata*, the *haori* does not close or overlap, but rather is held together by a string connecting the two flaps. In ancient times, the sleeveless *haori* used to be worn over the armor of the samurai. This jacket is usually black and underneath it wears *"Hakama,"* the pleated trouser skirt with vertical stripes. The male *kimono* for *Shinto* weddings is called *"montsuki."*

After offering the *sake* to the parents, the most emotional and important moment of the whole ceremony takes place: each of the bride and groom must make a speech where one speaks about the other, highlighting the virtues and the best of their spouse, and what they hope in the new way to travel together. Then the bride and groom make their sacred offering to the *"Sakaki,"* a tree that grows in the mountains whose branches and leaves are used for the *"Tama-Gushi,"* which literally in Japanese means 'jewel skewer' and is essential in the *Shinto* sacred rituals.

This tree is often planted as a sacred tree in *Shinto* shrines.

Next, the relatives follow the couple in entourage to carry out the photographic report. At the end of the photo sessions, it is time for the banquet, and the bride and groom change their clothes. The bride puts a more colorful and brightly printed *kimono*, and the groom usually changes into a western suit with jacket and tie. This is when the reception is held and the guests, who are usually numerous, are received one by one: distant relatives, friends, neighbors, co-workers, etc.

After the welcome greeting, everyone sits at the banquet to enjoy the variety of dishes, and a toast is made in which the bride and groom stand up as *"husband and wife."*

During the banquet, the newlyweds pass by the tables thanking the guests for their attendance, and offering gifts to each one called *hikidemono,* at the same time that the guests deliver theirs, which are always special envelopes with money for the newlyweds (the Japanese are always very generous at weddings).

The celebration continues with *karaoke* and lots of drinks, ending with the cake and a final speech by the bride and groom thanking all the guests for attending and for the money deliveries. Two bouquets of flowers are offered to the mothers and a red carnation to the fathers to be placed in their respective lapels. The parents also thank everyone for attending the ceremony, and the bride and groom depart for their honeymoon.

We had all that already organized down to the last detail. In Japan there are many specialized agencies that plan everything related to weddings. We had hired an agency in *Nagano* for "*Shinto* wedding in *Shirakawa-go.*" And we already had all the clothing and multiple accessories chosen and reserved, as well as the banquet and gifts for the guests.

We were just waiting to set the date, which depended on the availability of the temple, and we were still waiting (this usually takes weeks or months...).

We also had hired another agency specializing in "western weddings" in *Shinjuku,* since we wanted to celebrate it where we lived and worked, and thus, be able to invite friends, colleagues, bosses and employees of the company.

This agency also organized everything in a luxurious hotel downtown and included: the chapel, a large banquet hall, even the rental of the typical Christian wedding attire and all the accessories you wanted to hire. I chose a beautiful white dress, princess style with a sweetheart neckline, white shoes, a bouquet of lilac flowers, and a simple headdress with a tiara. You choose even the hairstyle and makeup!

Takashi-san decided on a beautiful black tuxedo very modern and shiny, in which he looked very handsome and looked like a dandy.

All this meant a big investment, to which we had to add our honeymoon, which would last eight days in the famous "city of love," in Paris (France).

A year before, our appreciated and respected "friend" *Karate* Master: Isamu Kobayashi Sensei, (who moved from *Okinawa* to Paris with his wife Sophie-San) had come. He had to come on personal business and had a day off before returning to Paris. So, he called us (which made us very happy!), because he wanted to see us and also wanted to surprise his childhood friend: Yagami-San (my boyfriend's father). We invited him to come to our residence in *Shinjuku* because he was very close, in the city of *Shibuya*. He passed a Friday night with us at our house to go together to *Nagano* the next day, on Saturday, to my in-laws' house.

Yagami-San's joy at seeing Kobayashi Sensei was incredible. He could not believe it when he opened the door, and saw him in front of him, after thirty years without seeing each other (although he had seen the photos we took of him when we were in *Okinawa* with him). They were both very excited about that meeting. This visit was something very expected and desired by them, and it made us very emotional, which made us all end up crying. There was an age difference between them.

They talked about how Yagami-San was the oldest and that Kobayashi Sensei was very young and impetuous, and that for that reason he was always keeping watch and controlling him until, with *Karate,* later, he calmed down and centered himself. They continued talking endlessly for hours, catching up since they last saw each other and how Kobayashi Sensei was doing in Paris with his wife.

Sensei had set up his *Dojo*, his *Karate-dō* school in the center of the Parisian city. He said that he was doing very well, and that the students in the West highly appreciated the Japanese Masters. He confessed that he was very happy and content, although sometimes he missed very much being in *Okinawa*, on his island, where he was known by everyone. He had brought us all some French presents, a detail that we all thanked him very much.

We told *Sensei* that we would get married the following year, and that we wanted to invite him and his wife Sophie-San. He told us that of course they would come! But, in return, we had to go on our honeymoon to the great "city of love."

To which we replied that the trip was already organized to go to Paris, that one of the reasons was because he was there precisely, and another because it is the "ideal city for the honeymoon of two lovers and newlyweds."

« Kobayashi Sensei was very enthusiastic about the announcement of our link and our trip to Paris. »

Everyone at the company already knew of our firm decision to officially marry and start a family. They were, like us, waiting for us to have a date.

They also knew about our search for a *"minka,"* which is a house or private residence built in one of the many Japanese building styles, so they were all passing us properties they found for sale. We did not stop going, in our free time, to see and visit houses.

One Saturday, which we did not go to *Shirakawa-go*, because we had two arranged visits with the real estate agency that helped us find a house, they showed us a beautiful new house, recently built, with a modern design on the outside, a large garden and a fence beautiful.

As soon as we arrived at the place we fell in love with it! But when we visited it inside, it was even better: Impressive!

It was Japanese style inside, very modernized and elegant, with two huge and very spacious floors. It was 130 m² by plant. All partitions, windows and doors were *"shōji"* (traditional type of door in Japanese architecture). These function as room dividers and consist of translucent Japanese paper with a wooden frame. They are designed to slide open. They are a must in a traditional Japanese-looking home. All interior and exterior doors were the same.

On the upper floor there was a large master bedroom with full bathroom included in the room, and access to a beautiful upper terrace with porch. There were three more bedrooms and another huge bathroom between the rooms (ideal for our future children...). The staircase to access the plants was very elegant and with comfortable steps. On the first floor at ground level, it had a wide typical Japanese *"Genkan"* entrance, to take off and leave shoes, giving access to a spacious and huge living room with access to the garden and a huge outdoor terrace; there was an immense kitchen with another side exit to the outside, with a small room for assistant or babysitter, and another complete courtesy toilet. It had very good high quality finishes.

On the side of the house, there was a garage for two cars and a space for gardening tools, etc. The roof of the house was a beautiful Japanese clay tile with glossy finish, authentic modern Japanese architecture. It was surrounded by a beautiful totally flat garden of 880 m².

He had a lot of space to train, to build a *Dojo* and teach Martial Arts to other disciples and to "our future children", which we knew would be two; and if a girl came: *"onna no ko"* and a boy: *"otoko no ko,"* would be perfect!

« The house really was very beautiful, we were stunned and very surprised, and we both fell in love with it as soon as we saw it!

The situation was very good, in *Shinjuku,* very near of *Kagurazaka,* 1 min from the station exit, with very good access to transport and the main cities. As for the underground subway lines it was 1 minute walk from the nearest subway station, with 2 access lines and 5 minutes to *Shinjuku* station. It only took 5 minutes to get to and from work each day!

It also had nearby: 2 supermarkets 2 minutes away (one in front of the station, the other only two streets away from the house), 2 big pharmacies, coffee shop 1 minute away, bakery 1 minute away, 24 hours convenience stores, *Byōin* (hospital) 5 minutes away, a *Sentō* (Japanese public bath) only 3 minutes away, the *"Zenkokuji Temple"* in 5 minutes...

It had it all in our favor!

It was the perfect place and house for us. Since we both liked it very much, Takashi-San didn't want to see any more houses. The problem was that it was over our budget. We had to talk to the bank again to see if this increase was viable, and redo the new numbers for the mortgage. We agreed with the real estate company to give us a few days to respond.

And it happened that, two days after seeing the house, while we were waiting for the Bank's response, Takashi-San's boss, Saitō-San, called him to his office, and after asking him how we were and how everything was going for us…, he subjected him to a kind of interview with many questions related to his work and his communication projects, especially digital ones.

He then explained the company's famous 4B theory:

The first step is *'Good to be,'* to act with honesty and sincerity. The next step is *'Good to do,'* to perform one's job in the right way. If these two steps are fulfilled, we can reach self-realization that is *'Good keep.'* And once we have fulfilled all the requirements, the economic reward will arrive, the *'Good to have.'*

Takashi-San confessed that he did not know why he was telling him all that, nor whether the meeting was for good or for bad, or whether there were mistakes in his work or in any management, and he kept waiting to hear his made mistakes... when, suddenly, he said:

"I am fully authorized by company management, and if you have no objection, I would be honored to promote you to be part of the *systems analyst group.*"

My boyfriend didn't know what to say because he wasn't expecting a promotion like that for at least five more years!

As there was confidence they talked about many other things, among them he told him about the house we had seen, and the price that exceeded the mortgage budget, to which he replied:

"Now you will not have any problem with the bank for that amount, so go and buy that house for your wife and your future family or you will have a problem with me if you don't!"

Outside the office, all his coworkers were waiting for him and congratulating him. He called me on my cell phone and I ran to the elevator and went up to the 22nd floor... and there he was with his companions and with joy in the air!

I went to him and congratulated him (I couldn't hug or kiss him there in public, I held on...!). I stayed there looking at his smile and his eyes, which kept attracting me every moment, when he told me:

"We already have the house! Make an appointment with the bank for tomorrow. Saitō-San is, right now, preparing the documentation for the bank manager."

I was stunned and unable to utter a word.

« Something always came up, some breeze or moderate wind, which helped us to continue sailing on the ocean of life. »

Takashi-San's new position was very important, he had to be part of a large team of specialists in information and communication systems; they are real engineers in fields like programmers, financiers, auditors, etc.

Only the group provides the necessary knowledge for the creation and analysis of systems projects, which is done for the users, and responds with absolute efficiency to the true interests of the company.

As a multinational company with extensions and subsidiaries throughout Asia, Europe and the United States, the position carried the label: "passport ready to travel when needed."

But from what we were informed, except for serious problems, the trips usually lasted three or four days. So we assumed it, although Takashi-san that part of separating us... did not like it at all!

We went to the bank the next day with the new documentation, and they did not put any impediment to access the mortgage for the new higher amount. In fact, we carry documentation of the new house, and the director of the entity said that it was a good investment and congratulated us for it. When we left the bank, we called the real estate agency giving them the good news that "we were buying the house," and all the machinery started up immediately.

It was summer when all these events, one after the other, were happening in continuous movement: New promotions at work, new responsibilities, new house, wedding preparations, etc., there were many changes...
Yoshida Sensei kept saying that changes were growth, that growing was my duty, and that in full growth I could not weaken; that I should use weakness to control strength, and that I should use that strength to accept the changes that were happening.
And, in that I was, accepting the changes and growing with what life offered us, and of course, thanking the *Kami* or Gods for all this: the small successes, the happiness and the infinite love in which I lived with *'the man of my life.'*
We were the envy of all the couples and marriages we knew. We never argued, never got angry, simply because there were no motives in our hearts.
However, Japanese people also do not tend to argue directly. When there are problems or they see an argument coming, they tend to become quieter and more discreet as a disagreement occurs. Japanese people always seek respect from their partner. As for friends and companions, they always seek to be listened to without interruption, which makes even a verbal argument almost impossible. In public, just as affection or expressions of love are not shown, neither are expressions of disaffection or disagreement. This does not

mean that, in their homes or in a private place, either party of the couple wants to express their disagreement with the other party. We usually use the silence until we are in a position to express our bad feeling without hurting or offending the other person, or we may let it go because we comes to the conclusion that "it's not worth it..."

It is "the Japanese philosophy" that is committed to the pursuit of well-being and happiness, and although many do not achieve it, they are willing to try until the end.

We didn't have any kind of problems, we understood each other perfectly, one look was enough and we knew what the other was thinking.

Like when the bank called to set the day and time to seal the purchase of our new residence. We looked at each other and knew what we felt and what it meant to us: apart from of being owners of a house, being still so young people, it symbolized the imminent change that was already taking place, it was already happening...! And we could not pronounce any words, we could only cry, hug, kiss and... We let all the emotions flow for a while...!

The first day of September arrived, and we already had the multitude of papers stamped with the Bank (where the first owner was the bank until we finished paying in a future), but the papers said that "we were the owners of a residence," and this already served us, it was enough for us!

The "keys" were handed over to us on the spot. We immediately went to "our new home" and Takashi-San again did the honors of crossing the threshold by taking me in his arms, and as there was no furniture, he laid me down on the floor, he placed himself on top of me, and we rolled around hugging around the immense hall. We were like crazy!

Then we made a list of everything that was needed (the bank adds an extra amount to the total of mortgage for repairs, reforms, furnishings or the purchase of a vehicle), and it was a very long list...

We had already shown the house to the families the week before, with the favor of the real estate agent, who very kindly agreed to open the house so that they could visit it. And both families liked it very much, especially because there was room for them and for many children, and that made them even more enthusiastic. They were marveled with the house just like us. Both parties offered their help, but we totally and flatly refused. They were already helping us with the expenses for both weddings, and we didn't want them to go to any more efforts for us.

While we were busy furnishing the new house, one day Yoshida Sensei informed us that the Temple had already given us available Sunday dates to choose from; this was: November 22 or December 6 (and that was thanks to my father, because there was no dates on Saturday or Sunday until the following year).
We still continued in the apartment (although we had already given the legal notice to leave it), until we had the essential furniture to make the move. We had to choose a date as soon as possible, but we wanted to talk to the agencies we had contracted to organize the weddings; to know if it was better one day or another for them or if it didn't matter, and we chose the date...
I knew that Takashi-san did not care one date or another, because for him it was a long delay already; he wanted to get married for years already, so it was going to depend only on the organizers.

At last we were able to tie up all the loose ends, and it was decided that on November 22 would be the *Shintō* wedding at the *"Myozen-ji Temple,"* in *Shirakawa-go*, which would be attended by all the relatives of the bride and groom, including distant relatives, closest friends, and also acquaintances of the place. And, the Christian wedding would be the following Sunday in *Tokyo*, in *Shinjuku*, which would be attended by the rest of the friends, acquaintances, colleagues and employees of the company, and of course, the family members who wish to attend.

Thus there would be a week between one and the other and we would go more rested, since the distances between the Japanese Alps and the capital did not allow us to do them in a row.

Our good friends: Akira Tanaka and his wife Masako Tanaka (they were our same age and had a six-year-old son) they offered to help us with the new house.

We wanted to use part of the money from the bank (belonging to reforms) to build a *Dojo*, a training room for *Budō* (Japanese Martial Arts) in the garden of the new house. Tanaka-San's father is a Master of traditional Japanese carpentry (considered an art in Japan), specialized in the construction of halls or tea houses and large residences, so he was the ideal professional for the construction of our Japanese *Dojo* with wood assembly without nails (traditional construction).

I was very fortunate that my father, Yoshida Sensei, designed it and offered to personally take care of the process together with Tanaka-San's father, also called Tanaka-Sensei for being a true Master in the woodworking art.

And Masako-San, who was and is a beautiful person, dedicated herself to finding everything we needed in furniture and decoration. We would tell her what we wanted: the color, the type of material, etc., and she would bring us the catalogs. We chose what we liked and she was in charge (she had house keys) to buy it and have it deliver and installed. She also collected and packed things from the apartment and took them in her car to the new house.

« They were a huge and invaluable help to us. She is a sun of a woman! They know how grateful we will always be to them, and for the thousandth time: Thank you Masako-San! Thank you Tanaka-San! Thank you Tanaka Sensei! »

Her husband, and our friend, Tanaka-San, also worked very hard helping his father in the construction of the new *Dojo*; and he was also in charge of checking the electricity, water and gas installations so that everything worked well, and he also helped put up bookshelves and pictures together with Takashi-San.

My parents were coming to the new house; they controlled the construction of the *Dojo*, and did various tasks inside and also in the garden; my mother planted lots of plants and prepared spaces to fill them with flowers next spring.

Takashi-San's parents were a bit older, and we didn't want them to make so many long and frequent trips to come to the capital, but even so, they were coming to help.

We all did everything and we were all in a hurry but organized.

The month of October arrived and everything was almost ready; in a week the rental apartment had to be vacated.

By that time, the wedding invitations had already been printed and sent to all the guests; there were around 300 people between the two celebrations: the *Shintō* and the *Christian*.

It is the Japanese custom that all guests respond by confirming their attendance or not.

We also had already booked the flights for our "honeymoon" in Paris, as well as our stay at the *"Brach Paris Hotel"* from November 30 to December 7.

A hotel that we loved (when we saw the pictures in the travel agency), for its elegant Parisian style with exquisite decoration and views of the famous "Eiffel Tower;" and also for its incredible restaurant, which had a lot of prestige and had been awarded several times.

It simply seemed to us the perfect hotel!

Although Isamu Kobayashi Sensei had offered us his house, something that we thanked him with all our hearts, he understood that for a "honeymoon" it was not very appropriate for us to stay at his house with them. In addition, we wanted to feel free to get to know and tour the city, although of course, we would meet them on different occasions and spend a few days in their company. He and his wife Sophie-San understood this perfectly, and agreed that the hotel we had chosen had been a magnificent selection. Anyway, we would see with them before in Japan, at our wedding.

One day, we decided to have a meeting with all those who worked and helped in the new house to inaugurate it.

We celebrated a great meal thanking everyone: the great help they had given us and for making it possible *in record time.*

We all toasted to happiness and love in that new home. There was also a "special" toast from our respective parents: *"Kanpai!* For us, our love and for seeing the *future children* run and grow in the garden."

The house looked very beautiful and we loved how everything turned out. It was all a dream come true!

We settled in and felt that it was "our place," "our nest," "our present and future;" it was: "the complete happiness in our private paradise." From this moment on, Takashi-San every time it had to say: 'let's go home,' he always said: 'let's go to our paradise,' and he said it everywhere and to anyone who was present: "Let's go my love, let's go to our paradise;" what's more, he loved to say it!

Only the *Dojo*, which was still under construction, remained to be completed. I was so looking forward to seeing it finished and to put all my weapons, paintings, degree certificates, the *Tokonoma* or altar, etc. on it!
In the house I had an exclusive closet with all my training clothes or *Gi*, which are many and varied over so many years: many obi or black belts, a large number of pairs of *tabi* or shoes to train in the *Dojo* and outdoors; some are special for the Art of *Shinobi* or *Ninja*: to climb trees or to climb rocks, swampy or watery terrains, etc. There is a great variety of *tabi* depending on their use, and I really wanted to use it all again.
Two minutes from the house there is a large wooded area with parks and a large pond. It has a soothing beauty.
Autumn was at its peak, it was about mid-October. The forests, at that time of year, are dominated by deciduous trees and offer a unique chromatic spectacle, enriching the landscape with an infinite number of hues.
It is the moment to enjoy the *"momiji"* (the change of color of the autumn leaves), and in silence, contemplate the burst of colors observing how the trees begin to lose their leaves and assist to the *"momijigari"* (to the hunting of autumn leaves) allowing ourselves to be seduced by that moment of changes and contrasts that nature gives us.
« How I missed my village and my mountains! »

There was a lot of desire and temptation to go into the forest, well equipped, and practice in nature; so that same weekend I dedicated myself to merging with that forest and with the nature of the place.

I walked it, listened to it, observed it, ran and jumped between its rocks and slopes, I climbed some of its trees, I recognized the whole forest and its hidden corners and hiding places...

I saw some hares that ran freely, and also I glimpsed between bushes a red deer (typical and normal to see deer in the area, because there are also many signs indicating it).

At times like this I forgot that I lived in the city. Japan has these contrasts, from full frenzy it is passed to the most absolute silence of its parks and forests; where nothing is heard but the sound of nature and the surrounding animals, and where the Japanese spend hours relaxing the stress caused by the fast and hectic pace of the country.

« For the Japanese: it is a symbiotic relationship with the environment in which one species benefits while the other is not affected. »

The next day I went again with Takashi-San and we enjoyed together that beautiful and natural corner that was so close to "our paradise." We get ready and go into the forest. He wanted to take it as a *"gotonpo"* training that is: the use of natural elements in their environment, taking advantage of nature.

It happened that while climbing a tree, he misused his technique and fell from a couple of meters high; although he only received a couple of scratches and did not suffer any injury, it served him not to trust, because he did it as if he was very self-confident, and was not aware that everything always has to be taken into account; there is always something that can go wrong or happen.

You should never trust anything, as in life: "You have to remain attentive to everything and be alert to react to the unexpected." For him it was a good lesson because "he learned that there are always points, obstacles or things that are sometimes not seen, but are there if we know how to observe well.

That situation and teachings of that day, led us without realizing it, to talk about life and death. Takashi-San brought up in the conversation a phrase of the Greek sage Socrates: "The man who thinks only of living, he does not live."

We talked that he also said: "Knowledge is the main part of happiness" or that "There is only one good: knowledge and there is only one evil: ignorance." We also commented that our Japanese culture also says that: "just like living, dying is part of the cycle of life," as a generalized thought in the population. However, I pointed out that this in many cultures, including the western, was difficult to accept this thought; which in my way of thinking this gave way to fear and suffering, due to denial of a reality that we already know but do not want that arrives, nor do we want to accept it, or what is the same: "the fear of death / to die."

He said that he accepted to die but of "old and together," after living a full life; when his body and mind weaken and he can't longer able to fend for himself...; he made it clear that this was his desire and purpose, and that he would be happy if it happened like this, because it was the only way he accepted death for himself and for the rest of human beings, the loved ones and the worthy (he said it very seriously).

My transmission, at that moment, was that my life was full of light and love, so I wanted to live intensely the here and the now, because our life together had so much sense. That the train only passes once; and he and I caught it and got on it in time. And that, for this, we had to give thanks every morning: for existing, for being healthy, for having been born, for having known this world, for eating every day, for having a family, for being surrounded by wonderful people, for living in a democratic society, for having rights, for having a job, for having learned and acquired such incredible knowledge...

"There is so much we have to be thankful for...!"I said happily.

I added that I did not believe that I had chosen the circumstances of my birth, nor the where, nor the when, nor the how, although I did think that all this had influenced the way in which I live, and in the way in which I will stop living; and what I also knew was that my *Senseis*, my parents, had and have had to do with my whole being, with how I am and how I live. And I ended up telling him:

"The range of life is very wide, and everything fits in it; let us always live life as if it were the last day and let us love each other as if there were no tomorrow. "

"All right!" he said, "I like that thought but we will both die together as old, very old seniors, as a very old man with a very pretty old lady...!" (He said it with his characteristic indelible smile).

Instantly, that great and deep conversation was closed and sealed with a passionate kiss in which we melted for a long time until we arrived at the bedroom, where our bodies took the control, surrendering intensely to passion and desire. It was a beautiful and intense moment, which was engraved in our feelings, because we gave ourselves with frenzy in a very passionate and vehement way. We truly merged into one.

That same day we decided that, just before the first *Shintō* wedding, we would stop taking measures on birth control, we would not put up any more barriers. We would let nature act on its own and bless us with our first child when considers it appropriate.

« Our new home had been well inaugurated in 'every' possible aspects! »

Every day we received replies from the wedding guests confirming their attendance to the event, even Isamu Kobayashi Sensei with his wife Sophie-San confirmed that they would come from France, but they would only stay for the *Shintō* wedding in *Shirakawa-go*, because they could not stay one more week to attend the Christian wedding in *Shinjuku.*
Takashi-San's parents would have them lodged in their house. So they were going to be very well taken care of.
« I don't remember any response of non-attendance. »

We were very comfortable in our new house, the *Dojo* was going a little slow, because Tanaka Sensei did it as a favor on his days off, and only came on weekends (he was also very detailed and perfectionist). When he came we were all there helping. We had a good time and we had a Japanese barbecue (a gift from Takashi-San's parents), where we made *"Yakiton,"* based on pork or *"Yakiniku,"* made from beef.

One of those wonderful days, after lunch, Yoshida Sensei asked me to go for a walk together. We went to the forest near home, and so I showed him where I enjoyed of the *"momiji,"* the change in color of the leaves of the trees in the city. As we walked among the trees on the fallen leaves on the ground by the autumn, he asked me about my feelings in this new stage of life, about to get married and in my new home. I told him how happy I felt, that he should not suffer or worry about me, because I was the luckiest woman and daughter in the world, that I had everything and could not wish for more. I also told him that, for that same reason, sometimes I felt afraid, because he had taught me that you could not have everything in life, and yet I had everything....
The *Sensei*, smiling, said that: "it was certainly scary but that I had achieved everything by myself, with my effort and

dedication, and that is why I should not be afraid because nothing had been given to me, that I had earned it and it was deserved; that I just had to stay alert and enjoy the bliss; that I should not let myself be carried away only by my heart, because I would lose my natural instinct, and that instinct is the one that would allow me to protect everything I love and myself."

« I understood that he wanted to look into my eyes to see through them, and make sure his daughter was happy because only then would he be happy too. He was in charge of carving and polishing what is now represented in this figure, and for that, I will always be grateful to him! Every time I am with *Sensei* I feel blessed. He emanates something that penetrates inside, in the inmost depths, and then I feel re-emerge; I feel safe and protected by his side, like when I was a little girl. »

In those days we were a little worried about my in-laws; they had some health problems, nothing important, but we had to be attentive to them, and we were pending that they made their medical visits and had their check-ups.

One morning at work, after a meeting, the company informed Takashi-Sensei of his first trip in his new position. A French affiliated company, located in Paris, was having problems with the data processing system.

Takashi-San had to implement and adapt an algorithm and debug the system for its effective use; as well as perform a data computation to solve the problem that was presented in that office.

His trip to Paris would mean being away for four days: from the 10th to the 14th of November. We said it was a coincidence because we had to go on our honeymoon on November 30 until December 7.

He would travel to Paris twice in the same month!

He would hardly have any free time because these problematic situations take many hours of intense work; one hardly has time to eat. Only the preparation, before leaving, kept him working in the office until after 8:00 p.m. every day.

Takashi-san said that he would like to be able to greet and see Kobayashi Sensei, and he hoped to find some time since he had spoken with him on the phone, and the Master was looking forward to seeing him if only to "take a delicious Parisian coffee together."

So, while he was preparing his imminent task and working every afternoon at the company, I decided to look for some gift for Kobayashi Sensei and his wife Sophie-San. I would look at something that they could keep as a nice memory.

I walked all over the *Shinjuku* shopping area looking, until I found in an alley, next to the central post office, an old traditional store of *"obi"* (Martial Arts belts). In this kind of places belts are sold and embroidered; so I chose a good black silk belt (the highest quality) and ordered an embroidery in gold thread with the name of the *Sensei: Isamu Kobayashi*, in *Kanji* (Japanese calligraphy). It would be ready for the next day. It is always an honor, for any Master, to accept an *obi* with his name engraved on it, even if they have many.

I had also seen a pottery house where they apply one of the famous traditional Japanese decorative techniques used in making utilitarian pottery. The name of the technique is: *"rakū-yaki,"* which means 'fun' or 'happiness.' The *rakū* is a complex alchemy where the four natural elements intervene:

earth, fire, water and air, resulting in unique and incredible pieces. It is an ancient tradition with its own beliefs.

In some prestigious parties or social gatherings, attended by *Zen* Buddhist Masters, all the attendees drank tea in clay vessels (glasses and tea cups) made by themselves and decorated them with oxides, causing a mono cooking in ovens called "Baskets." Using red clay at approximately 900 degrees Celsius, fascinating tones, textures, hues and colors are finally obtained; and there is never one piece the same as another with this *rakū* technique. I bought a tea set for two, and request that engrave their names on the cups with *Kanji* paint, so each one would have their own personalized cup. They would appreciate it, and I liked to think that every time they drank tea in them they would remember us, forming so a kind of connection across the distance.

The next day I had the gifts collected and ready for our respected friends. Takashi-san really liked very much the chosen details and he was sure they would like them too.

That last weekend, before his trip, we decided to go to *Shirakawa-go* and *Nagano*.

We were at his parents' house, sharing with them; helping them in everything and avoiding giving them any kind of work, because although they seemed to be fine, their health was delicate and they had to take good care of themselves a lot. After lovingly pampering them, in the late evening we took the train and bus to *Shirakawa-go* and slept at my parents' house, because we wanted to wake up there and enjoy the autumn scenery of the place.

We stayed late into the night talking to my parents. The four of us were so comfortable that none of us wanted to go to sleep, so my mother said:

"Let's go outside under the *Sakura!* I carry blankets and we'll lie under the tree."

We went outside, it wasn't cold that night. We did put some blankets on the fallen leaves of the *Sakura* and covered ourselves with another one on top. My parents together and hugging; Takashi-San and I held hands.

We were looking at the clear sky full of stars through the branches of the *Sakura* tree depopulated of its leaves. I still felt that *"goodbye"* in my body, and I was saying to my dear tree in my thoughts, mentally: "Yes! It's true that I left this place to live in another, that I didn't see it every day but that came twice a month; that there was certainly a little "physical goodbye" but that my dear *Sakura* would always be in my heart wherever that I be."

I requested it not to make me feel that *goodbye* pain every time, which I had not stopped feeling it since just before I went to live in *Tokyo*.

While I was having my mental conversation with the tree, Takashi-San commented:

"It seems that Haru's *Sakura* wants to tell me something but I don't understand it," he said it with a nostalgic tone.

"Takashi-san, don't you know that the *Sakura* only talks to Haru? Don't you know that it hasn't forgiven her for departure yet?" Sensei said.

"That's why I feel it crying, that's...! Cry for her!" replied Takashi-San.

"Certain!" I said. "It doesn't forgive me that I am gone. We should transplant it to our house in our garden and so it would be with us, what do you think of the idea?"

"It should be done next winter while the tree sleeps," commented Kimura Sensei. "It is true that the *Sakura* and Haru are very much interconnected. There is no doubt about that, but don't you feel that it announces something...?"

We were all silent for a while, and after a few minutes my father energetically got up and left.

After a short while my mother retired too, and I asked Takashi-san to go to sleep that I would go soon.

I connected with my *Sakura* and opened my heart and my mind. I sat in the *Seiza* posture, the traditional kneeling posture, and I don't know how long it passed until I felt like a prick in my heart, a slight sharp pain; ; then I knew that this *goodbye* that I had felt for so long was the "pain of suffering." I knew something was going to happen to me at some moment. I understood that the *Sakura* had been warning me for a long time.

After a while, I felt a few drops of water falling, a gentle drizzle on my face and my hair. I opened my eyes and saw how the sky had been covered with clouds and the stars were no longer visible. It was beginning to rain softly. I closed my eyes again and saw that the rain was the tears of the *Sakura* and that they were gradually turning pink, and each time the pink became more intense until it became completely red, a dark red....

  "It was tears of blood! The Sakura was crying tears of blood over me! It was its crying!"

That image scared me and I opened my eyes again. I was glad to see that it was not raining blood and that the soft rain was transparent. With my pain still in my heart, I paid my respects to the *Sakura* and went to sleep.

« At night, that image came to my dreams over and over again. I could barely sleep. *I only felt the crying of the Sakura!* »

  The next morning, when I got up, a little late, they had all gotten up. They were outside because it was a beautiful autumn day, with bright sunshine and mild temperature.

I said good morning and they told me to have tea and some lard toast that they had prepared for me; that we were going on an excursion. Soon after, we went out walking and crossed the village, passing by the temple where we were to be married in exactly two Sundays. We did the honors of paying our respects and obeisance, thanking and asking for our wishes. I lit incense and gave myself to the *Kami*, Gods. My wishes were always the same, except that, in that occasion, I asked for the wedding, our union and our love, in addition to my own protection along with that of all mine. I begged and pleaded, while holding in my hands the *"Omamori"* (the protective amulet given to me by Takashi-San in that same place five years ago, when I introduced him to my parents), which I promised to always carry with me as a protector, and never before it had failed me.

We continued walking; I had not commented on anything, not even to my boyfriend, what happened to me at night. Yoshida Sensei hadn't uttered a single word yet.

There, I felt happy again for this treasure of our planet Earth; this gift that has been given to us human beings for our delight and joy. We all remained in silence for a long time, each one with oneself, admiring the colorful and peaceful picture of the place. Takashi-san took my hand and squeezed it tightly as saying: "I won't let you go. I have a good hold on you." I transmitted to him: "I will not go anywhere without you. I am here with you, by your side." Later, when we spoke about it, we confirmed that this was exactly what we were saying to each other through our hands.

On the way home, I finally heard my father talking. He was answering my mother's questions about the shrine; they talked about the wedding and the banquet dishes. When we arrived, it was a bit late, so we ate quickly to catch the trains back to *Tokyo*.

We would not see each other until the wedding, although I would come the day before to leave from my parents' house. Takashi-San would go to *Nagano* the same day; he would stay at his parents' house and they would leave from there the next day, to go together to the Temple.

My mother reminded me of everything we had to prepare with the hired agency: the *Kimono,* makeup, hairdressing, etc.; that we had a lot to do and she kept telling me to rest a lot the days before to be radiant on that day.

I did not know what to say to *Sensei* because I was sure that in the night under the *Sakura,* he felt or saw the same as me, and that is why he had gotten up so suddenly and left without saying anything. I was surprised that he did not speak at any time about what happened. We always talked about everything, and I didn't know what to do because he had barely looked at me all day.

« I know him well, as he knows me, and I knew that he felt and perceived the same as me! »

Suddenly, when we were leaving and we were almost at the door to leave, he turned to Takashi-San and said:

"Takashi-san, I wish you have a good trip. Take good care, please! Are you sure you can't postpone the trip, son?"

"I would like not to go, Yoshida Sensei, I assure you," Takashi-San replied. "Don't worry, I'll be careful and I guarantee that nothing will impede me from coming back because I have to marry with your daughter as soon as I get back. We'll see you at the wedding. Thanks Yoshida Sensei! Thank you Kimura Sensei!"

Yoshida Sensei hugged Takashi-san while saying:

"Nothing will make me happier than to see your marriage, my son! I wish you a safe journey and very good luck."

It was the first time that my father hugged him and called him directly "son," "my son." He surprised me! Following, my mother hugged him too and wished him "bon voyage," in French.

Then, my father turned to me and put his hand on my shoulder as he said:

"My dear Haru, I hope you are well while he is away. Always keep in your mind that the life is sometimes like smoke, and although the water is always transparent, sometimes it is colored to attract our attention. Remember the changes and prepare your body and mind. The warnings are blowing with the wind. And always remember: If you need me, I will always go wherever you are and wherever you want, you know it, right?" (It is difficult to translate the Japanese used to express certain words so full of philosophical meanings).

"Thanks dad!" I replied as I looked into his melancholy eyes. "Don't worry, I'll be fine and I promise I'll stay vigilant. We'll talk again, thank you!"

I said goodbye to my mother and we hurried to the train station.

Back to "our paradise," not even in the hours of train ride we had on the way, did I comment him anything about my let's call it "feel" or "vision;" I didn't want to worry him now that he was leaving. We always told each other everything, but I considered that I would tell him when he returned, because he had a lot of confidence in "my predictions" or "feelings" (he called it "mental power"), and did not want him to have that in his head. So the conversations were about our parents, the weddings and how he was handling the preparation to solve the Paris office system.

The night before his departure, we packed his suitcase together. He wore three shirts, one for each working day, a suit of jacket and pants with another equal pants to change, two ties (that I had given him on the last day of Valentine's Day), several underwear, a trouser and T-shirt for to be comfortable in the hotel room and some Beefroll-type loafers (which he liked so much) to go with the suit, since to the airport he was going dressed casually and comfortable for the multiple hours of the plane.

He would arrive in the afternoon /evening at the Paris airport (according to the change in European time), so he would go directly to the hotel. He would not put suit until the next day to go to the company's branch office.

We added the gifts for Isamu Kobayashi Sensei and his toiletry bag.

I also put in his suitcase, without him seeing it, a *"love card"* (in Japan they sell cards for everything) so that he could find it when he unpacked his bag at the hotel. It was a personal love card, with metallic silver effect with the *Kanji* for *"eternity"* (the pictogram looks like the letter 'K'), combined with the *Kanji* for *"love"* that expresses *"eternal love"* and it wore in the background a *"Sakura"* or *'cherry blossom'* as a decorative element symbolizing the spring, the renewal, and the ephemeral nature of life, that remind us to treasure what we have and take advantage of each day.

I added a note in my own handwriting, the translation of which would be:

Love makes there is no distance in the world
To separate us
For our eternal love
And for our union I will be waiting for you
I am your Sakura, your ever spring,
Haru

The next morning, November 10, his flight was leaving early in the morning, and I accompanied him to *Narita* airport. I asked permission to enter the office later, as I wanted to be with him until he left. We did not let go for a moment; we went hand in hand all the time and we continually hugged each other, although the latter is not usually done in public in Japan. It was the first time in years that we would both sleep apart, and four days seemed like weeks...!

At the last moment we kissed and we both cried while telling each other how much we loved each other. At one point, he showed me his *"Japanese crane ring"* and said:

"Look Haru! You gave it to me! It is life and eternal love! It is longevity, as well as temporality. And it has always given me good luck. I'll be fine, though I'll miss you every second. Before you know it, I'll be back. Please don't worry for me. You have take care of yourself and be attentive to weather that they are warning about in the next few days. I'll be following it too, and calling you. I love you, my love!"

With my right hand I wrapped his hand caressing the ring while with the other I touched my *"Mokume Tsuba"* pendant as I told him:

"It is the union of our hearts and the value in the life. We are united forever and I will have the necessary courage to endure our separation. Besides, we have to get used to it because you will travel often. It's just that this is the first time, my love! We'll pass the test, and I'll be here waiting for you. And don't suffer for me, I'll be fine!"

We kissed passionately, and then: he began to walk away. I watched him through the glass. Every few steps he turned around and waved his hand saying goodbye; I raised mine and did the same. I was wrapped in tears, and kept looking at him without looking away until I stopped seeing him.

« The love of my life was leaving... and I was there: immobile, totally paralyzed, looking at infinity... ALONE! »

I don't know how much time passed; I only know that, suddenly, invaded me that feeling of farewell and immense loneliness, perhaps because, in truth, I had never been alone. I always lived with my parents and after with Takashi-San. I didn't understand that four days of separation made me feel as if I would never see him again... I decided that I had to change that feeling, and that I had to be attentive and pay more attention to myself due to the vision of the *Sakura*.
I took a deep breath and went back to *Shinjuku*, back to work... ALONE!

At the office, everyone was encouraging me, and said that it was only a few days, and that when I realized it Takashi-San would already be back.
I tried to focus and stay focused, but I just wanted to hear my boyfriend's voice as soon as he landed. He had just left and I was already missing him.
At work everyone was talking about the "typhoon" that was coming.
For days, the news had been announcing the arrival of a typhoon in the country for the following day. The typhoon season in Japan is usually in the months of May to October each year. However, being November, it was not surprising that strong winds with torrential rains would hit the coasts due to the country's geographical location. They usually don't last more than a couple of days. Japanese typhoons occur very frequently, but the vast majority of them are not noticeable on the ground; although at times, the effects of their passage can be devastating, leaving behind great damage, capable of paralyzing cities and airports. Some can cause even more damage and destruction than earthquakes.

This was what everyone in the office was talking about that day. The company informed all employees that if the alert level was raised the next day, many railway lines would be closed, and in that case, we would stay in our homes protecting them until the alarm was deactivated.

At the end of the working day I went directly to "our paradise." I only thought of "my beloved" and wished the phone would ring to know that he had arrived safely. Takashi-san insisted that he would leave me a message, because in Paris it would already be late afternoon, but in Japan it would be well into early in the morning, and he did not want me to wake up to answer; but that when I got up I would listen his message. We agreed that we would talk the next day (always calculating the time difference). But I thought: No way...! That I would pick up the phone no matter what time it was...

I spent the afternoon at home preparing everything for the arrival of the "typhoon," because during the morning various types of alerts were already being issued. I put all the security shutters and secured everything on the outside, just in case.
The Japan Meteorological Agency (JMA), that same afternoon, put several prefectures in the center and east of the country on alert for torrential rains and strong winds due to the imminent arrival of the powerful typhoon originating in the Pacific; it is expected to make landfall the next day around 10am in the eastern region of *Kanto*, where *Tokyo* is located. The red alert had been decreed (second highest level). It was a storm, classified as "strong" and with gusts of wind of about 215 kilometers. It was expected to cross the east and northeast of the island of *Honshū,* the largest in the archipelago, and return to the Pacific after 48 hours.

The Japanese have some specific apps in our cell phones that communicate the different alerts that are established in the country; with the information updated at all times through notifications, whether for earthquakes and tsunamis, or news alerts related to the weather, such as: typhoons, torrential rains or volcanic eruptions. As well as all the updated information on the status of rail services, and the status of any train, metro or bus line can be consulted live.

My phone informed me that about eight lines could be suspended the next day.

So, I saw myself at home "alone" in the face of that national emergency, and possibly I would not go to work for the next two days, so it would be even worse. This situation made me to miss Takashi-San even more. To all this, I had to add the concern I had for my "vision," and I couldn't stop thinking if it meant that my life was in danger because of the typhoon. I dedicated myself to securing the house as much as I could, and took a lot of measurements inside as well in case the roof flew off or collapsed.

I knew I wouldn't sleep that night; I would be on guard and vigilant, while waiting for the phone to ring. I didn't stop thinking if I had left me something important to secure in the house for when the typhoon hit land the next morning. I prepared myself to live a state of survival inside my own home.

It was four thirty in the morning and the phone rang. It was Takashi-San:

"Hello Haru! Why aren't you sleeping? We agreed that I was leaving you a message. I have already landed, and I am waiting for the luggage to come off the conveyor belt. What about tomorrow's typhoon?"

"How glad I am my love that you have arrived safely! The typhoon is on red alert level two, it will make landfall at 10am. I have spent all afternoon and part of the night securing the house and taking all the measures that I could. I have created a kind of *bunker* in here, you should see it my love!"

"That's fine! Any precaution is always little. Try to sleep and rest what you can Haru. I'm so sorry not to be with you there..., and in a situation like this, so worrying and dangerous, that I feel like going back right away".

"Quiet dear, don't suffer and don't worry! Everything is under control! I'm going to be fine and safe, because I am not going to leave or move from here. I will not go to work, and I have enough provisions for the two days that the alert is expected to last. Please, go to the hotel and rest from the trip, because tomorrow you have to be clear and focused to carry out your task. Now I feel calmer and I will try to rest. I promise you my love!"

"All right, I leave you trusting that you will rest. I will call you in the morning, which will be around 3:00 pm in Japan, and you will tell me how the typhoon is and how you are, although I do not doubt your strength. I love you, my love, and I already miss you so much..., you can't even imagine how much...!"

"I want you to know that: Me too, my love! You don't know how much I miss you since you left my side! All my love is for you, until tomorrow!"

After talking to Takashi-San and hearing his voice, I was able to relax and get some sleep.

When I woke up the next day there was already a strong wind, the typhoon was approaching. I took my *"Omamori,"* my lucky charm (a gift from my boyfriend) from my bag, and put it in the pocket of the sweatshirt I was wearing. I reached inside and clutched it tightly, feeling its protection.

I spent time to meditation and concentration; I burned incense before the *"Tokonoma"* or private *'altar'* at home; this is the most honorable place in the Japanese home. It is the main element, the focal eye that is always connected to outer nature providing the proper balance and communion between heaven, man and earth; or between the sun, the moon and the stars: the constant necessary energy of nature. While I was in that moment of meditation, the typhoon became stronger and more dangerous, but I kept calm while I heard its force and many other noises outside, things that flew and fell...

After a while, the torrential rain was falling together with the strong wind; it seemed like the end of the world and it did not cease for an instant.

I started to train in the living room, as that helped me not to be so aware of the scandalous infernal sound, until it was 3:00 pm, and punctually: Takashi-San called!

It was early in the morning for him, and he was on his way to the office at that time. Apart from saying good morning to each other and talking about how much we had missed each other, we talked about the typhoon situation that had him very worried. I commented to him how hard the wind was blowing and how it was destroying everything, but that I was fine and in the house everything was holding up well, for the moment... I tried to keep him calm so that he could focus on his work: solving the problems that existed in that branch office, to which he arrived at while we were talking. He also told me that he found my *"love card"* inside the suitcase; that he really liked the detail, and that it helped him sleep. He thanked me, and commented that he carried it in his work briefcase (which is almost like his portable office), and that this way, every time he opened it, he would see it and make him feel my presence.

It was very pleasant and reassuring to hear his voice, to feel that he was smiling and to imagine him in my head with his incredible and indelible smile. This gave me an immense joy and happiness in my whole being.

I was concerned about the problem with the Paris office, that it could be excessively serious and would take longer than expected. When he called again, he would know what he was up against and if he could solve it in those days. Takashi-San, the night he landed, told me he would call his parents when he arrives at the hotel. Nevertheless, I also called them to see how they were doing with the typhoon and to talk about their son. They remained cooped up at home and were fine.

My parents had also called asking if Takashi-San had called me and if he had arrived safely in France. They also worried about me because in *Tokyo* the typhoon was much more virulent than in the Alps area, and the televisions did not stop showing the disasters caused and the number of people injured in many places. There was still no talk of the dead at the moment.

I was relieved with every call from Takashi-San, especially knowing that the branch office problem would be solved in two days. We talked as often as the time difference allowed. Normally we communicated before he beginning in the morning at the office and at noon (European time), because the afternoon there was already the night in Japan, and we had to wait until the next day to communicate again. The important thing was that he was fine, his work too, and that the systems would be ready in the time he had planned. That was good news, and we were happy to know that he would have a whole day off to spend with Kobayashi Sensei, with whom he had already spoken and they kept in touch. He was in the office until 9:00 pm, and he had dinner in the same hotel or just next door where there was an Italian restaurant. He did not enjoy the place because he was tired after so many hours. That is why it made me happy that, at the end, he had a whole day to enjoy the beautiful Parisian city, although in a few days we would return to it together. I always tried to reassure him about the situation in Japan, but he also followed the news and was informed of the horror that was happening here. He did not stop lamenting for having left me alone in the dangerous situation that was taking place, and saying how much he loved me, and how much he missed me or how much it cost him to sleep thinking only of me. He said me such beautiful things, that he made his words reach me to the soul and that I feel, one the one hand, happy to have him in my life, and on the other, sad for his absence.

In those two terrifying days that kept me in constant tension, I only thought about keeping myself safe. The news, on the different television networks, already spoke and warned of more than a hundred injuries, and the landslides north of *Tokyo* had left several people missing and three deaths. Torrential rains and extremely strong winds also left many areas without electricity. Tens of thousands of people followed the evacuation recommendations and were received in refuges (in all areas of Japan there are safe areas of refuge in emergencies situations, and they are always prepared and equipped to receive to the citizens by districts).
In the area of our home, the place of refuge haven was a 3-minute walk away. I had everything planned in case I had to evacuate.
The second day of the typhoon was much stronger, and I felt that the house was going to collapse and it would fall on me. I had a really hard time; I did not dare to move from my *bunker* space for fear that it would collapse and crush me.
I did not let go of my hand my "protective amulet," my *"Omamori."* I tried to keep me calm so I could react in time at any moment. My parents kept in touch with me at all times; and Takashi-san was having a hard time because he knew how the situation really was, and he didn't stop sending messages to make sure I was okay. It was a horrendous,

terrifying and of authentic panic situation, a true state of emergency!

« I really feared for my life. I had thoughts about death like: that maybe I couldn't choose when to die, or maybe I could; or maybe I had the time to reflect on what that meant watching the moment comes, or maybe not; or which are the kinds of things that matter and worry while I am alive, but which will surely cease to be important when I am dead; or nothing matters anymore if I do not exist; or am I going to die now? And is that why I have had such a wonderful and fortunate fleeting life and so full of love and happiness? Or was the vision I had of the *Sakura's* tears of blood on me was my destiny and I had to accept death…?

Honestly, I thought and think that, believing in destiny can make us lose control over our life and ourselves, and that is not beneficial. I believe that we must be aware that we are masters of our own actions, and that we must be strong in the face of adversity and be prepared for everything, but always with the spirit of struggle, the struggle for survival, for keeping us alive. And if it is true that destiny is written before, let it not prevent us from fighting until that moment. It is said that our actions make us what we are and that what we are leads us to act... »

I fought to overcome the horror caused by this weather phenomenon and I remained strong, attentive to everything and at all times. I barely slept; it kept haunting me to think that if I did the roof might collapse, and kill me for not having seen it coming. The infernal hurricane sound got into my brain. I used to turn off the electricity for fear of a short circuit, and I would turn it on from time to time to charge my cell phone or prepare myself something to eat.

I was mostly in the dark with a couple of candles and a flashlight. I just thought it would be different if Takashi-San were by my side. At least I wouldn't have been cold because we would have spent it hugging, keeping the warmth of our bodies. I occupied my mind thinking about our love, about our life from the first day I saw him in college, what we had traveled and how far we had come. In the strong union that we had created between us until we reached the point where we could no longer live without each other...

I thought too many things... I spent many hours alone, huddled in my *bunker*, missing him...

Finally, after 48 hours (just as the experts predicted) the wind began to stop and the rain was no longer so intense. I felt that I was already safe. I thought that if everything had held up during the worst of it, the house was already not going to give way when it stopped. Or yes! It could be that the foundations were distended by the great amount of water that fell... But the light was already visible after the disaster, ruin, chaos, devastation, calamity, catastrophe and disgrace for all the human lives that were lost during the strong cyclone.

The deep respect and feeling felt for the victims, in whatever situation occurs, can never be expressed in words. The sorrow and pain, or sadness and shock that overwhelm us in such adverse circumstances, are also part of the fragility and transience of life: *"the hanami."*

The calm after the storm began to be felt on that new day with its new dawn. I was looking forward to Takashi-San's punctual call first thing in the morning, because (although he would already know because he followed the news and weather maps on his cell phone) I wanted that he to be very happy and calm given that everything had already happened, and I was well. Let him know that everything in the house held up well and hardly caused any major damage;

not even the half-built *Dojo* was affected. It passed the great test! From that moment on, everything consisted of waiting that lower the level of the large amount of accumulated water, and for everything to return to "normal" little by little. And, since nothing had happened to me, I was very happy because *"I didn't die"* in the typhoon... I resisted! I was very much alive and I was anxious to transmit on that joy to Takashi-San, as it was going to be his last day in Paris.

He had told me the day before that he would go to the branch office the next morning to finalize some details, and say goodbye to the employees. And that, when he finished (he had already spoken with Kobayashi Sensei) he would notify *Sensei*, and then they would meet in a nearby restaurant that they had agreed, and that *Sensei* would come accompanied by Sophie-San for to eat together. He also told me that, after lunch, they would go to the Kobayashi marriage's house to have coffee and spend the afternoon together, because they had already made plans for his last night in the city.

It made me happy to know that he was going to be in the best company that day at "Le Grand Paris," and finally, he was going to enjoy and relax a little, because he had really deserved it.

That same morning, Takashi-San's parents called me to know, now that the worst was over, how I was feeling and how everything was in the house, and of course, if I needed anything. They were fine too, nothing had happened to them, just some plants from the garden destroyed and uprooted. They also spoke daily with their son; they knew that he had complied and solved the problems of the Paris branch, and that he would spend the day with Kobayashi Sensei and his wife. They gave me a lot of encouragement because the next day their son would be back.

My parents were also calmer, since they suffered for me because I was alone in the face of the horror that had occurred in the country. I commented to my father that I could now be "calm" and that "he would not suffer any more for me," because I had "survived" the great disaster and I was fine, especially because "my love" would come the next day. His answer surprised me because he said: "That he did not fear for my life at any time, that he knew that I would know how to take the appropriate measures and care in a situation like that. That he knew that I would be safe, but that I had to prepare myself for the changes that were going to take place very soon in my life, not for die."

I told him about my "vision" and he replied: That "they were tears of blood on me," but that they did not mean my death, that they could mean that my joy of living, the light of my life, would undergo great changes; that some event will bring out my sadness and my tears, and that I take into account that: he is not a "visionary" nor "me neither;" that they are warnings of misfortunes or tragedies but that they do not have to be about me necessarily, but that they affect me very directly, or that they can refer to problems at work, an accident, etc.; usually something that does not depend on oneself, which is external."

Because of that way of perceiving "of the one who was born before," is the reason he asked me to be attentive to the changes around me, because something bad could happen or that would affect me directly in some way, but that I should not fear for my life, and from this he was totally sure and convinced.

« The conversation with my father made me feel even worse, because while I believed that it was about my life and depended only on me, I did not suffer for anyone else. But if this was not the case, then: What could happen? Who or what should I protect? How could I avoid some tragedy or event without knowing what or whom to confront? »

After that moment, just when I was with those thoughts that caused the conversation with Yoshida Sensei, Takashi-San's call rang out. As always, I was filled with joy and we talked for a long time before he came into the office to say goodbye to everyone. We conversed about the happiness of the end of the typhoon, of everyone was fine, of the beautiful day he was going to have with Kobayashi Sensei and his wife..., and that he would then return to the hotel to collect their gifts, which he was sure they would like a lot. We also talked about it was the last day that we would be separated, that the next day we would be together again, and that we would not take off from each other for an instant. He commented that he was not going to be able to bear so much traveling and being separated from me, which he would talk to his boss when he returned about the trips. That he did not care to work whatever and where he was, but as long as he could have me by his side or it does not mean to be separated. I told him that we would already study how to do it, that the important thing was that tomorrow he would return, and we would celebrate it by going crazy with love and passion. After, as usual, telling each other many times how much we loved each other, he ended the conversation by saying:

"You know Haru, my beloved! it was not enough for me to carry your *'love card'* in my briefcase, nor to take it out every night in the room when I arrived and have it on my heart when sleeping, so I carry it in the inside pocket of my jacket so that be all the time next to my heart; in this way I feel that our hearts beat together, I feel you with me, I feel you inside me, and it reminds me that I don't want to and I can't live without you. I never want to be away from you again, not even for a single day. You have taught me many things and I have learned some, and one of them is: how ephemeral life can be, like the *Sakura* flower; so I don't mind earning less and never moving up in the company, because nothing matters to me more than you and our life together."

My tears welled up and when he finished I could only stammer: *"Watashi mo onaji,"* 'me too, the same.' Then I pronounced the terms: *"koi,"* which expresses 'passionate love,' what you feel; *"ai"* defines 'deep love,' that which we devote time to build up over time itself, and, in the middle *"ren ai,"* which marks the transition from the state of passion or passionate love to the state of 'true love.'

And we said goodbye until the next and last call that he would make to me, just before or during his meeting with *Sensei*.

« Talking about love and romantic feelings in Japan is not limited to how to simply say: "I love you;" and for this reason, the language possesses something that goes beyond words; are expressions with deeper and more philosophical meanings, making it difficult to translate as they are more than mere words. I already explained that we played with those 'terms' and their *"Kanji"* (the ideograms of the Japanese writing), thus being able to form meanings that transcend beyond, giving them a meaningful, private and intimate concept. All that conversation, without knowing why, I recorded it exactly in my mind word by word, and I embedded them all in my soul and in my heart. »

That same day, in full calm after the catastrophic cyclone, most of the railway lines were reestablished, but I decided to ask for the day off work, because I wanted to clean and collect everything accumulated in the house. There were many tree branches scattered everywhere, as well as: woods, posters and traffic signs that had been blown up, along with pieces of sheet metal, fences and different objects of all kinds... I also wanted to remove all the security shutters and tidy up everything that had been mounted inside (just in case part of the ceiling and roof tiles came off); check all the installations, and try to make sure that the accumulated water had an outlet because the earth could not absorb any more... I had a lot of work to do and Takashi-san was coming back the next day from his trip. I did not want to leave him all that work to do; I wanted him to see everything a little better, and he could rest from the long journey. So, I got down to business for hours.

I was exhausted because there were so many things of different heavy materials to move and remove, and I decided to take a break to prepare some food. After eating, I lay back on the couch and turned on the television to get some rest. But there were only news and images of the catastrophe and disasters caused by many areas of the country, which saddened me so much that I cried for a long time, especially for the victims and the people who had lost everything.

It was very hopeless and emotional to see so much destruction. It made me think that we cannot fight against the forces of nature and its ferocity; that we are like a mosquito before an elephant's foot.

« How insignificant is human existence and how exposed we are to the blows that life gives us! »

I felt so sad that I went to the *"Tokonoma,"* the *'home altar'* and sat in *seiza*. I wanted to pray for the deceased, the injured and the people who were suffering so much. I spent a long time invoking and praying for them. Then, I thanked our luck and the protection that was granted to us, not only to me, but to the *love of my life* and our families and loved ones. I gave myself to the gratitude to the *Kami* or *Gods* and meditated, reflected and connected with my unconscious in order to have a pleasant meditation session. After all, it is a mental exercise in reflection that is done on something in particular, be it spiritual or physical. I achieved to obtain a total mental well-being; my mind remained calm just like the emotions (of the moment and the situation experienced) that stabilized until I reached a state of full consciousness and absolute peace.

I had been deeply immersed in that state of well-being and fulfillment for quite some time when…, suddenly! The "vision" of the *Sakura* crying *"tears of blood"* came back to me; but that "drizzle" was becoming a "brutal" amount, more and more "torrential," like the amount of water from the recent "typhoon," and all of me was completely *covered with blood*. Blood that ran over me like a waterfall... and I felt a sharp, like the tip of a cutting edge, wounding and very strong *"pain"* in my heart, until I fainted or I went into a state of unconsciousness...

« I have never known how long I remained senseless, faded away... »

When I came to, my heart rate was very low and my heart was beating very slowly (known as bradycardia); I was aware that the electrical system of my heart had suffered some damage, and I was having trouble breathing. I needed, quickly, to restore a normal heartbeat. So, I took a deep breath through my nose and got up to drink water, lots of water, and keeping my head straight, started up and down the stairs; I breathed slowly, repeating the exercise several times, until I noticed that my heart regained its heart rate and was beating normally (I acted as one should in this type of situation when the heart rate is slow, less than 60 or 50 beats per minute).

Once recovered, I was assaulted by the fear of what happened, of the pain felt, like death was stalking me again..., but if it was not about me, then: Who was it about? I looked at the clock, and in an hour I would speak with Takashi-San. It would be our last conversation until the next day before catching his flight. I had time to find out how healthy all the people most relevant or significant to us were: our close and distant family members, friends, co-workers, neighbors, local acquaintances, etc. I spoke with each of the people that I remembered; I thought of someone and dialed their phone number. I greeted them and asked them how the person, their family, her environment and those close to they were in health. I did not get any negative or particularly worrying responses. All the people I knew were fine. I couldn't think of anyone else to call. I made a great effort not to forget anyone...

I kept feeling that sharp pain, like something stabbing inside of me, and I needed to talk to *Sensei* again.

I called him and explained the "new vision," what had just happened to me, and how I then became worried about everyone, and had been trying to find out if anyone I knew had been hurt or something malicious had happened; and that I had found nothing and nobody for me to worry about. And that: "I felt a lot of pain!"

The *Sensei*, when I finished speaking, asked me:

"Have you spoken to Takashi-san again today?"

"Yes, but we will talk again for the last time in five minutes, because we won't be in contact anymore today until tomorrow when will he be at the airport, before getting on the plane. He is meeting Kobayashi Sensei and his wife at a restaurant, and then he will call me. Why do you say it?"

"I don't know...! But if he is fine and you don't know anything about anyone else, I can only pray for his trip: for the flight that goes well and that no accident or adverse circumstance happens, my daughter," he said while I heard my mother cry.

"Why is mom crying?" I asked.

"It is that we are feeling your pain; therefore we believe that you are feeling the pain of another person."

"My pain is too strong daddy, and I can't think anymore! Now when I talk to Takashi-san I will insist him that he take measures and action, and that if he feels or sees anything, that he cancel that flight. At the airport we will be connected all the time, I will not leave him not for an instant, to see if the two of us together are able to predict or feel something, and we can avoid any misfortune... It no longer occurs to me anything else, except to tell him directly not to take that flight and to wait one day or two more... What do you think? Can you think of anything else? If you feel anything, please let me know!"

"Of course, daughter; I'm going to the *Dojo* to meditate. I call you anything."

"All right, I hang up that he is about to call me, and I still don't know whether to tell him all this!"

While I was holding the phone in my hand and waited for his call, I already began to think that this pain in my heart had to be for him, for the person I love the most in this world, my "true love," my "eternal love."

More and more I convinced myself that he might be in danger. I thought that surely when I felt it, that could have been *"the moment"* in which something bad had happened to him.

I was getting very nervous because Takashi-San's punctuality was rigorous (like all Japanese people), and he was already several minutes late... I couldn't wait any longer and I called him... The phone didn't give a signal!

I thought that maybe he was going by taxi to the meeting point with Kobayashi Sensei, and he was passing through an area with bad coverage or he didn't charge the cell phone and would have run out of battery... I made more than ten attempts! And decided to call Kobayashi Sensei's phone (at this time, they would already have found each other, and would be together in the restaurant), but nothing, he was no signal either…! I thought then, that they were together in an area without coverage, but I was surprised because I knew that my love would not forget to call me, and I also thought that the restaurant was located in the center of Paris, a modern and growing city architecturally and technologically, so I ruled out that they were in a possible no-coverage zone.

I thought and thought...! Takashi-San did not say the name of the restaurant, he said that he had it marked on the map of the city that he carried on his cell phone, and that it was about 4 or 5 minutes from the company.

I called his hotel and it was also impossible; only a recording came out saying: "the lines are busy, try again later..."

I looked at the address of the Paris company (*rue Royale*, in the *Champs Élysée* district) and traced the radius of the 5 minutes of distance as well as the journey on my cell phone to try to locate the possible restaurants in that circle, and...

Suddenly, jump on my mobile in the Upnews (an application that, among its contents, includes the most important breaking news in the world, and the application itself notifies them directly) a *"red alert"* of very important news:

"Last minute: bombing in Paris!" *"Terrorist attack in Paris!"* (This on a background highlighted in red)

I started desperately looking for information to find out: in what area had it taken place and at what time...? It was only known that there had been an attack in the city, but I couldn't get any more details because it had happened so recently.

Suddenly, the application notifies again:

"A second attack has taken place in the city of Paris just minutes ago!"

I kept calling Takashi-San and Kobayashi Sensei and they still continued without giving signal... I turned on the television to watch the news, and I called my father again, desperately telling him the news. He told me that he had been calling me because he clearly felt the *"danger of Takashi-San."* I told him: *"Me too!"* *"I had felt myself die,"* and *"that was my pain."*

It was a chaotic moment and my pain did not let me think. My father was trying to reassure me that he would try to get more information about the attacks, especially where exactly they had taken place. On television the news was still confusing: in the first attack the terrorists had immolated themselves, and in the second they spoke of two or more explosions followed (all the exact details were not yet known).

I kept calling my boyfriend, *Sensei* and the hotel (in case he had returned). I wanted to have the idle phone just in case he called me, and that seemed impossible, because everyone wanted to know if Takashi-San was fine and if I knew what happened in France. I asked them to please: *leave the line free;* and that I would call them as soon as I knew something.

The attacks continued! Every 15 or 20 minutes there were attacks in different areas of the city!

I contacted the French Consulate and the French Embassy in *Tokyo*, as well as the Japanese Consulate in France, and the Japanese Embassy in Paris.

I also contacted the Consular Emergency Division. They still couldn't answer any questions. I could only leave the personal details of Takashi-San and mine, and that they would call me when there was more information. The media confirmed that: The killings on Parisian soil *"were an act of war by the Islamic State."*

I felt totally desperate, I kept calling my boyfriend and Kobayashi Sensei incessantly; their cell phones still didn't give a signal. I decided to prepare myself, thinking that he might be injured, that he was in one of those areas and had been hit.

«I could not and did not want to imagine another ending in any way! »

Our bosses also called asking for him. When I explained my desperation at not being able to locate him, they offered me all the company's help. The company was going to make inquiries and contact, at high levels, to find out about the status of their employee, and they promised me that as soon as they knew something they would let me know immediately.

Takashi-San's parents were very worried and were also attentive to what had happened. They had also been unable to make contact, and knew nothing about their son.

My mother, also convinced that something had happened to my boyfriend, wanted to come to *Shinjuku* to be by my side, she didn't want me to be alone living all that despair. I insisted that she stay in *Shirakawa-go*.

Immediately after the attacks, the country was declared at the "red alpha" level, the highest level of alert issued in France since World War II. For that reason, after two hours, the country's borders were temporarily closed.

I spoke to Yoshida Sensei again and he confirmed that "I was right" regarding what I said and felt, because he had also felt Takashi-San's suffering; that he could be injured, and that for the moment, we should think about that until knowing more…

They both insisted on coming home and I didn't want to, because I needed to focus on finding him. I wanted to search the hospitals where the wounded could be being transferred, and call one by one until I found him...

Two hours had passed after the first news of the attacks, when I received an unknown call with a prefix from France. It was Isamu Kobayashi Sensei!

He was very distraught and shocked, and could hardly speak. It was a complicated conversation, because I only asked about Takashi-San over and over again. Until I understood that I had to keep quiet, let him talk and listen to him... He told me that he was talking on the phone with my boyfriend, telling him that they were on the way and that in 2 or 3 minutes they would arrive to the restaurant; that Takashi-San was already arriving, that he told him that he was crossing the street and would already be at the entrance; he told him that he would be sitting at a table on the terrace of the restaurant waiting for him, and also told him to come calmly, because in the meantime, he was going to call me, and that just at that moment an *"immense explosion"* was heard, and the communication was cut off. His phone stopped working and people started running everywhere. An agent took him and his wife by the arm and put them inside a bank branch. He said that more and more people were coming in seeking shelter, then *"two more explosions"* were heard very close to where they were, and they had been held there for two hours, until it was safe to leave. When they were able to leave the place, little by little, they guided them to go backwards, away from the place. That the whole area was completely cordoned off and he hadn't been able to approach the place where Takashi-San was, or ask anyone because no one knew anything. That he looked for other ways to go to the place, but that it was impossible for him to get there because everything was full of police, military, ambulances, health personnel... Both Takashi-San's phone as well as his own: they did not work and he did not know why (he supposed it was from the shock wave). That he was going to the hotel in case he returned there, which he thought was most likely, and he was not going to move from the hotel until he know about him, because no civilians were allowed in the area. And that he agreed with Sophie-San that she would go hospital by hospital to ask one by one: if Takashi-San was among the injured transferred; since they saw a multitude of ambulances in continuous movement.

Sensei was so worried and so heartfelt that I noticed his suffering and pain. I just said:

"Thank you *Sensei!* Your help from there is essential and very necessary. We have to find him; we have to know about him...! I am strong to do whatever it takes but I know that 'I am dying by the second,' and I only think about catching a plane to go find him myself, because from here I feel useless and powerless *Sensei*."

"No Haru-San, no!" He exclaimed loudly and clear. "Now you must be there; you speak perfectly French so don't stop talking to the embassies and consulates, because they will be receiving front-line information. This is a real chaos and disorder, but at some point we will know of him. I'll try to get another phone and if not, I'll call you from anywhere else. You will see that we will find him soon, although I understand that for you it is already too late. You have my commitment! I will call you!"

"Agree! I will be waiting!" I said trusting him.

« I could see with total clarity in *Sensei* that he was going to give himself up and take full charge of the situation. It also seemed to me that he felt guilty, perhaps because he decided the place or because he was safe for not having arrived earlier... Whatever he thought, I don't blame him for anything and never thought nor would ever think such a thing. My vision, in all things, is broader, and I never look for a culprit in any circumstance or event in life other than myself. I never accuse or judge anyone other than myself. »

Night came and the news continued with the horror and chaos of the chain terrorist attacks perpetrated by Islamist suicide bombers. It was still too early to give figures of deaths and injuries in the media, but one could sense that it was of "extreme gravity." The attacks occurred in different parts of the city; there were several explosions, and other attacks with shootings in the middle of the street at people who were in restaurants or on terraces (people who were quietly enjoying and living their lives ...).

All this also reminded me of the attack with "sarin gas" (chemical weapon) that took place in the *Tokyo* subway, perpetrated by members of the *Aum Shinrikyo* group in March 1995. The terrorists, coordinated, committed five attacks on several subway lines. More than 5,000 people were affected; they managed to kill thirteen, fifty were seriously injured and about a thousand suffered from the poisonous effects of the gas. The founder of the "Supreme Truth" sect, Shoko Asahara, considered the mastermind of the deadly attacks, was executed by hanging (the method of execution established by Japanese law, for the murder of 27 people in more than a dozen crimes), along with six other lieutenants close to Asahara.

Japan lived a moment of catharsis, the executions of the seven members of the sect took place in four cities of the archipelago (Tokyo, Osaka, Hiroshima and Fukuoka), which brought relief to the families of the victims but concern to the authorities, what provoked the reinforcement of security for fear of possible reprisals from their followers.

News reports continued that French security forces were focusing their efforts on identifying the terrorists killed in the attacks, while searching for other attackers that could have fled after the attacks. They had already confirmed that they had several detainees involved in the different attacks. This suggested the great speed and professional diligence with which the French police forces were working, together with thousands of army soldiers who were mobilized to the different areas of the attacks.

It was the next day, and I hadn't slept at all because I spent the whole night talking to hundreds of places in France. It was daytime there and the day after the attacks (the day after the horrible massacre). Takashi-San hasn't been located yet. There was no news from him, and my hopeful thoughts were mixed with the cruel pain and sadness that invaded me. The numbers of the victims were increasing; they already spoke of more than 100 deaths and more than 400 injured...
That same day a heartfelt and painful tribute was also organized in *Tokyo* for the attacks in Paris: The French Ambassador to Japan spoke about the terrorist attacks in France. The French Chief of Cabinet, the Governor of *Tokyo*, as well as the Japanese and French diplomats, in a gesture of condolence and solidarity with the French people, held a solemn special ceremony at the headquarters of the French Embassy in *Tokyo*, to which attended by many local people. This was followed by a minute of silence in meditation and prayer, as an expression of mourning and condolences. After the event, a small group gathered outside *Shibuya* Station to sing the *Marseillaise* together, as a tribute to the French people and the victims. The entire city of *Tokyo* also showed their respect and solidarity by illuminating the *Tokyo Tower* and *Tokyo Skytree* in blue, white and red, the colors of the French flag.
« I would have liked to attend but I was not there for anything else other than to seek and find the love of my life... I was already praying for everyone constantly since the beginning of the hecatomb. »

Every hour, every minute and every second that passed, the situation was worse, and nothing that I heard, read or did could alleviate the suffering and pain that I was enduring.

I felt bad, very bad, too bad... And I didn't know what to do to change it! My state was that of a person who was alive until, suddenly: I felt like I was dying...!

« In this type of event, the moments of uncertainty are the hardest: hours and hours of waiting..., of calling everywhere, of not knowing anything..., of searching in hospitals, of waiting for the lists of the deceased.... There is so much pain and suffering in families... that cannot be narrated or explained! Human suffering has no measure. »

The phone of an unknown number rang and my heart began to beat very fast, uncontrollably; it was a very negative, harmful, evil feeling...!

I answered in an anguished, preventive and trembling voice:

"Moshi moshi" (we Japanese use this term when answering a phone call and it would have the meaning of 'Hello,' 'Tell me' or 'Hey').

"Hello my dear Haru-San," it was Kobayashi Sensei! And instantly, I perceived his tremulous voice, his nervousness and anxiety. "I wanted to be the one to give you the news, just as I promised you. We found him Haru! We have him! But I have the feeling that you already know: THEY HAVE KILLED HIM! HE HAS BEEN KILLED!"

His voice was cut off by his crying as he tried to pronounce the words; I remained motionless, listening in silence and with my tears that flowed in a torrential way, as if it were a waterfall, and I kept listening to him: "As he did not return to the hotel and Sophie did not find him in any of the hospitals, we waited for the lists of the deceased to be made and to communicate where they were being taken. As soon as we knew where the bodies were being transferred, we decided to go there, and with the help of a policeman (a student of mine) we could see the exposed bodies… and I found it there Haru! I found Takashi-San! I have identified him perfectly and we have even been able to see his passport," *Sensei* was crying again and it was difficult for him to speak, while I kept listening silently like a corpse. "I'm so sorry, Haru! I would give anything to not to have to give you this news. I was hoping for another outcome with all my heart. I don't know what else I can say to you at this moment; just express my regrets and my condolences, as well as my utmost respect and those of my wife, who is totally dejected by this tragic and unfortunate ending. Now I have to call Jiro-San (Jiro Yagami, Takashi Yagami's father), as a friend I must to do it! I have to communicate it to him as well! I also want you to know that, when we arrived at the place, the ambassador, the consul and some *buchō* (heads) and *shachō* (of the presidensy) of your French company were there. They were talking with the medical staff and some agents of the French National Gendarmerie Intervention Group, so you will soon receive news and communiqués informing you the discovery of his death. I can only tell you: 'Be strong Haru, stronger than ever, please!' Are you there? Are you alone? Are you all right? Please answer...!"

"I am here, I have listened, I have heard everything..." I replied with great effort and wrapped in tears, "I would like to tell my in-laws, because I fear for them, they are not in good health conditions and this news can be catastrophic. It's about their beloved son! They won't be able to bear it! They worry me! I love them very much!"

"I know, don't worry, you seek calm and cry all you can. Now you must do that Haru: cry until you have no tears left, do not hold them back, let go of them, release all the affliction and pain! Take all the time you need... Forget about the others for a moment and dedicate yourself to assimilate and assume the situation. I take care of everything! Do not suffer even more! You will talk to them later, so you will also give them the time of pain and crying. I will call you again. Promise me you'll be alright!"

"Thanks for everything *Sensei*, I just died again! And I can't promise anything," I said babbling, and hung up.

What I felt is indescribable, what you never wanted to hear arrived, when they tell you that there is a corpse, that "yes!" which corresponds to *"him..."* And then, the pain gets stronger and you think you can't bear it because you think: that he will never come back; that you will not feel his caresses, his hugs, his kisses, nor will you see his eyes or his smile anymore; that you will not be able to touch him, nor take his hand, nor be near him; that he will no longer be by your side in bed, never again!

I warned that my body was sinking into the earth to the deepest subsoil, being totally buried under it!

I relived my death for the second time, because I died with him at the same moment that he died...! We die together...! When he fell, I also fell, just when I was meditating and I had the *"vision,"* the *"omen"* or *"the cry of the Sakura,"* raining blood on me... and that was the exact moment of his death. I fell and passed out at the same time he fell...! So much blood was the pain and horror of so many people who perished in that same trance, in the same situation of terror; and the great and sharp pain was the suffering I would have to endure.

« *'I lived and died in the same day.'* The *Sakura* had been revealing to me for years a 'goodbye' that I did not understand or did not know how to feel. It showed me the fragility of life, with its *'hanami'* (the fall of its flowers). This one said me to enjoy the life of harmony, happiness and beauty that I had because it would be fleeting. And, at a given moment, just like the beautiful flowers it would wither. *The crying of the Sakura* had been showing me and warning me for a long time...! »

My precious life so full of love and happiness came to an end. Nothing made sense to me anymore. Without his presence, without him, my existence had no reason to continue.

I was sinking, I suffered and I was dejected...!

The pain became more unbearable...!

I remember screaming his name over and over again:

"Takashi...!" And I didn't get any response, and asked him incessantly: "Why? Why did you leave without me? Why have you left me here alone and lifeless? How am I going to live without you...? You promised that we would be together forever...!"

« My face was cracked with so many tears that furrowed it, and my soaked eyes could barely see, but I didn't care because I no longer had anything important to look at; I only had his image present before me with his indelible permanent smile, and all his words sounded in my mind going cross my senses. I did not want to stop feeling him, I refused! I didn't want to hear anyone but him in my head and in my heart. Either way, all I wanted was to be with him, to feel next to him. It hurt so much more when I thought about how he would have liked to die. *He wanted to die of 'old man' and 'together!'* He was very young and we had a lot to do. We had to *'handcuff'* within a very few days. I really believed that soon we would be 'husband and wife' for life and we would have two children... How was I going to bear all that? How was I going to be able to get up every day...? »

I don't know how much time passed, but it was hours… I had turned off the phone and when I turned it on, I had calls from all over the place and from many people.

I worried about my in-laws (they had been calling me too). I called them and we just cried, it was very hard and sad...; none of us could utter words, but I was relieved to hear them, even if it was only their crying that I heard on the other side. We agreed to talk at another time when we can speak words and think.

My parents hadn't stopped calling either. They were immensely worried and distressed. They called again and I answered to tell them only: that I was there, that only that: I was...! And I hung up...!

I wanted to continue being alone with Takashi-san. I didn't want to and couldn't talk to anyone. Our world, our life and our eternal love had been attacked and I had no one to fight against. It was a fight against a non-existent enemy, invisible and unattainable for me.

My thoughts of rage were mixed with my own guilt for not having known how to protect what I loved most.

I had dedicated years preparing to fight for life in an era of peace, knowing that the war was out there: in the protection and survival itself. There was no armed enemy who came to kill me directly and could defend me. I just thought that the hidden enemy had always been there and we did not see it, and that it will continue to be and we will continue not to see it: the killers of life, the terrorists who are the real threat to our security and freedoms, will continue to be out there. Their attacks, due to their exaltation, their nature or their prolongation in time generate a total collapse in our society, and this concept is well understood by all the citizens of the world. It's the terrorist hyper-reality!

There are people who have chosen to die in their own way and at their own time, because they could not bear to be alive, but there are also others who died without having chosen how or when (as was the case with my boyfriend). And, in these cases, the husbands and wives, the children and the rest of the families are left "hoping that he comes back so that, together, we can say the last goodbye to him," and offer him the inner peace that allows others to live the rest of their lives with certain serenity.

We do not know life without death, and just as we accept life naturally, it is difficult for us to do the same with death. In the spiritual sense, fear is the motive and the cause, a substitute for the courage that will lead us to accept reality as it is, or the courage that will allow us to be the masters of our life and our death. If we accept that we are born to live and live to die, we will find the energy, the strength, the engine that starts and makes you wake up every morning, even though being awake hurts too much.

And whether out of fear, courage or desperation, if I wanted to live, I had only one way: Acceptance!

Sooner or later, whether we want to or not, we will see and feel others die. Sooner or later, whether we like it or not, we will die. These realities are inevitable for all human beings. *"Feeling myself dying"* was terrible, and I made no excuses to bear the sentence that had been imposed on me, because I felt guilty for not having avoided it; I was willing, if I didn't die physically, to live with it for the rest of my days for the rest of my life.

All this time that I spent alone with my thoughts, pain, tears and desolation, I remained sitting in the *seiza* posture on the floor in front of the *Tokonoma*, the personal altar of our house, hardly moving, without drinking or eating. I was weak, very despondent and depressed, so I made the decision: *"I had to do what had to be done."*

I had to gather my courage and bravery, hold on to "acceptance," and by Takashi-San, if only for him and his parents, I would keep my weakness and fragility only for me, and take charge of the situation. I turned on the phone and complied, returning calls to the embassies and consulates that

had been trying to reach me to give me *"the fateful news"* and pertinent information. I also called, to answer the large number of times that he had called non-stop, to Takayama-San, my boss (who gave me his condolences on his behalf, on behalf of Saitō-San, my boyfriend's boss, who also had called countless times and was very shocked by what happened, and on behalf of all managers and employees); of course, I thanked the company for everything they did in Paris, looking for him and informing me, and I asked them for one thing only: *"Time!"* I needed time to take care of everything: I wanted to personally take charge of attending the *"recognition of the body and its repatriation to Japan."*
« As we had not yet married, I needed a "certificate of cohabitation" and the express "authorization" of Takashi-San's parents allowing me and consenting to this performance "on behalf of the family," due to their state of health. »

I was very lucky that the company told me: "All right!" that I should take all the time I needed, and what's more, that they wanted to offer me all the help and support. They asked me to allow them to take care of: all the necessary paperwork, all my expenses and the costs of repatriation. That it would not be necessary to do it through the government policy for the repatriation of citizens (whose cost is then borne by the individual), because it would be done privately, and the company would bear all the expenses through its own insurance companies: Takashi-San was an employee, who was the victim of a terrorist attack while performing his job duties for the company. Therefore, they wanted to take care of everything and fulfill their honor. And they asked for "my permission" to take care of everything. That I do everything I should and need; that I did not worry about anything, neither the time it took me or the expenses; that I say them when I want to fly to Paris, that they would send me the plane ticket (in first class), and that I would decide if I wanted to choose the hotel in which I wanted to stay (or did they?).

In addition, if my in-laws agreed, they would send their lawyers to *Nagano* to sign the appropriate documents, so that I would have all the necessary documents with powers of attorney and permissions to be able to carry out all the necessary procedures in France. And that, the "certificate of cohabitation," would be drawn up by a *"Kōshōjin,"* 'notary' in a few hours; upon arrival in Paris, I would not have to worry because I would have a *"Shain,"* 'employee' who would be at my disposal to assist me as a driver and in whatever way I wanted or needed.

« The offer, the resolution and the prompt disposition of the company to take care of everything, encouraged me a lot (because I was not expect it!), and gave me a vital boost of energy. »

I quickly spoke to my in-laws again (they were a bit calmer, assimilating the facts ...). I explained everything to them; I asked them to please not to go through the hard trance of traveling to Paris; to let me take care of everything, and that the company will visit them to prepare the necessary documents... They told me *"yes to everything!"* They were satisfied and encouraged me, thanking me for my bravery and my decision. They also stated that they were at my entire disposal, but above all: *"bring our son home, please!"* These were the words of request and supplication words of his parents and I responded: *"I promise!"*

I spoke to my boss to tell him that my in-laws were satisfied, and he told me that he, along with Takashi-San's boss, would fix everything right away!

I also called my parents again to let them know that I was feeling better, and to tell them that I would take care of

Takashi-San's repatriation. But when they answered the phone they told me:

"We arrived at your house; we have just arrived at the station. In two minutes we'll be at the door, so go opening...!" « It was clear that I left them very worried when I hung up the phone, after answering them with a simple: "I was..." That is why they did not take long to leave *Shirakawa-go* to come home to *Tokyo*, accompany me, and not leave me alone in those difficult moments (something totally logical). »

I opened the door, and the three of us embraced in a heartfelt and intense way where everything was expressed, and there were no place for words. We broke up, letting everything that still continued inside all of us emerge.

We stayed like that: Crying and hugging each other for a long time because they, in reality, were holding my weak and collapsed body, which lay totally dead only supported by my father's strength.

Immediately after, my mother went to prepare me something to eat; they had come loaded with bags. They said the first thing was for me to eat something; they knew I hadn't eaten anything since the news.

My parents told me that they had already spoken with the wedding planning agencies communicating them of the tragedy, and everything had already been canceled; they also met, before coming home, with the Temple priests and were praying with them for the loss of Takashi-San; as well as they also prayed for me that I would have the necessary strength to help me endure the tragedy of his death.

They agreed with my decision to want to take care of me to bring and accompany my boyfriend's body back home, but they insisted that they would also go with me to Paris, because they weren't going to leave me alone. But, I was so insistent that I should do it alone, that in the end they understood it and gave up.

That same day Isamu Kobayashi Sensei called, to whom I communicated him my decision to go, with the support of the company, to Paris to repatriate the body. He was happy for me and my in-laws, but insisted that I would not be alone in a hotel, that I would stay at his house. He and my parents agreed that it was the best thing to do, but again, I imposed my wishes of wanting to do everything my way. I greatly thanked Kobayashi Sensei and his wife Sophie-San for their offer, and I promised him that we would be together a long time, but that at certain times and at night I wanted to be alone with my pain. However, Kobayashi Sensei promised my parents that he would take care of me.

I was contacted by the Japanese Ambassador and the Japanese Consulate in France (the company informed them that I would go on behalf of the family, since there was no other direct family member), and they explained to me what the whole process would be like, and that it would take days to complete it due to the high number of deaths.
The first thing would be to go to the mortuary chamber for the identification of the body; there I would be accompanied by them. Then, the autopsy would be performed with forensic analysis and post-mortem DNA testing (for which I had to carry swabs with samples of the oral epithelium, that is: saliva; in addition to: toothbrush, rooted hair, nails, some garment, etc.). And, after all that, all the procedures for the repatriation of the body would be initiated.
I was also informed that the French authorities had committed to prioritize and expedite all the procedures for the victims' families, so that they can take their loved ones home as soon as possible.

The whole process could take between one or two weeks, due to the high number of victims. Once the administrative procedures with the relevant Embassy and Consulate have been completed, the body of the deceased will be transferred. And for the latter, it was also necessary to comply with the Regulations of the French Mortuary Sanitary Police, having available: all transfer requests, medical certificates (including cause of death and autopsy), judicial authorization and specifications for the transfer, such as, for example, the sealing of the coffin properly to travel in the hold of the plane, or in the case of "cremation," with the corresponding certificate of incineration ("Cremation Certificate"), as well as the box or case for the transport of the ashes, including on the outside the name of the deceased.

All this I learned in a fast and unthinkable way; I had all the information and all the steps to follow for the repatriation of a body. It was just that when they spoke about: corpse, deceased, body... for me it was "¡Takashi-San!" A person still alive in me, it was the love of my life that was being talked about, and it still hurt me deeply... but I had to assimilate all that... preparing myself for what I was going to live...

I had my travel suitcase ready in which I put, properly packed (according to the instructions), toothbrushes, hairbrush, sponge and shower cloth, and some of Takashi-San's clothes for DNA testing.

Our bosses showed up at home, and gave me all the documents: various certificates (including the "certificate of cohabitation as a couple with Takashi Yagami"), special permits (exclusively for "entry into Paris" of the relatives of the victims of the attacks) and the corresponding authorizations from my "in-laws," *the Yagami family;"* all signed before "Kōshōjin," the 'notary,' at the French

Embassy in *Tokyo* (with the presence of the French Consul and Ambassador). All the necessary documentation was there, together with my open airline ticket (in order to close the return date myself when the whole process was finalized, with the respective judicial authorizations). They had also sent copies to the Japanese Embassy in Paris of all the documents.

I was leaving the next day, early in the morning, on the first flight. By the time I get to Paris, it would have been around 50 hours since the first attack took place. I was somewhat nervous and uneasy. I spent the remaining afternoon and night with my parents. My mother had been in charge of answering all my phone calls all day, speaking with those who were concerned and offered their condolences; in this way, she freed me from going through that trance with so many people who wanted to show their affection in those hard moments.

The three of us were together meditating and praying before the *Tokonoma*, or altar. It was good for us because we were able to relax a bit.

We talked after many things, and what I would have to live when I arrived in Paris. They cooked a nice dinner and I managed to eat some. My body was strengthening and recovering little by little, and although my mind and spirit seemed to recover somewhat, nevertheless, my heart, emotions and feelings continued crying and suffering inside me; in the same way as in the first moment, when *I felt myself dying.*

And is that a large part of me was still dead, and I would follow him forever and ever...

They understood what was going on inside me; they exalted my courage to face the hardness of the situation that I would still have to experience, and that I would do it and go through it alone (although this was still very hard for them to accept, since they kept insisting until the end to accompany me). Seeing that I did not change my mind, they told me that they would stay in the house until I returned. They thought that if I needed anything, or if there was some problem to be solved, or they had to fly quickly for any reason, it was better to be in *Tokyo* to move more quickly.

And so, they took care of the house too, repairing and collecting the damage, which still remained in the garden left by the strong typhoon.

The next day I woke up at dawn (I had managed to sleep a few hours) for the trip and said aloud:

"I am going to you, my love! I am going to find you! I'm going to bring home, to your house, with your loved ones. I'm coming for you my eternal love...!"

My parents accompanied me to the airport, and there was a special feeling in the atmosphere; it seemed like when parents say goodbye to a soldier son who goes to war to fight. It was a strange feeling! Just before boarding, Yoshida Sensei said:

"I have full confidence in you Haru. As always: Do what you have to do!"

"Thanks! I will do exactly that! I love you both very much!" I answered while I hugged them.

"We love you too, daughter!" My mother replied.

And we merge in another strong and emotional hug the three of us together.

As we stood there the three of us, I couldn't get it out of my mind that, at that same point, I had been with Takashi-San the day he was leaving and we were saying goodbye. I remembered everything we said to each other and the kisses and hugs we gave each other. And I realized that I had already lost count of the kisses I owed him since the last one I gave him, precisely there, at that point, in that same place...

On the plane I had many hours of flight time to think, too many...! My mind kept going back to the memories stored in my memory, to so many and so many moments of our life together. Images, conversations, intimate moments... Everything crowded into my head, and it comforted me to relive it again, but when I came to myself and realized that I was traveling to meet him..., reality showed me the harshness of the situation. I was going to an encounter where I would no longer see him smile, where I would no longer hug and kiss him, where we would no longer talk... And once again, sadness completely invaded me.

I asked the company that I wanted to stay in the same hotel as Takashi-San, and if possible: in the same room. I wanted to feel everything he lived in his last days, during which we were separated for the first and last time.
They were the only days, that in our life together, I was without him and I wanted, somehow, to recover them, to fill them... Madness or torture! But it was my desire.
My only wish! To live what he lived!

Kobayashi Sensei and Sophie-San wanted to meet me at the airport but I asked them: please not to do so!
I told them that once I was settled in, I would get in touch with them. As I had the *"Shain,"* 'employee,' sent by the company to pick me up and take me to the hotel, I wanted to live all that alone (just like Takashi-San did).
Upon arriving at the Paris-Charles de Gaulle airport, one could already breathe the horrible tragedy that had occurred. It was fully guarded and protected by a large number of

French security agents. The country had been in a state of emergency since the jihadist attacks, and a strong security device had been deployed. Hence, there were many controls, and since the country's borders were temporarily closed, you could only enter with a 'special pass that, in my case: I had it, as a family member of the victims of the attacks. Three days of mourning had been decreed and I arrived on the third day. The sadness, pain and suffering of the country were still felt. I felt very united to the general feeling of the Nation.

There was a man holding a sign with my name in the departures terminal. I approached him and we made the corresponding introductions and greetings. His name: Katsuo Harada (*"Katsuo"*: 'victorious child,' *"Harada"*: 'meadows, field'). Everything about him reminded of an elegant 38-year-old Parisian (Japanese-style) with a slender figure and average height. He had a very well-groomed face, very short hair and a good-looking appearance. As his name suggests, he looked like someone victorious.

He immediately took my luggage, and we drove to the parking lot where he kept the car. He drove directly to the hotel, passing through many police checkpoints along the way. From inside the vehicle I looked out over the city, and there were hardly any people to be seen on the streets. It was noticeable that the rhythm of the city was very different.

There is no doubt that the capital of France is one of the most beautiful and spectacular cities in the world. It is also called "The City of Light" ("La Ville Lumière"), for its fame as a center of culture and the arts, and for its early adoption of urban lighting historically.

That light had been covered in black mourning; it had been tarnished and stained, dyeing of red its streets that had previously been cheerful and full of colors. The always fascinating city had been brutally attacked, and it was crying the horror experienced, as it tried to make its way through and overcome the impressive massacre and the terrifying scenes it had suffered.

It was a pitiful journey, the feeling of which penetrated to the depths of my soul. My heart shared all that feeling with all Parisians.

We arrived at the hotel, it was a beautiful and very robust building; a very friendly bellboy welcomed us, took the luggage and accompanying us to the reception.

I asked Katsuo-San that he could retire, that I still had no plans and that I would call him when I needed him. He insisted that it was his job and that he could stay there all day, and I told him that there was no need, that I would already let him know.

I made sure that the room was the same as Takashi-San had been in (all the reception staff showed me their condolences), and they informed me that all their things still remained in it, since the authorities had ordered that everything it remained as is until the investigations were finished (something that I was totally unaware of). They told me that they spoke with them due to my request to occupy the same room, and it was authorized it because they no longer had to come. Likewise, they informed me that a gentleman from the OTARU NHK GROUP COMPANY came, who left his card, and he ordered them not to remove anything from the room; to leave everything in the same state, that the person who would occupy it would be his wife, and she would take care of the belongings. And that was how they had proceeded.

They offered me all the help I needed, "anything!" They said. They were very kind and courteous to me. They escorted me to the room, opened the door and left.

They understood that it was a special and intimate moment to live it in solitude.

It was somewhat shocking to enter the room, and see that there were his things, his clothes, and everything that he did not have with him on the fateful day. I got very excited looking at and touching his belongings. There were analysis papers and drafts of the work he was doing there, in the French branch, next to his laptop. It was, as if he was going to come back, as if, from one moment to the next, he was going to walk through the door and I give him the great surprise of having come to be with him.

I lived a movie of pure fantasy. It was the state of "emotional shock" that I was suffering; is that: I did not expect the room with his things and just as he had left them...

It took me a while to get over all that.

After a while, I decided to unpack my luggage and put things away. I saw, in the bathroom, his toiletry bag and that some objects were missing (toothbrush, hairbrush, his razor ...), they were elements that the investigators had collected for the identification tests, since the hotel gave notice that this client did not return on the day of the attacks.

When I tidied up my things, I took a bath. I was tired from the trip, but I had to talk to Kobayashi Sensei. I called him, confirming that I had arrived safely, and he told me about the next day's program to go to the "burial chamber." When I told him about the room, he was also surprised that Takashi-San's belongings were there, and he was concerned about how it had affected me. I asked him to be calm, that it seemed good to me to find the room with all his belongings. We agreed that we would go with Katsuo-San (the *Shain* or company employee) the next day, and we would pick him up at his home first thing in the morning.

I was barely hungry, it was time for dinner, according to the European time zone, and if I wanted not to suffer much from 'jet lag disorder,' I had to make an effort to get used to the new schedules and to adapt the biological clock, the one that controls all of our systems.

I also wanted to stay strong to get through what was to come, so I went down to the hotel restaurant.

The waiters, very kind, expressed their heartfelt condolences and indicated me the table where my boyfriend had breakfast, lunch or dinner, because he always occupied the same table. They told me that he was a very correct and educated man, who always smiled and thanked for everything (something normal in the Japanese for our ethics and courtesy), but yes, that was "my love," no doubt about it. And, of course, I sat on it and thanked them with all my heart for their words and feelings. They said they would always keep it reserved for me for as long as I stayed at the hotel (that was nice of them and all a detail). They also congratulated me on my perfect French; this yes that my mother would have liked to hear it, because whenever we conversed either in French or English, she always corrected me something.

The truth is that languages make everything much easier when traveling to another country, and in a situation like that, it would have been much more difficult for me if I had not been able to communicate well.

I was living what he had lived! Talking to the same people! Eating at the same table and sleeping in the same bed! I was hugging his clothes perceiving his smell, his scent, and my brain tried to process all that...

« Was it something magical, or was it something dark and gloomy? »

I spent the night with my thoughts focused on him, missing him and crying his absence. The vivid images kept spinning in my head: the first time I saw him at the university sitting under the tree looking up at the sky; the first time I looked into his eyes, when we introduced ourselves; his first smile, our first look or conversation, our first kiss, our first intimate act; our trips together to so many places; our houses and our illusions, or our wedding plans, our children and all our dreams...

I spoke to him without waiting for an answer, but I needed to tell him how I felt and how much I loved him, even though he already knew it...

I kept telling him how much I regretted his absence from this world for that tragic cause; and I asked for the thousandth time, his forgiveness for *not protecting him and for not being by his side,* because if it could not have been avoided, *we would have gone together.*

The next day I would have to see him in a lifeless, inert body, or as one would say in Japanese: *"Kojin,"* *'occised,'* which comes from the word *"occisus"* and *"occedere,"* which means exactly: *'killed,'* *'cut off,'* *'assassinated.'*

Therefore, *"Kojin"* defines it very well. It is very precise and correct. It applies to a person who has died a violent death due to some tragic cause, such as an accident or murder.

Takashi-San, my boyfriend, the love of my life, was a *Kojin,* was brutally "murdered!" And tomorrow I would see him for the last time!

I think I had only slept a couple of hours when the alarm clock rang. I got ready, and took my folder with all the documentation that could be requested, as well as the package, properly packed, with the samples that were requested for the post-mortem DNA tests.

I went down to the restaurant, to "our table" (the one that was reserved for me). I wanted to call it so in my mind, and basically I took a coffee and a real 'croissant' for breakfast.

Katsuo-San arrived, with the Japanese punctuality. I gave him Kobayashi Sensei's address and we went to pick him up.

He was already at the door of the building with his wife. As I got out of the car, Sophie-San ran up to me and hugged me tightly, offering her condolences and expressing her regrets. She did not release her hug. She was offering her understanding for my loss and pain, conveying her trust, empathy and support. I thanked her very much; it was very meaningful and very heartfelt (I could see Katsuo-San, who inside the car was moved to see the scene).

The *Sensei* greeted me with the Japanese etiquette, I reciprocated; and then he pounced on me, wrapping me tightly in his arms and merging us in a hug full of strong emotions and enormous feeling. I felt that I suffered a great pain and suffering; it's more: I could perceive, through his energy, a "feeling of guilt" that I did not understand. He was not guilty of anything at all. I thought we would talk about it some other time...

I transmitted to him with silence and my intense embrace, my gratitude for being there, for having found him, and at the same time, my unbearable inner pain.

He felt it and said in my ear:

"No Haru, no! You are alive!"

"No, Sensei!" I answered sobbing, "I died with him on the same day, at the same instant. This is only my physical body. I have come to do what I have to do: take him back with me to his home with his loved ones, who wait full of pain for his return to give him their last goodbye. And I need to see him one last time with my own eyes! I need to say goodbye to him!"

The three of us got into the car, riding in the back seat in total silence. I was sitting in the middle between the two of them, and they both held my hands conveying calm and support.

We arrived at the place, a pathology building, near a medical school. Katsuo-San stepped forward and addressed some people standing at the entrance. As we approached, he introduced us to these people. They were: the Japanese Ambassador to France, the Japanese Consul, the forensic doctor, a specialist psychologist and two agents from the Scientific Police Services, experts in identification.

After the presentations, we walked down a corridor; everything was painted white and gray. The atmosphere was cold and somewhat gloomy, although very clean.

I was taken to a room with the psychologist, whose job was to prepare me for the situation I was to face, and what I was going to encounter. It was a room painted white, with a metal table in the center and several white chairs. There were no windows, and an intense white fluorescent light allowed the psychologist to clearly observe the face of the person in front of him. He asked me some questions to catch my mental state as well as my condition, and the knowledge I possessed about the deceased in question. He then explained the condition of the body and asked me if I was able to see and recognize it. I nodded firmly and confidently.

I had been preparing myself psychologically for this moment. I was fully aware that identifying Takashi-San's deceased body would be the first confrontation with the reality of "the death of the love of my life." And that is why, in such a difficult moment, the preparation for the identification situation could have a great impact on the subsequent grief process. I knew that, from that moment on, acceptance and my mourning would begin. After the conversation with the psychologist, the medical examiner came by, and asked me a series of questions about details of Takashi-San's physical appearance. The objective was to make a "spoken portrait" as complete as possible, but focusing more attention on the search for exclusive and specific features of that person such as: tattoos, scars, moles, deformations, features or characteristic marks that help an identification that does not generate doubts.

Then we all went together to another room: the refrigeration and exposure of corpses for identification; which was the storage area for human corpses awaiting identification or extraction for autopsy. The bodies were refrigerated to slow decomposition.

It was a very cold room, at a very low temperature, lined with white tiles on the walls. There were several stretchers scattered in the room, some had bodies in bags and sheets on top. A large steel cold room, full of compartments with doors, occupied the entire side wall. In each compartment there should be a body. They opened one of those doors and took out a stretcher with a body and a sheet over it.

At all times, the psychologist was next to me, but at that precise moment, he withdrew enough to allow me some privacy, as did the rest of the people present. The expert police officers asked me if I was comfortable or needed anything, and tell them when I was ready.

I nodded my head, and the medical examiner pulled part of the sheet that covered his body. The frigid climate of the room and the cold that his body, gave off caused an icy sensation that penetrated me.

I just stared at him without saying anything. After a few seconds or a minute, I don't know…, I asked permission to touch him and they nodded.

I opened the whole sheet to see him completely: his body showed many traumas and there were serious injuries in the extremities, craniofacial structures, thorax and abdomen. I also observed multiple lacerating wounds, with fractures, cuts and burns produced by the propulsive effect of the explosion, explained the forensic doctor; and also that due to the violence of the explosion, which had deadly effects, all of his internal organs were affected (generalized blast).

I observed in many places a large number of shrapnel injuries with great forcefulness at the points of impact. The entry holes were irregular and of different shapes, as if from different objects, with large hematomas around the holes.

Traumatic injuries could be clearly seen all over his body. He was truly mangled and replete with bruises, abrasions and puncture lacerations.

My mind was filing and photographing every inch of his anatomy. I took his hands, touched his body and his cold face, which had wounds, cuts and two shrapnel entry holes in his cheeks. My tears flowed across my face, and I saw them fall on the body of my beloved, there: inert, torn, fractured, destroyed, broken and murdered.

Inwardly, I spoke to him; I told him that I was very sorry, that he should forgive me, which I would love him all my life, that it was not his fault; and that I forgave him that he had left me alone, but that I was never going to forgive myself for not being by his side, nor for not having died of old age as he wanted. I told him that in six days it would be our wedding and that we had to get married, as we had desired so much: to spend the rest of our lives together; I told him not to worry because he would be my husband forever. I also said him that he would live with me in my memories, and that I was saying *"goodbye"* to him, only physically, because I would always keep him present in my life, in my head, in my heart and in my spirit. I said goodbye hugging him and whispering to him:

"Until always my love, my eternal love, love of my life! Thank you for having existed, for teaching me and giving me so much love and so much happiness. We will continue forever united by 'that' so special and unique that there is between us."

I kissed him on the lips and on the forehead.

Sophie-San and *Sensei* gently took me by the arms indicating that "I should finish that moment." Apparently I had been there long enough and no one had interrupted me or bothered me or said anything. Anyway, I wanted to ignore them all and feel like it was just him and me.

I slowly withdrew from his body, while keeping his hand held, and Sophie-San took my hand caressing it and separating it from Takashi-San's hand.

It was time to "Identify," which means exactly "to recognize," to confirm to all those present that: Yes! That body corresponded to the person of TAKASHI YAGAMI, without any doubt.

This was a "direct recognition," which had to be complemented with the support of other techniques, since the "recognition" is not definitive proof of identity.

Apart from the recognition of the corpse by witnesses or relatives who "give a satisfactory reason for their knowledge," the results of the studies carried out by specialists (forensic doctors and members of the security forces, as well as experts in the field of identification, fingerprinting, dentists, anthropologists, radiologists, as well as specialists in clinical analysis, etc.) will be missing. That's why, at that time, I had to deliver the package with Takashi-San's samples for post-mortem DNA testing.

They had to perform the autopsy and I requested the "cremation" service with a "certificate" to take the ashes to Japan. I made the decision without hesitation, because I would not carry my boyfriend's body to his parents in that state. They also explained to me that after more days, even if it was refrigerated, the state of the body would worsen even more. I wanted to spare my in-laws the harshness of seeing his son like this, because the image was very cruel and painful.

Then we went to another area, and the agents showed me the belongings that he carried with him: a Japanese passport (his photo and his data were stained with blood and with breakages, illegible, but the sheet with the Paris entry stamp was visible), a pen (which was a gift from his father on his last birthday), my love card (torn, burned and bloodstained, which I put in his luggage, and he placed it in his jacket pocket on that same morning of that "fateful day"), and his "ring of the Japanese crane and the *Sakura*," the cherry blossom (the one that I gave away him, and that he had never removed from his right ring finger, the one that he pointed out to me the last day telling me that it would protect him ...).

All that surprised and shocked me greatly, and wrapped me in sadness and pain. Once again my tears flowed incessantly...

The agents said that I could keep the ring, and the rest would be delivered to me in the next few days. I was very excited about the ring and thanked again for all the attention. I put the ring on one of my fingers, and I wouldn't stop touching it!

We said goodbye to everyone thanking them for the exquisite treatment, patience, delicacy, as well as by everyone's respect and understanding.

The Ambassador told me that, when everything was ready and prepared, he would contact me immediately, so that I could choose the date of return to Japan, and let him know if I wanted to take the ashes with me or not.

I knew that all this was going to take time, so I had to accept that we had to wait....

We left there, and Sophie-San said we were going to her house for lunch. I preferred to go to the hotel, I was not ready to eat after what I had seen and experienced; and I wanted to be alone... I needed it!

It had been a very hard moment and that was also why they did not want to leave me alone. But I needed to be with myself and assimilate the images that I had in my head. They were images that were superimposed on all the memories that came to my mind when I thought about him.

I remembered him always beautiful and smiling, and at that moment, the image of him was dark and sinister. I had just seen the body of my beloved disfigured, broken and destroyed!

I needed to digest and absorb that horrible and harsh experience.

On the way back, nobody said anything; it was a mourning silence. I touched the Takashi-san's ring on my finger, and thought: I gave it to him with the meaning of "the temporality of life" and the symbols of peace, beauty, longevity, loyalty, love, good luck, rebirth and eternal life...; then: What had happened? Where was all that? Where had they gone...?

We left *Sensei* and Sophie-San at their residence. Before they got out of the vehicle, I asked them for the address of the restaurant where they had agreed to meet Takashi-San.

We continued on our way and headed to the hotel. When we arrived, I told Katsuo-San that I wouldn't need him anymore, and that I would let him know. He showed me his feelings for the situation we had just gone through. He understood my state and withdrew feeling enormous concern and sadness.

I discovered that the hotel had a side door (for service); I noticed that I could go in and out, and decided to use it. That way I did not have to go through reception and I would not find anyone, since my state was discouraging and disheartening.

Alone in the room, I lay face down on the bed and I completely broke down. I burst into tears without being able to remove those frightful and monstrous images of my beautiful and elegant beloved, of the one who was to be my noble and handsome husband the following weekend, of the one who would be my eternal love.... And they had killed him, murdered him and destroyed his body so that we would suffer the horror, terror, repulsion, aversion, fear, chaos, panic, cruelty and the monstrosity of their acts which they call bravery....

I wanted them to arrest all those murderers, who did not immolate themselves, and to pay for their assassinations and their crimes.

I was feeling the hatred and rage, as the images of his pierced, wounded, cut and bruised body of violet color crowded into my mind with his face deformed and partially disfigured.

I told myself over and over again that:

"There was no reason in his whole life for him to end up like this, in that inhuman way!"

« What is the point of a situation of extreme pain and suffering in which all efforts to reduce or avoid it reach a limit? All the efforts I made came to an end. I was aware that the pain mechanism has, above all, a biological sense; it is part of our human condition and the state of shock, in itself, is a protective mechanism. »

It hurt me to have those kinds of repulsive feelings, because I was brought up not to wish evil on anyone or to despise any human being; I was educated in the utmost respect for all people regardless of race, religion or color; to not judge or criticize the actions or thoughts of others.

The *values* in Japan are from ancient times. The norms and codes of conduct in society are clear, unambiguous, uniform and precise, and are based on a series of fundamental principles that direct and govern the behavior of our lives.

We have what we call: the *"code of ethical values,"* which is based on: Respect *(Sonkei)*, Loyalty *(Chūgi)*, Honesty *(Shoujiki)*, Humility *(Kenkyo)*, Solidarity *(Rentai)*, Patience *(Konki)*, Gratitude *(Kansha)*, Austerity *(Taibou)*, Harmony

(Chouwa), Integrity and Honesty *(Shōjiki)*, Perseverance *(Kinben)*, Unity *(Wa, Otagai)*, Order *(Chūmon)*, Benevolence *(Jihi)*, Honor *(Meiyo)*.

Ethics is linked to morality, and helps us to differentiate what is good or bad, permitted or desired, with respect to an action or decision.

A code of ethics, therefore, sets standards that regulate the behaviors of people within a society. And although ethics is not coercive (it does not impose punishments or legal sanctions), the code of ethics supposes a norm of obligatory fulfillment, inherited from the spirit of the *Bushidō,* which does not remain only in the warrior class, but also transcends and penetrates widely into the Japanese citizenship, acquiring the character of national morality.

The *Bushidō* was the code of conduct of the samurai, which advocated the cultivation of martial virtues, a sense of honor and indifference before the pain and death; and this came to permeate the soul of all the Japanese people, which explains the mentality and customs not only of ancient Japan, but even of the current one.

Each and every one of the teachings of my *Senseis* or Masters, who were my parents, came to my mind, and all those that the art, culture, the search and desire for learning, as well as those of life itself had transmitted to me. I was trying not to get carried away by those feelings, remembering my training and preparation. I had to extract those horrible images and remember Takashi-San as he was: beautiful, happy and smiling.

I knew it was good, even being alone, to express and bring out the emotions and pain. I also knew that I had to accept the reality of the loss; I had to adapt to a life with Takashi-San absent forever, and I had to reposition him emotionally in order to continue living....

For all that, I took a bath of beautiful memories and beautiful images of our life together, our wonderful trips, our funniest moments, our loving games... I tried, with the memories, to give comfort to my mind, if only for an instant.

The sun had set and it was already getting dark in "the city that never sleeps." From my window, the view of the capital was dazzling and it was perfectly lit inviting me to walk through its streets.

I went out for a walk, it was cold, and I could perceive that the beautiful city still breathed the smell of tragedy, pain and suffering. It was a dense air, there were very few people in the streets, and there was hardly any movement. The Parisians stayed in their homes; there was still fear... I was struck by the fact that many stores were not only closed, but were also boarded up with metal sheets and wood.

Paris was still in mourning, the city was sad and mourning could be felt everywhere. It was a climate of fear, and there were many police on the streets especially plainclothes: watching, attentive and keeping guard.

I walked in the middle of that sad light until I reached the "place," the restaurant area, the same one where Takashi-San arrived to meet death; right where the second terrorist attack in the country took place and the first explosion of the total of three that exploded in the same area.

He was killed by the first explosion, right there, where I was exactly: in front of the restaurant. There were still the signs (tapes, fences, delimiters, etc.), and the bloodstains which were marked on the asphalt and on the wide sidewalk, and which had already turned a dark ocher color.

I had read that the people of the place, the next day, placed flowers and many rose petals, as a way to cover those bloodstains and honor the dead. Others were among chalk circles with messages written by children, witnesses of the horror. (The Parisians were united in grief, and expressed their condolences in the places where the different attacks took place).

There were also the remains of candles next to the traces of terror that dotted the whole place, which continued its dark and sad mourning. Some people as they passed, stopped and looked saddened at the entire cordoned off area, crossed it and hugged each other to cry.

It was the desolation, affliction and pain interspersed with the hope, confusion and faith.

The restaurant was almost completely destroyed; it was practically collapsed and half walled up, with iron and beams to maintain the structure of the building. It was a devastating and sinister image.

I was trying to visualize that day, that moment when Takashi-San was crossing the street to the terrace of the restaurant, talking on his cell phone with Kobayashi Sensei. I imagined him clearly: smiling, happy and content with the meeting they were going to have...; I also remembered the words that *Sensei* commented about the conversation they had, when my boyfriend told him:

"Take it easy *Sensei*, now I'm going to call my beloved Haru!"...And suddenly...! There was a strong "detonation" while a stele dissolved in the air due to the energy that was generated at the point of the explosion and, at that moment, he must have suffered a strong commotion, because the shock wave caused a significant amount of damage that is lethal due to the dispersion of energy and air pressure.

I wanted to feel what he felt in the place where he suffered it, and I was left with that, at that precise moment, I was in his thought because "he was going to call me!" And I "was waiting for his call", so we were connected: me in his mind and he in mine...

When I felt and suffered his unbearable pain, when I lost consciousness, when I saw so much blood on me...! I preferred to think that I kept all his pain; that he did not feel anything; that he fell and did not suffer.

I looked at all the bloodstains on the ground, while I touched his ring on my finger, as if wanting to find out or feel: Which bloodstain was his? I wanted to know: Where had he been lying and bleeding to death...?

It might seem somewhat lurid or immoral, but it was my way of wanting to feel everything he experienced in his last moments. Suddenly! in a certain puddle, right in the middle of the wide sidewalk, almost in front of the entrance of the restaurant, about three meters away, I suffered again that stabbing pain in my heart...

I put my right hand with his ring on the point of pain, on my aching heart, and closed my eyes, feeling him...! Then, I put my hands on the floor over the stain that I wanted to believe belonged to his blood, to his body. It had two pink hearts drawn with chalk and the word "amour" (it was clear that it was a child's handwriting and strokes). I remained there, crouched on the ground, and I felt the pain in my heart gradually ease up.

« I really felt that Takashi-San had been lying on the ground there, at that exact point, and that some of that spilled blood was his. It was an "emotion," a "feel" or "perceive." This is something difficult to explain because the feelings, sometimes, are ineffable (cannot be expressed in words) or unspeakable. I wanted to believe in my sensitivity and I fully believed it! »

I stayed a few hours in the place; I had seen a *kiosk* a couple of blocks away, which sold bouquets of flowers.

I went back there, and bought all the bouquets that the man had for selling. When he asked me: "Why I bought them all?" I answered him (pointing to the place of the attack): "That in that corner my boyfriend had died along with many other people; that I wanted to put flowers to honor and pay my respects to all the fallen, and that it was my little tribute."

Then, the gentleman was surprised, but very kindly said he would help me, that he would close the stall and that we would take them together (I would have had to make several trips by myself); we put them in a cart. I also bought him all the newspapers that talked about the tragedy. We went together and placed them on the sidewalk, next to the entrance of the restaurant, so that they would not disturb the step to people. On the stain, that I thought belonged to Takashi-San, I put two bouquets on the children's hearts. Some young people passed by and offered to place the rest of the bouquets. They did it with a lot of feeling and respect. We did a minute of silence, and those of us who were there hugged each other and cried without knowing each other. It was emotional and very beautiful, personally for me. I thanked them with all my heart for the special moment that was lived and felt there, thrilling and moving us all.

I hadn't eaten anything all day. I went to the hotel restaurant for dinner. I had to eat! I had to be strong!

The television was on in the dining room; they were giving news about the attacks, and the waiters quickly went to turn off the television when they saw me come in, and I said:

"No, it is fine! Leave it, please! Do not worry about it. Thank you very much."

I saw the news of new information about the different attacks, new arrests, and the effects and consequences that they had caused. They showed images and more images of the horror that happened. The investigations and the mourning of the people continued in all parts and places of the Nation.

I don't know how, but I got dinner something and went up to my room.

I turned on the TV, and all the channels were talking about the attacks. I left it, and took a bath, while I heard the information from the police about the terrorists. I thought about going the next day to the police post in charge of the investigation to ask questions, and find out more about the facts.

I called Kobayashi Sensei and told him about this. He replied that he did not know where or who was conducting the investigation, but that he had a student who is a police officer (the one who helped them find out where Takashi-San's body was), and that he would know more. We agreed that he would talk to his student, and he would tell me something soon.

I had finished my bath when he called me back to tell me that the next day was the agent's day off, and that we could meet him in the morning. *Sensei* said that he would come to pick me up at the hotel, and we would walk together to have the meeting and talk with him. And he warned me that he didn't want to hear any excuses; that we would spend all day together.

After recognizing the body, I had called my parents and my in-laws. To these, of course, I did not tell about the horror that I saw. I told them that the body was intact and perfect; that his son was beautiful and that it was as if he was asleep. I didn't have the courage to tell them any macabre details. I thought I would call them back, in other moment, to somehow explain that I would carry his ashes and not his body. I did tell my parents the truth, and they gave me strength and advice to overcome it. Above all, they told me that I had to forget those images and always remember him as he was in life.

Hearing the news and reading all the press I had brought with me, I had a more complete idea of the real situation that happened, and of the terrorists; as well as at what point were the different lines of investigation at that moment. According to official sources, it was speculated that four attackers had immolated themselves in the first attack. In the second attack, there were three explosions that were detonated from a distance, and two of the three executors, who were supposedly together, had been arrested. It was unclear if one of the group members had managed to escape. There was a high alert about this *"armed terrorist"* who could have sought refuge in the Parisian streets or who could have fled the country quickly, before the closing of the borders. They also reported four more detainees who opened fire on people who were on the terraces of various bars and restaurants; that four other individuals had opened fire on the police and had died...

I tried to sleep and rest but my mind kept thinking about what I had experienced so far, about what I had seen and heard in the media, about the place and the point where everything happened, about the stabbing pain I felt again right there, about the images that I had to replace in my mind... Everything kept spinning into my head and I had to fight to cope and accept that so it was, that it happened so, and that I had to continue living. I had to wait to take his ashes with me, and close that horrible and dreadful stage because that was why I had come...
In the end, I managed to sleep until the alarm clock rang.

As soon as I got up, I got dressed and went down to breakfast. I wanted to have a better day. I wanted to be the strong person that I had always been. I wanted to be the *Budō's Master,* the *Sensei* that Takashi-San liked, and whom he admired for her wisdom and attitude towards life. I didn't want to let him down because, furthermore:

That was really ME!

When I went down, Kobayashi Sensei was sitting in the reception room, reading the news press. We greeted each other effusively and cheerfully. He accompanied me to breakfast. He was very happy because I looked better and more animated (I had put on a little make-up). I said him that the previous evening I had gone to the restaurant place, and told him everything that had happened to me, and with all the details. He was very impressed. He commented that he believed that he, in my situation, would not have had the courage to go to the fateful place and do what I did, that he would not have wanted to live that experience, because he believed that so he would never be able of get over it. He expressed that my courage exceeded of the brave and that this could, at times, be dangerous and that it was clear that he could not leave me alone... We laughed, and when we finished the delicious breakfast we were served, we walked towards the *Montparnasse* area. This area of Paris is where the Montparnasse Tower, the Catacombs and the important and busy Gare Montparnasse Station are located. It is a residential and commercial area with its incredible *Boulevards.*

As we walked through the streets, I thought that Takashi-San and I would be doing the same thing on our honeymoon.

« How is the life…! We were both in Paris, in the city of the light and love as we both wanted, but not as we had planned: on our honeymoon both. We were both, but not together, not as lovers, not as husband and wife. We did not fulfill our dream and our greatest wish... »

We arrived, through a quiet and cheerful street, in front of a large wooden gate with a *"Torii,"* this is: a 'traditional Japanese arch' or 'sacred entrance gate' of a *Shinto Shrine*, and a small bow must be made before crossing them. They are of an intense red color, which act as a transition between the earthly and the sacred world. There was, just above it, a sign that read *"Dojo Karate-Do"* and underneath the kanji for his last name *"Kobayashi."* We bowed in respect and entered. It was a *Dojo,* a training room, clad in wood and bamboo with a *tatami* (the type of Japanese rice straw floor) green color. In front was the beautiful wall of the *Tokonoma* or altar, with a *"Kamidana,"* a miniature wooden domestic *'Shinto altar,'* which stood out on a raised shelf along with other ornamental elements such as vases, bells, incense and five candles in front that symbolize the five natural elements: *Chi* (Earth), *Sui* (Water), *Ka* (Fire), *Fū* (Wind), *Kū* (Emptiness). These five essential elements called *"Godai,"* in Japanese culture, come from Buddhist beliefs, and are applied in the teaching of Martial Arts. The characteristics that define each element are focused on self-knowledge, thus indicating attitudes and conditions. All *Martial Arts Dojos* have their own *Kamidana*, which represents this philosophy and helps disciples to prepare the mind for integral learning. The Kobayashi Sensei *Dojo* transmitted calm and serenity; there was a good "feeling" or sensation, which was perceived throughout the space.

I remembered our *Dojo*, in our house, still unfinished and interrupted by the arrival of the typhoon, and by the unfortunate and tragic situation that had brought me to the city of Paris.

I felt very good vibes and it made me want to put on a *Gi* or martial clothing, and start training… Kobayashi Sensei told me: "It's your home; you can come whenever you want!"

His words were an honor for me and I sincerely thanked him, making a reverence (courtesy of Japanese and martial salute).

We were talking about the photos of the predecessors and founders of *Karate-Do,* photos of him competing in Japan as a young man and about the different Martial Arts: their origins and the present; of the weapons of *"Kobudo"* or *'the way of the weapons of the warrior'* of *Okinawa,* as it had a good representation and collection of them. We went into his office, a small but comfortable room, filled with more pictures with photos and more weapons on the walls. He had a small desk with chairs and a small Japanese couch. He lit a kettle to heat the water and make tea. At that moment some bluebells rang, it was the front door bell. *Sensei* went to open the door. It was the person (the student, police officer) that we expected.

They came to the office and *Sensei* introduced us. Let's call him: *"Pierre"* (to keep his anonymity). We bowed and the officer offered me his sincerest condolences. We sat down, while Kobayashi Sensei prepared tea for everyone.

He was a tall man, corpulent, robust, muscular man, with the appearance of iron health. He must have been in his 40s, brunette with very short hair on the sides, almost shaved, and a little longer at the top (like a soldier). He had a strong and confident voice. A very good looking and quite attractive man...

I thanked him for all the help he gave *Sensei* to locate my boyfriend's body, because thanks to him, *Sensei* and his wife were able to access the place where they had taken all the deceased, and he was able to search among the bodies until they found him. That saved us a lot of time in the search and I expressed my great gratitude to him. He said that for *Sensei* he would do anything, and that when he explained that he was looking for a compatriot and friend, and that he was right there in the place talking to him at the time of the explosion, nothing more was needed: he ran out to find out where those who had not survived were being transferred, temporarily; and took him to the scene, as Sophie-San had confirmed that he was not among the wounded who had arrived at the hospitals.

We talked about the attacks and the information about them. He contributed some more data that had not yet been released in the media.

Sensei served tea. Pierre-San said that most of the attackers were "individuals with a long history of antecedents" that "they were under police surveillance," and that "they had them under control;" that one of them "had just been released from prison after serving a sentence for crimes of terrorism" previously, who on this occasion, was killed during the shootout that took place against the police when they were surrounded. He also said that these terrorists were preparing to wreak havoc throughout the country with more attacks, if they had not been prevented. That it was thanks to the great anti-terrorist device that was quickly activated and installed that it did not cause more tragedy, due to the effective coordination and intervention of the different police and military forces.

But in my head some questions and some concepts not understood were spinning, so I asked to him:

"What do you mean: controlled and guarded? If this was so: How is it possible that they organized and carried out the attacks if their movements were guarded? What kind of surveillance is that? How is that possible...? Excuse me Pierre-San, but: I DON'T UNDERSTAND…!"

"I know it is not easy to understand," Pierre-San said, "the list of people under surveillance is very large here and in all countries. It is not that they are guarded 24 hours; only the movements in and out of the country and where they are going or where they return from are controlled. There are not enough agents anywhere for total control of so many people."

"With all due respect," I told the agent, "I still don't 'understand,' maybe because I am Japanese, or maybe because my dedication and learning in the *Budō* forces me to understand in order to know how to react and act. I can understand that there are not a million policemen for a million illegal people, but I cannot understand that there are illegal aliens in a country. In Japan there are no illegal persons. No one can enter illegally. Just like here: I have entered legally with my passport, and the border control controls where I stay and what I have come to. Legally, I am a tourist who cannot stay in France for more than three months. If after three months, I have not left the country, the competent authorities come looking for me and expel me. Is that so, right? It is well, that's how it works for everyone! So, how is it that for those people the same thing does not apply? But it is the same, let them come by whatever means; if they are stopped and they are not legal, how are they allowed to stay or how can they rent a house and move freely? Do they have some kind of approved Visa…? In my country it is not possible to stay illegally without some type of Visa for studies or work; you can only stay as a tourist with a time limit, and there is passport control. I believe that border laws are universal!"

"I know that it is very difficult for the Japanese to understand," answered Pierre-San touching his head and looking for a way to explain it better. "I know about your culture and ethical standards, but your laws are very different from those of European countries."

"Excuse me, but you are also talking about the fact that some of the detainees had already been detained before, and that they had antecedents... But I have also read that some will spend "a few years" deprived of liberty, and back to the streets...! And this is because "those" did not press the button or the trigger directly... In Japan they would have the death penalty without any kind of doubts! There has been a horrible slaughter, as if there was a war going on; hundreds and hundreds of people have been killed and injured, how come some of them will only be in jail for a few years and that's it?

How come there are more people under surveillance who could be potential terrorists? How can someone like me understand those laws? What justice can I ask for, and not just me, but all the relatives of the victims of this terrorist attack and others like it…?"

"I understand you Haru-San," he replied, standing up. "Believe me, but they are very different countries and you will not be able to understand our judicial systems no matter how hard you try, because I already tell you that many things are done wrong, but they are legislated like this, and if the laws are not changed this is what we have, and throughout Europe it is more or less the same. I know from Kobayashi Sensei that you are trained and educated, in addition, in the martial world and that you are a Master just like him, and apart from being Japanese, you have a superior philosophy of life, which I would already like; but you should not worry: the laws will apply to them and they will have the right to a judgment. I just hope we finish catching the missing ones, all those who participated, and we are about to do it!"
Kobayashi Sensei chimed in saying:

"Suppose that I understand, which I don't, but: those who have a criminal record and have committed other terrorist attacks, they get out of prison, in how long…? And quickly, do they attack again? But aren't they under surveillance...?"

"I know!" said Pierre-San. "I know what you think and I know how difficult it is to understand what is not understandable, but I repeat that today's world is like this, and the laws and rights of people are what there are. We limit ourselves to comply them and with the orders that are given to us."

"Agree!" I exclaimed. "I think that we would not get out of a loop of questions whose answers would not give us more than incomprehension and even more questions. But...

what about the fled terrorist who is being sought and is feared because he is armed? Is it true that he is the one who remotely detonated the explosions of the second attack?"

"Yes, there were three. They were together," answered the officer. "They are the culprits of those consecutive explosions. We caught two of them, the third escaped. Some images from a camera on the street, moments before the attacks, capture to them together, and the one who fled carried in his hand what we believe to be the detonator. The three 'were under control,' they had a record, but until now they had not committed any notable act."

"What is the name of the fugitive?" I asked.

"Omar Sabbag. Did you know that 'Omar' means 'the devout'?

"What do you intend Haru-San?" said the *Sensei* frowning and looking deeply into my eyes...

"Nothing, just to know!" I said, shrugging my shoulders as I kept talking and looking at Pierre-San. "Nothing we talk about here is going to leave this place. That's why I ask these kinds of questions: Do the police have any clue as to where he might be? Isn't it possible that he had time to leave the country before the borders were closed? Because he had two hours to do it...! And there is time to go to the airport to catch a plane..."

"No! We know for sure that he has not left the country. He is here, in the city of Paris," said firmly. "Of that we are totally convinced for the moment. All possible addresses of contacts who could have given him refuge are being searched. We will catch him sooner or later. There is another terrorist who participated in the attack with shootings, and we also have a track of him in Belgium, and we are already closing in on him. We will capture them all. Have confidence. The country's police forces are doing a great job."

"Is there any possibility that I could see the recordings from that camera where do you say that you can see them before the explosion?" I asked.

"They are part of the investigation and are in the police station. I don't think that's possible Haru-san!" he said very seriously.

"Can't you make a copy to show me?" I dared to ask.

"I'm sorry, what you're asking is not possible; it's illegal, but you can stop by the police station tomorrow and I'll see what can be done. I'll talk to my superior."

"Please, tell your superior that I just want to see if my boyfriend is seen on the on-site camera footage before the explosion," I said, thinking that would be a good reason.

"Give me your phone number and I'll call you tomorrow," said Pierre-San very kindly.

"Agree! Thanks for everything! I really have liked to meet you and talk about all this. I will always be grateful to you," I said bowing before him.

Pierre-San left, and *Sensei* and I were left alone.

He suspected something and said: "What do you pretend? What do you have in mind?"

I replied that "nothing," that I just wanted to know and have more information, because it was logical to wish that all the guilty to be caught and pay for their multiple crimes.

He was not very convinced of my answer..., and it is that Kobayashi Sensei was right...

Things were happening in my head, things that were part of my nature and my training.

« I believe in the justice, especially in the universal justice. But I also believe in doing what is right. And, above all, I believe in the value of life. The life is the most valuable asset and no one has the right to take the life of another human being, but I also assume the right to defend one's own life and that of one's loved ones, if they are in danger of death. And I think that whoever kills another human being, other than for this condition of extreme defense, has lost the right to live in society. »

I decided to change the conversation because I also sensed that *Sensei* felt responsible for Takashi-San's death, and I could not bear for him to have that feeling under any circumstances, so I started the conversation calmly:

"And you *Sensei*, how do you feel about the situation we are living?"

"I am saddened and very sorry for her passing. I never thought that something like this could happen, that I would live through something as terrible as this. And the worst thing is feeling powerless."

"I know you think a lot of things, like you should have chosen another place to meet with Takashi-San or things like that..."

"That's not exactly it! Sophie-San and I wanted to go to another place that we know a lot about, but he insisted that it be that restaurant because he had seen it (it was a spectacular and very big place right on the corner), and he told me that, in the company, the managers had told him that the food was wonderful and that he could not leave Paris without stopping by that restaurant and tasting *"La Soupe À L'oignons"* (an emblematic dish of the traditional French cuisine, which is made with *'small pieces of bread, meat broth and caramelized onion'* and the *"Boeuf Bourgignon,"* also very traditional, which owes its name to its two key ingredients: *'the ox and the wine,'* two emblematic products of *Bourgogne*). And I said, "Okay, we'll go to that one!" In fact, we wanted him to visit my *Dojo* after lunch, and then we would come to our house to prepare a big dinner for him. My wife had everything ready; even I bought a good *Sake Nihonshu* (Japanese alcoholic drink made from rice). The idea was: "to celebrate your wedding!" That was our thought to say goodbye until we meet again in *Shirakawa-go*, at your *Shintō* wedding, and then we would meet again here on your "honeymoon". That was the plan. Maybe if I had insisted on going to the other place..., which was in the other part of the city, where there was no attack, he would be alive...! That's what I think!"

"But you can't blame yourself *Sensei!* He chose the site! You just wanted to satisfy him. Honestly, you shouldn't torment yourself, much less blame yourself. I have not thought of anything like that at any time. Look at me; I had warnings long before, and was unable to avoid it. Believing that the danger was about me, I neglected him! I did not understand that the warning was about the pain and suffering that I would experience, and not to avoid what would happen. I have wanted to understand that I couldn't help it. You couldn't either. Honestly, I think no one could (although inside I did feel guilty…)"

"You speak great truths Haru-San. I think your words are accurate. I hope in time to accept the inevitable myself. It was hard to find him there among the corpses! It was hard to give you the news, and on the phone... It was very hard to also say the same to Jiro-San (his father) and Natsuki-San (his mother). I have not had children, but I can imagine what something like this must be like. And I am also able to imagine what you are going through. I remember when I met you both in *Okinawa* I told you that you had a very beautiful and wonderful life. It was enviable. I have never seen a couple as harmonious and happy like you two. Do you remember that you gave me a gift and a letter from Jiro-San?"

"Yes *Sensei,* I remember that you read the letter, smiled and put it in his pocket."

"The gift was a *"furoshiki"* (a 'traditional cloth bag or sack that is used to wrap and transport all kinds of objects'). When we were little it was our bag of treasures. We had to find very special stones, which were not common, and every time we found one, we ran to find the *furokoshi* to keep it with the rest. We kept it well hidden so that no one would see or take away our treasure. The note said that: "I will keep the *furokoshi* because when his son was born, this became his only and most precious treasure. And when my 'greatest treasure' is with you, I will be calm, because I know that there is no one better than you to keep him safe and take care of him." You know what those words from Jiro-San mean, right?"

"Yes, of course! But it was while he was in *Okinawa!* I think there is no lack of honor here on your part *Sensei*. An unexpected and unpredictable situation has occurred."

"No, Haru-San, I did not return the note (according to our traditions and code of ethics: if you return the note it means that you do not accept the commitment, otherwise it is your obligation and duty until death). He entrusted his son to me and I accepted. I accepted the responsibility of taking care of his most precious treasure when he was with me. This is for a lifetime until my death, not for a moment. You know well the strict code of our conduct. Not only did I not take care of him, but I had to tell him that, just when I was on my way to meet him, he was killed! I didn't protect him. I did not take good care of him; I had to take care of and save his most precious treasure even with my life! That was the commitment I made by not returning the note!"

"You couldn't help it *Sensei!* I know Jiro-San doesn't feel that way. I know he would tell you the same thing that I am saying you here and now. So don't think about it again. Jiro-San still has his best friend in you. He has even told me that on several occasions since I have been here."

"The time is what will help us all to bear our burdens and pains. Regarding my lack with Jiro-San, it will be he who, in due time, will save my honor or not. And I will face it with total loyalty. But now I am worried about you. I think that, given your experience, training and mastery in the Arts of *Budō* (Martial Arts) and the Arts of *Ninpō* (Ninjutsu), I fear that you will do some craziness that will not lead you to a good end. I see in your eyes your restlessness and I see some vengeance, is that so Haru-San?"

"I do not feel the desire for revenge *Sensei*, but I would like to have him in front of me, to look him in the eyes and know: What does he think, what does he feel when he takes the lives of others in a cowardly way...? I know that it is something that I will never be able to understand, but it is enough for me to try to know how and what does someone like that feel. I just want that, to look into his eyes and for him to look into mine. And then, ask him why and for what. Is it too much to ask?"

"Yes, it's too much to ask! Of course you are asking a lot and an impossible. As you rightly say: You will never be able to understand it! We, normal people, cannot understand such actions against the lives of innocent people, in any way. There is no possible explanation that would convince us to support such acts or crimes. Therefore, what good is it going to do you?"

"Just having him in front of me and looking into his eyes, as I said before, would be enough for me. It's only that!"

Sensei kept telling me that nothing was worth it and to discard anything in that sense, because it was very complicated, being the security forces deployed all over France, and especially in the capital. In addition, military forces and civilian police were also deployed. I assured him that he could be calm, that I was neither crazy nor a heroine. That I only expressed my desire and feelings...

We went to his house. Sophie-San was waiting for us, because she had prepared a Japanese meal and a French dessert. It was true that I had eaten very few times since I had arrived in Paris, but it was because of my emotional state; because to tell the truth, French food is fantastic, it has great and high quality dishes.

Upon arriving at their house, Sophie-San, as elegant and kind as always, opened the door for us. She gave me a big hug, and showered me with compliments and praises. We were in an authentic French-style dwelling; it was a fourth floor of a residential building of a good size and very large and spacious, with many windows to the city and a fantastic light that illuminated the entire room.

They served tea and, while she finished the meal, she insisted that I had to eat it all, that she had put a lot of seaweed and a lot of vitamins and proteins, because she said that I was in the bones. I offered to help Sophie-San in the kitchen but she wouldn't let me, threw me out of the kitchen, and sent me to the living room to sit down. Kobayashi Sensei sat across from me and poured the tea. He told me to tell him the story of that Takashi-San ring, which he thought was a beautiful jewel and that he knew the meaning of it, but wanted to hear the full story.

I agreed to tell him that it was my gift when Takashi-San was celebrating *"Seijin No Hi"* or "Coming of Age Day," 20 years old, in *Nagano*, and that he dressed traditionally with *Hakama*. That he, on that day, was handsome, and at a time when we were alone, in the middle of a big party, I gave him my gift. When he opened it, he was surprised and amazed, while exclaiming: "It is a Ring of the Japanese Crane!" I told him that it had been made by an artisan jeweler expressly for him in gold. And, that to add more symbolism and special meaning, I had added the "cherry blossom," and so it would always will remind him of me. For him, the *Sakura* was also very important because it was related to my name. And for all that, it was special to him, and he had never taken it off since that day.

"How do you feel about wearing it now?" asked *Sensei*.

"I don't really know that. I have mixed feelings. Because, on the one hand, it would have to stay on his finger forever, but how his body will be cremated, I have thought that it is better to have it myself and feel it with me. Although, at the same time, it reminds me of 'the temporality of life,' and makes me think..."

"You know well that nothing is permanent or eternal, everything is transient and fleeting. We can say that everything is transitory, but that it endures and remains in time."

"We always believed that our love would be eternal, even knowing that life would not. I still believe it, and I will keep his love alive in me eternally, because this love was not transitory, and yes, it will last in time."

"The relationships that one can maintain in life are all subject to this condition of temporality, let's call it: fleeting, temporary, ephemeral...This is the rawness of existence. It is the natural reality."

"All that I know well *Sensei*. The *Sakuras*, with their *"hanami"* (the falling of their blossoms) show it to us and remind us every spring. My own name is imprinted on it and my own *Sakura* tree has been showing it to me for years."

Since the table was already set, Sophie-San ordered us to change seats and start eating.

She served a *"ramen:"* it is one of the most popular Japanese soups both inside and outside of Japan. It is made with *dashi* broth (fish broth) combined with *shio* (salt), *shoyu* (soy sauce), *miso* (soy paste), or *tonkotsu* (pork bone), and is served with egg noodles that including pork, boiled egg, bamboo shoots, *wakame*, bean sprouts, *nori* seaweed and many more...

I let them know that it was exquisite and tasty, but they forced me not to leave any in the Japanese bowl.

Then she brought another dish that was popularized by *"Sumo"* wrestlers in Japan. It is a staple food that increases training capacity, and contains a lot of protein. It is the specialty: *"Chanko nave"* and it is prepared with meat, fish, vegetables and tofu, it is an ultra caloric dish!

Sophie-San had proposed to herself that I will recover in one day what I had lost since the day Takashi-San left us. And with this meal she got it. She didn't allow anything to be left on the plate...!

And then she presented an incredible French dessert, the *"Paris-Brest;"* they explained to me that it was a very popular dessert in French gastronomy. It was a choux pastry cake filled with muslin cream with praline and sprinkled with laminated almonds. Sophie-San told that it owes its name to a famous cycling race that took place between the cities of Paris and Brest in 1891; that some twenty years later, *Durand*, a pastry chef from *Maisons-Laffitte,* decided to pay tribute to the race and its cyclists by inventing this gastronomic marvel. Both the appearance and the delicious taste were extraordinary.

It was a generous and magnificent meal, Of course I recovered...!

We were chatting about *Okinawa,* about life there in Paris, and that Kobayashi Sensei had adapted very well, and they were happy. The *Dojo* was going well for him; he had many students and was happy, and his French was also improving a lot. He said that the difference in mentality was what cost the most, because when teaching the philosophy of Martial Arts or *Budō,* it was difficult for him to assimilate it to the European and Western character. He was talking about the rhythm: the French had a very fast rhythm for practice, but the mental part was not so fast; that the fusion of body and mind was difficult for them; that they understood it but find it difficult; and that this also has to do with the rhythm of life, the rush to live, the rush to learn, rush for everything and... The stress comes as a result. We commented that Westerners have many things in their favor, but that they do not take advantage of them enough and forget themselves. They dedicate themselves a lot to others and to superficial things, and along the way they lose about themselves and what is truly important: living authentically, living fully being aware. It was getting dark, even though it was still afternoon; I was tired and wanted to go to the hotel. I had things on my mind, and I needed my meditation space. So we ordered a taxi and I thanked them for the wonderful day they gave me, and the excellent food. In exchange, they had to let me invite them to lunch the next time, and we agreed that I would call them.

Back in the hotel room, I decided to do a couple of things I hadn't done yet: open his briefcase (his portable office) and the room safe. Takashi-San and I used one same code for everything: passwords, cell phones, computers, cards, etc. Thus, both one and the other, we could freely access any device or carry out any management. I took the briefcase, opened it, and took out his laptop and started it up. He had changed the background image on the screen. Before leaving on a trip, he had a picture of the two of us summertime in *Venice* on a gondola. Now he had changed it: it was a close-up photo of me in the previous spring next to my *Sakura.* In that picture, I am looking at him while he takes the photo, and I hold a blossoming branch in my hand next to my face, and I smile at him. To smile...! How long had it been since I last smiled...! I supposed that he looked at the photo and that it made him feel better. There were more papers and drafts of the work he did. In a pocket of the briefcase I found a small folded paper (I noticed that it was paper from the notebook in the room, and with the name of the hotel printed on it). I unfolded it and it was for me, it said: "My beloved Haru: accept this ring and grant me the honor of being your husband for life, forever. To be together with you is my only wish. That you are my wife is the greatest pride and glory that I could obtain to complete happiness and our eternal love, do you accept?"

My tears again…! I deduced that he thought about buying the wedding engagement ring (we had talked about it, and agreed that no, that only the alliances of the wedding, which we already had reserved). He wanted to buy the engagement ring! I kept thinking about his wish and became saddened. Just in case, I took a good look at all the corners and pockets of the briefcase, but no, there was nothing… I opened the hotel safe, and found an envelope and a small gift-wrapped package, and I thought: "Oh, it sure is the ring!" I opened it! I was very nervous, and yes! It was a beautiful white gold wedding engagement ring cut with an exquisite Halo cushion. I put it crying on my finger and answering him: "Yes," "I accept to be your wife for life," "I accept to be Mrs. Yagami," "I want to resign my surname Yoshida to take yours," "Yes to everything…" I spent some time talking to him and asking him why a lot of things, knowing that I would get no answer. I had to go back to acceptance! I took the envelope from the safe, and in addition to money, there was the purchase invoice for the ring for the customs declaration upon arrival in Japan. It was expensive! And he had bought it on his last day in Paris, after saying goodbye at the office, and before going to the appointment with Kobayashi Sensei and Sophie-San.

He returned to the hotel to leave it; took the gifts of the Kobayashi marriage (the *obi* or engraved black belt, and the *Raku-yaki* ceramics), and he left again towards what would be his appointment with death, his destiny...

"My poor love!" I thought between myself with a shrunken spirit.

I took off the ring, along with the note that I was sure he had been rehearsing... and put it back in the safe.

I was aware that it went up and down, that I filled me with energy and I break me down again. My sensitivity was on the surface and everything affected me; I knew I had to get over it; I had to apply all my wisdom and knowledge of the body and mind to stay awake and alert.

The city still feared that there would be new attacks, it was still in a state of alarm, and I could not allow myself not to be on guard and attentive.

Besides, I wanted to do what it dictated, not only my heart but also my *Budō* spirit, what was part of me since I was born, what was taught to me by Yoshida Sensei, and in this I concentrated:

There are the *"5 Shin or kokoro,"* which are the *"5 principles or mental states of the warrior."* These 5 spirits build the mind of a warrior. It not only applies to practice in a *Dojo*, but it also applies to the state of mind, strengthening our interior to face every situation in life no matter how difficult it may be, because the "martial way" does not consist solely of personal defense, it is much more: it is the way of improvement and inner growth.

The *"Shoshin"* spirit is the mind of the one who remains attentive to see everything as if it were the first time, free from prejudice. It is humility and an open mind to teaching to continue learning, because the moment we stop learning, we begin to die.

The *"Zanshin"* spirit is the alert mind, an elevated state of consciousness, where everything is perceived and everything is felt. This is the concentration necessary for the action to be correct. We connect with everything around us, not in a single part but as a whole.

The *"Mushin"* spirit is the mind no-mind; it is attention devoid of judgment or thought. It does not judge, there is only acceptance without anger, without resentment, without remorse and without fear. The warrior needs to accept the reality in which he finds himself in order to modify it. It identifies with the flow of water *(Mizu)*. The mind, on its own, always flows without getting bogged down in vain or unproductive thoughts, allowing us to find the right action. Reflection on life is good but it is necessary to let go of that burden, and let the water calm down to get back on track.

The *"Fudoshin"* spirit is the unshakable mind, immobile mind. It is the beginning of courage and serenity. The mind takes us away from fear.

It is the calm before the storm. The mind is in full control. *Fudoshin* represents gaining mental strength to face every situation in life. Bravery and calm boost the courage and valor needed in difficult situations.

The *"Senshin"* spirit is the enlightened compassionate mind. It is the result of transcending the other four states of mind. The absence of fear, anxiety, useless thoughts and the acceptance of reality in order to act, make the mind abandon the need for conflict. It is the harmony with the universe. It is a mind free of judgment, alert and aware, stable and fluid.

« Staying focused and preparing my mind on these basic principles to know how to act in the right way gave me the courage to stand up and continue the *'way'* or *'Do.'* »

The next morning, the French police officer Pierre-San called me. He told me that I could stop by the central station of the *Police Nationale* (National Police) at any time in the morning.

I had to talk to my in-laws that I would not carry Takashi-San's body to Japan, that I would carry only his ashes. I had to tell them that they were not going to be able to celebrate the first and second phase of their son's funeral with the wake, and the subsequent cremation ceremony.

There was no way I was going to allow his parents live through what I! I decided, on my own, that they were not going to have that memory because no parent should outlive a child.

They would remember him as he was in life: beautiful, handsome and with his incredible smile, which is why I "piously lied." I told them that the coroner had called to tell me that all the tests and the process would take days and that the body would be deteriorating and decomposing, so, in his opinion, he advised us that the cremation should be performed there and his ashes repatriated. And that I had replied that I had to talk to my in-laws to make that decision. My mother-in-law thanked me; she commented on it with her husband, and she replied that everything that seemed good to me, for them too. I told them that I supposed we should prevent their son's body from arriving in bad conditions. To which they replied that I was right, that we should avoid the decomposition process, and that they preferred to remind him as he was like in life. I showed them my total agreement with the decision that had been taken and that I would report it to the forensic right away. They thanked me for making them part of the decision and I thanked them for their trust and support.

Now I felt better! Despite the "trick and deceit," because I had made that determination without counting on them, and even if I did it for their health and well-being, I did not have the exclusive right; it is more: it had to be their decision. They are his parents! They did have full rights!

I called Katsuo-San to come pick me up and take me to the police station, but first I invited him to a good breakfast. I really wanted to evaluate him; I wanted to know what level of trust I could reach with him. As Japanese, I knew some of the virtues I could count on, but he had been in France for five years and I didn't know his way of life.
It was very interesting talking with him. It helped me to get to know him and observe him better. I was able to know that his silence was assured, because he had no orders to receive, except mine; that he did not have to report or explain anything to any boss or manager. That his salary was fixed, whether he worked or was at home; that they assign a person to him and he puts himself at his service for as long as it lasts. Then, they would assign him to another person or client and that was his job. He also let me know that I could order him whatever I wanted, and that he was available 24 hours a day. He commented that he was paid very well, and that he preferred to earn his salary and not be at home. He knew the city perfectly; he said: "Better than a taxi driver!" He also told me that he had a Japanese girlfriend who worked at a university teaching the Japanese language, and that they were thinking of living together because their relationship was serious and stable.
Little by little, I would see to what extent I could count on him.
We went to the appointment at the police station. He left me at the same door, everyone was watching (I told him to park the car in a discreet place, and that we would try to correct that and not attract attention again).
Upon entering, I asked for Agent Pierre-San and they led me to a waiting room. After several minutes, he appeared

apologizing, and it is precisely that he was arguing with his superior about allowing me the viewing of the cameras of the place of the Takashi-San attack. He said that his boss had told him that he wanted to meet me, and then he would decide... He took me to a large office and a man came in. He introduced us and we sat down. He gave me his heartfelt condolences, and we talked a bit about the tragedy and the events that happened in the city. He also informed me of the state of alarm, and reassured me that he was convinced that there would be no more attacks for the time being. He seemed like a good man, and was very concerned that I was comfortable at all times, lamenting my loss on several occasions. He explained to me that there was a lot of pressure from the institutions to search for the only Japanese man who was listed as missing, and that the investigations were well advanced and would soon be completed. All means had been deployed and all available agents were tirelessly dedicated to solving and capturing all participants and collaborators in the multiple attacks. They had many detainees, apart from those who died immolated in the acts and those who fell in direct confrontations with the security forces. Then, he asked me why I wanted to see those recordings and what I expected to find. I replied that I just wanted to see if my boyfriend was seen before the explosion; I would like to have his last image alive in the beautiful city of Paris, because our honeymoon would have taken place here in a few days, since we were going to get married in four days. And my words and my face had an effect on him... He agreed! He ordered Pierre-San to take me to the technical room, and let me watch the images of the explosions of the second attack in the restaurant area. We were in front of a screen the two of us alone. I saw a quiet city on a normal day. People were walking on the sidewalks, some in pairs talking, others with shopping bags or talking on their mobile phones, and at a certain point: he pointed to the three terrorists who were walking together. You could see how nervous they were as they kept looking to all sides continuously and lowered their heads. He stopped the tape, and pointed out to me the two who had been arrested and the one who had fled. I asked him to enlarge the image of that one, the one called Omar, who I wanted to see his face (he didn't like the idea very much, but he did it). When he zoomed in, he showed me how he was holding the detonator in his hand, and it certainly looked very clear (he showed me one that they had right there saying it was the same type, and the one normally used by those terrorists), which was exactly the same as the device he had just shown me. He enlarged his face more and I looked at him very carefully. I looked at all the details. I made a mental drawing photographing him in my mind: his hair, the features of his face, his eyes, nose, chin, jaws, mouth, eyebrows, wrinkles, etc., including a "mole on the left cheek" (because I knew that I could not ask him to print the face of the murderer for me), and so I perfectly recorded every feature of the skeletal anatomy of his face. I asked him to decrease the plane and I took note of his body structure: I calculated his height, his weight and I divided the parts of his body making a diagram, and fractioning it through the clothes to calculate his physical complexion; I observed with attention his body postures and his way of walking. I already had a complete mental picture of the *"assassin" who actuated the detonator of the bomb that killed Takashi-San.*

In that recording my boyfriend was not seen in any frame. He turned on the second one, which showed the area of the restaurant from the front, the side of the road, and the three terrorists were again seen together crossing to the front, as if to move away and activate the remote control once they were at a safe distance. I told him to stop the image. It was him! He had just crossed and he was holding his cell phone to his ear (it was when he was talking with Kobayashi Sensei; when he was telling him that he was crossing, and that he was already arriving at the restaurant). And he disappeared from the image... He was never seen again... It was an instant of barely two seconds! And then, suddenly: the devastating explosion...! It was barely visible, with so much white smoke that it threw a huge fireball into the air and generated a mushroom cloud. You could see how the deflagration destroyed vehicles, parts of buildings, and stones and objects were seen in the air. Some volatile pieces looked like clothes between the dust and smoke (I would say that I could also distinguish remains of human parts flying in the air...). They really were very harsh images. The recording was cut there. It was concluded that it was clear: Takashi-San must have crossed with the terrorists in the pass of pedestrians…!

The images of the devastation reminded me of the one caused by the atomic bombs of *Hiroshima* and *Nagasaki,* although these were of a greater magnitude and disproportionate and transcendental dimension, but it seemed to me that I was experiencing a similarity in the context of war, in a warlike conflict in the country. The devastating horror caused was tremendous.

My blood ran cold completely!

« On any scale or dimension, the death of human beings is of equal transcendent and of utmost importance. Only one human life is equally relevant. »

There was a map of the city on one of the walls of the room we were in and it had many markings on it. I asked Pierre-San if he could point out the areas of the addresses where the logs had been carried out to interrogate and locate the terrorist "Omar Sabbag." He pointed out perfectly explaining the places, areas, buildings, houses, warehouses, etc., that had been registered, and the arrests made at road checkpoints of terrorists trying to flee to *Belgium* or other European territories. I asked questions to find out the areas where the majority of Muslims were concentrated, as well as the shopping and mosques areas of the city. Especially from which were the places where he had been most likely to obtain refuge. I wanted him to tell, everything that he could tell, to a civilian who is in mourning waiting to be handed over the ashes of his loved one and who was one more victim among hundreds, to return to her country as soon as possible; and that soon he would not see her again...

« That was what I pretended to make see. That was my role on the scene. »

Other agents came in offering me coffee. They must have seen my body tremble. I thanked them, as my body was making an effort to maintain its internal temperature since the blood flow had been reduced, and the freezing cold made me shiver (some scenes were frightening and terrifying).

They wanted to meet me, and know why I wanted to go through all that. Pierre-San explained and summarized my presence there. They all regretted the situation and believed that it was not good for me to have seen the images. They said that some of them became ill and even vomited.

After I had been there for quite a while, I decided that they had already dedicated too much time on me. My body temperature had regulated. I said goodbye to everyone and thanked them for giving me such personalized attention, and I also thanked them all on behalf of Takashi-San, and for the work they were doing with such dedication.

Katsuo-San noticed sadness on my face and insisted, asking me to tell him how he could help me; that he was there for whatever I needed and wanted to do things for me. I talked to him about not attract more attention. Not to leave me at the door of the places. We would park the vehicle, from that moment on, in underground or covered parking lots and we would go walking to wherever we went; he would leave aside the Japanese courtesy of greeting and opening and closing the doors, neither of the car nor of the places (something that, in Japan is very normal, but there it seemed that you were someone important or of a certain social level); at the hotel he would pick me up and drop me off in the side alley, where the service door was located, and that when it was closed I would go to the main entrance. It was about moving and going unnoticed. He nodded to everything, although he admitted that the lack of courtesy was going to cost him a lot, since for the Japanese, this means bad manners and lack of ethics, something very serious in social behavior.

I asked him for a map of the city. He took one out, and on it I marked all the areas that Pierre-San told me about. I asked him if he knew those areas well and to tell me about them. He marked some that were very dangerous and, for that reason, he was unaware of them. I asked him if we could go through them with that vehicle. He replied that no, it couldn't go with a car like that in those places. We would attract attention and get mugged, for sure. But he commented that his girlfriend's car was a small and simple car, quite a few years old, that did not attract anyone's attention, and that we could use it whenever we wanted, because she took the bus to work, and hardly used it. So, we decided to change vehicles and visit those areas.

We spent hours touring those places, not very suitable for visitors, but it helped me to observe the lives and how people from the Islamic world or Muslim world coexist, and how they intermingle in society. Places with a large number of mosques located in many areas, and with a lot of movement of young people around them.

It was curious to see, in the heart of Europe, the proliferation at a dizzying rate of neighborhoods, sometimes small towns or entire cities, known as *'no go'* ('don't enter'), in which if you are not Muslim it is better not to enter, and where the police refuse to set foot unless they are armed to the teeth, and where ambulances do not enter without an escort... These are areas governed by Islamic law.

The feeling one get when you arrive in the Parisian suburb of *Saint Denis* is that you arrive in a totally different country. The Islamic ethic, of Islam and Muslims, is palpable in the atmosphere; storytellers of prophets in the Holy Quran and Belief in Allah: these were some of the books that were exhibited for sale in the shop windows of the bookstores in this neighborhood.

Saint-Denis is divided into 40 administrative districts, known as *'communes,'* of which 36 appear on the official list of Sensitive Urban Zones (ZUS) of the French Government. It is a multi-ethnic place. More than 100 nationalities coexist in that district, although the majority population is that of Muslims. Thus, it was common to see in its streets women covered with the veil or *hijab*. It also has one of the highest unemployment rates in France, and has become a cradle of mujahedeen, that is: guerrillas fighting for their faith. In fact, the terrorists who blew themselves up in the first attack were from that neighborhood, and also from where an anti-terrorist operation was subsequently carried out that ended with multiple arrests, and three dead who were planning another attack, according to Pierre-San.

Katsuo-San said that: "The French Police had a very difficult job in that neighborhood, which has always been considered one of the most violent and dangerous areas in France, especially when night falls." And he added that, in recent years, *Islam* had occupied a large space in *Saint-Denis*, and in other places, such as the French town of *Lunel*.

As we toured some of its streets, we could see abandoned and demolished buildings, along with some boutiques dedicated to the sale of veils and *burkas*, as well as warehouses full of food products.

Another area with a "bad reputation" was the *Roubaix* area in the north. This was the area with the highest poverty rate in France. The person allegedly responsible for having manufactured the bombs that were used in the attacks on the French capital lived in this area, according to the French press.

Roubaix was "the first French city with a Muslim majority," published a newspaper. And, the only terrorist who fled from those who attacked Paris had resided there temporarily, and what is more: "He was booked for crimes of drug trafficking, possession of weapons and violence."

I had already a fairly broad idea about that other world, but there were many places we didn't dare to pass (with our Japanese appearance), although inside the car we did put on caps (which Katsuo-San's girlfriend had in the trunk) and sunglasses. At no time did we get out of the vehicle.

It was not difficult to circumvent the encirclement of the police in such a large area, as we could see on the map, which extends along the border with Belgium, a neighboring country which, we observed from a high area, could be easily accessed on foot or by bicycle.

It got late, it was beginning to get dark; we had not eaten anything and we had only stopped, in a safe place, to fill up the fuel tank.

We went back to the hotel and I invited Katsuo-San to stay. I asked them to prepare us something to eat before he left to do the cars change, and he would have the rest of the time free until the next day.

We were very hungry and they prepared us a *"Cassoulet,"* a pout of white beans with pork ribs, in a clay pot, which was delicious.

After finishing eating, Katsuo-san started asking questions. He wanted to know: Why we had been in those places? Why take that risk? That he didn't care, but he wanted to know what I was looking for... He begged me to trust him, that he didn't tell nothing to anyone, not even to his girlfriend, about his clients or his work, and that he would do anything because he wanted to do it for Takashi-San and me. Then, he told me that he got to know him at the company. They were introduced by another companion in the office, and they talked about the typhoon that was happening in Japan; that they told each other where they were from; that Takashi-San told him about where his family lived, and that he lived in *Tokyo* with me; that he was worried, because I was alone with what was happening there; and that he wanted to finish his work to go home, because he had to marry with the love of his life.

He saw him again the day before the attacks; everyone there was happy, because he had solved some kind of problem, and they were congratulating him. That he went to the bathroom and Takashi-San came in after him, they greeted each other and talked about the success of his work, and then, he asked him if he knew of a good jewelry store nearby in the area, and that he pointed out a well-known one to just two apples from there. He thanked him and said goodbye, wishing him a safe return trip.

"What a coincidence!" I thought. It turned out that Katsuo-San was the one who pointed him to the jewelry store where he bought me the wedding ring!

I chose to tell him that I wanted to find my boyfriend's murderer, the only terrorist who had not been caught and who was also: the one who pressed the button and detonated the bomb. I told him some details and the information I had, and that for that reason, I had asked him to take that tour through the areas to which he and the rest of the attackers belonged. He was astonished saying it was madness and suicide. He commented that he knew of my mastery as a Martial Arts expert, and that he practiced for eighteen years *Karate* in *Nara* prefecture, in the *Kansai* region, on the island of *Honshū* in Japan. He, repeatedly, said that these were very dangerous individuals; that I had already seen the areas where they belong, and that, in addition, the news also said that the fugitive was armed and that he was highly dangerous; that we had run a great risk going through those places, and that I had already been able to see how there were streets that were impossible to cross or pass. He remarked that, in those areas, not even the police did go there and that we had been very lucky. I told him that I understood and to be calm, because I would never put him at risk again. Then, with a worried face, he expressed:

"With all due respect, Yoshida Sensei: It's crazy and some impossible! I don't even know how you could have thought of something like that... Besides, what do you want to do? Kill him? We are not like those people, we are not capable of killing anyone, and we are not murderers like them."

"Take it easy Katsuo-San! You are right, it is a crazy! And we are not like them, and much less, murderers. I just want to find him, to have him in front of me and look into his eyes, and that he look into mine, and to be able to ask him: Why? How does it feel to have killed innocents who never did anything to him?"

"I can really understand your pain and what you feel, but you have to get it out of your head, and let the police do their job."

"I'm sure that sooner or later they will catch him. That is why I want to find him sooner. Don't worry; I'm not going to get you into this."

He kept his head down, in thought and in silence. After a minute he said:

"It still seems madness and a suicide to me! But count on me. If you are going to do it, I'm not going to leave to you alone, but I hope that, at some point, you give up and quit."

And he rubbed his head, as if to say: "What am I saying or doing ...?"

"Thank you for your support and trust; I will count on you for some things, but not for others. I will not put you in danger; besides, you live here now."

We put an end to the conversation and I told him that the next day I wanted to go to the Japanese embassy; that he could go home to rest. He's gone...!

I went up to the room, showered, changed and went shopping at a department store nearby. They were huge and you could find everything. I bought dark clothes, especially black, comfortable and warm, comfortable and warm shoes, hats and caps, wigs (I had to buy a special gel to be able to collect my long hair under the hairpiece); I got day and night glasses to hide my slanted eyes (I had observed in the area what kind of glasses the Muslim women were wearing); I also bought "hijab" (veils that cover the head and chest that Muslim women wear), and a fabulous and magnificent binoculars with high definition video camera, with a telescope and color screen, very light and of a comfortable size to carry hanging on top (with it, you could visualize and record with great clarity from more than 1000 meters away). It was truly extraordinary!

Loaded with the purchases, I passed by the "fateful place" where Takashi-San was killed. I stood at his bloodstain. The flowers were scattered by the wind, but the two infantile hearts and the word "amour" were still painted. I recorded and photographed it with my cell phone. I mentally spoke to my boyfriend and promised him that I would find his "killer." I stayed there for a while, and visualized his last moments, walking towards the restaurant, crossing the avenue, talking on the cell phone with Kobayashi Sensei and thinking about me, about calling me... and right there... The end of his young life! How sadness invaded me! What pain I felt in my heart!

I returned to the hotel with my thoughts and feelings, and sensing a deep melancholic loneliness wrapped in disconsolation and unhappiness. I put an end to that exhausting day. I needed to rest, although not, without continuing to think about my beloved and the short image I had of him (in the recording of the cameras) finishing crossing the street and finding: the terror, horror and death.

The next day, Katsuo-San picked me up and we headed to the Embassy; I wanted to talk to the Japanese Ambassador who had been very kind to me.

I waited and he received me. I wanted to know how the various tests and autopsy of the body were going, and if he knew when everything would be ready and finalized for repatriation. He replied that he did not know, but made a few calls and there was still no definitive date since all the forensics were saturated with so many deceased. He told me not to worry, that he would let me know as soon as the whole process was finalized. Then, he told me that I should present the "request for compensation" for physical or psychological damages, or death in terrorist attacks, since family members, persons in an affective relationship analogous to that of the spouse, or other persons living with the victim on a stable way, were fully entitled to be compensated by the French Government.

I said: No! I did not want to submit any application for compensation of any kind! I explained to him that I was resigning, but could not speak on behalf of his parents, and that he should talk to my in-laws, in case they wanted to request it. I also expressed him my wish that I only wanted "justice," and that since there was no death penalty here, I asked that none of them ever be released from prison. "That is what I wanted: *Justice! Not money!* It is, because for me there was no money in the world that would pay for the life of my traveling companion and future husband Takashi-San."

The Ambassador explained that he was obliged to inform me of my rights, and that he did not intend to offend me, and that the "certificate of coexistence" presented, gave me the right to be recognized as a victim of the terrorist attack due to the death of the cohabitant.

We said goodbye, agreeing that he would contact me when everything was ready to be able to collect and take me my boyfriend's ashes. But I'll have to count one more week, at least..., but it could be a little earlier.

I left somewhat enraged and went back to the hotel!

Back in my room, I turned on my boyfriend's computer, and started studying the maps of the areas that we drove the previous day by car with Katsuo-San. I was following and viewing around, as much as I could (because there was not much information on the internet about those places and neighborhoods). I opened dozens of maps and found one that was hand painted by a Muslim. It had a lot of details: street names, shop names, familiar names on doors, and signs or symbols that I couldn't figure out what they mean, but I photographed them in case I could show them to someone.

I was able to clarify, by comparing with others, zone by zone, that it corresponded to a place in an industrial suburb, just a few hundred meters from the *Saint-Denis* area. I focused on that place; the information on the networks said that it had become, in recent times, a residential locality inhabited entirely by Muslim immigration. I also read that several terrorists had died there in an attack that took place years ago in the Nation. I also found articles that said that this was the place where those in charge of finding young people to radicalize them went, because being unstable people, they were easily convinced. They called that particular place: *"le quartier sans nom,"* 'the unnamed neighborhood.' After hours, my instinct made me focus on that point and I searched as much as I could. I copied the maps I found and the hand-painted one onto a USB stick. I went down to reception and printed them all. I took the opportunity to order something to eat in my room. I was dedicated to making a plan and developing some strategies to reach my objective, my goal. I needed it to be: specific, realizable, attainable and limited in time.

I had to use intelligence, to study how a jihadist terrorist thinks and sees the world. Their motivations are always foreign to us. The idea of *terrorist jihad* as a religious imperative, and the conviction that their act is effective, together with the fact that its success is manifested with the proclamation of the *caliphate,* helps them to channel those emotions, along with the feeling of crisis or identity conflicts. Their codes of behavior and their ways of acting are not ours… I also had to consider hatred, a main element, but not exclusively towards Westerners who are called "the infidels," but among themselves due to individual motivations.

They are usually in the company of others and not isolated or solitary. They are usually integrated into cells, groups or networks, and remain confined until they carry out their attacks in the selected territory.

It is a type of ideology characterized by the frequent and brutal use of terrorism, in the name of a called or claimed:

jihad, which its followers call a *"holy war"* in the name of Allah.

Getting a profile of the killer and understanding how his mind thinks in order to become him was my first step.

For starters, the terrorist Omar Sabbag, as well as the two who accompanied him, did not blow themselves up, which meant that they clung to life, that they wanted to live, so they weren't able to take it away, not even for Allah. Perhaps, because they were not authentic warriors, and with the criminal record they had, it could be said that they were criminals who made the leap to murderers. Surely, in those moments, he felt more important in front of his own, he felt like a hero or a brave man; now he had sown real fear and horror...

Whatever he felt, he did not become a "martyr," he did not immolate himself and he remained in hiding.

He was a "coward!"

"Where would I hide if I were him?" this was the question I asked myself for the second step.

I had to make a stop to talk to my parents and my in-laws who had called me and left messages.

I spoke with everyone, and it felt good to hear from them and to have them tell me different things. For them, I was simply waiting for the entire process of forensics, criminology and the Prosecutor's Office to finish, and the order for repatriation was given, and so it was! So they encouraged me to endure the waiting time. My parents were still at my house in *Tokyo* and were working on the construction of the *Dojo*. They wanted it was finished when I came back, and it to give me some joy among so much unhappiness and misfortune...

I also had messages from Sophie-San inviting me to go shopping and spend time with her and his husband.

I also had several messages from my boss, who on behalf of all the employees and colleagues of the company conveyed to me everyone's concern, and interest in how I was doing. I returned the call to him back and he was glad that I was well, and wished me that the wait would end as soon as possible, but that he had "good news" to cheer me up, and that is that *my project*, which was being tested in different locations in Japan, was having a lot of *success,* because it was helping many local families and small businesses. Many were affected who lost everything with the "typhoon" that devastated in the days before the tragedy in Paris. So it certainly gave me a lot of joy, and it was like a shot of adrenaline for my emotional state.

The city of Paris was slowly recovering its rhythm. There was still fear and that was reflected in daily life, as few people were still seen in the streets and many armed police and military patrols were still watching over and carrying out controls everywhere; which gave me greater security and tranquility, because it was very difficult for the terrorists to make any movement or other attack with as much surveillance as there was in the whole country, even the borders of all of Europe were under rigid controls.

Night fell and I wanted to go reconnoiter the terrain in that area. I had thoroughly studied and memorized all the maps. I would make use of *"Hensojutsu," 'the art of disguise,'* a Japanese Martial Arts skill, especially *"Shinobi"* or *"Ninja."*
In some *Ninja* clans, in the *Art of Ninjutsu* it was known as the *"Shichi Hō De"* or *'seven ways of acting or walking'* (the way in which one person plays a role very similar to that of an actor by impersonating another kind of person). It refers to the *seven attitudes,* which are the basis of seven types of

costumes, based on seven ancient professions, such as: priest or monk, samurai or *yamabushi* (warrior monk of the mountains), merchant, craftsman, artist or puppeteer, farmer and local citizen. To accomplish this, the *Ninja* studied sociology, observing people in other cities for a period of time until, like the actors, he could blend into the crowd.

The *"Kunoichi"* or *"female ninja"* were specialists in *Hensojutsu* due to the importance of close contact missions. It also included the art of camouflage in nature such as: a mesh covered with leaves, herb, mud, bark, etc., or the manipulation of shadows, shapes, light, etc...; as well as: adapt and become part of a rock, a bush, a tree or "merge" with the foliage or the environment and "visually disappear." It had to be practiced and learned until you mastered it expertly. This is different from other methods in that the *Ninja* only needs to appear as "another person" for a short period of time. A good *Ninja* should be able to impersonate anyone in terms of appearance. It is the method and technique of disguise in all its facets.

The *Hensojutsu* was used to enter the various social spheres, to hide or even to penetrate protected or inaccessible areas, which is called "infiltration" technique. This Art was one of the most important for the complete training of a *Ninja* and it was performed in an intense and complete way, because the *Shinobi* had to assume completely the role of the disguise he adopted on each occasion: habits, language, gestures, skills, ways of walking and behaving..., since, a merely physical disguise, it was ineffective and could be easily discovered.

« The mastery of this Art would allow me to frequent any place and converse with any person, without putting my person or my identity at risk. ».

For that night, I chose a boy's costume, wore dark men's clothes, I put on a wig with short male hair, a cap and special polarized night vision goggles (I had the problem, as a Japanese, to hide my slanted eyes, the issue of using colored lenses would not work for me in the West), and the normal sunglasses at night was not appropriate or normal either.

When I went shopping, I tried not to forget any details for the various costumes and uses, as well as taking into account day and night, cold and rain... Before shopping, I had looked on my cell phone at the weather and moon phases for the next few days, and I was going to be lucky, because I wouldn't have a full moon for a few days, and the complete and utter darkness would be my ally.

I requested a taxi service, and as I knew that these did not go into those areas, I looked on the maps which were the best points to get off the vehicle, and from there, I would walk... As I was dressed as a boy, I prepared my phone translator to communicate with the taxi driver (implying that I did not understand or speak any French), and thus I did not even have to open my mouth. Luckily, the hotel's side service door was open (I had been observing and controlling it for days, and had concluded that it was never locked, for now…). I went out, and had agreed for the taxi to pick me up at the next corner, so that it would not be viewed from the hotel, as there were cameras at the main entrance.

As I got out of the cab, I visually searched for the landmarks I had marked on the maps. Once I got situated, I began to walk towards the widest street of the entrance in "the neighborhood with no name."

I wanted to go inside to see what it was and if there were people outside the houses... It was a gloomy neighborhood, poor, lacking and underprivileged; there were barely two small bulbs of dim lights on the entire street. On both sides there were very humble dwellings, some seemed about to collapse and the ground floors were places that, by day, were businesses and shops. There were very few people: three young men, two older people and two young girls passed by on what was the main way. Then, the street made curves at variable angle, like a zigzag, and I arrived at a point that was a sort of intersection of four roads in all directions, according to my compass watch, because they indicated the four cardinal points (this was probably what the signs in Arabic said: south street, north street, east street and west street). More than streets, they were roads or paths: dirt, narrow and full of old houses that were inhabited. You could hear people inside them talking in Arabic. On those roads the only lights were inside the homes. I was already favored by the scarce penumbra, the darkness and the shadow games.

The hand-painted map matched perfectly! I tried to read, on each door, what looked like the familiar name of those who lived there, but it was Arabic and they were very deteriorated or old, and besides, they were not going to be of any use to me without knowledge of the Arabic language.

With my fabulous binoculars I located a hill with some kind of antenna tower on top, not very high, but enough to observe the whole neighborhood from that position. I headed towards it, crossing fields of weeds and brambles. From there, I had an almost complete view of the whole neighborhood. I settled down and began to observe, taking advantage of the opportunity to study my newly acquired optical instrument: The binoculars, which had a lot of functions...: I could focus and zoom in to the windows and see inside each building, or I could zoom, enlarging the image and record on video or take pictures, and all through the touch screen. I thought: It was perfect! I had the technology at my service! I entered, through them, in many, many houses looking for "the devout." (I decided that, apart from terrorist, murderer, criminal or coward, I would also call him "the devout," since that was what "Omar" meant, as Agent Pierre-San told me, and I would avoid pronouncing his name if possible). After two hours I saw a large group of young men, between 20 and 30 years old, leave... I counted twelve people and they must have come out of some kind of meeting. With the binoculars I checked them, zooming in and focusing one by one, and none of them matched "the devout" or "assassin." As they walked, they separated and seemed to be heading for their respective homes, except for two of them, who left the neighborhood towards the area, which we could say "safe" or "normal" of the *Saint-Denis* district. They walked without stopping until I could no longer see them, because of the buildings that blocked my vision and the enormous distance. I looked back at the house from where they had left; I observed three people inside: a man and a woman, both elderly and a young man in his 20s, as if it were the family set. They were talking until it turned into a loud argument, and the young man left slamming the door, leaving the neighborhood as well. An hour and a half later, the first two men who had left the neighborhood returned, entered a house together and opened a light inside. A few minutes later the light went out.

I had arranged to meet the taxi driver, in the same place where he left me, at four o'clock in the morning. There were 35 minutes to go, and I decided to start descending the hill.

I had located with the binoculars another way down full of creeping herbs, to the "safe zone," so I wouldn't have to go through the neighborhood again. I hoped the taxi driver wouldn't fail me! Luckily, he arrived punctually. I put an end to my first nighttime foray there.

The next day, I got up later than usual, something logical after having returned at dawn, but I wanted to continue studying the area during the day.

I dressed like a modern Muslim woman and practiced how wearing a *hijab* or veil with large sunglasses, like the ones they wear, and a bag of their style, too. I collected my hair and put on my glasses, putting the veil in my bag next to my binoculars to go down to breakfast at the hotel restaurant.

I had requested a cab, again. On that occasion, I asked to be dropped off near the place, just where I had seen a *"bibliothèque municipal"* (municipal library). I thought it was a big place where I could go in and use the toilets to put my veil on, and go out without anyone noticing. I went out with my veil on, ready to see by day what I had seen the night before. My cell phone wouldn't stop ringing and I put it on silence. I changed my natural way of walking, which was somewhat different from the bearing of the Arab and Muslim woman. I verified that nobody noticed me, and that I did not attract attention.

It was very different from the night. There were many people on the street shopping in the food stores. A dilapidated building housed many people inside; I realized that it was a small mosque, and that it was the center of the community where the faithful, not only did they go to pray, but it was also a full-time school, dedicated to teaching both Islamic doctrine and general knowledge. That is why there were children and young people inside.

I wanted, from the outside, to look at the *Imam*, the leader. I could see him only for a moment and I left. I arrived, again, at the crossroads of the four directions. There was a group of girls playing. They were speaking French to each other and I sat down to watch. One of them fell while jumping; I got up and went to her. In French, I asked her if she had hurt herself and she said yes, pointing to her little foot. I looked at it and it had a slight sprain without major problem, and I practiced a technique of *"shiatsu,"* originally from Japan. It is a technique, which uses the pressure of the fingers at certain points with the objective of balancing the energy of the organism; thus achieving the correct channeling of the "vital energy" *(Chi)*. She told me, smiling, that it no longer hurt, that I had cured her! I told her to be careful and rest her foot for a while... She thanked me, and I took the opportunity to ask her if she knew or had heard the name of *Omar Sabbag* and she replied that she knew many Omar. I described him to her, and she said he could be the Omar from the fruit shop at the beginning of the street. We said goodbye and I went down again to the fruit shop. I was outside looking at their fruits and I heard someone shout out: Omar! And a boy answered and attended to the man. He was not "the devout!" I saw that there was an area, on the other side of the neighborhood, with more separate houses and fields, and it was accessed from there, from the same neighborhood, by a very narrow stone alley. A lady was walking towards there, and I did the same after her at a fairly prudent distance. The short alley ended, and its continuation was through an open *"path,"* as in the middle of the countryside with large fields of cultivation. The lady, who was in front, stayed in a crop and began to gather herbs; I continued for to see how the area was with those houses that I saw a couple of kilometers away. Halfway down the trail I stopped to look through the binoculars; I was alone and I was not in anyone's sight. Yes, it was like a small village more scattered and I could see what looked like a church or hermitage. I arrived at the place, walked from one piece of land with a house to another. There was a great distance between them. It was getting late, and I decided that I should go back.

Now, in the "safe area" of *Saint-Denis* (here I also had to be very careful: not to be identified as a tourist; I should not take out a map in the middle of the street; I had to act very sure of myself as if I knew the place; not to carry valuables, and do not do things that would attract too much the attention), I went into an underground car park; there I took off my veil (I looked like a Parisian! I changed my sunglasses, too), and when I left again, I saw a restaurant where was read: *Crêperie.* I was eager to eat the famous *"crepes and waffles"* of Paris! I knew perfectly the ingredients of this cooked dough in the shape of a disk and browned on both sides: flour, eggs, milk, oil, salt or sugar. There were different varieties in sweet and savory.

I tasted them all...! They were exquisite...!

« Takashi-San had also tried the *crepes,* and I remember him saying that he planned to pass "the honeymoon" eating them every day, that he would not get tired because there were many kinds and flavors... »

I was able to observe that police patrols passed quite frequently, just as I detected several plainclothes policemen (I had already identified some in the morning), behaving as such (if you are a good observer...).

I could see that they were many more than in the morning. They controlled, dissimulating, those who entered and left the 'neighborhood with no name.'

While I was enjoying the crepes I called Katsuo-San to come find me. I indicated to him that he should enter an underground parking lot in the area, and that I would go to him in there, so as not to attract the attention.

I called Sophie-San, and we decided that the two of us would spend the afternoon together, and then: they would accept my invitation for to go the three of us, together with Kobayashi Sensei, to dinner that night at a good Parisian restaurant.

We drove to her house to pick her up. She really liked going with a chauffeur like Katsuo-San, she often said jokingly. She enjoyed it when he opened and closed the door for her; she said that she felt like a celebrity or a famous person.

She told me that we were going to a special place to pleasure ourselves. I thought of an *Onsen* or *Sentō* (Japanese public and thermal baths) or something similar in Paris... But no, it was a "Institut de beauté" or 'beauty salon,' and as she said: "To dedicate ourselves!" performing: facial and body treatments, pedicure, manicure, circulatory massage to finish with another relaxation and wellness massage... In one of the massage sessions, I was aware that I had managed, for the first time, to relax and feel good about myself, feeling me float, almost happy…! But then something in me jumped…! Alerting me! And telling me: "But... What are you doing? How dare you feel good? You have no right! You have to suffer your grief and your sentence! You have to feel the pain! You have to keep mourning her loss and pay for your guilt! You can't feel good even for a single instant...!"

It was that feeling that did not allow me to relax, because I had no right to wellness... I had my own sentence to fulfill and I was not allowed to relax or not suffer pain...

I had to concentrate my mind on the *"Fudoshin"* spirit and the *"Senshin"* spirit in order to have total self-control of my emotions, and achieve my own inner peace, even if only for a few moments...

When we finished, they made us up and left us beautiful and radiant!

From there, we went to pick up *Sensei* at his *Dojo*, who was finishing his classes to go to dinner together. As they were my guests that night, and so we had agreed, I chose a restaurant that I had seen on my cell phone and had been very impressed: the *"Restaurant 58 Tour Eiffel,"* located on the first floor of the Eiffel Tower. It offered a magnificent panoramic view of Paris. It seemed like a great choice to them! I would take the opportunity to see the tower, since I had not yet approached it. That Parisian monument, symbol of France, seemed to me a beautiful structure designed of iron. It stands out imposing, being the highest in the city and the most visited in the world; becoming, due to its spectacular nature in the symbol of the capital. Its more than 300 meters represent an iconic and controversial architecture! And its unique silhouette has made it an emblem of Paris. The restaurant was elegantly designed, and I found it the perfect setting to share a pleasant evening with these wonderful friends. We enjoyed great comfort and tranquility, as well as a tasty French meal with all the lights of the city diffused and represented before our eyes. I invited Katsuo-San to sit at the table with us, too. I didn't want him to wait alone for any more hours again. He had already endured almost two hours of solitude in the car when we went to the beauty salon. I felt bad for him...!

All of them made an effort to make it a pleasant moment and tried to distract me a little, telling anecdotes and happy moments that had happened to them in Paris. I forcibly moved my lips as if I was smiling just like them, but in my mind there was only Takashi-San. I imagined that evening was with just the two of us alone, on our honeymoon having dinner with the views of the city... How beautiful it would have been...! Enjoying our love and happiness, just as we had dreamed and wished... And in front of us, with the views of the city, was the majestic hotel we had booked for our honeymoon with a view of the Eiffel Tower. There it was, seeing it from the Tower, the impressive *"Brach Paris Hotel."* Kobayashi Sensei realized that my mind was elsewhere and said:

"Haru-San: Why don't you share something with us and free yourself up a bit?"

I told them that I had found the wedding engagement ring, along with the words that Takashi-San was going to use when handing it to me, and that he had bought it the same day, just before the tragedy. I also commented to them that Katsuo-San, coincidentally, had been the one who pointed him to the jewelry store. And I asked him to tell them how it happened. And he explained to them his meeting with him at the company...

Sophie-San replied afterwards:

"You should not be sad! Quite the opposite! Everything has to make you feel good, because you have been happy, you have known true love, and each test of his should give you happiness. Not everyone gets to know it, nor feel it, or live it. You have been lucky! And you have to live your grief, of course, but thinking in the future and remembering with pleasure and joy everything you lived with him."

"Don't be afraid to smile," added *Sensei*. "Takashi-San loved you so much that he couldn't bear to see you like this. He would want you to be happy, to be his habitual Haru, his spring, or isn't it…? You just need time for it to stop hurting so much… But you are strong and you will bear it. You've been preparing your whole life for this, even if you didn't know it. Today, I have spoken with Yoshida Sensei, your father, and although he is suffering for you, for not letting him be by your side at this time, for your loss and for your pain, he is not at all worried about your overcoming. He told me that he prepared you very well to face death and life, and that you only need to recover your mental and spiritual state to re-harmonize and balance your emotions. He also told me that you need to be alone, that you like to be alone to fight, that this is your way... So we will be sensitive to your way of handling your pain! And we will leave that you be the one to call or visit us whenever you want or feel it, do you want us to do like this?"

"Yes," I answered, "that's fine with me. I thank you for everything you do from the bottom of my heart. I know why you didn't want me to be alone today, I know exactly what today is, I know you have tried not to make me feel lonely and sad. You wanted to accompany me on this "day" especially. And I am fortunate for that, to have you, not only as friends but as part of my family. I love and appreciate you with all my soul. My father is right, he knows me well, and yes: I want to be alone and I promise to call you when I feel like it. Please accept my humble and sincere apologies! Thank you very much!"

They all showed understanding and utmost respect for my feelings.

We finished the magnificent dinner and the evening, thanking the exquisite treatment and the magnificent service of the restaurant.

Back at the hotel, I noticed that I was tired, since the night before I had only slept about four hours, due to my night incursion plus the morning that I also spent in that inhospitable territory. I needed a good sleep cure. But I knew that, precisely on that day, it was going to be difficult, because in that early morning at 3 a.m. in Paris, it would be the time of my *Shinto* wedding in *Shirakawa-go,* my beautiful village (The Kobayashi couple knew perfectly well that it was the day of "our wedding". They had to be in Japan to attend, as they already had their flights booked. That was the reason why they did not want to leave me alone on that appointed day and they tried to do as much as possible to distract me and cheer me up…). In the temple that saw me born and grew up, at 11 o'clock in Japan, I would be handcuffing with Takashi-San, my eternal love. We had spent so much time choosing all the details, with so much illusion so that everything would be perfect…, that it made me very sad to think about it. We did not become husband and wife, that was what we both wanted so much; and my tears were running down my face again. Between us, we always feel like we were married. But we were also very excited for our families, and for the desire to have children and to form our own family.

« I stayed, lying in bed with my loneliness and pain quite a long time, thinking about him and me, and imagining our beautiful ceremony, our happy wedding day and our happy life together... until I fell asleep and dreamed... »

I woke up the next morning at 7 o'clock. I had managed enough sleep to stand up and also felt strong. I dedicated 20 minutes to meditate, to thank the *Kami* or Gods, and I concentrated on staying alert and letting my instinct guide me; I wanted to get some light in that new dawn.

I decided that day I would disguise myself as a normal Parisian woman, without attracting attention. I dressed combining in black color the upper part and military green pants, with a winter anorak coat in a greenish-black; medium length wig with brown hair, a black sports cap and sunglasses. After a powerful breakfast, I took a taxi again and the same route, starting from a different departure point. During the journey I received a call; it was the agent Pierre-San. He was just calling to know how I was doing and worrying about me. I asked him if there was any news, and he told me that they had covered the entire *Roubaix* area, which bordered on *Belgium* (this was the area we saw on the first day, which Katsuo-San and I drove through, and we said the neighboring country could be accessed by bike or on foot). He said they had the entire area totally under control, because they knew he was hidden waiting to find a way to cross the border. He commented that they were totally convinced, also because that was the plan he had with the other two detainees who were with him: "to cross through that area together to *Belgium* because there they had a dwelling to hide in for a time..." He also told me that, the day before, there were policemen in *Saint-Denis* asking French neighbors about the fugitive and that they showed a photo of him, but that nobody recognized him, nor had they ever seen him... Only an elderly French woman who lived alone, but who according to the police officers was not in a good mental state and seemed to be somewhat psychotic, said she recognized him and that he had been with her on the bus, but then began to ramble, and they left her without giving her any credibility. Also, because they located him in the surroundings of *Roubaix* (which is 200Km from *Saint-Denis)*. I tried to get him to give me the address of that lady, which would be in the report of those agents, and he asked me: "If I was thinking of going to see the lady..." To which I replied: "No!" I thanked him for his call (in a dry, cold tone), and hung up on him.

I continued with my plan, and made my way to the scattered little town with the houses so far apart and with its cultivated fields, where I had spotted what looked like a remote hermitage or church. I walked bordering the entire area on the outside, through the fields of crops, without entering the center of the 'neighborhood without a name'. Something in me was directing me: feeling, prediction, instinct... After an hour I arrived at the hermitage. I was able to clearly distinguish its difference with a church, architecturally. Also, being in the countryside and unpopulated, I had no doubt, although they symbolize the same thing and perform the same function. The size and number of people who live in the community is the real difference with a church or basilica. This was the local parish, a small building like a chapel with its altar. The old door was open; its closure consisted of the fact that the door's own wood was swollen from humidity and the passage of time. In this way the neighbors could come to pray to the image present on the altar of the Saint *"Saint Dionisio of Paris,"* the *'Headless Saint'* or simply *'Saint*

Denis,' who was a bishop of Paris (the first) martyred together with two of his companions during a persecution, for which he became a martyr. I read this in a writing located at the foot of the figure of the Saint. There was a door at the back of the hermitage on the left, but it was closed; it had an iron lock with a key hole. I felt someone approaching and I decided put myself on the wall, next to the entrance door, standing naturally, and thus being protected when the wooden gate will be opened. This way, when the person came in, I would be behind. She was an elderly lady. She went to the figure of the Saint, lit a candle and knelt down to pray. In silence, I walked until almost the second row of pews, an also I also knelt taking the prayer position, waiting for the lady to finish her prayers. When she saw me, she would think that I came in later and that she hadn't heard me. The lady finished and turned. At that moment I stood up, like I had finished too; I went to her to light another candle and greeted her. She corresponded, and I commented that it was a very beautiful chapel; then she told me about the place, she even told me that she had married there when she was very young. I asked her if there was no priest and she said: 'no,' that he had died years ago and no substitute was sent. I pointed to the closed door and she said that behind it there were some steps that led to an underground room that was occupied by the person in charge of maintenance, cleaning and lighting. She said that this person had lived there for ten years; that he had passed away the previous year and since then it has always been closed.

In that place: "I was feeling things inside me!" The lady left and I went outside. It was an isolated place and very few people must have to come up to here; moreover, there were about two kilometers to the nearest field with a house. And that was the direction the lady took when she went out... It was a long way if the majority were older people, so very few should come here. I looked outside, in the area where the underground room of the hermitage was. There wasn't any kind of window or anything like it, but a wide tube about four meters high and about 18 inches in diameter did protrude from the wall, at ground level, with higher eaves for the purpose of a hood and natural ventilation.

On the north side of the hermitage, about 800 meters, there was a group of eucalyptus trees and a variety of pine trees, with many shrubs around them. It was an extension of approximately 200 square meters. Enough to camouflage myself, to think and to observe...

What the place made me feel, and the story of the "martyred Saint" together with his two companions after being persecuted, reminded me of the three terrorist friends (who went together in the police recordings). The two companions arrested and the "martyr" (a person who suffers persecution and death for defending a cause, generally religious, or his ideals), seemed to sound like the same story. In a context of different religions and facts, the meaning coincides. And to the questions: Where would I hide if I were him? Where would the police never look for an Islamic terrorist...? And, if we add my theory that he must have been a "coward," because he chose, unlike others in his group or terrorist cell, not to immolate himself and run away... that confirmed to me that he should not like being alone either. He needed to be close to his people so that they would feed him and keep him informed.

To all this my answer was:

"This is the perfect place for 'the devout,' that assassin coward!"

His relatives or friends were from the 'neighborhood without a name;' they could come up to here perfectly or send a Frenchman, who would have radicalized, so as not to attract attention, every few days to bring him food, clothes, information, etc.

My feeling was getting stronger, although in those moments, I was also sure that there was no one in there in that underground room. I sensed with total certainty that the place was empty. I stayed crouched there, behind the bushes between the great trees, vigilant and attentive. I took the opportunity to look at my cell phone, because when I was on my "mission" I always turned it off or put it on silence. I had a message from Pierre-San apologizing and giving me the address of the old lady of *Saint-Denis*, warning me that it was a waste of time because she was sick in the head. I knew that by hanging up on him the way I did, I would get him to have an unfounded feeling of guilt, as it was provoked by me, and it worked! Almost two hours passed and no one approached the place.

I decided to go back to the "safe zone" of *Saint-Denis*, and ask for the address that Pierre-San had given me of the lady.

I went to a restaurant on the main avenue called *"le petit jardin,"* a pleasant space with a patio, a terrace and a rather surprising small and coquettish garden in the back. I cleaned myself up a bit in the washroom and sat in the back garden. There was a splendid winter sun. I ordered the *'Plat du jour,'* 'Dish of the day,' a huge combo plate of large cheeseburger, garnished with potatoes and vegetables. While I was eating, Katsuo-San called me. He was concerned that I was not requesting his services; he said that he knew I was out there, alone, looking for the terrorist, that he wanted to be by my side, that I not to put him aside, and that he wanted to come wherever I was. He asked please and begged in every way possible. I told him: "Agree!" But he should come with his girlfriend's car, dress casual and that he does not look for me, but to a half mane westerner with brown hair, a black sports cap and sunglasses. I met him at the restaurant, so I could finish my tasty dish quietly.

When Katsuo-San arrived, he approached doubtfully, he wasn't sure if that woman was me. I had to nod to him. The first thing I told him was that we let's speak in French (that I was a Parisian woman and he a Japanese man who lives and works in Paris, because his French was perfect). He said he would never have recognized me, that I looked like a western woman with the glasses and the hair. He was stunned by my costume! I really got lucky with the shape of my face, since Asian faces are generally wider than Caucasian faces, but they vary a lot depending on the genealogical origin. In my case, my face is narrow and oval with the cheekbones upwards and not outwards (like most Japanese people). It looks more like a Filipino face, in fact, when I was a child I was asked if I or my mother were from the Philippines, and it is that in my mother's family tree there was a branch of Filipino origin. That's why that without my slanted eyes, the shape of my face seems Caucasian.

Katsuo-San was a bit angry, because I was not counting on him. I explained to him that I had already made it clear that I would not expose him in this issue, that it was only my matter; that it was not going to involve anyone, and even less to those who reside and develop their lives in Paris. I made him understand that: "I will go…" "I will disappear…," but the others (referring to him and to Kobayashi marriage) stay. He insisted on not leaving me alone in my battle, although he did not share what I did or how I did it, but he did share what I felt.

I summarized to him what I had been doing and my intuition of the "place" where "the devout" had his hiding place. I warned him, in advance, that I didn't want to hear him say things like: "go to the police and tell them;" so he no longer expressed it. I also informed him of the address Pierre-San had given me of the French lady, and why I wanted to speak with her. He said that it was very close to there, and that we could go walking. He thought the same as the police: that if the lady was mentally ill, we could not pay any attention to what she said or to the fact that she recognized the photo, nor that she saw him on the bus. I told him about the human mind and how to recognize a person with psychosis: the first thing we would see is disorganization in thought and speech, false beliefs that are not real (delusions), as well as unfounded fears or suspicions. If the brain is affected, the medication is essential because it remissions those episodes. I explained that if the persons are in that phase of symptoms remission because they have their medication under control, they can see and speak clearly if you use counseling and some psychotherapy (a communication process that helps the patient to correct and modify his behavior and thoughts, directing his mind towards what is real keeping hallucination and possible fears away). Katsuo-San said that how could I know so many things, that I was young to know of so much and of everything... I sanctioned his words because I hardly knew anything. I still had so much to learn and to know...! I have always feared that I would not have time in life to obtain a minimum of wisdom, knowledge and understanding before dying, before leaving this world.

We were in front of the door of an old but preserved building; we knocked on the corresponding floor and door and a lady answered. We told her we wanted to talk to her and she opened the door for us. We went upstairs and she was waiting with the door open. We introduced ourselves with made-up names and he invited us in, which we seemed something daring for her safety (she shouldn't act like that with strangers). We sat down, and I spoke a few words to see her mental state, and she seemed balanced. Then, I reminded her that the police had come to ask her something, and she immediately answered: "Yes!" And that they asked her about a boy (she even remembered Omar's name!), and that she replied that she did not know any Omar; then, they showed her a picture of him and she said that she did not know the guy, but that she saw him on the bus the day before. He wore a gray sweater with a hood that he wore all the time to cover his face; also that he was with another more browner, and that the one in the photo spoke French but not very well, that's why she noticed him, and also because he did not raise his head from the ground. That the young man got off at the same stop as her, the one that was about 50 meters from her house, and that he continued walking down the street, with his head down and his hands in his pockets. She also told the police that he was surely a criminal from the 'nameless neighborhood.' I was just redirecting her, and she spoke firmly and confidently on her own. She did not hesitate at any time. She offered us a coffee. I asked her if she had any kind of medication at her age, because I found her very well. And she told me that she was not so well, that she had had two episodes of hallucinations two years ago, and that she had a very bad time, but that she had never had another attack, and that she believed it was thanks to the medications that helped her to control it. And that she never forgot of taking them, because she was afraid that this horrible episode would happen again. This meant that her psychotic break was stabilized by the medication. She believed that we were another class of officers (because when she spoke she meant "the other cops..."), and she thought she was helping to catch a criminal. We thanked her for her cooperation, and before we left, gave her a few safety tips and an order to "never open the door to any stranger."

Even to Katsuo-San it was clear that the woman was in good mental health. We commented that, most likely, the woman was honest in telling the police, just as she did with us, about her episode of hallucinations and the medication, and therefore, the agents discarded her as a credible witness, assuming her mental instability.

« It was a very serious 'mistake' for not observing better and paying due attention to the witness! »

It was very useful for me to verify her testimony because I saw it and felt it as totally credible, and it helped me to know that the "murderer Omar Sabbag" remained in the area, close to his people, and not more than 200 kilometers away where the police placed him. It also helped me to know that my instinct was right, that it had not failed me.

I told Katsuo-San that I would return to the hermitage to check if there had been some movement given that it was getting dark, and in the morning there had been no one, and it was very possible to detect some activity at night in that isolated place.

He commented that he would come with me and that he would do whatever I ordered.

We walked, skirting the outside, to the place, and when we were approaching it, he asked:

"Is here? But this is Catholic!"

"Have you ever seen a Muslim enter a Catholic place?" I answered him with this question.

"No! Never!" he answered firmly and confidently.

"That's what I thought!" I told him. "Doesn't it seem like the perfect place for a fled Muslim terrorist? Who would look for him here?"

We are located in the set of trees and bushes. I ordered him to opt for a comfortable position that allowed him to remain motionless and silent, because if someone approached, he could not move a single branch. He understood this, and we stood there observing as far as our sight reached. I hadn't brought my binoculars, because I didn't have my bag or the wide coat that allowed me to hang it up and hide it. But we had four eyes!

After about an hour, we saw a person approaching in the darkness of the path that led to the hermitage. That person was getting closer and closer. Despite still having a dark night, as he got closer we could see that he was wearing a blue anorak coat with a hood that hid part of his face. He was a young man in his twenties, considerably taller and thinner than "the devout." He was carrying two bags that appeared to contain food supplies. He came to the door of the hermitage and stood in front of it, leaving the bags on the ground. He was restless, looking around in all directions. Several minutes had passed, when suddenly, we saw another individual emerge from the north face, as if he had come through the fields of cultivation, and he headed to meet the other in front of the entrance. They were both in front of the door. This new individual also wore the hood, but it was from the gray sweater he wore under a wide army green jacket. My attention was fixed as when a cat has detected its prey, the mouse. I realized that it matched the description given by the lady we had visited: the gray hooded sweater. Moreover, due to his height and way of walking (I had noticed well in those details in the police recordings); I clearly and perfectly identified him as "Omar Sabbag," even though I only half saw his face when they turned on a flashlight. They spoke for a moment and said goodbye. The taller young man turned around, and with empty hands shoved into his pockets, he went back the same path that he had come. The one who looked like "the devout" carried a dark sports bag across his shoulder; he looked both ways, and immediately pushed the gate going inside with the bags.

Everything in my body was announcing to me that it was him, that I had found him, and that he was not going to escape me. All my alarms went off, and everything in me merged with the brain activity that shot up at high speed.

« My state at that time, could be compared with the behavior of Japanese honey bees, which, due to brain activity, organize themselves together to assemble their secret weapon, allowing these insects a very effective defensive strategy, as well as unique and spectacular to fight against their greatest adversary: the hornet. When they feel attacked, they form a real living ball and surround their enemy, generating their killer heat until is completely suffocated.

What desire did I have to embrace the "cowardly murderer" like that! »

He remained inside, didn't make any kind of noises. I ordered Katsuo-San not to move or breathe, while I approached to the other side of the hermitage, where the ventilation duct was; I put my ear and could hear, albeit very low, the sound of what sounded like a murmur of Arabic words, as if they were prayers. He was praying!

I went back to the set of trees. I put my cap on Katsuo-San and ordered him to follow the other young man, who we still saw walking away, in absolute silence, naturally and at some distance; only to see where he was going, whether to a private house or some other place. I ordered him not to approach him under any circumstances, that he had to be totally invisible to that person, and that I would go to meet him. I wanted to wait a little longer, because I wanted to make sure that the killer was going to spend the night there. They brought provisions for at least a day or two, so it was to be assumed that the next day he would continue in the mosque. I listened again, and verified that the silence, through the ventilation duct, at that moment was total and absolute.

I was tempted to push the gate but it creaked a lot, even though I was sure he was in the room with the door closed on the inside, I didn't want to risk him hearing the noise.

The other night I was in the place until 4 a.m., no one was there or came. I still didn't know if he came every night or if he also had another place...

I went in search of Katsuo-San to the 'neighborhood with no name,' which is where everyone belonged and moved, and from where the path that led to the hermitage was taken. I found him hiding in a corner of the main street of the neighborhood, he pointed me to the house he had entered, and it looked like a private home. There were people inside and we could hear them speaking in Arabic. We decided to leave because we had managed to know a lot, and above all: I had confirmed my theory!

We went to the hotel, I was very satisfied and happy because: I HAD HIM, IT WAS HIM, I HAD FOUND HIM!

I invited Katsuo-San to stay for dinner with me at the hotel restaurant, as he was quite excited about what he had done, and for my intuition in the investigation. He saw it with his own eyes, and he still didn't quite believe it...

We entered through the side door of the hotel and went up to my room. I had to take off my wig. Katsuo-San handed the cap back to me, and waited while I fixed my hair in the bathroom, since I had to put a large amount of gel to be able to collect so much hair under the wig, after it was very difficult to undo it. I had to use a lot of shampoo to remove all that gel. I dried it a bit with the hot air from the dryer, and we went down to the restaurant.

During dinner he asked many questions, he wanted to know why and how I fixed my attention on that area and in that neighborhood that had already been searched by the police, and likewise it was completely discarded by them.

And, about the fact of no one would ever think of looking for a Muslim in a Catholic building, this had left him totally astonished, because he said that it was something that resulted from an incredibly logic, but that nobody would ever think about it, because they would never set a foot in a Christian place under any circumstances (except this "coward"). He kept asking how that crazy and accurate thought had occurred to me. He was incredulous because in a few days I had achieved what he himself called "an impossible and madness." Now he wanted to know what I was going to do, when and how... I replied that he was not going to know or participate any more, that with what happened that day he had already exposed too much. It had turned out well, but we were not going to tempt to luck or fate. When his adrenaline was regulated, I told him that that day concluded the end of my wedding day with Takashi-San in Japan, and that this was my gift to him: "finding his murderer" as part of "my marriage offering." Katsuo-San was shocked, regretting what I must be feeling inside. And that, on that same day, I found him precisely... and my offering... He was speechless him and remained silent with moistened eyes, as did I. We finished dinner, and he accepted my decision that he would no longer participate in "my mission" because it was mine and nobody else's. I thanked him for his help, interest and support. He, as a good Japanese at the service, guaranteed his silence and insisted, once again, that he would remain on standby for whatever and whenever. He ended up telling me that he understood my feelings and that he respected me immensely for it. He withdrew until further notice.

In my room, alone again, all my thoughts crowded once more in my mind: my non-existent wedding day that had ended a few hours ago, see and find the killer, to be so close to him...

My core beliefs and values of life reminded me of the exploits, history and the transmitted teachings of ancient Japan. Because along with those fundamental virtues and values, the *"Bushidō," 'the way of the warrior,'* in which I had been trained and formed, also followed with utmost respect the justice, benevolence, love, sincerity, honesty and self-control, as its maxims. The justice was a fundamental principle in the samurai code: crooked ways and unjust actions were considered degrading and inhumane. The love along with the benevolence, were supreme virtues and worthy acts, because there was no greater glory for a samurai than to be able to help others. Sincerity and honesty were as valued as their lives. The *"Bushi no ichi-gon"* or "The word of a samurai," transcended a mere pact of trust. When a samurai gave his word, it was his own life that he put as a guarantee, reason for which no pact, task or mission of a samurai was ever recorded in any writing.

The samurai also needed complete self-control and stoicism to be fully honorable. He was not to show signs of pain or joy in public and endured everything inwardly, since he was forbidden to moan or cry. He always showed a calm, serene demeanor and a mental composure that did not allow any passion to get in the way.

This hard and demanding education was necessary to become a true warrior.

With all this in my thoughts I asked myself the following questions:
- Would I do something denigrating and inhuman?
- Would I be failing to help others?
- Would I be breaking my word in any way?
- Was I ceasing to be honorable?
- Was I bearing it all inwardly?

- Was passion getting in the way of my mental attitude?
- Was I a true warrior...?

      I have known what it is to feel "love" but I had also just known, for the first time in my life, what it was to feel "hate" towards someone. But what happens when these two feelings are felt at the same time? Why could I feel so much love for someone and so much hatred for another human being at the same time? They were totally opposite emotions that were inside me. They were conflicting feelings facing each other and in two different extremes.
It was like feeling happy but sad at the same time.
"Love and hate are not blind, but they are blinded by the fire that they carry within." —*Friedrich Nietzsche.*

      My training and my values, as well as my philosophy of life were at stake, it was my litmus test for to know myself at the edge of the thin red line that separates us of the good and the evil, of the just and the unjust.
I couldn't put aside what I had felt inside of me: "death." I did not forget that I suffered the pain that is felt "when dying." I, who had only known good fortune and happiness in all its magnitude:
"I lived and died in one same day, with him, on that day!"
I had to get some rest and relax my mind; but all my thoughts were still focused on the love of my life and the wonderful existence that we had, until the day it rained so much blood from the sakura on me, covering me completely and causing me so much pain; until the day they killed us both....
      Dawned and I got up pushed by the need to continue with "my mission." I planned that I would visit the hermitage during the morning several times and at different times, as if I were just another parishioner in the area.

I needed to check if during the day he stayed there or went at dawn to another hiding place, and only came back at dusk to feed and spend the night, which was what I thought he was doing...

My costume from that day in the morning consisted, again, in a simple and devoted French woman from the small village with its fields of crops. I chose a wig with slightly wavy hair and in a red tone, with simple clothing and without superfluous ornaments; I also put on a wide straight-cut coat that allowed me to hang my fabulous binoculars inside without them being seen or noticed. This time, I wanted to bring his face as close as possible to be absolutely sure that he was "the devout" without any kind of doubts.

I wore some super glasses, which covered almost half my face, with a headscarf wrapped around my neck in the purest Parisian style of the 50's and 60's in the West. So I could appear to be a woman of more years.

I left, like most of the time, through the service door of the hotel, without anyone seeing me. I walked a couple of blocks and stopped for breakfast. After, I called a taxi, which dropped me off in another part of *Saint-Denis,* since I took into account that, every day, the police cars patrolled, in addition to the plainclothes officers, who controlled to those "registered" and "controlled" from that area.

I walked to the hermitage by another path, taking a additional detour around the outside of the district, but I wanted to know which side of the chapel he would go out, since the murderer, on the previous evening, had suddenly emerged from the north face.

I had to recognize and identify the limits of the surrounding territory, and thus, avoid any kind of possible unexpected surprises.

I went through meadows and fields with those houses widely separated from each other, and I found three abandoned. I inspected them, and they seemed to have no signs of movement. They lacked doors and windows. The habitability seemed impossible with the cold of the time. I checked several routes and came out on the North face, the same way he had gone out the night before.

I also accessed and inspected the west side of the hermitage. There were several possibilities: he could come from some of the isolated inhabited houses, or from outside the area that adjoined several kilometers away with a well-to-do and elegant neighborhood of the city (something that I discarded due to the lordship of the place), from the 'neighborhood with no name,' (where the police do not enter), or from the 'safe zone' of *Saint-Denis*, as I did (also unlikely due to the continuous police surveillance). After analyzing everything, there were only two unique possibilities that I was going to consider.

I entered in the hermitage; there was no churchgoer at that moment. I walked over to the lockable door of the underground room. I checked that it was closed. I looked through the key hole, the key was not placed inside, and even though it was dark, I visualized a couple of steps and a cement or concrete wall. This meant that he had left by locking with the key from the outside.

I studied the hermitage well, and imagined where I would place him so that I could look into his eyes and he could look into mine. I observed, next to the Holy Martyr, a metal and oil glass lamp with a wick. It was almost full of oil, and beside it, there were some long matches to light it. I thought that it would have been placed there by the parishioners to have some light if they needed it. I thought it would already serve me to see our faces, and not have to maintain the cell phone flashlight or another in my hand.

"The hands must always be free...!"

I went to the entrance gate to try to open it, so that when I pushing it, it would not make any noise, but there was no way to eliminate the creaking of the wood. During the day it was no problem, but in the silence of the night everything is different, and the sounds are perceived with greater clarity and distinction.

I left the hermitage; I walked by the surroundings and the path. I climbed high up the thickest and largest tree in the group of trees, where I camouflaged myself to observe from the heights, with the binoculars, in all directions and the maximum possible distance. I could see up to the house, where Katsuo-San said the young man who he followed entered. After an hour, I decided to leave the place to come back later, and I stayed hanging around the *Saint-Denis* area. I was walking around, like someone who goes shopping in the district, and played to detect the agents who were in plain clothes. It was easy because they were doing the same as me. Suddenly, I seemed to recognize the leader of the mosque from the 'neighborhood without a name,' and I was controlling him. He had entered into a bookstore and I went in, behind him. The man looked at the books, and I did the same until I caused some of them to fall next to him. I excused myself in French, and he said me that nothing was wrong in acceptable French. He helped me pick them up. I thought about starting a conversation and ending up asking him if he knew someone named: "Omar Sabbag," but I concluded that whatever the answer was, it would not be positive because they could alert him. It was preferable that he continue to feel safe and stay in the area. For what I let it pass…; I left the bookstore after buying some postcards to dissimulate my action.

I returned to the hermitage and placed myself on the last bench, at its outer end; in case someone entered I would have a full field of vision. Kneeling in prayer position, I put my brain to work because I was worried about the time I had. I couldn't stop thinking: How long would "the cowardly murderer" keep doing the same thing? What if today or tomorrow he changes places? What if he decides to leave the country and cross the border...? That uncertainty of not knowing what his plans were in the short term worried me, since it could cause a change in the current situation, the one I was calculating and controlling...

But I was also aware that I should not rush.

No one passed through the place. I went out and looked for another spot different from the group of trees that would allow me, when it got dark in the afternoon like the day before, to hide and camouflage myself to keep watch.

There was no more populated area, but between the trail and the north side, where he had emerged, there were some tangled wild bushes, a variety of blackberry, not very tall but dense, which you would skirt so as not to step on them, because they were thorny. I prepared a place for myself to lie down on the ground when I returned later, in the dark.

I went to the "safe zone" again; looked for a restaurant where I could eat something and wait until dark to return.

I turned on the cell phone. I had messages from my mother, my in-laws and the police officer Pierre-San; all wanted to know about me, and the agent also wanted to invite me to dinner when I want it.

Evening was beginning to fall and gradually darken. I went to occupy my new surveillance site in the chapel.

It was the most uncomfortable place, the thorns and spikes were digging into my legs like needles. As I was lying down and covered, I had less vision but was totally invisible. The time passed, and at the same time the day before, no one came. I looked in all directions with the binoculars and did not see anyone in the whole environment. I began to wonder if he had already changed of places and plans.

I was afraid of losing him! Thirty minutes later, in the distance from the beginning of the 'neighborhood without a name' path, an individual as coming. With the binoculars I was able to zoom in and enlarge the image, and I started recording as well. I could see him perfectly. It was a man, the same young man as the day before, only that he had changed his coat, it was brown and without hood. He was wearing a black sports cap. He was carrying a bag, probably with more provisions. He kept getting closer, never leaving the path. I looked the other sides to see where "the devout" would appear. I saw someone approaching from the west face, the same area that I had checked earlier that morning. He changed his approach: the day before he appeared from the North face and this time from the West. It meant that he was careful not to repeat the same route or the same time schedule (something logical in a concealment strategy with possibilities of follow-up). I kept recording everything as I watched him, bringing his face closer and zoomed in, enlarging it... It was him! But to make sure I looked for the 'mole' on his left cheek, and there it was...! It was the 'mark' that left no doubt as to his identification. He was wearing exactly the same clothes as the day before.

I continued recording them both... The other individual arrived at the entrance of the hermitage, and without letting go of the bag, stood waiting and looking everywhere. After a few moments, the two meet at the entrance. They open the door and enter, closing it again. Two minutes later, the young man who had brought him the supplies comes out, and returns along the path at a brisk pace.

For the "murderous terrorist" it was time to regain strength and sleep, hiding where he knew no one would look for him. Nothing was heard. He was very careful. But I could feel and smell his fear and cowardice; I saw it perfectly with the binoculars when I enlarged his face, his eyes and his look....

That night he would no longer move. He was there, locked in that room. Since I was not there all day, I assumed he was leaving in the early morning or at dawn, before any parishioner could come.

So I decided to end the surveillance and return to the hotel. On my way back, when I turned my cell phone back on, I had more calls and messages. One message was from the Japanese Ambassador to France, telling me that he had news and to contact him as soon as possible. I called him and he told me that, in the next 24 hours, the ashes of Takashi-San would already be at my disposal to collect them, and that he, in person, together with the forensic doctor, had selected the vital bones, for the later traditional ceremony in Japan, which will be placed together with the ashes. I was glad that I could finally take Takashi-San home, but on the other hand there was "my mission," which I had not yet accomplished.

In the hotel room, I took a long relaxing bath while I thought about carrying out "my mission."

I wanted to go in the early morning, before sunrise to keep an eye on my target: "the devout," to see when he left the hermitage, where he was going and what he did until he returned at dusk.

I had to buy an "urn" for my boyfriend's ashes, as I was not going to allow them to be transported in a simple travel case, like the one I was shown when I went to the burial chamber. And I had to finish the "mission": Inexcusably the next day! It would be the last night I would have to conclude my personal fight, to finalize and fulfill my most longed-for wish to have Takashi-San's "murderer" in front of me.

I prayed to the *Kami* or *Gods:* that he would still be there the next day, that he would not change strategy or location.

I plotted the plan in my head and finished my bath.

I went down to dinner at the restaurant. The waiters were very nice to me and always asked me how I was doing. They always treated me wonderfully. I informed them that, in 24 hours, I could collect the ashes and end my trip. One of them asked me that he had read that the Japanese put the bones of our deceased with the ashes, and if I could tell him how that worked. I explained that not all the bones were put, and that in Japan, death is seen as something that is impossible to avoid; it is the beginning of a new stage. After watching over the deceased, by law he is cremated, and by the belief that the body returns to earth after death, while the spirit remains and moves independently of the state of the body. The relatives collect the bones from the ashes and transfer them to the urn using large toothpicks. This is known as *"kotsuage,"* and it is the only time in Japan when it is appropriate that two people to hold something at the same time with chopsticks, whether made of wooden or metal. In any other situation, holding something with chopsticks by two people at the same time is considered a major social error, since it is reminiscent of a funeral. The foot bones are collected first, and the head bones last. This is done to ensure that the deceased is not face down in the urn. The hyoid bone, which is located in the neck, and is the intersection between the pharynx, jaw and skull, is the most important bone of all. The ashes can be divided and shared among more than one urn, and these can remain in the family home for a period of time or can be taken directly to the cemetery. Before and after the funeral, the family mourns and shows their respects for the deceased. A white lantern is placed outside the house as a sign that they are in mourning. The dynastic relatives place them on the family altar of the house, along with the photographs of the deceased, and every day the family members offer incense and prayers to their deceased.

They were surprised with the explanation, and said that it was clear that they were very different cultures, and I replied that this was the curious and beautiful thing about the world, that each place has things to teach or show us, and we must learn from each of the differences and always respect. They let me finish dinner quietly. When I finished I went back to my room. I had a lot to think about. I looked on the internet for a funeral shop where I could buy the urn to transport the ashes the next day. I thought a lot about this, about having Takashi-San's ashes with me. I felt that it meant that it would be the only physical thing I would have of the man that I loved so much, and whom I caressed and hugged..., something that I would never do again. With all this feeling, I had more wishes to put the "culprit" in front of me, but I knew that hatred and anger are not good allies in the real fight...

I called my in-laws, and told them that in two days I would finalize everything and organize the return with the ashes of their beloved and only son. They were happy that I would soon return with the love of their lives.

My parents felt the same, they were happy for the soon return and very eager to be together living and accompanying me in the duel. My father asked me if all the terrorists had already been arrested, because the news there said that some had escaped to *Belgium*... I told him that I had understood that only one had fled, but that I believed that he had already been arrested or that he had died, that I was not very aware of the information. And he said: "Ah! All right, then, are you all right?"

« My father knew me better than anyone else in the world. He knew what I felt. He knew my pain. He knew what I was like and there was no need for words between us. »

I set the alarm clock for 4 a.m., and I request a taxi for 4:30 a.m. When I woke up I dressed in black completely, I gathered my hair in a bun, took my night glasses and a black wool cap. I also took my binoculars and went to the corner where I asked the cab driver to pick me up. We arrived at *Saint-Denis* and I quickly headed towards the hermitage, hoping that he was still there and had not left the place before my arrival.

I wanted to see him come out! I positioned myself in the set of trees to have a better view from afar, and see what he was doing and where would he go. I waited, and at 6 o'clock, he came out with the crossed black bag (the same one, that he didn't carry in the afternoon, but he did carry the night before). He had changed in his gray hooded sweatshirt for a dark blue one, but the rest of his clothes and shoes were the same. In a calm way he started walking on the north side; he did not look anywhere, he felt safe... I followed him; I enjoyed performing my movements in *"Shinobi iri"* (technique of walking and moving in silence, specialty of the *Ninja*). Since I was a child, training in nature was like a game for me, although this time, it was not... It was immensely important that he continue with that security that he showed: "he believed that no one saw him and that he was alone." Hence, it was crucial not to make any kind of noise or sounds that were not part of the environment. He crossed the fields of the houses, one after another, in the same North direction until after 14 minutes which changed direction to the West. He went through the wide fields, dodging and avoiding approaching the houses until, suddenly, he went directly to one of the houses and entered it.

His tour lasted a total of 22 minutes, always maintaining the same light step.

I placed myself hiding in the land in front; it had an abandoned and totally collapsed house. The house he had entered was old but in good conditions and habitable. With my binoculars I watched through the windows. He had turned on the light when he entered. From where I stood I had a perfect view of him and the interior. He was in the kitchen; he took out food from the black bag he was carrying. He was preparing breakfast... and he began to eat quietly! Another man appeared in the house, and then another... The three of them were in the kitchen and each one was preparing their own food. Two more came out walking through the house. And yet another individual sat in an armchair in the room that appeared to be the living room. There were a total of six people, all males, living together in that house... It seemed that, one by one, they entered what could be the bathroom (that area could not be seen because there was a wall in front), as they came out with a towel, drying themselves. They all passed to that living room, and on a carpet on the floor of the room, they got on their knees and touched the floor with their foreheads for Muslim prayer. They were all part of the same group and gave refuge to one of their own... However it was, it was certain that he moved with and among their own... He was in their zone from the beginning! He probably stayed in that house all day long protected by his friends. And, at night, for fear of searches and police interventions, he would hide in the "Catholic hermitage," where no one would look for a Muslim or Islamist.

That had been his only plan! And this proved that I was right in saying that he was a coward and that he was afraid.

While they were praying in the house, I left the place on the east side, skirting the outside until I arrived to the main road of *Saint-Denis*. I already knew the area well and I was able to orient myself perfectly, both during the day and at night. It had dawned already and I took a taxi back to the hotel.

There were no people on the streets. The city was still asleep...

I had breakfast and went back to my room. I changed my clothes. I called Katsuo-San to pick me up, and we went to the funeral store that I had located on the internet.

I was met by a very kind man. I chose the "wooden urn" for cremation ashes. It was the most beautiful of all, with incredible finishes and double customizable plaque to engrave an inscription in honor of the deceased. I called my mother-in-law to tell her about my choice, in case she preferred something different. She let me know that the wooden urn with double plaque was a very good option, that she liked it very much, because they could put one inscription and I could put another. I told her that I wouldn't know what to put, and she told me not to worry, that we would do it together when I got back, and that she wanted me to buy that urn if I liked it.

I bought the urn and went back to the hotel to drop it off. I called Pierre-San to accept his invitation for a meal, if he was doing well in two hours (lunch time in Japan: 12 noon). He said, very happy, that it was perfect for him.

I called my boss in Tokyo to inform him that Takashi-San's ashes would be delivered to me the next morning. He told me that the company had already been informed, and that they were waiting for me to confirm the date for the return flight. I told him that the day after of the delivery, on the first flight, it seemed perfect to me. He replied that they would get to it immediately and he would call me again to give me the details. He informed me that I did not have to worry about anything, that I simply I should go to the company's counter, and that they would have everything ready there. He also notified me that I would have the airline's authorization to carry the urn with me (since that was what I had requested) and not in the cabin.

I finished my calls, and with Katsuo-San, we went to Kobayashi Sensei's Dojo because he had already told me from the beginning that when I had to go collect the ashes, he would accompany me. I knew he would be at his school and wanted to communicate it to him personally. He received me with real enthusiasm and joy. Upon entering I greeted the *Tokonoma*, the altar.

I saw, on the wall of weapons, some ropes of different styles and sizes. I took one between my hands and we began to talk about the *"Art of Hojōjutsu"* or *"Nawajutsu"*: it is the traditional Martial Art of Japan in which the opponent, whether a prisoner of war or a detainee, was tied up using a rope. The main reason for tying someone up was to keep prisoners alive and prevent them from escaping. Another objective was to ensure that prisoners were presented, and brought before a judge to be tried for the crimes they had committed. The *Nawa* (rope) is part of the so-called *Torimono Dougu* or arrest and detention techniques. In Japan, the *Hojōjutsu* was incorporated into the training and knowledge of the samurai and was integrated into their combat skills, but before it was a specialty of *Ninjutsu* or *Ninja*.

Some of the ropes used were only about 30 centimeters long, while others were more than 10 meters long; being the latter used today by police forces, called *"Okappiki"* or *"Doshin."*

Most of the ropes were made of braided linen, but hemp and silk rope were also used. For the latter, use was made of the *"Sageo"* or *'cord'* of the *"Saya"* or *'sheath'* of the *Katana*, which was attached to the *"obi"* or *'belt,'* having very varied techniques and uses.

The police forces carry the rope in such a way that one end of the rope protrudes, called *"Torinawa"* or *'capture rope,'* which allows the prisoner to be quickly detained and immobilized to transport him to the interrogation post, to the court or to his execution. The techniques make it possible to arrest multiple attackers tied together, so it requires an important knowledge of human anatomy, and in particular, of all the joints since, on occasions, it does not only seek to immobilize, it also takes care not to cause severe damage and even provoke a sensual reaction, which is called *"Shibari."* Although these techniques have been supplanted by the use of metal handcuffs, in Japan many Martial Arts Masters continue to teach the *"Art of Hojōjutsu,"* and it is an important part of the curriculum, even today, of the modern police of the country.

We talked for a long time about this discipline and the use of the ropes, while I continued with a braided linen rope in my hands, which was thin but very consistent. It was about 7 meters long, and I liked its touch (it was the same material and touch as one that a *Kobudō* Master had given me, when I was very young), to which *Sensei* referred explaining that I was holding the one that for him had a lot of significance, because it was given to him by his *Hojōjutsu* Master, as a memory when he studied its handling years ago. I went to leave it in its place again, when he told me:

"No Haru-San! It will be an honor for me that you have it. Passing it on to you will honor me greatly. Maybe someday, sometime, it will be useful to you."

"Thank you very much *Sensei!*" I replied bowing and holding the rope between both hands. "The honor is and will be mine. I will have it and keep it as a treasure."

"Remember that your eyes are very communicative and transparent. Do not forget that your look, always mysterious, is very special my dear Haru-San. I beg you to take care of yourself at all times, and never forget that you always have me here."

We said goodbye until the next day that we would go together to the forensic pathology building. I told him that I was going to have lunch with his police student, and that way I would thank him and say goodbye to him.

I went to the appointment with Pierre-San. He was already there, standing by the entrance of a Japanese restaurant (he had wanted and chosen it), the "Matsuyama" in the center of Paris. We greet each other and enter. It had a beautiful interior decoration of *"Sakura in bloom"* or 'cherry trees' (something that haunts me even in Paris!), with an elegant and discreet air. It had a great specialty in *Sushi* dishes. They offered us a welcome cocktail and gave us the menu. Pierre-San said that he was in love with Japanese food and especially *Sushi;* he explained to me that for him it was more than just a meal, that it was a state of pure energy. We ordered: *"Maki"* (rice rolls wrapped with seaweed), *"Sushi"* (slices of raw fish with rice) and *"Sashimi"* (slices of raw fish). In reality, the service was excellent and the fresh fish was of a very good quality. We were talking, while we enjoyed savoring lunch. He asked me how I had been all those days in Paris, and if I had had the courage to visit and get to know it. I told him that no, I had not been in the mood, since my state of pain and mourning prevented me from doing so; that *I had come to do what I had to do,* that I would repatriate my boyfriend the next day, and that he could finally return and rest in his country and in his home. He lamented that we had met "in and by" those circumstances, and that he wished it had not been so, but that it was only the fault of the terrorists and no one else. He took the opportunity to tell me that six more had been arrested, and that they had found the explosives that they had prepared to commit more attacks, for which a few more attacks had been prevented and aborted. And that, due to the speed of the police and military operations, they could not continue and did not take place, because what they really intended would have caused thousands of deaths and an uncountable number of wounded; which would have been much more catastrophic and of an inhuman magnitude.

His face reflected the fear of that magnitude that could have occurred, as well as the tiredness and exhaustion, for which I told him:

"The police and military forces have done a great job successfully and with great speed, there is no doubt about that, and all sources at the international level acknowledge this. All of you have left your skin, from minute one, for days and nights without rest. The citizens will appreciate, value and they will be grateful, I am sure of that. It is that everything lived has similarity to a state of war. It is what it seemed when seeing the images, and thanks to the fact that they did not commit all the acts that they had programmed and they have been aborted thanks to your interventions. You can only be proud of yourselves!"

"Of course, you are right: it is the same horror of a war," Pierre-San said.

"It's worse Pierre-San, because in a war you know who you are fighting and facing, when and how. These terrorists do not confront, they do not warn, they are cowards and they kill only innocent people, by surprise and treachery. They don't face the army head-on; they don't have the courage for that. It is hatred, evil and criminality, which takes away their right to live in the civilization with the rest of the citizenry."

"That's right Haru-San, but they are there, in many cities and countries, and it is with what we have to live in the future."

"We always end up talking about the same thing, and neither you nor I, can put an end or solution to all of that. But maybe we can contribute with our little grain of sand in that enormous global mass, who knows...! For my part, I thank you for your friendship and your police work, as well as to all the security forces that have dedicated all their efforts, and more, in catching the culprits and preventing a greater tragedy, with many more victims..."

"As soon as he tries to cross the border... That one falls! It's a matter of days or weeks…! I promise you that this individual will pay it too, Haru-San!"

"I'm sure YES! Thanks for everything appreciated Pierre-San! It really has been a true honor meeting you."

"The honor has been mine, Haru-San! And, once again: I'm so sorry! I also want you to know that I share your pain; I don't know what I would do if I found myself in your place. You have shown to be a very strong woman. I wish you all the best."

We finished lunch and said goodbye. He wished me a good trip and said that maybe he would visit Japan, to which I replied that he would count on me if he did that trip, that I would be his guide, and take him to the best *Sushi* in the country.

« Pierre-San, besides being a good policeman, is a good man, very honest and kind. When we said goodbye, I left thinking that it would be great to see him again in Japan, some day... »

I headed quickly to the hotel; I had to prepare my last night of "mission," my last chance!

I quoted Katsuo-San for the next day at 9 a.m. in the morning to go collect the ashes. The Ambassador also called me to tell me that he would be present and that we would meet there.

Already in my room, I made myself comfortable to prepare. I meditated to prepare my body and mind for what would be the most crucial moment of my philosophy of life and of the *Budō* or *'way of the warrior.'*

I concentrated all my energy on "the devout," on the murderous terrorist, so that he would continue in the same place, that he would stay there one more night, that he would not change his plan, that he would appear one more time, just once! There was no more time. The clock ticked and set the time. In a few hours the moment I had most wanted after the death of Takashi-San would take place: to have in front of me the murderer, the culprit, the terrorist who pressed the button and detonated the bomb that killed him, the one who was still free and hiding like a coward. He would be in front of me to look into his eyes, for him to look into mine, and look at the man who he snatched me. I wanted to show him *"the mistake"* that he committed, and ask him: What does he feel after causing the death of so many innocents...? Pleasure...? Does he feel more of a man...?

I showered and prepared myself by dressing slowly, very slowly..., while my mind became conscious, and it was unified with my body to have a correct action at the precise moment. I took off my *"Tsuba Mokume"* pendant (gift from Yoshida Sensei and Takashi-San) and the *"crane and cherry tree ring"* (from Takashi-San).
I dressed totally in black, very comfortable and I would wear, in due time, the *hijab*, the black *veil*, but not as a Muslim but as a *Ninja,* as a *"Kunoichi"* (ninja woman), as a hood or *Zukin,* which is ideal to hide the face and leave only the eyes visible (which was the only thing the "murderer" had to see of me). I also wore polarized night glasses to move around the area (not to show that I was Japanese woman in those neighborhoods, for safety reasons), until I reaching the hermitage. I placed on my belt the *nawa* or rope (a gift from Kobayashi Sensei), like the Japanese police, with the end sticking out of the belt, to pull on it at the moment of taking out and using the rope. I had my hands free. Everything I

needed to carry: passport, money and my *"Omamori"* (the lucky charm, gift from Takashi-San that I have always carried with me), I wore it on my seat belt (special for travelers) with an inside pocket and attached to my body. I took a picture of Takashi-San from my wallet and put it in my pocket.

My plan consisted of attacking the two individuals by surprise (if the same situation as the previous nights occurred) when they are in front of the gate of the hermitage, at the precise moment they are going to enter and push them both inside; disabling the individual who carries to him the supplies by "knocking him out," that is KO, with an accurate and strong knock, either behind the ear, in the neck, in the throat, in the solar plexus, kidneys, nose... This would depend on the many and varied "circumstances" that occurred. Since you cannot plan exactly a specific technique or movement because nothing is fixed... Everything is changing...

And to the "criminal," I would make that my sudden and crushing entry project him forward and he would fall face down (prone position); I would keep him under control to frisk and disarm him (the police announced him as dangerous and armed), and I would proceed to tie him up to place him in front of me.

That was all I could foresee beforehand. From then on, I had to count on all the unforeseen events and possible changes: that more than one person would come to bring him supplies, that the routes and schedules could change and be different, that the weather could change too, that no one would come to the hermitage that night, that he could stay in the other house with the other individuals, etc.

My mind prepared for all the unforeseen. The only sure thing for me was that "it had to be that night."

At last, it began to get dark in the early afternoon of my longed-for day. I had called a taxi, as usual, and it drove me to *Saint-Denis*, leaving me at another point (I always had in mind that, each time, they left me in a different place), even if it meant walking more. You never know who is watching (to begin with, I knew about the civilian agents who were guarding the area...). To get to the hermitage, I also always changed my routes and accessed through different places bordering roads or crossing fields full of bushes, on the outside of the sector, which also took more time and difficulty.

I arrived at the chapel, after a long detour, and decided that the best position to act most quickly was the area of the group of trees and shrubs, the one that had less distance to the gate of the entrance to arrive quickly on them at the precise moment that they pushed the door.

I placed between the bushes, took off my glasses, put on my veil as a *Ninja* hood, put on my gloves and waited, asking the *Kami* or Gods, to give me the opportunity, that let him appear and grant me my wish... That I was asking for an innocent and good man, who never hurt anyone, who only loved, and was killed without having fulfilled his dreams: to handcuff us and die of old age.

I had spent more than an hour without moving, begging and waiting to see the routine of the previous days. They were delayed, and I wanted to think that it was logical since they also changed the schedule. Forty minutes later, I spotted a person taking the path leading to the hermitage from the 'neighborhood with no name.' I hoped he was the one of the supplies. It was still far away, and I didn't bring my binoculars so as not to carry anything on me. That night my eyes would be enough! I did not see anyone else appear anywhere. The other individual was still advancing at a leisurely pace, approaching, and I could see that he was carrying the bag of provisions.

I was happy because the gods had heard me!

As he got closer I could see that he was not the same as the day before; this man was shorter and chubbier He was wearing a wool cap and no hood. I still didn't see anyone else approaching from the other side. I was attentive, because I could feel him but I still couldn't see him. I was looking at the other man who was closing the distance, and I already had a good vision of him. He was bare-faced, with a very dark complexion and a short beard. He was about 30 years old and of Arab ethnicity. Finally, "the devout assassin" appeared from the west; he was walking at a lighter pace than the other individual. He was wearing again the same outfit as the day before and with the hood trying to cover his face. They were each approaching to the hermitage, but... 200 meters before, "the assassin" intercepted the other individual on the path...! They barely greeted each other and he took the bag of the other. He turned around and went alone to the hermitage. The other one, also turned around, and went back the way he had come.

I thought to myself: Well, one less! So much the better!

"The devout" was walking calmly, but looking to all sides, towards the entrance of the chapel. He stood in front of the entrance door. I was right behind his back, ready to go out at high speed, but in silence. He had one hand busy with the bag. He put his arms on the heavy gate to push it and... Just at that instant, I fell on him from behind using *Tai-Ken* (hit with the body) taking me to him with the door ahead, hitting him, at the same time, with the elbow in the cervical, performing a technique in movement or form of projection called *Taki Otoshi Nage* which means: dropping in a "cascade" or crushing, in the form of *"nagare"* (to flow like water, to let oneself fall to drag our adversary in the fall), projecting him and causing him to fall face down with his face against the ground, causing him pain and daze.

Then I let the whole weight of my body fall, supporting and hitting with my left knee on his back, while I grabbed his arms from behind dislocating his shoulders and maintaining control of his arms and back, my other leg controlled his, exerting pressure *(kyusho)* on vital points of his legs. All the control and pressure applied, together with the dislocation of arms and shoulders, caused him great pain. Exercising total control, I pulled the end of the rope or *nawa* from my belt by pulling on it, and proceeded to tie him. I entwined the rope between his arms, chest, neck and his crotch (pressing very hard on *Kinteki* or testicles, causing him great pain), and I knotted it conscientiously, with specific knots learned in the Art of *Nawajutsu* or Art of rope-tying the opponent. I frisked him and found his gun on his right side. I took it from him, and kept it on my back tucked into my belt inside my pants. He also carried a good-sized pocket knife in the inside left pocket of his coat, which I put in my pocket. He had no documentation of any kind, no money, only a large metal key in his right front trouser pocket (a key I assumed was from the iron door of the room where he was hiding in the chapel), which I also kept. He couldn't move, he was stunned by the blow and the fall. After a couple of minutes he began to babble, muttering words in Arabic... I took him and dragged him across the terracotta tiled floor of the chapel to the front, next to the Holy Martyr, the place of the oil lamp with its long matches (which I had checked the day before). I lit the wick; I could already see his surprised and stunned face. With one hand I grabbed the oil lamp, and with the other I dragged him four meters to the door of the locked room. I put the lamp on the floor, and took out the key that I had found in his pocket. I opened the door; there were about four steps to the wall and a landing on the stairs; I grabbed the oil lamp and I pushed him kicking him; he rolled down in a bad way; another six rungs more, and in the same way, I kicked him and he continued rolling... I went up and closed the door from the inside. Someone could come and... Nothing and nobody was going to take that moment away from me!

The room was disagreeable, it was full of garbage and many paper plates and plastic cups, used and dirty. There were a couple of gas bottles with a stove, several buckets of water, and many soda cans everywhere. There were clothes hanging off and thrown away. On one side there was a single bed, a table, two chairs, and a stool. I sat him on one of the chairs, undid some knots to have more rope, and I tied him securely. He was still groggy and sore. I waited a few minutes and asked him:

"Is your name Omar Sabbag?"

He uttered a few words in Arabic...

And I hit him, warning him that I knew he spoke French. I repeated the question once more...

"Yes! So what? Chinese whore or whatever you are...!" he said with an aversion face and in a jocular and cocky tone, still stunned...

I took out of my pocket the picture of my boyfriend; I put it in front of his face forcing him to look at it, while I said to him:

"Take a good look! This person has been killed by yours, your people, but you pressed the detonator. You killed him along with hundreds of other people. What do you feel? I want you to tell me, how and what does it feels like to do something like this?"

He spoke again in Arabic and that time I made him feel the pain in his body, using the *"Kyusho Jutsu"* (the human being possesses vital points or meridians, which help us to disable or even kill an individual, as well as it also allows to alleviate or cure certain ailments; there are more than 300 points throughout the human body...), and I applied pressure on the vital point: *Sonu*: point located at the base of the neck, above the sub-sternal or clavicular hollow (at the level of the thoracic center). This point is very painful and can cause death if its pressure is not controlled.

"Stop it! Stop it!" He screamed in pain and showing signs of difficulty breathing. "What do you want me to say you, Chinese whore? Who was that, your boyfriend? The worst thing is that you were not with him and you would have died too, Chinese whore bitch!"

"That was your mistake!"

"What mistake?"

"Me, I was your only and worst mistake!"

"If he's dead, I'm glad, and now what...? It's the Holy War!" he said, while he still suffered from the pain caused.

I applied pressure on another point located in the free spaces of the 11th and 12th ribs (which cause fainting) with control, because I didn't want him to faint. I wanted him conscious at all times...!

"Stop it now! Aaah! Stop it! You are a fucking Chinese woman...! Tell me what do you want from me?" he cried choking with pain. "What do you want...?"

I looked into his eyes, making him look into mine. I wanted him to read what mine were telling him, and I also wanted to see inside his own to know what someone like him felt (apart from the pain caused by me...). I wanted to see if there was any humanity in his spirit. I wanted to know if someone like that could have something inside his being that would prevent me from executing him (all the teachings, values and transmissions received were swirling in my mind...). I took the photo of Takashi-San again, and I put it back in front of his eyes and said:

"This is for him and for the hundreds of people you have killed, that is, if you have not killed more previously... I have only been able to see in you an unscrupulous murderer, who does not feel or respect the lives of others, but his own. You are afraid to die, which proves that I was right: you are a coward! You have not even killed yourself for your cause. You don't fight to the death for it, so you lack courage and value. You make a war and you are not even worthy of being called a "warrior," because you are very far from being one. What I have said: you are just a coward and a monster! I would like to know: why do you kill innocent people?"

"Why? Because I want to and I can! This is because all of you are unfaithful to the doctrine. All governments must be subdued, because there is no other God than Allah, and Muhammad is our prophet. This is an all-out jihad against the West, and the only way to rehabilitate them is by murdering, killing as many as possible until you all submit. This is my mission! It's my only mission!"

"Do you consider yourself a martyr to the cause of jihad? Do you expect the reward of going to "paradise," which you call "garden of souls" by murdering? And that there you will be immortal and live surrounded by luxury? Is that what you think...?"

"The "final judgment" will come and all the humanity will disappear because all of you are cursed! I will be rewarded, yes! And it will be because I will have contributed to spreading their message by fighting the infidels to the death."

"Oh yeah...? So, why aren't you suicidal? Why didn't you immolate yourself? Don't you want to go to the Garden of Eden like others of your same cause?"

"Not yet, I have to keep fighting for the cause! Eliminating more infidels and causing more terror to the hostiles. Has it been clear to you already, fucking Chinese or Filipino, or whatever you are...? Nothing would satisfy me more than putting a bomb on you right now and watching you volatilize in the air. Is this the answer that you wanted? Tell me, what do you want now?"

Despite his bad French, and his complaints of pain as he spoke, I understood him perfectly. With my serious countenance, in which he only saw my cold gaze, I answered him:

"Look me in the eye! And listen carefully to the answer to your question: 'I want to take your life just as you took the life of my beloved and the lives of hundreds of other innocents!' Now, I know how you are and how you think. Now it is clear to me that you do not deserve to live among us humans. But, you know what...? Despite everything ..., I am going to do something good for you: I am going to help you to reunite with yours and you can receive your reward in paradise."

"You're going to kill me! Aren't you? Is that what you're going to do?"

He pronounced with difficulty, due to the pain he continued to feel from the applied pressure points; at the same time that his body was already trembling, and his eyes, now yes! They were wide open...; and that hesitant and arrogant smile had already disappeared...

I paused, a moment of silence, a crucial moment..., while I looked into his eyes, in which I only saw hatred, barbarism, contempt and more deaths... (He kept waiting, in fear, awaiting the sentence...) until, with total conscience and impartiality, I ended up telling him:

"I give you the option to do it yourself..!. Or I will!"

There was again a long, dark and sepulchral silence, until the only sound was a fluid through his vibrating body.

I disappeared into the darkness...

Satisfied, I said to myself:

"I have done what I had to do!"

"I am a true Kunoichi!"

I went back to the hotel. I took a long and careful bath, rubbing my whole body and feeling that my stay in Paris was coming to an end… Then, calmly, I bagged all the clothes and accessories that I had bought for "my mission." I wanted and had to get rid of them. I also had the courage to pick up Takashi-San's clothes from the room. I lowered all the bags exiting through the side door of the hotel, and I walked a couple of streets to put everything in a container, which I had already seen of "clothes for humanitarian aid."

Back in the room, lying on the bed, I mentally spoke with my boyfriend, I told him about it..., and although it cost me a lot, I managed to fall asleep soundly.

The next day a beautiful winter day dawned. On my cell phone I had messages from my boss giving me the time of the flight, and the company with which I would travel the next day back to Japan. I got ready and picked up the wooden urn. The time had come! I had to collect Takashi-San's ashes. I went downstairs for breakfast, and Katsuo-San arrived, who told me to forgive him, but he had to tell me that I was very pretty and radiant. I thanked him and we headed to pick up the Kobayashi's marriage.

They were on the sidewalk of their house waiting, and as soon as they got into the car: the same thing, they showered me with compliments and flattery. *Sensei* showed me the chopsticks that he carried to transfer the bones from the body to the urn.

We arrived at the pathological building, that building with internal cold. When we entered the Ambassador was already inside, he was talking to other people. He signaled for us to wait in the living room. He went with those people down the long corridor and returned after a few minutes. He led us to another room, where the medical examiner and another doctor were also present, and they showed me, placing it on the table, a metal box. I stared at that sad and cold grayish metal box... The coroner opened it, and showed me the chosen bones from Takashi-San's body along with the ashes. The Ambassador and Kobayashi Sensei took my wooden urn and passed the ashes; then, the *Sensei* with the chopsticks transferred the bones one by one placing them according to the anatomical shape. I preferred to reserve that honor for the funeral ceremony in Japan, together with my in-laws.

A bailiff entered the room to hand me the Cremation Certificate, and placed a sticker on the outside with some numbers and the name of the deceased: *Takashi Yagami.*

They wrapped the wooden urn in plastic with a special seal and handed it to me, placing it in my hands.

They also handed me the rest of his belongings because the investigation was closing: his Japanese passport (stained with blood), the ballpoint pen (gift from his father), and my love card (torn and bloodstained).

They all made me the Japanese greeting with reverence and gave me their condolences, regretting the circumstances that had occurred, and wishing me a safe return trip.

At that time, the Ambassador handed me the rest of the official documents for the "repatriation."

With my heart broken into a thousand pieces and the urn in my hands, I thanked everyone present and on behalf of all the relatives and loved ones of Takashi-San for the respect, the attention to my person, as well as for the intensive work and dedication they had showed all the time.

We all left with sadness on our faces and the silence as the only ally, towards the vehicle that would take us away from that place. Sitting in the vehicle, I had the urn with the remains of my boyfriend on my legs and held with my hands on top, as if I wanted to embrace what was inside...

Sophie-San took out a very nice bag and said:

"Let's put the box in here, is it okay for you?"

"Seem right! It's very pretty!"I said nodding and putting the box inside.

"It's for the trip, so no one will know what's inside; they will only see a nice bag."

I kindly replied: "Thank you Sophie-San!"

I told Katsuo-San to stop at the restaurant of the explosion. I wanted to share and show Kobayashi Sensei and Sophie-San the exact place where Takashi-San died. There were still remains of the flowers that I had left, along with others that had been left by Parisian citizens, scattered all over the sidewalk. I showed them the blood stain that I felt was Takashi-San's, with the two childish hearts and the letters "amour" which were becoming more and more erased as the days went by. Sophie-San said that we show a minute of silence and respect in his memory; that we speak to him mentally and we show him our affection. There we were all three concentrated, and when I spoke to him: I told him that here he had lost his physical life, but that he was already with me and we were returning home together, to "our paradise", as he liked to call it; that "I had done everything that had to be done", that he could now feel at peace, and that his blood spilled on the ground would fade with time... but that all those feelings we had were never going to be erased, nor were we going to forget all the love that we live... When we opened our eyes again, there were more people around us praying and others paying their respects in silence.

And it is that still Paris continued crying to its dead, to the horror suffered. There was still pain, sadness and darkness in *"the city of light."*

Sophie-San had prepared a meal on the occasion of saying their last goodbye to Takashi-San (which is normal in Japan, since ceremonies are held in honor of the deceased with a lot of food, sweets and sake), for what we headed to their house. She made many Japanese variety dishes, many sweets and Kobayashi Sensei offered exquisite rice *sake*. We set the table; we placed a plate for Takashi-San and served him food and a cup of *sake*.

To finish, Sophie-San took out a bouquet of beautiful fresh white roses; she handed each of us a rose to place in front of Takashi-San's plate, and at that moment, we wished him: "a good journey in peace to the afterlife".

Kobayashi Sensei said the following words looking towards his plate full of food with the flowers spread out in front:

"I am convinced that you are already at peace. Travel happily with the same happiness with which you have lived. You go full of love just as you have loved. Find your place in the afterlife!

Then, he lit incense. In the act, Sophie-San and I took our incense, and the three of us put it together in the bowl of sand in the center of the table.

The smell spread throughout the room!

I appreciated the detail that they wanted to say goodbye to Takashi-San; it was a gift and an honor. It was time to say goodbye to them and it was a very long farewell, full of very sentimental and emotional moments.

We agreed that we would meet again in Japan very soon, and when I was already at the door about to leave, *Sensei* whispered to me:

"I hope, dear Haru Yoshida Sensei, that the 'nawa' (rope) has been useful to you. It was my gift to both of you!"

"Ossu *Sensei!*"

« The term *Ossu,* of Japanese origin, is a daily expression in the world of Martial Arts; it is used to replace expressions such as: thank you, delighted, bye, understood, I agree, that's right, hello, etc. It is exactly a contraction of two words: *Oshi:* literally means: "push," symbolizing the spirit in combat, with a positive and determined attitude.

Shinobu: means "endure, resist, and suffer," which expresses courage and the spirit of perseverance, always keeping the morale high.

The result is *Ossu*, which is pronounced *Oss*, literally says: push resistance, push suffering, which also means patience, determination and perseverance. »

After the farewell, I returned to the hotel where I would spend my last night in the city that experienced one of the most tragic horrors in the annals of history.

When saying goodbye to Katsuo-San until the early morning that would take me, for the last time, to the airport, he wanted to know what happened to "my mission…" I stared at him in silence and he said: "Ossu Yoshida Sensei!"

I went up to my room. I prepared my luggage; I had the travel suitcase ready along with the urn bag that would travel in hand with me. I made the appropriate calls to the families and spoke to everyone for a while. I already felt at home! It would be a question of hours...

I had dinner at the hotel; it was my last night, and I said goodbye to all the employees who had treated me so well and so excellently, thanking them for their understanding, compassion, as well as all their cuddles and tenderness towards me.

When I finished thanking them, they applauded me! I felt ashamed, but: I smiled!

The alarm clock rang, it was still night, and after getting ready, I stayed a moment looking at the room and the bed where he had been before me, where his things were when I arrived, where I had felt him all the time, where I had mourned his absence and his loss so much, where I missed him and talked to him every day and every night... I breathed deeply…! I took my luggage, closed that door, and handed over at the reception the key that would jealously guard "the secrets that happened there."

Katsuo-San was waiting; he took my luggage and we set off. I watched the beautiful city, still dark with its bright lights, during the journey.

I was finally at Paris-Charles de Gaulle Airport!

It was 7 a.m. and my flight was leaving at 9 a.m.

Katsuo-San was carrying my travel bag, and I was carrying my hand bag (so pretty from Sophie-San) with the urn. We went to the Japan Airlines Corporation, or JAL, counter. I was informed that my reservation was in first class, and that they were fully informed of my situation. The flight attendant showed me her heartfelt condolences. No one had asked me for anything but I presented the official repatriation documents and from the urn; the flight attendant asked me if I wanted to carry the urn with me or if I preferred it to be in the captain's cabin. I said that: "It would go with me!" She affixed a carry-on duct tape and another that read: "Fragile."

Katsuo-San and I went to have a coffee in the VIP lounge. There was a great buffet and drinks in a large comfortable and relaxing space. We sat down and talked about how life can suddenly change, and take a 180 degree turn without wanting or expecting it. He told me that he had never experienced such a situation with any client, nor had he been with someone like me. That having met me, in such a hard and difficult situation, had taught him a lot. That sharing with a *Budō Sensei* had been "a unique experience," and he was very grateful what he had learned in those days; and he wanted to make it clear that he would not forget me, and that everything in me surprised him: my person, my philosophy, my courage and bravery...

« I think that is surprising what seems unknown and mysterious, but that was part of my education and training throughout my life. Perhaps I had a different existence than the common one and that was surprising, even for the Japanese. But he did not ask again about the end of "my mission." His silence from what he had seen, heard and experienced, was guaranteed. I have always had a deep respect for him and a big thank you. I hope he will be a happy person! »

The plane took off heading for our home. Takashi-San was with me in my seat; I did not separate myself from him. I had him with me, next to me at all times. I had too many hours of flight time to think and I thought a lot, and about everything. I observed "the city of love and light" from the air, and it seemed impossible to me, with those wonderful views, that a tragedy of such magnitude could have occurred. Through clouds, as the vision of the place receded, I prayed and prayed for all the innocent human beings who lost their lives in such an inhumane and cruel way.

In my mind the sorrow of our dreams and illusions loomed. We should have come to Paris together, to enjoy our honeymoon after celebrating our two weddings; we had to walk in love and happily through the beautiful streets of Paris, visiting its monuments and tasting its gastronomy ... "That was what it should have been and was not."

It turned out that he came to die and I came to pick up his inert body, observe his bloodstain on the ground, and do what I never believed I would do...

Hugging his ashes, I fell asleep and rested for a few hours, until the stewardess tried to touch my bag, and I suddenly woke up! She was surprised by my quick and abrupt reaction. She just wanted to move it a bit so that I would be more comfortable and not bothers me.... We both apologize!

When I woke up again, I thought again. I knew that, upon arrival, I would face my daily life, living the mourning with the families, the ceremony and the funeral of Takashi-San; to suffer the loneliness and the longing of a love that surpassed all barriers: an infinite and eternal love; a full and happy life, that had been taken from me by the criminals of a society built by ourselves. I knew that I would live very differently from this moment on: on constant alert. This, which was taught to me since my childhood, I learned suddenly in a real experience, in a way that was engraved with suffering and pain forever in my soul and in my heart. The life put me to the test to show me who I really was...

Upon my arrival at *Narita Airport* I was pleasantly surprised. They had come to receive me my parents: Yoshida Sensei and Kimura Sensei, my in-laws: Jiro Yagami and Natsuki Nagami, the *"Kachou"*: Shiro Takayama (my Boss) and Hiroshi Saitō (Takashi-San's Boss), the *"Shitencho"*: Kenzo Suzuki (Director of the company) and the *"Shachou"*: Yoshio Manaka (the President of the company).
Everyone felt and expressed enormous emotion when they *"received us,"* putting an end to the long wait. I handed the urn to my in-laws, who with contained passion took it in their hands. They hugged it tightly, with feelings of joy and pain intermingled with the affliction and shock of holding their son in their arms.
It was a very emotional, painful and bitter situation! I felt anguish and anxiety for them... You could still see the furrows on their faces from so much they had cried during all those days... and they kept crying with him in their hands...

The representatives of the company had put at the service of the family an "ostentatious limousine" with which we all went to my house.
There, they had prepared the farewell ceremony, with food, sweets and *sake*, typical of our traditional customs (as well as

the one celebrated with the Kobayashi marriage for the farewell: the last goodbye).

We arrived at our home, "our paradise," accompanied by everyone.

It didn't look like a typhoon had passed when I left. Everything was beautiful. I could see the *Dojo:* it was finished!

It was bigger than it appeared when it was half built. "Awesome!" was the first word that came to mind. And there was something else... that stood out spectacularly between the house and the *Dojo: "my Sakura;"* it had been moved from *Shirakawa-go,* and planted in our house: my precious and beautiful cherry tree! The *Sakura* that had lived with me since the day I turned eighteen years (a gift from my parents), and they had also placed the stone plaque (which was the gift from companions *budoka* training from Yoshida Sensei's *Dojo*), under its branches and next to its great trunk. When it bloomed in spring it would reign in the garden with its exuberant flowering I thought, as I admired it. It kept reminding me that it taught me, with much anticipation, that nothing would last, that beauty would fade and that happiness was ephemeral like the petals of its flowers and the life.

Hugged by my parents at all times, I was contemplating the work they had been doing. They told me that even Takashi-San's parents came to help finish the *Dojo*, being in mourning, and waiting for their son's body...!

« How can I not love in-laws like them? How could they not have all my respect, love and admiration...? »

When Kimura Sensei opened the door of the *Dojo*... I cried and put my hands to my heart! I had no words to express what my eyes were seeing. There was, just in front, the *Tokonoma,* that stood out in a spectacular way; it is the honorific wall of the *Kamiza,* a *Shinto* altar that means: "seat of the spirit." It is the main part of every Japanese *Dojo*, since it is the place where the *Kami* or Gods reside, the point of reverence, respect and purity. Next to it there were two very large pictures, with photos of Takashi-San. The top image was a photo in which I am performing a technique on him and he has the "pain face" caused by the control that I am applying to him. He always said that when I chose him to make of *Uke* (it comes from *"ukeru"* which means 'to receive,' and is the passive person who "receives" the technique when the *Sensei* shows it), I caused him more pain than to the others. That was not true! I did the same to everyone! It was a very nice photo; he loved it, because his face reflected the pain that he felt, and he said that it was real and he was not pretending. The second picture was when Yoshida Sensei and I deliver him the 1st Dan Black Belt, which made him so happy. I remembered his face and his great emotionality on that day; it meant so much to him...!

Inside, noble and aged wood reigned, recalling the old Japanese style. It was fully decorated, with all my weapons placed in the gunsmiths that hung on the walls; the paintings with my martial photos, titles and graduations, the *Kakejiku Shodō,* with Japanese calligraphies and paintings; the *tatami,* the rice straw mat covering the floor, was a beautiful and elegant green. It was perfect!

I was very moved to know that so many people had been working, despite the pain and the adverse circumstances. And all this was for me, to make me feel good, to see the dreams of Takashi-San and mine fulfilled, even if he was missing. But he was just missing physically because I felt him with me, by my side at all times...

We were together in "our paradise!"

My mother, before retiring to attend to the others who were in the house, said that: "She had been anxious to see my face when I would see the *Dojo* that I deserved everything, because I had shown my courage and bravery before the worst situation that can be endured in life. That she was very proud of me, that we would be together to remember him and mourn him and that she felt that I, very soon, would return to being the happy woman I had always been." She hugged and kissed me with the tenderness of a mother.

Yoshida Sensei and I remained alone, in total silence, contemplating the *Dojo* and the photos of the ancestor Masters, located on the *Tokonoma,* next to the altar.

After a few minutes, he looked me in the eyes and said:

"Your mother has told a great truth. For both it is a great honor that you are our daughter. I admire the courage you have shown to overcome and fight with the difficulties that life sometimes gives us to test us. We couldn't be or feel prouder of you, daughter!"

"The honor is mine *Sensei*. I have been honored to have you as my parents and mentors. I have been fortunate throughout my life. And I owe it all to you two. Thanks to the teachings that have been given to me, I am here today. But I don't know how I am going to live alone, and with this pain that I still feel, I miss him so much dad!"

"You have us Haru! We are here to ease your pain. Takashi-San's absence will become bearable with the passage of time. Now you must carry your grief as you feel it, and let the rest flow naturally, do not force anything. Let yourself flow like water and do not resist. You must be flexible like bamboo so that the strong wind does not break you. And give yourself time; do not be in a hurry because you will continue to love life. I know it. By the way, how was everything in Paris?"

"Well daddy, I did what I had to do."

"I know, I have no doubts, I trust you completely, my daughter!"

« We never spoke of that subject again. *Sensei* didn't need any explanation. He trusted that he had taught me well: I would always do what has to be done and what should be done. »

We went inside the house; it was decorated for the "farewell" in tribute to Takashi-San (the funerals in Japan are "celebrated," in a good way of course, with multiple decorations in honor of the deceased). There were flowers from the *Sakura* of silk (because it was winter), placed all over the house next to the photos of him. A large painting with his photo, almost one meter high was in the middle of the living room, being the fundamental piece of the decorated with a close-up of him, where his eyes and his incredible and infinite smile that characterized him so much stood out. Around it hung branches of *Sakura* blossom around the edges of the image (his parents had placed the wooden urn with his ashes at the bottom). And, as tradition dictates, in front of him a table full of food and drink with Takashi-San's plate in the place that he always occupied (it consists of celebrating his last food and drink together and for the last time). Takashi-San's parents (who had come two days ago to receive us) and my parents (who had stayed in the house from the day I went to Paris until then), had taken care of everything, and gave themselves very much with dedication and love. They had worked hard to make everything perfect. My in-laws did the honor of serving the plates and the *sake* cups to everyone. I noticed a lot with what affection and delicacy Natsuki-San served her son's plate. After toasting him several times, the president announced that the company, in the Takashi-San department, would place a picture with his image and a plaque that will remind us that he died in the attack in Paris while working for the company. In this way he would always be present, and neither he nor the act of terror and horror that occurred in Europe would be forgotten. We all appreciated it. It was an honor! Immediately afterwards, I got up to thank the company, and especially those present, for everything they had done for him, for me and for the family. That I would never have expected so much, since they had taken care of everything, of the repatriation and of me. I was also grateful for the speed with which they solved all the necessary procedures, as well as the facilities and attentions that I had had in France... a fact I will never forget. I promised to work tirelessly. To which, quickly, the President said: No! And he added that I would work as I had worked up to here, that I did not owe anything, and that they were the ones who were indebted to Takashi-San forever. The Director added that we are a family, and we laugh and cry together for what happens to any of our relatives. Takashi-San's boss, very shocked, spoke a few words about his character, what a good worker he was... and that he would miss him very much. My boss chose to highlight my bravery in going overseas alone and bringing him back home; he lamented how hard it must have been for me to face a loss and something of that magnitude.

We toasted again, and I thanked my in-laws for the trust they placed in me, for the support that they had given me at all times, as well as the fact that they were there preparing all this and collaborating in everything. I told them how much I loved them and that I would always take care of them, if they would allow me....

Natsuki-San said: "You are a daughter to us. Besides, you were our son's love and happiness. We know how much love there was between you two. Our son would want us to love you; that is what we have done and that is what we will continue to do. The love of his life is our love."

Jiro-San added: "He wouldn't forgive us for not taking care of you. You were everything to him. I agree that you are a daughter, we have been blessed. You have four parents Haru, don't forget!"

I was very moved, because they are very important in my life and we made the last toast to him, all of us directing to his huge close-up photo. Then, I handed them the pen (given to me by the judicial police) that Takashi-San was carrying when he passed away, and which had been a gift from his father on his last birthday. He was very happy and cried, because he knew how much he liked it, and he thanked me very much.

The bosses left; told us to rest that the next day the limousine would return to take us to the *"Hanazono Shrine"* a temple in *Shinjuku,* where the funeral would be held. My in-laws and parents were staying at home to sleep. They chose that temple because my in-laws thought that doing it in *Nagano* would mean a lot of distance and many hours, and that for their friends and acquaintances it would also be more complicated, and they even said that for me that after the long trip, and being all in *Shinjuku,* they preferred to reduce so many movements and hours of travel.

I slept that night in our house, and although my parents and in-laws were also in their rooms, I was in our bed, alone, and feeling the emptiness of home without him. I cried him even more, although it cost me a lot because my eyes could not with more tears; they were swollen and stinging every time because they had cried already too much. But I didn't care, I wanted to do it. I longed him and I missed him so much...! The pain did not cease and each beat of my heart was like a blow, as if nails were driven into me with a mallet... How every blow, each beat of my heart ached...!

The next day, we got up and dressed for the occasion. The etiquette for mourning (*mofuku*) is a black dress for women and a black suit with a tie of the same color for men. Before leaving the house, I told my mother-in-law that the inscriptions on the wooden urn were missing, and that she had told me that we would do it together. She explained to me that because we couldn't do it on time, and that we were going to distribute the ashes, she bought two urns: one for her and one for me. We would distribute the ashes and bones. And she thought that I would save the wooden urn for when we decided to put part or all inside in the moment of burial in the cemetery, and by then, we would engrave the inscriptions in time.

« In Japan, the ashes of the deceased can be divided among more than one urn. For example, some ashes go to a family grave, and others go to the temple or even to a burial grave in the cemetery. Depending on local custom, the urn may remain in the family home for an indefinite period of time or it may be taken directly to the cemetery. In our case, we each took an urn with bones and ashes to our altars at home. We would wait that the bones would completely decompose, and then we would put some ashes back in the wooden urn to be buried later in the cemetery. »

The limousine was waiting outside the house and drove us to the *Shinjuku Shrine*. My in-laws carried the two ceramic urns to perform the ceremony. I carried the wooden urn with Takashi-San's ashes.

We got to the temple and there were a lot of people. There were all of our friends, relatives from different parts, and company colleagues from the *Shinjuku* headquarters.

The monk made a small ceremony of a few minutes, and we returned to say goodbye to Takashi-San once again.

In pairs, my in-laws first, and then me with each one, we both picked up a bone at the same time with chopsticks, and we placed them in one urn and then in the other, dividing the bones. Afterwards, we divided the ashes between the two urns. At the end, they took one urn and I took the other, holding them in the hands.

Something that cannot be lacking in all funerals is the burning of incense, or *shōkō*: first, take some powdered incense (*makkō*) using the thumb, index and heart of the right hand, raising the palm inwards to the level of the forehead. After, the incense is spread in a burner (*kōro*), keeping the fingers on top of the container.

All the attendees participated in this special moment where only the most absolute silence reigned, giving their last "goodbye," and wishing for Takashi-San a "safe and good journey to the afterlife." They paid their respects, one by one, to all of us, their families, and took their leave leaving the temple.

When everyone had left, I spoke with Jiro-San about the situation and Kobayashi Sensei's feeling, regarding his lack of honor for not taking care of his son by accepting responsibility for the note delivered in *Okinawa*. My father-in-law was exalted in surprise, saying that he did not make him the note in the sense of accepting a commitment for life, that he made him understand that the childhood treasures had changed, and that his son was his greatest treasure. He did not imagine that he would have taken it that way! And of course, he kept thinking that there was no one better than him to take care of other, and that he had never thought badly or had ever blamed him for what happened. He assured me that he would speak to him that same day, and I not to worry, because he would take away him that erroneous duty and feeling, and thus returning his honor.

My in-laws and my parents went straight to the station, returning to their homes in *Nagano* and *Shirakawa-go*, just as I had asked them to do. They understood that I wanted to be alone to cope with his absence.

I walked to "our paradise" with my urns, the wooden one (to keep until burial) and the ceramic one to put on our family altar at home.

« An image of the deceased is placed on the family altar in the home. Some homes have a *"Butsudan,"* 'Buddha's house,' a wooden closet with doors that enclose and protect a religious symbol or image as a sanctuary. The doors are opened to show the icon during the prayers. Candles, incense burners, bells, and trays for offerings are placed. Other homes have a *Shinto* Shrine, called *Kamidana,* a domestic altar (in my case). After, the home shrine is closed and covered with white paper to keep impure spirits away from the dead. »

After arranging the home altar, I dedicated hours to his memory and prayed for him and his spirit. I ended up meditating to strengthen my body and my spirit, too.

I placed a white lantern (Japanese tradition) outside, at the entrance door, as a sign of mourning.

Then I went to the *Dojo* and in a gunsmith, just below the picture of Takashi-San when the delivery of his black belt, I placed the *nawa* or rope, gift from Kobayashi Sensei (gifted to him earlier by his *Hojōjutsu* Master), which he gave to me with honor hoping it would be "useful" to me at some point and that "it was his gift to us." The honor was mine and I promised him that I would keep it as a "treasure."

« That *nawa* or rope in the *Dojo* next to his picture was a symbol towards Takashi-San's honor. »

After a couple of days, I got back to my new life, going back to work every day, as I did before everything had stopped in my world.

A previous life that I neither wanted nor could forget.

I always carried with me my *Omamori,* the amulet, a gift from my beloved and the love card (which I placed in his luggage when he left for Paris) broken, burned and stained, because it reminded me of the beautiful words he said to me when he found it. They were words that have always remained in my head and in my heart.

At the company they treated me with great attention and affection. I felt sheltered by everyone. I was adapting and my project was a success in the cities where it had been proposed. From "pilot test," it went on to become established in the official organization.

The work was compensating me with joys my inner sadness and loneliness, when I returned to our home, to "our paradise." The autumn passed, as did winter, and gave way to spring. My *"Sakura"* sprouted with great strength after being transplanted. I placed under, in its shade and its vibrations were very positive. It gave me peace, harmony and well-being, as it had years ago. I whispered to it and it conveyed love to me. Soon, we would experience the first *hanami,* the rain of its flower petals, in the new place for both of us. I longed for that moment, because my *Sakura* would no longer cry *'tears of blood'* over me; they would be *'tears of love,'* which will mark a new stage, a new beginning and a new life.

One day, sitting in the rocking chair in my living room of my house to rest, and with my legs resting on a seat, I turned on the television and was giving the news reports. On one of its channels they said:

"The Islamist terrorist, who has been identified as Omar Sabbag, the only participant in the latest attacks in Paris who was still in search and capture, has been found dead. It is believed that he had been dead for about five months, and according to police sources, everything indicates that a few days after committing the attacks, he could have committed suicide."

Hearing this, I put my hands on my balloon-like swollen belly; I caressed it, and noticed certain frenzied activity. He was already responding to external stimuli and to my voice. In a soft voice I said him: "Did you hear my *"little one?"* *Mom* always "does what needs to be done" and will always protect and take care of you, and your *Dad*, "my eternal love," will always be watching you, even if you can't see him.

The *"little Takashi"* already weighed about 700g and was almost 35cm. He liked to move and play. In the last ultrasound I had seen his face and I could see him smiling perfectly. He had the incredible smile of his father!

Before spring comes to an end, a being born of true and authentic love would come into the world.
I had something very important to live and fight for.
I would love eternally again.
Although I would never be able to overcome or forget
"that moment," in "that instant" in which:
"I lived and died in the same day!"